Th

The dark-blue BN... ...5 P.M. and parked... ...e window and place... ...n his knees.

He removed the gun from the case; he checked to make sure the capsules were loaded and in place. Then he looked through the telescopic sight and focused the crosshairs on Travers' front door. He checked the range; seventy-two meters, well within the gun's effective range.

In a few moments the lethal poison brewed six thousand miles from London would be propelled at high speed into the body of Robert Travers. It would paralyze his respiratory, cardiovascular, nervous and muscle systems. Within a second or two he would die . . .

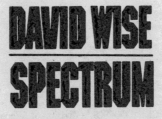

DAVID WISE
SPECTRUM

PUBLISHED BY POCKET BOOKS NEW YORK

POCKET BOOKS, a division of Simon & Schuster, Inc.
1230 Avenue of the Americas, New York, N.Y. 10020

Published by arrangement with The Viking Press
Library of Congress Catalog Card Number: 80-17418

ISBN: 0-671-44266-X

First Pocket Books printing October, 1984

10 9 8 7 6 5 4 3 2 1

POCKET and colophon are registered trademarks
of Simon & Schuster, Inc.

Printed in the U.S.A.

To Christopher and Jonathan

SPECTRUM

Chapter 1

It was hot outside, and the late-afternoon sun beat down mercilessly. In the white glare, there was not a spot of shade anywhere to shield the man who walked up the steps of St. Anthony's.

Inside, the church was cool and dark. Mike Kolchak paused for a moment to let his eyes adjust to the dim light. He wiped his brow, and realized, without surprise, that his hand was shaking.

There was a font near the door. He dipped his fingers in the holy water and crossed himself. Silently, his lips formed the ritual words. "In the name of the Father, the Son, and the Holy Spirit."

He moved hesitantly down the side aisle, pausing halfway to the altar. He genuflected, crossed himself quickly once more, and knelt in the pew. After a moment, he looked around, in a way almost hoping that he would see one of Perella's men who would order him to leave. But the church was empty, except for an old woman kneeling at the communion rail.

Kolchak bowed his head, pretending to pray. That was a

sin in itself. He knew he was taking a risk coming to the church on a Saturday afternoon, when confessions were heard, for he might be seen and his purpose suspected. But he had to talk to someone. The secret was burning inside him. And a priest could be trusted, even if no one else could.

He rose, made his way down the aisle a few feet, and entered the confessional. He knelt, pulled the little white curtain aside, and peered through the cane grille. He could make out only a dim outline of the side of the priest's face. But from the thatch of prematurely gray hair, he could tell immediately that it was Father Hanlon. He was a young priest, new to the parish. He could not have been much more than thirty, which was Kolchak's age. That might make it easier.

Kolchak put his lips as close to the grille as possible. He spoke softly. He was not sure whether the heavy velvet drape that served as the door to the confessional would muffle his words completely were anyone to enter the church and sit nearby.

"Bless me, Father, for I have sinned. It has been six months since my last confession. These are my sins. . . ."

He paused, but the priest remained motionless, waiting.

"I've been stealing something from the plant where I work, Father." Kolchak licked his lips, and stopped.

"Go on."

"I work on the production line at NUFAC. You probably know what they make—enriched uranium for the government. The stuff is pressed into little metal pellets, Father, not much bigger than rabbit food. It's easy to take out." Kolchak looked through the grille, but he could see no reaction from the priest, whose face was mostly in shadow.

"About three months ago, Father, these guys came to town. Nobody knows from where; they're not from Pittsburgh or anywhere else around here. Real tough Italians, mafiosi. They started hanging around Mama Leone's. A lot of guys from the plant go in there for a beer when their shift is over. These new guys played it cool, Father. At first, they didn't say much. But pretty soon the word went out, you know, that these Mafia guys would pay five hundred dollars for half a pound of broken buttons. That's what we call the pellets. That's a lot of money, Father. Mama Leone let these guys use the back room, and they were around there a lot. So, finally, I go back there and I talk to this big, heavyset guy who seems to be the head man. Perella, Angelo Perella. He buys me a glass of beer. He asks about my family and about my church. Like a job interview. Then he asks why do I want the money? I told him the truth, Father. I told him I needed it for my wife and kid, for the car payments, and for doctors' bills. So this Angelo grunts and he thinks for a long time, and he sips his beer. He doesn't seem in any hurry to deal. He tells me to come back in a couple of days. When I do, he says, okay, they've checked me out and I'm in. Then he says if I talk about it to *anyone*, even my wife, they'll cut my tongue out. He says that's what they do in Sicily, and they'll do the same thing here in Apollo to any of us if we talk or make any kind of trouble."

The priest spoke quietly: "How long have you been stealing from the plant?"

"About two months, Father. I asked them if they wanted me to take a few pellets out every day in my Thermos jug, you know. The metal in the Thermos would shield it, in case they used a Geiger counter at the plant exits. They hardly ever check us, but once in a while they do. So Perella says, 'No, you'll need special equipment and we'll give it to you.' I know it sounds crazy, Father, but a few days later they give me this jock."

"A what?"

"A jock. It looks ordinary but it's specially made. It's got two very thin layers of brass inside. He says to put the pellets in the metal lining, because brass will fool any Geiger counter, Father, and he knows they never do a body search at the plant. Father, I'm scared. I want to stop, to get out. But I'm afraid if I stop, they'll kill me." Kolchak was crying.

Father Hanlon spoke very gently: "Everyone experiences temptation. But God is understanding, and God is forgiving. If you were not a good man, you would not be here."

"Thank you, Father."

"God is not so much concerned with the past as with the future. Is there any way you can put back the things you have taken without incriminating yourself?"

3

"It's too late, Father. I've already been paid for three pounds. I took the money and I spent some of it."

"Then you must give the rest to some good cause, a charity. And you must certainly stop what you have been doing."

"I will, Father. I was even wondering if I should go to the police, or the FBI. They have an office in Pittsburgh."

Father Hanlon shook his head. "You are under no obligation in the eyes of God to incriminate yourself. And you must consider your wife and child. They need you to work and provide for them."

"Father, you have to understand. These guys could blow up cities. They must be planning to make bombs with this stuff. I don't know what else they would want it for."

"You may be right. But God does not ask that you go to prison for your sins. You must tell these men you will not steal anymore, that is over for you. I want you to say the act of contrition now. For your penance, you will say ten Hail Mary's."

Kolchak bowed his head. "Oh my God, I am heartily sorry for having offended you. I detest all my sins."

"Ego te absolvo," the priest intoned, *"a peccatis tuis in nomine Patris et Filii et Spiritus Sancti."*

Father Hanlon had finished giving absolution.

"Thank you, Father."

"Go in peace."

Kolchak's legs felt stiff as he stood up. He was not a big man, but he was strong, with the rough hands of a worker. His people had come from Silesia in the 1890s to work in the anthracite mines near Wilkes-Barre. His grandfather had been killed in a mine disaster. After that, his grandmother had taken her young baby to live with relatives in western Pennsylvania. She had settled in Apollo, an industrial town twenty-five miles northeast of Pittsburgh on a bend in the Kiskiminetas River, a tributary of the Allegheny. Her son, Stanislaus, Mike's father, married young. He had stoked a giant blast furnace in a steel mill for forty years. He had died five years before, in 1960. Kolchak's mother had died two years later.

Kolchak was grateful for that in a way. If he were caught

4

now, at least his parents would not share his disgrace. He knelt in the darkened church, breathing in the coolness and the faint smell of incense. "Hail Mary full of Grace, the Lord is with Thee," he murmured. "Blessed art Thou among women and blessed is the fruit of Thy womb, Jesus. Holy Mary, Mother of God, pray for us sinners now and at the hour of our death, amen."

It was near dusk but still hot from the summer sun that had baked the town all day when Father Hanlon left the rectory of Saint Anthony's Church and walked across the parking lot in the rear. He had removed his cassock, but the black suit he wore was hot and it was soaked with perspiration under the arms. His collar felt tight.

He walked quickly to a metallic blue Plymouth and got in. He started up and drove north on Route 56 to the edge of town. He turned off on Vandergrift Road and slowed down after crossing the Penn Central tracks. There was no other car in sight. The area he drove through was almost deserted. Once, it had been a busy center of light industry, but the town had sprawled south along the east bank of the river, toward Pittsburgh. Now the area was mostly decaying warehouses, chain-link fences, and empty factory buildings. There were a couple of auto-body-repair shops and a junkyard littered with rusting, battered cars. A cement plant still operated on the west side of the road, but it was closed on Saturday, the fat-bellied trucks parked neatly in a row like hogs at a trough. The priest drove beyond the cement factory, then turned right through a gate, and parked behind a long, low building where his car would not be visible from the road. The large painted sign on the front of the building said Wholesale Meats. The paint on the sign was cracked and peeling.

He pushed a buzzer on the side of the building, near the loading dock, and a large, corrugated-metal door lifted slowly. He entered the warehouse, pushed another button, and the door clanged shut behind him. In the gloom, he could see the bright lights of the office at the far end of the building. He made his way toward the light, threading carefully past dust-covered dollies, piles of cartons, and machinery that he supposed must have once been used for slicing and packing beef and pork. The sawdust that still covered the wooden floor stuck to his black shoes.

He grasped an iron railing and mounted the steps that led up to the office. A big, heavyset man behind a battered wooden desk was on the telephone. He was smoking a large cigar, and gesticulating with it as he talked. In an ancient leather chair across from him, a short, slim, swarthy man sat with his feet propped up on the big man's desk. He was cleaning his fingernails with a knife, carefully running the point of the blade under each nail, and flicking the dirt on the floor. There were no decorations in the office except for a large, full-color girlie calendar on the wall over the fat man's head. The blonde in the photograph wore black lace panties and nothing else. She had huge breasts and rosy-pink nipples. The calendar was two years old, and dusty. Several of the pages had been torn off. The page showing said "July 1963."

The priest did not speak to the two men. He walked over to a small refrigerator, and took out a bottle of Coke. He removed his jacket, laid it on a chair, uncapped the bottle with a beer opener, and sat down across from the fat man, who was still talking on the phone. The priest put his feet up on the desk, lit a cigarette, tilted the bottle up, and took a long drink.

"Jesus, it's hot." He reached to the back of his neck, unsnapped his clerical collar, and tossed it on top of his jacket. He let out a long sigh of relief.

The fat man finally hung up the phone. "You don't look much like a priest without your collar," he said.

"I'm not, remember?" The man, whom his parishioners at St. Anthony's knew only as Father Hanlon, took a long drag on his cigarette and exhaled the smoke before he spoke again.

"Mike Kolchak is scared. He isn't going to hold."

"We know."

The big man, who was known in Apollo as Angelo Perella, although that was not his real name, flipped a switch on a tape recorder resting on his desk.

". . . I asked them if they wanted me to take a few pellets out every day in my Thermos jug, you know." It was

6

Kolchak's voice, clear as a bell. "Father, I'm scared. I want to stop, to get out. But I'm afraid if I stop, they'll kill me."

". . . Everyone experiences temptation. But God is understanding, and God is forgiving."

"Shit, you even bugged the confessional. Why didn't you tell me?"

"Need to know, Dickie, need to know. We can't take any chances in Spectrum. The tapes have routinely been going to Travers in Domestic Operations. He needed to know. You didn't."

The gray-haired man drained his Coke. "With Kolchak wobbling, we could be blown tomorrow. Besides, I don't know how long I can carry on as a priest. My Latin is a bit rusty. I think Father Filetti is beginning to smell a rat."

"You were chosen for this operation because the computer search showed you spent two years in a seminary before you came to us. You're doing fine. And don't worry about Filetti. He's only a parish priest. Towny Black set this whole thing up through the Diocese in Pittsburgh. It seems the bishop roomed with Trilby Gates at Princeton. 'Father Joseph Hanlon' is assigned to Saint Anthony's for six months. At the end of that time, he'll be transferred out. Poof. He'll vanish, and there'll be no record of him here or in the Diocese. He'll simply cease to exist. And Richard O'Donnell will disappear back into the Plans Directorate. Spiritually improved, I daresay."

O'Donnell drained his Coke and set down the empty bottle on the desk.

"Frank, what the hell are we going to do now?"

"We're going to do exactly what Angelo Perella would be expected to do. We're going to make an example of Kolchak."

"Frank, for Christ's sake."

"I'm not going to let one frightened Polack endanger the entire operation. There's too much at stake for the country. We're using Mafia cover; we're going to act like Mafia."

The thin man with the olive skin had not stopped cleaning his nails. But he grinned to himself, as though he enjoyed the prospect held out by the big man.

7

O'Donnell stood up, picked up his jacket, and slung it over his shoulder. He let his cigarette stub drop to the floor and crushed it with the toe of his shoe. Then he carefully replaced his clerical collar.

"What are you going to do to Kolchak?" he asked.

"Don't let your priestly cover interfere with your professional judgment," the big man replied. "What we do to Kolchak is for me to decide."

"Frank—"

"Call me Angelo when we're operational. It's good tradecraft. Otherwise you might slip up sometime."

O'Donnell paused on his way out the door. He turned, raised his right hand, and made the sign of the cross.

"God bless you, Angelo," he said.

"Fuck off."

Chapter 2

On Monday morning, Frank DiMario was back at his office in the warehouse. At forty-two, DiMario had already earned a considerable reputation among his peers. Dark-haired and somewhat jowly, he was a powerful man, heavyset but muscular. A swarthy complexion and hook nose added to his menacing appearance, and had led some of his associates to call him, behind his back, "The Hawk."

DiMario slipped easily into the role of Angelo Perella, Mafia hood. He had been born on Mulberry Street, in Lower Manhattan, the son of Salvatore DiMario, a restaurant owner who had migrated to New York from Pescara, a fishing port on the Adriatic. In the summer, when Salvatore could afford it, he liked to go back to Pescara, where he would visit his relatives and drive around the streets in a rented Cadillac, exulting in the role of the rich American and lording it over the townspeople. While Salvatore visited Italy, his wife managed their restaurant, DiMario's, on Mulberry Street. Real mafiosi often dined there; Vito Genovese regularly ordered the saltimbocca and a bottle of Valpolicella. Tommy Lucchese, known as Three-Finger Brown, was another frequent visitor.

Frank DiMario, although a first-generation American, was fluent in Italian, which had helped his credentials at Mama Leone's. He grew up tough, surviving gang fights with Chinese youths on Bayard Street, where Chinatown collided with Little Italy. He had learned to use his fists, and on occasion, a knife.

But he was bright as well as street-wise, and his father insisted that his son have the education that he did not. He sent Frank to NYU, and DiMario graduated from the campus on Washington Square, in Greenwich Village, in the top third of his class.

None of the workers at the NUFAC plant—the initials stood for Nuclear Fabricators Corporation—doubted that DiMario was exactly who he said he was, Angelo Perella, a Mafia don whom it would not be wise to cross. He spoke Italian, he dropped occasional references to his friendship with Vito Genovese and Sam Giancana, and he paid cash— $100 bills peeled off a huge wad—for the uranium pellets the employees stole. The slim mobster who accompanied him everywhere looked as though he would kill a man as easily as he would step on an ant. Tony Milano and Nick Canucci, the other mafiosi who hung around Mama's with Perella, were equally tough-looking.

DiMario was alone this morning, however, and he had locked the single door to the office so that no one could enter from inside the abandoned warehouse. He unlocked a desk drawer and pulled out a telephone, ordinary in appearance except that about six inches from the base of the phone the cord passed through a small, rectangular black box. DiMario dialed a number in New York City. It rang, however, in Washington, D.C., in an office on the fifth floor of a building on the south side of Pennsylvania Avenue only a block from the White House. The building housed a number of newspaper bureaus, law firms, and other commercial offices. *Newsweek's* Washington bureau occupied the top floor. The Washington office of the New York *Herald Tribune* was directly below, on the twelfth floor. The United States Information Agency took up the sixth and seventh floors. The entire fifth floor was occupied by what seemed to be a unit of the Pentagon. At least, on the board in the lobby, the office was listed as "U.S. Army Element, Joint Planning Activity, Joint Operations Group (SD 7753)." No such unit existed in the Army. The listing was a cover for the Domestic Operations Division of the Central Intelligence Agency.

When the telephone rang, in an office with a large picture window overlooking Pennsylvania Avenue, it was answered by a tall man who said something rather odd, or so it might have seemed had an outsider overheard him. "This is Mary Jane," he said.

"This is Alice," DiMario said. "I'm ringing through on the sterile number in Manhattan. I'm also on the scrambler, configuration one, so we're secure."

"Go ahead, Frank."

"Phase Blue is in a little bit of trouble. Mike Kolchak is losing his nerve. He's talked about the operation."

"To whom?"

"To Agnes. He went to confession."

"Thank God it was Agnes."

"We have the whole thing on tape. The courier plane is leaving Apollo in an hour. You should get it this afternoon."

As director of the newly formed Domestic Operations Division, Robert Travers, the man who had called himself Mary Jane, was not, technically, in the direct line of command for Operation Spectrum. Because Spectrum was a covert operation, it fell under the Directorate of Plans, headed by Trilby Gates, the deputy director for Plans, and his assistant, Graham Townsend Black. Gates had designated Black the officer in charge of Spectrum. But because the operation was taking place in Pennsylvania, on U.S. soil, in violation of the National Security Act of 1947, Robert Travers had, of necessity, been cut in. Towny Black and

Frank DiMario, the CIA officer in the field, could not have run Spectrum in the United States without the logistical support and the approval of Robert Travers. Even the courier plane bringing the tape to Washington belonged to the Domestic Operations Division. Trilby Gates and Angus Maclaren, the reclusive head of counterintelligence, had grudgingly agreed that DiMario report in the first instance to Travers, even though Black was ultimately responsible for the operation.

It was Towny Black who suggested that the parish priest in the blue-collar neighborhood in Apollo, from which the men would be recruited, be a CIA agent. Travers agreed. It was an ingenious safety valve and early-warning system, should any of the workers whom DiMario enlisted begin to waver. For the uranium-smuggling operation, DiMario had been careful to select only Roman Catholics who lived in St. Anthony's parish. Unlike Kolchak, most of the workers siphoning uranium from the NUFAC plant had Italian backgrounds. DiMario felt more comfortable working with his *compari*, which he pronounced, exaggeratedly and thickly, so that it sounded like "goombari."

Although Travers was shaken by DiMario's news about Kolchak, he tried not to let his voice betray his emotions. "We knew something like this could happen, Frank," he said. "After all, that's why we put O'Donnell in place. The problem is what to do now."

"I've thought about it," DiMario replied. "We're going to have to bring Kolchak in. Hurt him so badly that he won't dare talk anymore. It will have the added advantage of serving as an example to the others."

"You can't do that. If you target Kolchak, it will blow O'Donnell's cover. He'll realize the priest was one of us."

"That's not a problem. O'Donnell told him to tell us he won't steal any more of the stuff. You'll hear it when you get the tape. When Kolchak comes to us and says he wants out, *then* we can react. And it won't endanger O'Donnell at all. Kolchak himself will be telling us."

"How can you be sure he will?"

DiMario sighed. "The trouble with most of you guys in the

11

company is you're all a bunch of WASPs. If you were a left-footer, like me, you'd understand. Kolchak received absolution from Father Hanlon. He'll do what he says."

"Even if he does come to you, it still isn't the answer. Look, Frank, I want to protect Spectrum as much as any of us. It's a vital operation. But my division's involved, and it's very delicate. I don't want anything to go wrong. If you put pressure on Kolchak, it may get out of hand. You may end up terminating him. It's happened before. I don't want it to happen now, on my turf."

"We may have to slice his tongue off. We threatened that, after all. And we have to preserve our credibility. But we're not, repeat not, planning to terminate."

"You can't be sure what will happen. You remember what Bill Bradford did to that Estonian refugee he was interrogating in Wiesbaden three years ago?" DiMario remembered. Bradford had been giving him the submarine, holding his head in a bucket of water until the last possible second. Only he held him down a little too long.

"Billy Bradford is a wild man. It was a mistake."

"The point is, these things don't always go the way you expect. If the DDP terminates a target in one of your own ops, that's your problem. But I'm involved in this one, and I won't have it. Not in my division."

"Listen to the tape when you get it. Kolchak's threatening to go to the Bureau."

Travers exploded. "Damn it, Frank, you can't let that happen. Can you imagine what Hoover would do if he finds out about Spectrum? That old bastard would squeeze our nuts flat. For openers they'd shut down my division. The agency's not supposed to be doing *any* domestic operations. Before it was over, we'd all have to go. You, me, Black, Trilby Gates, Angus, perhaps even the director. It would be a total disaster."

"Then let us bring in Kolchak."

"I want to talk to Towny Black first. There must be some other way."

"There isn't."

"We'll get back to you in twenty-four hours. Meanwhile you're on a hold button with Kolchak. Don't forget it."

Travers hung up, replacing the receiver a little harder than necessary. He immediately picked it up and dialed a number.

A woman's voice answered.

"Potomac Historical Society," she said. "This is the library."

"This is Mary Jane," Travers said. "Tell him I'm coming over. It's urgent."

"Is he expecting you?" she said sweetly, with the razor edge in her voice that secretaries spend years to cultivate.

"He is now."

Travers clicked off. He put on his suit jacket, and moved quickly out to the reception area by the elevators. He nodded to the attractive young Chinese woman who sat at the desk and guarded the entrance. Only one door gave access to the suite, and she controlled it with a buzzer.

Travers took the elevator down to the lobby, walked out past the fountain on Pennsylvania Avenue, and turned left. He strode rapidly to the corner, crossed the avenue, and walked north up 18th Street past the Roger Smith Hotel. He crossed H Street and turned in a few paces until he came to the entrance to an old Victorian mansion. The brass plaque next to the door said Potomac Historical Society.

Graham Townsend Black, the assistant deputy director for Plans, insisted on operating from this building, rather than from headquarters across the river in Langley, Virginia. Four years before, in 1961, most of the agency had moved from the old OSS buildings on E Street, across from the State Department, to Langley. But there were still a dozen CIA units scattered in the downtown area, including Travers' Domestic Operations Division, which was deliberately located away from headquarters because of its ultrasensitive nature. Black, too, made a point of staying in town. He claimed he lost too much valuable time commuting over Key Bridge to Virginia. The real reason Black preferred to operate out of the building on H Street, Travers suspected, was that he could walk down the block to the Metropolitan Club to lunch with his friends. Since the Plans Directorate had almost unlimited funds, Trilby Gates, the DDP, indulged Black. Gates himself preferred his office at Langley.

Travers mounted the steps. A huge glass door covered with

iron grillwork barred his way. He rang the bell. After a moment, an elderly, gray-haired lady with steel-rimmed glasses peered through the door, then pressed a buzzer to admit him.

"Good morning, Mr. Travers," she chirped. "I didn't see it was you. My eyes must be getting worse. I was just making a cup of tea. Would you care for some?"

"No thank you, Miss Witherow. Perhaps another morning." Travers paused at the bottom of the marble staircase. "Don't drink too much of that stuff. Security may think you're working for MI6."

The gray-haired lady smiled good-naturedly.

"Oh my, Mr. Travers," she said. "You do joke so."

Miss Witherow did make good tea. She was also, despite her glasses, a crack shot with the .38 she kept in her desk drawer. The last time the staff of the library had taken their annual test on the firing range at Camp Peary, Travers had heard, Towny Black and the rest of the men on H Street had hit the targets—which were silhouettes of a male figure—in the arms, thighs, and legs. Miss Witherow's bullets had all pierced the heart.

Travers went up the stairs to the second floor. The icy secretary who had answered his phone call kept typing for almost a minute before she bothered to look up. She did not greet him.

"I'll tell him you're here," she said.

"Thanks," said Travers laconically.

Towny Black's secretary disappeared into his office. In a moment she was back, wearing her best frosty smile. "He'll see you now," she said.

Travers entered Black's office. It was always, he reflected, like stepping into the nineteenth century. The office was completely paneled in dark wood and two walls were lined with bookcases from floor to ceiling. Only the fact that it was July, Travers thought, prevented Black from having a log blazing in the marble fireplace. The assistant deputy director for Plans sat at a table rather than a desk. He did not get up, but he waved Travers to an armchair.

A tall man with even features and prematurely graying hair, Black was, as usual, flawlessly dressed in a dark-blue, pin-striped Ivy League suit, a button-down, blue oxford shirt, and a club tie. The assistant DDP was a man who spent a lot of time cultivating an air of studied elegance. The office, with its dark, antique furniture, reflected his elaborate taste.

Travers came quickly to the point. "Spectrum is in trouble," he said. "One of the workers DiMario recruited, a man named Michael Kolchak, has confessed to Agnes. He wants to quit, and of course Agnes had no choice but to advise him to stop stealing from the plant."

Black filled his polished briar with Dunhill's London mixture, tamped it down, and lit the pipe before he replied. "Then let him quit. Or is Frank afraid the man may be indiscreet?"

"That's the point. He's threatening to go to the Bureau."

Travers enjoyed watching Black lose a little of his composure, if only for an instant. The assistant DDP had removed the pipe from his mouth.

"And what," Black asked slowly, "does Frank have in mind for the unfortunate Mr. Kolchak?"

"I don't know precisely, and I'm not sure I want to know. But I've instructed him to do nothing without further authority from Washington."

"I don't see any point in delaying any preventive measures that DiMario, as the field officer, considers appropriate." Black fussed with his pipe, which had gone out, and relit it. "Surely, Robert, you understand the importance of Spectrum. Lyndon Johnson is distracted by Vietnam. While we're preoccupied with the Viet Cong, we may lose the Middle East. The Israelis must be given the means to secure their borders. You know as well as I do what an Arab-Israeli war could mean for our own national security. If the Israelis lose, the Middle East will become a Soviet playground. So we've got to allow Israel to become a nuclear power. We're giving them enough enriched U-235 to make six atomic bombs. At twenty-two pounds per bomb, that will require 132 pounds of weapons grade uranium, or sixty kilos, to be precise."

"And does the president know what's going on?" It was a point on which Black, Trilby Gates, and Angus Maclaren had been consistently fuzzy in their conversations with Travers.

"We are acting in his interest, and in the national interest, my dear boy. Part of our job in the Clandestine Services is to insulate the president from unpleasant realities. To provide him with plausible deniability, as it were."

"I understand that, and I agree. But we may be approaching a point where the risks of Spectrum outweigh the benefits."

"On the contrary. Up to now, at least, Phase Blue has been running like clockwork."

Travers had to admit to himself that it had. Spectrum/Phase Blue called for the transfer of the 132 pounds of weapons-grade uranium metal to Mossad, the Israeli secret intelligence service. Although Travers was not a physicist, he had found it necessary to learn the basic technology of nuclear weaponry in order to participate in Spectrum. In nature, he knew, uranium occurred as U-238, an element useless in itself for making atomic bombs. The fissionable material necessary for explosions was U-235, of which only slightly more than seven-tenths of one percent was present in uranium ore. To obtain more, the uranium had to be enriched. To do that, it was turned into a gas, uranium hexafluoride, and filtered minutely and endlessly in a complex gaseous diffusion process. This took place at a plant in Portsmouth, Ohio. From there, the enriched uranium in the form of a gas was shipped to Apollo, Pennsylvania, where the NUFAC plant converted it into uranium metal for the government. The little grayish-green metal pellets that Mike Kolchak had been smuggling to the CIA men, whom he thought to be Mafia hoodlums, were similar to the basic ingredients of Little Boy, the atomic bomb that had leveled Hiroshima. Sixty kilograms, the amount being smuggled to Mossad, would fit into a volleyball. It was enough to vaporize Manhattan island.

Towny Black had finally got his pipe going satisfactorily and he was rambling on in his self-satisfied way. "The operation has been moving smoothly. Every two weeks, Itzak Lev, scientific attaché of the Israeli embassy in Washington, drives to Pittsburgh to see his sister. She lives in Fox Chapel, one of the nicer suburbs. She is, of course, not Lev's sister. She is, in fact, Tamara Stern, one of the top Mossad agents in the United States. Lev is a bird fancier. When he drives to Fox

Chapel, his pet parakeet, whom I believe he calls Ben-Gurion, goes with him in a large birdcage. The cage rests on the backseat of his Peugeot between two suitcases. When he returns to Washington on Monday morning, the birdcage is much heavier. It contains ten pounds of enriched uranium pellets in the hollow tubes that form the struts of the cage. It keeps the pellets nicely separated. That way, too many of them don't touch and go critical. Jorgensen in the Technical Services Division designed the cage for Mossad and we're rather pleased with it. He got the idea from the fact that the specially designed steel drums in which pellets are normally shipped are called birdcages. A nice touch, don't you think? There is, of course, no danger to the parakeet. The system is quite safe unless Lev cracks up on the Pennsylvania Turnpike."

"What would happen then?" asked Travers.

"The uranium would go fizzle," Black replied casually. "It probably wouldn't blow up, but if it happened, say, around Somerset, Pennsylvania, the radiation would kill about ten thousand people."

"How would we explain that?" Travers asked.

"We wouldn't," Black replied. "At that point it would be the Israelis' problem. We wouldn't know anything about it."

Travers smiled. It was best to smile a good deal and be agreeable when dealing with Towny Black. "I appreciate your cutting me in on the paper for Spectrum. I realize the access list is extremely tight. But according to the latest operational summary I read, last Thursday, I think it was, Itzak Lev has been doing a lot of commuting. Mossad has already received seventy-five pounds. Instead of bringing in Mike Kolchak, which could cause all kinds of problems for my division, why not just shut down Phase Blue now? You're not so far short of the total amount scheduled to come out of Apollo."

Black smiled back at the younger man, but it was the slightly patronizing smile of a father helping a young son with a difficult math problem. "Phase Blue calls for 132 pounds," he said. "Originally we had planned to provide enough for five bombs. But Angus Maclaren pointed out there are six major Arab countries. We can always trust Angus to argue the Israeli viewpoint. But then, as you know, he handles the Israeli account for us, in addition to his other hat as chief of counterintelligence. At any rate, we are sticking to the operational plan. We certainly can't stop now."

He tapped the bowl of his pipe gently on a large glass ashtray. "In fact," he continued, "I've been thinking I may not pull Frank out immediately, even after Mossad receives its quota. There may be other possibilities."

"What do you mean?" Travers had been in the agency for almost a decade, but he could never quite get used to the elliptical way in which the senior people talked to each other. As though intelligence operations were all a parlor game, a charade, in which guessing the hidden meanings was part of the fun.

"Well, there's Africa. In the past ten years, thirty African countries have gained their independence. Eighteen of them in 1960 alone. Africa is the new battleground of the cold war. The KGB and the Chinese are extraordinarily active on the subcontinent. The time may come when we will want to help some of our friends there in the same way we are helping Israel now. We'll have to see."

Travers persisted in his objections. "Aside from Kolchak and Itzak Lev's driving abilities, there are other risks. Suppose the Atomic Energy Commission suspects there is Material Unaccounted For at Apollo. If the MUF is discovered, and they run a Diversion Path Analysis, the trail could lead right to DiMario, and from him right back to the Domestic Operations Division."

Black appeared unperturbed, as usual. "The last DPA they ran at NUFAC drew a big fat zero," he said. "Greenstein, the president of the company, convinced the AEC investigators that any MUF could be explained by the uranium picked up in the wiping rags and sticking to the pipes and the machinery. The AEC went away satisfied. They won't be back for a while."

Travers made one last try. "If Kolchak is badly hurt, or worse, the flap will damage my division much more than Plans. We're a new division. We can't afford trouble."

Black smiled his weary, patronizing smile again, and waved

a hand, indicating the meeting was over. Travers got up. He had reached the door when Black spoke.

"I'll tell Frank just to put a good scare into him," he said. "Nothing excessive. Moderation in all things, you know."

It was more than Travers had expected, and he thanked Black. He was genuinely grateful. When he passed the secretary in the outer office, she looked up and gave him another frosty smile. Travers smiled back. As he walked down the stairs, he wondered vaguely if she pissed pure ice water. It would certainly be a great convenience, Travers thought, in the summertime in Washington.

Chapter 3

Mama Leone's was about half a mile south of the NUFAC plant on the other side of the road. At night, it was usually crowded, mostly with regulars from the plant and other patrons from the working-class, ethnic neighborhood. Mama, a fat, black-haired woman with a hearty laugh, kept Iron City on tap, and in the restaurant part, she served her own lasagna, spaghetti and meatballs, and ravioli. Her customers joked that it all tasted the same because of the tomato sauce. Mama Leone used a lot of tomato sauce.

It was dark when Kolchak drove up to the restaurant and parked his Chevrolet. He could hear the jukebox blaring, and from the pleasant sound of the voices inside he assumed that the bar at Mama's was already fairly lively. Kolchak's feet crunched on the gravel in the parking lot. He had taken only a few paces when two men, who seemed to come out of nowhere, fell into step on either side of him.

Even in the darkness, the hulking figure of Perella was instantly recognizable. The slim, smaller man, who called himself Joe Vento, was with him, as usual.

"What's the trouble, Mike?" Perella asked in a casual, almost friendly tone. "You said on the phone that you couldn't make next week's delivery."

"I can't. . . . I just need to talk to you."

They were alongside a black Chrysler, and Perella opened the door. "Get in," he commanded.

The open car door blocked Kolchak's way in front, and Perella and Vento crowded in on his left. Kolchak spun around and saw that two more of Perella's hoods were standing right behind him. He recognized Tony Milano, who was tall, heavyset, and blond, and Nick Canucci, a shorter, husky man with a foreign accent.

"Why can't we talk inside?" Kolchak asked.

The answer was a fist that landed flat on the right side of Kolchak's jaw. He never knew which of the men hit him. The blow felt like a sledgehammer, and it left the side of his face numb. He did not fall down, but he lost his balance and slammed against the side of the car. Someone—he thought it might have been Canucci—shoved him hard into the back seat.

Kolchak sat up and put his right hand to his face. It felt wet, and Kolchak realized there was blood trickling out of the right side of his mouth. Two of the men had him wedged in the back seat between them. Vento got behind the wheel and Perella sat next to him. The car started up and shot out of the parking lot.

Kolchak managed to pull a handkerchief from his pocket and put it up to his jaw.

"What do you guys want from me?" he pleaded. "I've delivered three pounds. I used the jock you gave me and walked out the gates right past security every time. I haven't made any trouble. I just don't want to do it anymore."

"Shut up," Perella growled.

They drove on in silence for a few minutes and then pulled off the highway onto a smaller road. Kolchak realized they were going to the warehouse, the building that Perella called the *magazzino*. He knew the way, because it was there that he had made his deliveries and been paid off by Perella in $100 bills.

Over Nick Canucci's shoulder, Kolchak could see they had passed the darkened cement plant. In a moment, Vento spun the wheel to the right and they pulled up at the warehouse. Kolchak was frightened. His jaw ached and his hands felt cold. It was pitch-black outside, the moon now hidden by clouds and not a star in sight.

"Get out," Canucci ordered.

Kolchak did, but his knees almost buckled from the fear. He stumbled to the building, flanked by Canucci and Milano, who were half pushing him along. Perella punched a button and the big metal door clanked upward, then slammed shut behind them.

They were in total darkness, but Perella had a pencil flashlight. With its thin beam of light, he guided the group past the abandoned machinery and the boxes until they came to what Kolchak guessed must once have been a refrigeration room. Someone shoved him inside and Perella flicked on the lights.

The room was brightly lit by bare electric bulbs in white porcelain sockets in the ceiling, but the windows had been covered over with black tarpaper and tape, so that no crack of light would show outside. If anyone drove by, which was unlikely anyway in that almost deserted industrial area, the warehouse would have looked completely dark.

The room in which Kolchak found himself had almost no furniture. There were a couple of chairs, and a green garden hose connected to a tap in the corner. The floor was slatted so that water, or blood from the sides of beef that had once hung in the room, could run through the slats into a trough and down a drain. Along the walls, at a height of about seven feet, were a dozen meat hooks.

"Sit down," Perella ordered Kolchak.

Tony Milano, the hulking blond man, stood in front of the door, arms folded. His real name was Douglas Carlson. He was six feet four and weighed 240 pounds, an ex-Green Beret rumored to have beheaded his Vietnamese mistress with a machete one night when, claiming a sore throat, she declined to perform fellatio. No charges were ever brought, because the murder could not be proved, but Carlson left Saigon under a cloud. The agency picked him up. He was one of several dozen agents it used on high-risk operations that might require the kind of murderous skills Carlson had acquired at Fort Bragg and practiced in Vietnam. Towny Black used these men, but, privately, he referred to them contemptuously as "cowboys."

Nick Canucci, the stocky, shorter man, stood near the chair in which Kolchak sat. His real name was Marko Vujevec, a former Hungarian Freedom Fighter who had escaped from Budapest and made his way across the border to Vienna. He was taken by the CIA to Frankfurt. After lengthy interrogations, his questioners were satisfied as to his bona fides, and Vujevec joined the Plans Directorate. His face was a map of Eastern Europe, and he had not shed his Hungarian accent, but miraculously, no one in Apollo seemed to doubt that he was an Italian.

Joe Vento, the slim, little man whom Kolchak feared the most, was leaning against the wall, under one of the meat hooks. His real name was Dominic Salerno. Like DiMario, he had grown up in New York's Little Italy, and it was DiMario who had brought him into the agency. Vento had joined the Marines in World War II and fought on Okinawa. He had killed a lot of Japanese. He seemed to have enjoyed it.

Perella was leaning over the chair, his hawk nose pushed almost into Kolchak's face. "You don't tell Angelo Perella when you're going to stop," he said. "We tell you."

Kolchak did not reply. The bleeding had stopped but his face still ached.

"We're gonna teach you a lesson, Kolchak. We're gonna teach you how to dance. Get up."

Kolchak didn't move immediately and Perella slapped him hard on the face. Kolchak rose slowly to his feet.

"Take your clothes off," Perella ordered. "Strip."

"What the hell—" Kolchak stopped in mid-sentence. Perella was pointing a gun directly at his stomach. He took off his shoes and socks, then his shirt, pants, and jockey shorts. He stood stark naked under the bright electric lights. The warehouse was cold and he was shivering.

Perella nodded, an almost imperceptible signal. Agile as a cat, Tony Milano, the big blond man, moved swiftly away from the door, grabbed Kolchak around the waist, and lifted him up and toward the wall. Kolchak felt a searing pain in his back as a steel meat hook pierced the soft flesh between his shoulder blades. Milano released his grip and stepped backward.

Kolchak screamed in pain as the steel hook ripped deeper into his back, taking the full weight of his body. His feet dangled well above the floor. He hung there, helpless and naked.

"Take me down," Kolchak screamed. "Take me down you mother-fuckers!" He felt the blood running down his back and over his buttocks, dripping down his legs to the floor. The pain in his shoulder blades had spread. He felt like his whole back was gripped in a vise of steel.

Joe Vento, the little man, was approaching the wall where Kolchak hung, screaming. In his right hand, Vento carried a slim, three-foot-long object that looked a little like a gun. At its base was a box with a red plastic handgrip. A long white, Fiberglas tube extended from the box. Mounted on the end and wrapped in wire was a small blue plastic cylinder, from which protruded two round brass prongs.

"Let's see if he knows how to dance," said Perella.

Vento pressed the prongs of the electric cattle prod against Kolchak's stomach. He pushed a little white button on the handgrip. There was a buzzing sound, and sparks flew. Simultaneously, Kolchak's body jerked to the right and he screamed. It felt as though the prod had burned a hole in his stomach.

Vento touched the prongs to Kolchak's chest, and the shock sent a sharp, searing pain through his side. He gasped for breath. His feet and hands were twitching uncontrollably.

"He's not dancing too good," Perella said. "Try his balls."

Vento giggled and shoved the prongs under Kolchak's genitals. He screamed in agony, his body writhing, and his legs flailing the air. The pain was almost unbearable.

"No, no! Stop," Kolchak pleaded. "For God sakes, no more." His legs were still kicking at the empty air.

"He's dancing pretty good now," Vento said.

He sent another shock coursing through Kolchak's body. The red, white, and blue cattle prod he was using was called "Superboy." It was powered by ten D cells connected in series and delivered enough voltage to kill a rat.

Kolchak was moaning, gasping for breath, and pleading with Perella to take him down.

Instead, Perella nodded to Canucci, who had picked up the garden hose and approached Kolchak. He turned on the nozzle and sprayed his entire body. It felt ice-cold and Kolchak screamed as it hit him. The water turned red as it mixed with the blood dripping down Kolchak's back and ran through the slats on the floor.

"Fry his prick," Perella ordered. Vento, grinning, carefully placed the prongs so that they straddled the end of Kolchak's penis, and pressed the button. The water had turned his entire body into a conductor, and the jolting shock spread from his loins to his fingertips. Kolchak howled in agony, his legs kicking out and his body twisting against the steel hook that tore deeper into his flesh.

"Look at him," said Vento excitedly. "He's flopping around like a fish."

Kolchak was alternately screaming and moaning now. Suddenly, he was quiet. "Holy Mary," he whispered. "Mother of God." Then he threw up. Most of the vomit splashed down his chest and onto his stomach and legs. Abruptly, Kolchak's legs stopped flailing and he hung, limp on the wall, his chin down against his chest. He had blacked out.

"Clean him up," Perella ordered. Canucci played the hose on Kolchak's burned and bleeding body. Kolchak was still unconscious.

"Okay, Tony," Perella said. "He's had enough. Take him down."

Joe Vento looked disappointed. "Just like a fish, Angelo," he said. "He was floppin' just like a fish on a hook."

It was midafternoon the next day when the telephone rang in Robert Travers' office in Washington. It was long-distance and a poor connection. "This is Agnes," a man's voice said. "I'm calling from a pay phone at a gas station." Travers realized that O'Donnell was breaking security; he was not authorized to have direct contact with Spectrum personnel in Washington.

"What's the trouble?"

"You know the package we had been having some difficulty about?"

"Yes."

"Well, it's been badly damaged."

Travers felt sick. "How badly?"

"From what I understand, it was torn up pretty badly and burned. An electrical problem. I just thought you ought to know." There was a click. The caller had hung up.

Travers immediately dialed DiMario on the scrambler. There was no answer at the warehouse in Apollo. He kept trying at twenty-minute intervals, until finally, just before 5:00 P.M., someone picked up the receiver.

"This is Mary Jane," Travers said tensely. "Let me talk to Alice."

There was a long pause, and then a voice that Travers recognized as Douglas Carlson's replied: "I'll see if I can find him."

Travers heard footsteps and muffled conversation in the background. Finally, DiMario came on the line.

Travers did not greet him. "What the hell is going on there?" he asked.

"What do you mean?"

"You know damn well what I mean. What have you done to Kolchak?"

"Oh, Kolchak. I understand he's in the hospital. They say he got drunk the other night and had a nasty fall. Went over backwards on a wrought-iron fence and ripped his shoulder on a spike. There were some burns on his body, but he refused to tell the doctors where he got them. Said he didn't remember. He lost a lot of blood, but he'll be all right."

"You son of a bitch. You had no authority."

"Negative. The librarian called me the day before yesterday. He authorized me to do whatever was necessary to protect the integrity of Phase Blue."

"He told me you were only to put a scare into Kolchak."

"That's not what he told me."

"I'm going over to the library to check it out. You'd better be right, Alice."

"I'm right."

Travers hung up and left his office in a cold fury. This time, he did not bother to telephone Towny Black's secretary. She took one look at his face and made no attempt to bar his way into the inner sanctum.

Black did not seem surprised to see Travers arrive unannounced.

"I've been expecting you, Robert," he said. "Sit down, and spare me your recriminations."

Black pushed a button and spoke into the intercom. "Have Miss Witherow send in some tea, please. Cream and sugar, Robert?"

"I don't want any, thanks."

"Just the usual, for me, Patricia." He leaned back. "Well, Robert, I can see you're upset. I understand."

"You tortured an innocent man. You told me it wouldn't be done."

"I don't like violence, my dear boy. But sometimes in our business we have to use unpleasant means to achieve our ends. We are engaged, as Dean Rusk has recently put it, in a dirty, back-alley struggle. The other side does not play by the rules. The KGB would have shot Kolchak."

"We are not the KGB."

"Ah, but they have a point."

Miss Witherow knocked, and entered with the tea. The service was Royal Copenhagen. Black poured himself a cup, dropped in a lump of sugar, and added some milk. The silver teaspoon made a little clattering noise as he put it down on the saucer.

"I've been placed in a very awkward position," Travers said. "You've undercut my authority. I don't see how I can continue to deal with DiMario under the circumstances. I suggest he be recalled from the field and replaced."

Black took off his glasses and rubbed the bridge of his nose. He looked up at Travers. "As a matter of fact, Robert, I've been talking to Trilby Gates. He and I have agreed that

Domestic Operations is not your—forgive me—cup of tea. We both think you might do better abroad."

"I've only had the division for six months. It's much too soon for me to give it up."

"Crowley is leaving as station chief in Rome. He's being transferred to the Paris station. You're to be his replacement."

"I have no choice?"

"None, I'm afraid. The decision is made. You and Margaret will love Rome. We bankroll the Christian Democrats, as you know, and the Soviets are not at all bothersome. It's not Vienna, after all. You like art, don't you, Robert? You can arrange frequent inspection trips to our base in Florence. The Uffizi awaits you. The weather in Rome is glorious, and I can recommend some excellent restaurants in Trastevere. Margaret can give little dinner parties by candlelight, and your menservants will wear white gloves. She'll adore it."

Black had played his hand cleverly, Travers realized. He was offering him a major post, one that officers in the Plans Directorate fought for. It was transparently a means to cut him away from Spectrum, but after what had happened he no longer wanted to be a part of the operation anyway.

"I'll have to talk it over with Margaret," he said.

"Of course."

"And we'll need some time to sell our house."

"Naturally."

Travers got up and prepared to leave.

"By the way," Black asked, "who told you?"

"It's not important."

"I'd like to know."

Travers smiled grimly. "A little birdie."

Black seemed disconcerted. "Surely not The Hawk?"

"No," Travers replied. "It was Itzak Lev's traveling parakeet."

Chapter 4

The black Mercedes 450 SEL with the roof antenna swung off the Dolley Madison highway onto the long, sweeping access road. It slowed down but did not stop as it approached the gate. A sign on the chain-link fence warned, "U.S. Government Property. No Cameras."

A uniformed guard saluted and waved the driver on, but the tall, distinguished man in the backseat did not look up from the papers he was reading. They were stamped TOP SECRET-SCOPE, a special intelligence classification that meant the information they contained had been acquired by a spy satellite whirling over the Soviet Union twelve hours earlier.

Within a few moments, the car glided to a halt near the front entrance of a massive, white-concrete-and-glass building set among the trees. It was spring in northern Virginia, and the leaves were already turning from the pale-green shades of April to the darker hues of May. The director snapped shut his attaché case and thumbed the wheel of the combination lock. He squinted involuntarily as he stepped out into the sunshine and the cool morning air.

The Office of Security people had asked that he use the underground garage entrance, from where he could be whisked unseen to his office by a private elevator, but the director preferred the front door. It was a small gesture, but he liked to think it preserved the common touch, and made him seem more like the other nine thousand employees who toiled at headquarters. In fact, few people were there to observe the director's entrance; it was only seven o'clock, his usual arrival time. It would be another two hours before most of the employees were in their offices and headquarters came alive.

Although he entered this building every day, the director never failed to be struck by the eerie and unexpected silence that enveloped it. No other government agency of this size was set amid such pastoral splendor. Outside, not a sound could be heard except the hum of the building's air conditioners, the chirping of the sparrows, and the distant cooing of a mourning dove. Off to the right, a separate, domed structure housing a five-hundred-seat auditorium managed, in combination with the silence, to give the grounds a weird, almost Martian atmosphere.

Attaché case in hand, Graham Townsend Black strode through the glass doors and into the lobby, turning sharply left to avoid stepping on the huge, circular seal inlaid in the marble floor. In its center a fierce eagle's head glowered. Around the bottom of the seal were inscribed the words "United States of America." The words along the top said "Central Intelligence Agency."

Black had aged well. After sixteen years, his full head of hair was now completely white. It had been a long journey from the library on H Street to the top; President Anderson had named him director of the CIA in January 1981, only four months ago.

A guard seated at a desk in the lobby murmured into a walkie-talkie. "Station one. MK/Leader in the building." An indistinguishable reply crackled back.

The director walked the sixty feet to his little private elevator, stepped in, and punched the button for the seventh floor. A moment later, he emerged into a thickly carpeted reception room. It looked much like any corporate executive suite, except for the large glass booth to his left. At the entrance of the booth, an athletic young man in a dark-blue suit stood, balanced on his heels, with his feet apart and his hands behind his back. He had jet-black hair and his face was so pale that his dark lips seemed almost painted on. He might have been Italian or Greek; he reminded the director of a young Tony Curtis. The director wished that the Office of Security would assign a bodyguard who might at least *look* as if he had gone to the right schools. But that was the trouble with those OS types, he reflected; put them in an Ivy League suit and they still looked like something out of *West Side Story*.

Holly Corcoran was waiting for the director outside the door to his office, which was marked, simply, 75706. She wore a bright-red knit dress and a single barrette in her blond hair. She was smiling at the director, flashing her nearly perfect white teeth. Holly always looked as though she belonged on the beach at Malibu. She was in fact a golden girl from southern California.

"Good morning, Mr. Black," she said. "The National Foreign Intelligence Board meeting has been rescheduled for nine-thirty, so Evan Younger asked me to move up the staff meeting to eight-thirty. He said you'd approve."

"That's fine."

"The Special Coordination Committee meeting has been postponed until tomorrow. And President Anderson wants you at the White House promptly at three-thirty P.M. He expects to be briefed on Angola as soon as he wakes up from his nap."

"All right, Holly." It wasn't, she knew. Black detested briefing the president in his cramped, second-floor bedroom. Often, before dressing after his nap, the president sat around in his underwear, interrupting their conversation to take phone calls, while Black perched awkwardly on a narrow and uncomfortable Regency chair next to the bed. On one occasion, the leader of the Free World had summoned him into the bathroom and insisted that the director brief him while he showered. Black had shouted the CIA's secrets at the glass door of the shower stall, but he was not sure how much the president heard over the noise of the running water. The director's shirt had wilted from the steam; when he got back to Langley he noticed with dismay that his suit was baggy. Black took comfort in the knowledge that at least Thurlow Anderson was an improvement over Lyndon Johnson, who had sometimes required McGeorge Bundy, his national-security assistant, to confer with him while LBJ sat on the toilet. The mental image of the patrician Bundy being forced to listen to Johnson's musical notes never failed to give the director a chuckle.

Black would need a talking paper on Angola in his hands by 3:00 P.M., in time for the White House meeting; he would have to instruct his staff assistant to get the machinery moving. "Tell Evan I want to see him five minutes before the staff meeting."

"Yes, sir."

The director sat down at his uncluttered desk, and dismissed his secretary. As Holly turned and moved toward the door, the director studied her rotating rear end. It was one of the small joys of his day.

As she closed the door softly, he glanced down at that morning's edition of the *National Intelligence Daily*. In his rare public speeches, the director liked to refer to the daily as "a very exclusive newspaper with the world's biggest staff of reporters and the world's smallest circulation." It was an accurate description. As Washington slept, and information flowed in to the CIA from around the globe by radio and Teletype, the *NID* staff toiled through the night to cull the most important tidbits for the daily bulletin. The president got a copy with his morning coffee, and Black, the secretaries of State and Defense, the president's national-security adviser, and a handful of other top officials were on the access list.

The director riffled through the *NID*, but it failed to hold his attention for very long. The Soviet premier's diabetes had become worse in the past week. The prime minister of Israel would shortly propose to President Anderson yet another summit meeting on the Middle East peace negotiations. The director assumed this had been picked up on routine NSA telephone intercepts in Tel Aviv. An African leader who liked whips and chains had imported an imaginative new mistress from a Paris bordello; he was unaware that she was an agent of the KGB.

It was, Black reflected, the usual mélange of hard intelligence, gossip, and speculation; many of the items, he knew, were included more in order to titillate Thurlow Anderson and the other *NID* consumers than for their actual intelligence value. As long as the president read the *NID*, the theory went, he was at least aware that the CIA existed. The director had not appreciated it when Evan Younger had suggested they include a centerfold.

31

Black put the daily aside and began going through the neat stack of mail that Holly opened and placed on his desk each morning. Almost immediately, he saw the letter.

As he read it, a knot formed in the center of his chest and tightened. His hands felt moist.

The envelope, which Holly had clipped to the back of the letter, had been postmarked in Zurich two days earlier. There was no return address. The director examined the envelope briefly, then tossed it aside. He knew the letter would not have been written in Switzerland, merely mailed from there. It was, he realized, the work of a professional, the opening move in a potentially deadly chess game. He would have to react decisively, but he needed time to think. He could not afford to make a mistake.

He lit up his pipe, swiveled in his chair, and stared out the picture window for a long time at the rolling green hills and the thick groves of oak and maple that surrounded and screened the headquarters.

He had always enjoyed the bucolic view and the illusory sense of seclusion it afforded. Illusory, he realized, because in the winter, when the trees were bare, the headquarters could easily be seen from the Dolley Madison highway, especially at night, when the building was ablaze with lights. But it was spring now, and no intrusive sign of civilization interrupted his vision; he might as easily have been on his farm in Vermont as in Langley, Virginia, eight miles and twenty minutes from the White House.

The CIA had moved to this rustic setting in 1961, two decades before, when Allen Dulles was the DCI. The agency's headquarters had been built on the old Leiter estate. The CIA had bought up the surrounding land as well, and over protests, evicted the affluent suburban residents to insure perimeter security. Dulles had departed because of the Bay of Pigs. His successor, John McCone, thought the agency needed even more land for privacy. To justify the need, two technical specialists from the Office of Security had climbed a hillside, and using powerful telephoto lenses, taken photographs of McCone sitting at his desk by the same picture window through which Graham Townsend Black now gazed. The fifty-power blowups of the photos had even revealed the documents McCone had been holding in his hands, their TOP SECRET-UMBRA classification marks and their text clearly legible. Armed with the photographs, McCone had won his fight to buy up additional land. A physician named Jenkins whose property adjoined the agency had fussed, and there had been a little flurry of publicity, quickly hushed, but in the end the agency had had its way and the doctor had quietly moved to another house in McLean.

The director swung back in his chair. He looked around the familiar office with its teak paneling that so artfully concealed the hidden microphones, its thick carpeting, the white telephone on the desk next to the gold globe, and the red scrambler phone that he could lift, if he wished, and in an instant talk directly to the president. He savored the trappings of his office, especially the view through the picture window—from which he could occasionally see deer—and the title of Director of Central Intelligence. The DCI. The quiet power he wielded from this office was extraordinary. He could reach out almost anywhere in the globe from Room 75706. His decisions could mean life or death for men and women thousands of miles from here, most of whom would never suspect that the bullet that shattered a brain on a narrow street in Istanbul or the knife plunged into a stomach in some dark alley in Marrakesh had been set in motion from this quiet, air-conditioned office in Virginia, the birthplace of presidents, the cradle of democracy. He could, Graham Black realized, overthrow a prime minister before breakfast or snuff out the life of a minor KGB agent in Macao over afternoon tea.

Black enjoyed being the DCI, not only because he wielded great power but because his was *secret* power. His classmates at Yale had become corporate executives, or moved in the quiet affluence of the more prestigious Wall Street law firms. Theirs was ordinary power. They would never know the special exhilaration of Towny Black's world. Black the black operator.

The director also knew that no man could expect to occupy the DCI's chair for more than a few years; Dick Helms had lasted six, but there were special circumstances and the byzantine complications of Watergate. In time, Black realized, he would have to step down, perhaps at the end of President Anderson's second term. He would retire to the farm in Vermont, perhaps write his memoirs, as Allen Dulles and Bill Colby had done.

But at age fifty-nine, he was not ready for that yet. He had hardly settled into the job. Now, unexpectedly, a cryptic message from the past on a blue sheet of airmail paper threatened his power, his reputation, and his future.

He slumped in his high-backed chair, leaning his large head against the polished leather. He removed his glasses, closed his eyes, and rubbed the bridge of his nose with his fingertips in a characteristic gesture. He was a large man, over six feet, and a bit heavier than he wished, despite his regular lunchtime squash game in the CIA gym and the rounds of golf on Saturdays at Burning Tree when his work and the weather permitted. His features were even, almost handsome. He was sure he could have been as successful in the corporate world as his contemporaries, for he looked the part of a senior business executive. Which was half the battle.

The director sat forward, put his glasses back on, and stared again at the letter, at the thin blue tissue on which there appeared a single typewritten word:

SPECTRUM

He knew what had to be done. He reached for the buzzer on his desk.

Chapter 5

One month earlier, at Charles de Gaulle Airport near Paris, an attractive English girl in her mid-twenties waited in the Air France passenger lounge for a New York flight. She had straight brown hair that fell almost to her shoulders and wore large Givenchy sunglasses. She was simply but expensively dressed in a light-tan raincoat, a beige cashmere sweater, and brown skirt. Over her left shoulder she had slung a dark leather purse with a gold clasp that she had purchased the day before at Hermès. A small flight bag rested at her feet.

She might have been on holiday, but something about her clothes and appearance suggested it was more likely that she was traveling on business. Perhaps she was a young fashion consultant for a Paris couturier on a trip to the States, or a buyer for a London boutique. She was, in fact, none of these. Her name was Valerie Kerr, and it was no ordinary mission that brought her to the air terminal at Roissy.

"Mesdames et Messieurs, le vol Air France numéro quarante-deux, destination New York, Aéroport Kennedy, est maintenant prêt pour l'embarquement, porte vingt-trois. Veuillez présenter vos cartes d'embarquement au contrôle. Ladies and gentlemen, Air France Flight 42 for New York's Kennedy Airport is now ready to receive passengers at Gate Twenty-three. Please have your boarding passes ready." At the announcement, Valerie extracted her ticket and boarding pass from her purse, picked up her flight bag, and joined the line of passengers already forming at the gate. A few moments later, she was moving down the aisle of the huge 747 to

a window seat. She had been careful to choose the no-smoking section. Ever since she had managed to give up cigarettes a year earlier, the smoke bothered her. She settled in her seat, allowed her head to sink back into the soft cushion, and realized that it was the first waking moment in the past forty-eight hours that she had stopped running. Robert had insisted that she leave for the States from Paris, rather than London, and his directions had been explicit. She had left Waterloo Station two days before on the train to Dover. As Robert had instructed, she had switched cabs twice on the way to Waterloo. She had boarded the train at the last possible second, after a hundred-yard dash down the platform from the gate, past a surprised guard. The crossing was pleasant, the Channel not very choppy, and she had gone up on the upper deck to enjoy the sun, the blue sky, the sparkling water, and the smell of the sea. As the white cliffs receded, she felt rather wistful, as she always did when she left England and all that was familiar. This time, she realized, the nostalgia was tinged with a dark sense of foreboding. She was frightened.

The sea gulls were scolding and hovering almost motionless overhead as the ship eased into the dock at Calais. She carried her small suitcase down the gangplank and paused a moment on the pier, breathing in the sea air deeply, and glancing quickly but casually at the other disembarking passengers. She was sure she had not been followed. Robert's precautions were probably unnecessary. No one knows about us, she thought. Still, she reassured herself, Robert knew what he was doing; he had not become chief of the London station by making simple mistakes in tradecraft.

A bored official with a pencil mustache inspected her passport and looked her over with what Valerie felt was more than bureaucratic interest. *Cochon,* she thought.

"And what is the purpose of your visit to France, Miss Kerr?"

"I'm on holiday."

"How long do you expect to stay in France?"

"Just two days."

He motioned her into the customs shed, where a blue-uniformed *douanier* asked her if she had anything to declare.

Only a name, she thought. The name of a man in Washington. And it was not written down. It was in her head.

"Rien," she replied.

On the train to Paris, she dined on pâté, bread, and a half bottle of Beaune. She luxuriated in the white tablecloths, the gleaming silver, and the single rose in the vase as the green fields and hedgerows of Picardy swept by. She loved France, and she almost wanted to cry for the sheer pleasure of being there again. But two steely-eyed nuns in black habits and gold-rimmed glasses sat opposite her all through lunch, staring at her with what Valerie decided was disapproval, and she was determined to show no emotion in front of them.

At the Gare du Nord, she hailed a taxi, and told the grizzled driver to take her to the Arc de Triomphe. Both driver and vehicle looked like survivors of the Battle of the Marne. *"Ah, vous êtes anglaise,"* he crooned. Yes, she replied, in her best Mary Poppins voice, "I *am* English. And how lovely your city is." At the Etoile, after dawdling a few moments, she hailed another cab and told the driver to take her to the Tuileries. She strolled through the park and lingered for a long time at the carousel, watching the children, immaculate in their pinafores, laughing and squealing as they reached for the brass ring. She stood there, soaking in the calliope music, the almost hypnotic effect of the horses and giraffes moving lazily up and down in their mechanical gracefulness, and the laughter of the children. Then she walked along the rue du Faubourg Saint-Honoré to Hermès and bought the purse. It was late in the afternoon by now and getting chilly; she was tired and had played tourist long enough. She hailed a taxi and told the driver to take her to a café on the boulevard Saint-Germain. She sat at a sidewalk table and sipped an aperitif. After paying the check, she walked up to the corner of the rue des Saints-Pères, turned south, away from the Seine, and registered at an inexpensive hotel halfway down the block. The room seemed lonely without Robert and she did not sleep well.

After a quick breakfast of coffee and croissants in the courtyard of the little hotel, she had checked out and taken a taxi to de Gaulle. The jet's engines were whining now and the plane was accelerating down the runway. With a sudden surge, it lifted off and began climbing at a steep angle, the great engines screaming, straining, thrusting upward. When the seat-belt sign flickered off, Valerie released a lever, reclined as far as she could, and closed her eyes. She thought of Robert, of how well and passionately they had made love in her flat in Chelsea. That had only been two days ago, but already it seemed much longer.

The taxi dropped Valerie off at the Capitol, and she walked through the little park to the New Senate Office Building. It was early, but the sun was up and the day already warm with a promise of becoming unseasonably hot. She threaded her way through busloads of tourists—fat men in checked pants with cameras slung over their shirts; women in bright-green or pink slacks, carrying shiny, vinyl purses; crew-cut, towheaded farm children, many of them wearing turquoise alpine hats decorated with dyed feathers. The people of the world's greatest democracy, come to see their government in action. They would wander mindlessly through the marble corridors of the Capitol, seeing little and understanding less, then spew out along Constitution Avenue to lunch on hot dogs hawked from mobile stands by beady-eyed vendors who seemed to be constantly on the lookout for the police. Washington was beautiful in April, Valerie decided; the tourists were decidedly not.

She quickened her pace, and cut across the grass; she did not wish to be late for her 10:00 A.M. appointment at the Senate Intelligence Committee. She made her way down the long corridors of the Dirksen Building to Room G-308. The black, uniformed guard behind the old mahogany desk asked to see some identification. Valerie fished out her driver's license. He glanced at the pale-green-and-white card in its plastic holder, then checked her name against his manifest.

"Mr. Goodman is expecting you, Miss Kerr." He picked up the telephone, dialed an extension, spoke quietly for a moment, and then handed her a laminated-plastic visitor's badge. Valerie wondered whether the CIA itself could have more security; it seemed to her faintly ridiculous to go through all this rigamarole to see a staff member of a Senate committee. But then, this committee did deal in official secrets. The guard pressed a buzzer and motioned her solemnly through the heavy door. Inside, a plump, bespectacled secretary, also wearing a security badge, met Valerie and escorted her back through a rabbit warren of partitioned offices.

Their journey ended at one of the cubicles. A short, almost gnomelike man was hunched over a desk, reading a document. He stood up when Valerie entered, removed the cigar from his mouth, and offered a hairy hand. He was dark-haired, and dark-complexioned, and he peered at Valerie through thick glasses. His face was heavily pockmarked. Caliban in a Brooks Brothers suit, Valerie thought. He was so ugly that some women—Valerie not among them—found him handsome.

"Ben Goodman," he said, introducing himself. "Have a seat. Just move those books out of the way." Valerie settled into an uncomfortable typing chair, its stuffing visible through a large crack in the ancient green leather. The little cubicle, she noticed, was piled high with books and reports. Small as Goodman was, there was barely space for him, let alone a visitor. Electric typewriters were clacking away incessantly in nearby cubicles.

Goodman was smiling. "I didn't know Bob Travers had such a beautiful assistant."

"No, no. I don't work for him. I'm just a friend."

"Well, if he let you out of his sight, even for a few days, it must be important."

"It is, Mr. Goodman."

"Please—Ben."

"All right . . . Ben." Valerie smiled back nervously. Goodman, as Robert had explained, was the committee's staff member in charge of CIA affairs. Everything depended on his reaction. Goodman relit his cigar, blew a puff of thick smoke in her direction, and settled back in his chair.

"You've come a long way to see me this morning," he said. He leaned forward slightly. "As a matter of fact, it all seems rather"—he paused—"clandestine."

"Robert wanted it this way."

"Of course. The habits of a lifetime. But what's on his mind?"

Valerie took a deep breath. She had rehearsed this moment with Robert in the flat in Chelsea, and over and over again in her mind during the flight to New York. Still, she was tense.

"As you know," she began carefully, "Robert has built a brilliant career with the agency. But he doesn't get along with Graham Black."

Goodman sat up, alert. "I know that," he said, "and I've wondered why. Because Black spared him during the Halloween Massacre." Four years before, in October, Admiral Turner had fired literally hundreds of the covert-action people. Black was head of the Operations Directorate at the time, so he had selected the victims. Turner had practically wiped out the Old Boy network in the Clandestine Services. A clean sweep of the Ivy League. The adenoidal cries of horror were heard all the way from the Metropolitan Club to the Harvard Yard. But Black had kept Robert Travers. "How did he escape?" Goodman asked. "Did he go to Ohio State?"

Valerie was beginning to like Goodman a little, despite his outrageous male chauvinism and his foul cigar.

"No, Yale."

"Then it's a mystery. But go on."

"During all the trouble with the Church Committee, the Rockefeller Report, and the stories in the press day after day about CIA horrors, no one inside could have been more disgusted than Robert with what the agency had done."

Goodman minutely examined the ash on his cigar. "A reformer in the whorehouse," he said. "I've heard that song before, from others. Travers is high up in the Operations Directorate. He worked directly under Helms in the 1960s. He must have known a good deal about what was going on. The assassination plots, the mail opening, the domestic spying, the drug- and mind-control experiments, the wiretapping."

"Less than you might imagine, actually. He knew nothing about Operation Chaos; that was all in Counterintelligence, under Maclaren. The Technical Services Division handled the drug- and mind-control projects. Robert did know about the assassination plots. In some areas, I suppose he knew a good deal."

Goodman was beginning to look bored. "Of course he did.

And now, like a lot of others in the agency, he is protecting his ass. Was he upset because the CIA broke the law? Or was he really worried about how the disclosures tarnished the reputations of the agency people like himself who remained on in the top jobs?"

"Both," Valerie said firmly. "I'm sure there is some self-interest involved. But Robert believes in this country. I don't, particularly—it isn't my country—but he does. And he's devoted his life to serving it. Whatever he did, or felt in the past, he feels now that everything must come out. That the only hope for the agency is to start over with a clean slate."

Goodman nodded. "I agree. But not all the senators on the committee would. Most of them would rather not know any more details about what the agency did in the past. Water under the bridge."

"There is something too big and too dangerous to ignore. Robert knows the secret. He believes Black will go to any lengths to keep it from getting out."

"And what is it?"

"Robert can explain. But I can tell you this much: there has been a massive cover-up in the agency. People have been killed, or at least Robert suspects so. With all of the official investigations and reports, and with all due respect to you, Mr. Goodman—Ben—and the committee, this secret is something that you don't know about. At least you haven't been able to prove it, even if you suspect it."

Goodman looked at her sideways, like a sleepy crocodile lazing in the sun. He tried again. "And what, may I ask, is the agency covering up?"

Valerie leaned forward and kept her voice low. Goodman could barely hear her over the sound of the typewriters.

"It's complicated," she said. "And Robert hasn't told me everything. But it has to do with nuclear weapons."

Chapter 6

Senator Barry Owens of Colorado fiddled with a sharp-pointed silver letter opener on his ornate oak desk as Ben Goodman quickly briefed him. Even at age thirty-eight, after six years in the Senate, Goodman reflected, Owens looked totally out of place amid the brass cuspidors, the marble pillars, and the nineteenth-century splendor of the Senate. He was too contemporary. Handsome, with square, chiseled features, given to mod suits and a breezy, informal manner, Owens might more easily have been mistaken for a movie actor or a television anchorman than a United States senator. But his personal style was a product of his background; as a young lawyer in Denver, a Democrat, and a leader of the antiwar movement in the late 1960s, he had managed Brockway Macallister's unsuccessful presidential campaign, a moral crusade that was doomed from the start. Despite his candidate's defeat, Owens had gained national attention in the news media. *Time* magazine had called him "one of the bright new breed of hard-driving, skilled campaign managers who are remaking America's political map." All three of the major television networks had given him substantial exposure on the nightly news. In 1974, Owens had unseated Colorado's senior Republican senator in an upset victory. Despite his youth, he had won a place on the new Senate Intelligence Committee, and now he was chairman of the subcommittee on CIA. It was a tricky assignment, and it might help or destroy his presidential chances. Publicly, Owens disavowed any interest in the presidency, but he was pleased when the press sometimes compared him to John F. Kennedy. His aides assumed he was biding his time; he was telegenic, bright, and ambitious, and Ben Goodman—who was Owens' man on the committee staff—and the others around the senator, were bound to him, not only by loyalty but by their own private visions of moving with him into the White House one day.

Owens put down the letter opener and began tossing paper clips into a cup on his desk. "So Travers wants to deal?" he asked.

"So the girl says."

"What do you think he has to tell us?"

"Hard to say. Aside from the fact that it has to do with the agency and nuclear weapons she wouldn't say much. My impression is that she knows more, but probably not the full story."

Owens, in his shirtsleeves, leaned back in his chair, still tossing paper clips as he talked. "I can take an educated guess. Suppose the CIA has evidence that more third-world powers have secretly developed nuclear bombs—perhaps even tested them. But the administration is sitting on the story. Maybe Travers wants to leak it to us."

"Could be. But my instinct is that it's something else. It has to be something bigger. Big enough to have touched off a violent power struggle inside the agency. A cover-up. Assassinations. At least that's what the girl claims."

A buzzer interrupted their conversation. Owens picked up the phone. "They'll have to wait," he snapped. "And Karla—no more calls while I'm meeting with Ben."

He resumed his basketball game with the paper clips. "Fucking Sierra Club," he said. "They're out there waiting to lean on me about water. It's always your friends who take up the most time. Because you *have* to see them." He paused. "Ben, where do you think Travers is coming from? What's his motive?"

Goodman swung a leg over the arm of the stuffed leather chair and fingered his dead cigar. He longed to light it up, but never did when he was with the senator.

"For some time now," he replied, "I've been hearing rumors that Travers is very unhappy. I know he's been feuding with Towny Black, and probably Black has kept him overseas to get him out of the way. It's prestigious but it ain't Langley, if you know what I mean."

"What does Travers want? Does he want to come to Washington and testify in executive session?"

"Hell, no. He wouldn't have sent the girl. He's moving very cautiously at this point, holding back. What he wants— well, according to the girl, he wants *you* to meet with him secretly, in England. She says he'll tell his story, but only to you, in person."

There was a long silence. Owens tossed another paper clip, missing the cup. The clip went skittering across his polished desk and landed noiselessly on the thick, green carpet. "Shit, Ben, I can't do that and you know it. Suppose it leaks out? 'Senate CIA Watchdog Holds Secret Meeting with London Station Chief.' *The Washington Post* would love that one. Bradlee would weigh in with an editorial warning against senators with presidential ambitions who conduct foreign policy on their own. The chairman would chew my ass out and I'd be reassigned to the Agriculture Committee, if I was lucky. Thanks a lot, Ben."

"But suppose Travers really does have something big," Goodman protested. "On the order of Watergate. You could bring it all out, in televised hearings. It would mean a lot for the country, and a lot for you. You know damn well that if Sam Ervin had been twenty years younger, he would have been elected president after Watergate."

"I doubt it. Besides, I quote *Rolling Stone,* not the Old Testament. And you haven't told me how I could fly off to London without a news leak."

Goodman flicked the remains of an ash off his cigar. "Senator, the physical arrangements for your trip can be handled so it won't leak. I can manage it. That's not really the problem."

"What is?"

Goodman leaned forward and spoke slowly and deliberately. "The whole thing," he said. "It could be an operation. Directed against us."

"Jesus." Owens finally stopped playing with the paper clips and sat upright.

"Sooner or later," Goodman continued, "I think they'll try

it. I've felt all along they will. And suppose this is it? Suppose the girl works for the agency. And suppose Travers is really acting on orders from Towny Black? They suck us in with a phony story about another agency horror. You go for it, meet secretly with Travers, hold hearings, and the whole thing turns out to be false. The committee is discredited, the agency says the entire affair proves the Congress should leave the CIA alone, and Barry Cartwright Owens ends up back in Colorado practicing law—which is exactly where the agency would love to have you."

"You really think they would risk a thing like that?"

"Travers has run covert operations all his life. It's his business. His craft. And he's good at it. Who is to say that this isn't just another operation? Against the United States Senate. Or at least against the committee." Goodman paused, letting his words sink in. "On the other hand, the damnable thing is that this could be the biggest break we've had so far. If Travers is on the level, there is no telling where this could lead."

The junior senator from Colorado turned away from his assistant and gazed out the window for a long time, the silver letter opener suspended between his index fingers, its sharp point pressing against his flesh. The only sound in the room was the loud ticking of the antique clock on the marble mantel over the fireplace. After what must have been three minutes, he swiveled back and faced Goodman.

"I'll go," he said. "But you're coming with me." He punched a button. "Karla, send in my visitors." As Ben Goodman slipped out the side door of the senator's office and into the corridor, a delegation of five men and women trooped in from the waiting room. Senator Owens, smiling broadly, arose from his desk and extended a hand cordially.

"Hello, Arthur," he said. "It's really good to see you all again. Forgive me for keeping you waiting. I've been tied up in committee all morning. But if there's one group I always have time for, it's the Sierra Club."

Chapter 7

The sunlight was streaming in the living-room window of Valerie's little flat in Margaretta Terrace, and Robert was gently kissing her neck, enjoying the caress of her hair against his face and the smell of her perfume.

She pushed him away gently, laughing. "Rob, it's ten o'clock in the morning."

"You're back, that's all I know. I don't give a damn what time it is." He kissed her full on the lips, and drew her close to him, felt the softness of her body as she relaxed and then responded, holding him tightly around the shoulders.

"I missed you, Rob. Every moment."

"I thought you had Barry Owens to keep you company."

"Goodman never introduced us. I'll bet you saw to that."

"Not me. Goodman probably had his own designs on you."

"He needn't bother. What an extraordinarily ugly little man, Rob. I much prefer tall, handsome station chiefs." She kissed him lightly.

It was odd, Travers reflected. They had been lovers for eight months. They had shared every possible intimacy, and he had come to trust her—he, the professional, who trusted no one. And yet when they came together this way, after one or the other had been away for a short time, he felt a slight awkwardness, almost as though it were last September again, and they had just met for the first time.

It had been casual enough. Dick Austin and his wife had invited him to dinner at their home in Plaxtol. Dick was one of Travers' closest friends and best officers, and after ten years in London, he looked, dressed, and even talked like a

Brit. He was Travers' natural choice to handle the station's liaison with MI6 and MI5, and he did the job well. But Dick insisted on living an exurban existence in Kent, despite the long commute to the embassy. Both he and his wife, Diana, liked to garden. Dick had joked that a beautiful young Englishwoman would be dining with them, "but you're much too old for her." Diana had met her in a pottery class in Chelsea. The girl's father, Christopher Kerr, as it turned out, worked for MI6 under Foreign Office cover.

After they had met that night in Kent, Travers had telephoned Valerie. There were a series of picnics in the countryside, long walks in the rain, a weekend at a little inn in Devon, and Travers had fallen in love. He had not thought that could happen again, not since the divorce eight years earlier, and all the bitterness that he had felt. Now Valerie had entered his life, and the loneliness had washed away in the rain. He was astonished to find that he still could love.

He kissed Valerie again, lightly, on the cheek. "Darling, tell me how it went. Did Goodman buy your story? Is Owens coming?"

"The station chief," she mocked. "Always the professional. Rule One. When an agent returns from a mission, it is essential to debrief her immediately, while all details are still fresh in her mind. If the situation permits, the case officer should take notes—"

Travers interrupted by kissing her hard on the mouth. As he did so he unzipped the back of her dress and slipped his hand inside her bra. He felt her nipple grow hard. She was kissing him fiercely now, her fingers digging into his shoulder-blades.

"Let's continue this conversation in bed," he whispered.

"But I told you; it's only ten o'clock in the morning."

"Fuck you, Val."

"I'd like that."

She giggled, let her dress fall to the floor, and he followed her into the bedroom, admiring the curve of her buttocks beneath her white panties. Then they were both naked and he was kissing her breasts, her mouth, her thighs. She caressed him gently and moved her tongue teasingly downward along his belly.

He pushed her down hard against the pillow. "No. Don't. I can't wait. It's been four days and I want you now."

"Oh, God, Rob, so do I. Come in me."

He was above her, thrusting inside her, and her hips were pushing up to meet his, and then they were both coming together, like the waves crashing against the shore at Siasconset, where he had summered as a boy, and then, all too quickly, it was over.

They had both dozed for a time and then Valerie went rummaging in the kitchen, returning with a bottle of Soave and two glasses. She poured the wine and playfully pressed the cold glass against his ribs. He twitched at the cold, opened his eyes, and smiled at her.

"That," he said, "was worth waiting for."

She handed him a glass, and they both sipped the wine.

"You weren't so bad yourself."

"For an old man."

"You're not old."

"No, I suppose not." He grinned at her. "All right, Valerie. You have no more excuses. Tell me about Owens. Will he come?"

"Darling, I wish I knew. I did my best with Ben Goodman, but apparently you are not high on his list of Most Admired Spooks."

"What's he like?"

"As I said, short, ugly, very bright. Tough." She took a long sip of the Soave. "And not easy to convince."

"What did he say about me?"

"First of all, he seemed very suspicious that Black didn't fire you along with the rest of the Old Boys. Come to think of it, how *did* you escape, Rob?"

"Black couldn't fire everyone and keep the place running. And I'm good. Beyond that, there are things I know about him. You know what I'm talking about, Valerie—at least you have a general idea by now. What else did Goodman say?"

"Well, he assumed you were aware of and had even participated in some of the bad things the agency has done. He's cynical about your motives. I guess he doesn't really think you've changed."

"You know I have. I wonder whether every damn thing

I've done for the agency in the last twenty years was right. The bottom's damn near dropped out of my life. At least it had until you turned up and I learned to walk in the rain."

"But, darling, you're fighting back. You're trying to make things different." She kissed him gently on the cheek.

"I know, Valerie. And you've been extraordinary, and brave. I trust you and I couldn't do this without you."

"You don't have to."

"But I'm a realist. I've prided myself on that in every operation I've ever run. I know I can't win this one by myself, even with your help—and I don't want to expose you to any more risks than you've already taken. I need the Senate committee behind me, Val, or it's useless. Black will fire me before long, and the agency can write me off as just another disgruntled ex-spook. Marchetti. Agee. Snepp. Stockwell. Travers. And Ben Goodman thinks I'm playing games."

"Given your background, can you blame him?"

"I suppose not." He sighed. "But perhaps you've made them curious. Perhaps Owens will come. He's ambitious."

"There's at least a chance he will, Rob."

"If he does, this will be my swan song in the Clandestine Services. My last operation. Only this time the target isn't the president of a banana republic or some heavy-handed KGB ambassador in Zaire." He paused and drained his glass. "This time the target is the CIA."

He drew her to him, and they held on to each other for a long time, their naked bodies pressed together. After a while, Valerie was kissing him on the mouth, her tongue tracing the outline of his lips. He kissed her hard. Slowly, rhythmically, gently this time, they began to make love again.

Chapter 8

The movie had been rather boring, a girl-meets-fish underwater saga, but Senator Barry Owens felt good. Farrah Fawcett, he concluded, looked even better in a wet suit when viewed through the prism of four Scotches on the rocks, a passable airline meal, and several glasses of Chablis. He had chosen an aisle seat of the 747, which gave him ample room to stretch out his lanky frame.

Next to him, Ben Goodman was hunched in to the window seat, trying to read a paperback mystery. He was finding it impossible to concentrate. Every few moments he would close the book and stare restlessly out the window at the fiery jet engines or the cloud cover below. He chewed all the while on an unlit cigar.

Ben, Owens knew, was nervous about flying, but even more nervous about Robert Travers. "I sure as hell hope we're not being set up," Ben had growled as the mobile lounge at Dulles glided out to the aircraft.

The film ended and Owens removed his earphones. One of the stewardesses approached his seat and leaned over, her blond hair cascading down close to his face. The little pin over her left breast said that her name was Helfi Tannenbaum, and it had already been established in previous conversation that she was from Kassel, near Frankfurt, spoke four languages, liked to disco, and preferred the Atlantic run to the Far East, which she had also flown. "May I get you another glass of wine, Mr. Cartwright?" There was only a trace of an accent.

Senator Owens flashed the smile that hundreds of women in Colorado and a lot of other places had found irresistible.

"I'd love another glass of wine, Helfi."

The senator was carried on the manifest of Pan Am Flight 86 as "B. Cartwright." Under a standing arrangement with the State Department, members of the Intelligence Committee and their senior staff aides could, to preserve security, travel abroad under assumed names. They were able to obtain overseas airline tickets without showing their passports. Ben Goodman, who had purchased both their tickets, was traveling as "Ben Newman." They had left Dulles International Airport on Friday morning, and planned to be back in Washington on Monday evening. Constituents, casual visitors to his office, and callers from the press were told simply that the senator was out of town.

Goodman had booked them rooms in an obscure bed-and-breakfast guesthouse on Gloucester Place, where it was unlikely that they would be recognized. The day before, he had cabled Valerie at her flat in Chelsea:

SORRY ABOUT MUM'S ILLNESS. WE ARRIVING FRIDAY NIGHT CONTACTING YOU SATURDAY. UNCLE BEN.

Valerie had shrieked with delight when the cable came. She had pirouetted around the room three times, holding the message aloft, finally coming to rest by the fireplace. She kneeled on the hearth, opened the flue, and burned the cable. Then she dialed Robert on his private line, reaching him at the American embassy on Grosvenor Square.

"It *worked*, Rob," she said. "They're coming." She was cautious over the phone. "They'll be here tonight and they'll call me tomorrow. Dear Uncle Ben. To come all the way from St. Louis. Mother will be so pleased."

Travers felt the tension break inside him. He had waited for days for this news, hoping fiercely, yet unconvinced that Owens would come. Now he felt calm; he experienced the same sort of inner tranquillity that always came over him once an operation had begun. To be moving, acting, was what he always wanted, despite the risks of failure or personal danger. It was the waiting that Travers hated. Valerie's news had restored his confidence. But a flicker of doubt remained. He had to be sure.

"Is Uncle Ben making the trip by himself?"

"No. The cable said 'we.'"

"Good. I'll see you tonight."

"Kisses."

Valerie rang off and looked at the fireplace, where a little wisp of smoke still curled upward from the grate. She smiled inwardly at Ben Goodman's invention. Her mother was in fine health, except for a touch of bursitis, and was at that very moment probably puttering about her garden in Surrey, feeding the rosebushes, pruning the forsythia, and potting the impatiens.

Her mother loved the garden and the modest, two-story, mock-Tudor house in Epsom in which Valerie had been born and had grown up. Her father, Christopher—known as Kit to his family and friends—still took the 7:31 train to Waterloo Station every morning. In his dark suit, bowler, and furled brolly, he was indistinguishable from all the other civil servants commuting to London. But at Waterloo, instead of hurrying across Westminster Bridge beneath Big Ben, like the hundreds of other commuters headed for the government offices in Whitehall, he turned east and walked a few blocks along Westminster Bridge Road to Number 100. There, at 8:15 each morning, he entered Century House, which to a casual passerby might have appeared to be a high-rise luxury-apartment building over a Mobil filling station. It was in fact the headquarters of MI6.

Christopher Kerr worked there under Foreign Office cover. He was nostalgic for the old days, before the 1960s, when headquarters had been the Broadway, a grubby, nondescript building south of St. James's Park that was officially listed as a subbranch of the Ministry of Land and Natural Resources. He had much preferred the ancient building, with its creaking stairways, musty wooden furniture, peeling paint, and World War II posters still on the walls because no one had thought to take them down. The one in the corridor outside his office admonished: "Keep It Here! Keep Our Secrets Secret." Another, over his desk, had warned: "Careless Talk Costs Lives," a slogan illustrated with a dramatic painting of a tanker poised to slide beneath the waves to the bottom of the North Atlantic. He had grown rather fond of it, but he did not take it with him when they moved across the bridge. The new headquarters was all steel, glass, and concrete, a sterile spy house with none of the character of its predecessor. Moreover, it was too far from his club, the Reform, and the better restaurants. Sir Richard Whitworth, the current "C," and as such the head of MI6, still maintained the red-brick, four-story town house at No. 21 Queen Anne's Gate, which backed on the Broadway, but that was all that was left of the firm's former headquarters.

Valerie loved her father, as only a daughter can. She remembered the night many years ago when he had come home so proudly with his CMG. "Call me God," he had announced, repeating the standard jibe in the senior levels of the Foreign Office and MI6. Later, he had been made a Knight Commander of the Order of St. Michael and St. George. "Keep calling me God," was the phrase for a KCMG. And finally, three years ago, he had received the highest honor of all, the GCMG. He had arrived home in Surrey, poured his usual glass of sherry, and broken the news to Valerie and her mother: "I have the pleasure to announce that now even God calls me God."

Valerie smiled to think of how her father made light of the honors that he had worked so hard to earn. Her father and his colleagues, she reflected, still faithfully served the tattered remnants of empire. They manned the battlements in their bowler hats, armed with their umbrellas and their neatly folded copies of *The Times,* as though England were still in her glory instead of her dotage. To Valerie, men like her father were the glue that held England together. By refusing to recognize the drab reality of the present they managed to hold on to something of the shining past. They were shored up by their public-school educations, which in her father's time did not allow for gloomy thoughts about Britannia's rule, and even by the very names of the stations to which they commuted so loyally each day. Victoria. Waterloo.

Lord knows, Valerie thought, there was little else to hold on to. Christopher Kerr, as did all civil servants, earned only a relatively modest salary. Until Valerie was eight, the house in Surrey had no central heating and she still shuddered to remember the baths she had taken as a child. She and her younger brother, John, were each allowed only four inches of lukewarm water in the tub. So, just as her parents did, to keep from freezing to death, she had started each day with a steaming hot cup of tea.

There was one difference that set the Kerr household a bit above the others on the block. Christopher had met his wife, Katherine, in India, when he was stationed in Madras and she was a secretary in the consulate. They had married in India and brought back Jeela, a plump and good-natured woman with jet-black hair who had served as a combination nanny and housekeeper, a bargain-basement Poppins who had raised Valerie and her brother.

Perhaps, Valerie sometimes thought, she was in love with Robert because America was the great world power now. Perhaps Robert represented what her father merely symbolized.

"Oh, Val," she said half aloud, "don't be foolish. You love Robert because he is handsome, intelligent, and strong." And—she had to admit to herself—because, like her father, he was a spy. A spy who still believed. For all of Robert's doubts, and his determination to challenge the leaders of the agency, he still believed. At the very least he believed in the possibility of change, or he would not be risking everything.

Helfi Tannenbaum had picked up the microphone at the forward galley of the huge jetliner. "Ladies and gentlemen," she intoned, "Captain Endicott has flashed on the No Smoking sign. Please extinguish your cigarettes, fasten your seat belts, and place your seat in the upright position for landing."

Grudgingly, Barry Owens sat up and obeyed. Ben Goodman put on his earphones to seek reassurance in the pilot-to-tower chatter. He shoved the unlit cigar in the breast pocket of his jacket.

It was nighttime and in a few moments Goodman, peering out the cabin window, could see the welcome blue runway lights below. The big jet slowed, shuddered slightly, and set down as smoothly as a sea gull. Goodman barely felt the wheels touch the tarmac.

"We're at Heathrow, Ben," Owens said cheerfully. "You can relax now."

"I wish I could," Goodman murmured.

As they left by the forward exit, Helfi smiled broadly.

"Have a super time in London, Mr. Cartwright. You, too, Mr. Newman."

The three-hundred-year-old wooden cottage was set back on a hilltop at the end of a winding country lane. Approaching it, Valerie's little white Marina bounced up and down like a jeep, especially during the last half mile, where the dirt lane petered out and turned to grass, stones, and mud.

"Slow down, Rob," Valerie pleaded. "This isn't Le Mans."

Travers grinned but did not let up on the gas pedal. "I'm trying to save the Western world and you're worried about a broken axle."

"It's easy for *you* to say that. It's my car."

"We had to take yours. Mine's too well known and we can't afford company today."

"Excuses, excuses." Valerie leaned over and nuzzled Robert on the neck. As she did, the cottage came into view. Travers pulled over and stopped. They had to park at the bottom of the grassy slope about 130 yards below the cottage and go the rest of the way on foot.

It was a beautiful day, rather windy, but it had been perfect for a drive in the country. The fields were dark green after the spring rains. Yellow daffodils covered the hillside, dancing lightly in the breeze under the bright sunshine. The blue sky was broken only by a few gauzy wisps of high, windblown clouds.

They climbed up to the cottage, and Valerie stood for a moment at the top of the hill, smiling at the flowers and letting the wind play with her hair. "I wandered lonely as a cloud," she recited, "that floats on high o'er vales and hills. . . ."

"When all at once," Robert joined in, "I saw a crowd, a host, of golden daffodils."

"Darling." Valerie put her arms around Travers, stroking her cheek gently against his tan cashmere sweater. "I'll bet you're the only station chief in the whole beastly company who quotes Wordsworth."

"Nonsense, Val. We're not a bunch of double-oh-seven Philistines. The company is full of bright, educated people."

"They're mostly the analysts, from what you've said. The little men who sit in cubbyholes all day studying the railroad timetables from Pinsk to Minsk. Or counting cows in Kazakhstan. There aren't too many intellectuals in the Clandestine Services."

"That's true in general, but not always. Henry Souers, the station chief in Bonn, happens to be one of the world's leading musicologists. He's had six books published, including the definitive work on Monteverdi. He knows more about the early baroque composers than anyone alive. There are plenty of others like him. Angus Maclaren edited the literary magazine at Yale and founded a poetry journal."

"He's dead."

"Yes."

Valerie pushed open the wooden door of the cottage, and they went inside. Robert put some kindling and three logs in the fireplace, hunted up a match, and lit the dry wood. Soon a blazing fire warmed the room.

It was a simple and rustic place, but perfect for Valerie's needs. She had rented it for the past three years from her friends, Cynthia and James Sheffield, on whose farm it was located. The cottage was a mile from the tiny village of Stapleford Tawney, near Romford, Essex. Although it was less than an hour's drive northeast of London, the area was rural and the cottage completely isolated. There were no other houses within sight and no telephone. Valerie exulted in her good fortune; her hideaway was as remote and peaceful as if she had found a cottage in the Hebrides.

The Sheffields and their ancestors had farmed Crown land for more than two hundred years. Technically, they leased the acreage and did not own it, but in practical terms the distinction was unimportant, except that the farm could never be sold. The Sheffields were mostly engaged in truck farming, raising cabbages, beans, and other vegetables that they sold to the wholesale-produce markets in London.

It was an attractive and affluent area, in which the farmers owned large and comfortable houses, with polished Jaguars, and often one or two other cars, parked in their driveways.

Their male offspring were sent to Eton or Winchester and then up to Oxford or Cambridge. But it was always understood that one son would return to Essex to manage the farm.

Valerie used the little cottage as her pottery workshop. She loved nothing better than to work there alone for hours, turning bowls, cream pitchers, jugs, cups, and other pieces on her kick wheel. She had exacting standards, and she had to be satisfied with the form and texture of each piece, or she would discard it and start anew. The bookcases on each side of the fireplace were crowded with her work, some finished, some awaiting firing in the small gas-fired kiln she had built in a shed out back. She made only high-fire stoneware in warm, earth tones. She sold her work, which was excellent, to a store in Chelsea, in King's Road, and the income, while not large, was enough to keep her afloat.

Often, she would spend several days at a time at the cottage, immersed in her work. There was a small bedroom off the main room, and a tiny kitchen; it was all she needed. Since Robert had come into her life, however, the cottage had become less of a workshop and more of a trysting place. They had spent many weekends there, making love in front of the fire, taking long walks over the meadows, and dining out at the local pub, secure in the knowledge that they were far from any place where Robert's world might intrude.

It was precisely because the cottage was a sanctuary, reserved for her work and their love, that Valerie had hesitated when Robert suggested that they use it to meet with Senator Owens and Goodman. But the same isolation that made the cottage a special and private place in their lives also argued for its use this weekend for a far different purpose.

"I can't use any of our safe houses in London," Robert had explained. "Half a dozen of the people on my staff know the locations. And they're wired, of course. So it really has got to be the cottage."

Valerie had understood, and had quickly agreed. She had given Goodman the directions early that morning, when he telephoned her flat, and he seemed to get them right, although he had joked over the phone about whether he would be able to remember to drive on the left side of the road.

Travers was pacing up and down in front of the fire, looking at the readout on his digital watch every few moments. "They're late," he said.

Valerie's reply was to put a kettle on. Travers finally sat down when she brought tea. They sipped in silence. Travers was first to hear the car. After a moment, there was the sound of the engine stopping and doors slamming. Travers looked out the front window, and saw a tall, youthful man striding up the hill, and his short, older companion scrambling up the path behind him.

Ben Goodman was out of breath when he reached the cottage. Valerie did the introductions. Travers was pumping Barry Owens' hand. "Thank you for coming, Senator. I'm sorry that our business this morning won't permit me to receive you at the embassy."

"Well, I hope this trip was necessary," Owens replied, jovially but pointedly.

"Hear what I have to say," Travers said evenly, "and you can decide."

Valerie jumped in quickly to break the ice. "Would anyone like tea? We've already had a cup, but the kettle's still on. Please do sit anywhere, and excuse the god-awful mess. I use the cottage for my work."

Barry Owens settled into a rocker by the fireplace, across from Travers. He came directly to the point. "We're due back in Washington Monday, so perhaps we'd best get started. Ben tells me you have information of the highest importance affecting our national security. I'm here to listen."

Travers spoke quietly. "Senator, I hope you know that what I am doing isn't easy. I asked to see you only after the greatest soul-searching and inner debate. It's taken me a long time to reach this point. Years really. I know the risks. But I feel that what I am about to tell you has to be told. To the Congress, and, ultimately, to the American people."

"I understand."

"I've spent my whole life with the agency. I was recruited at Yale, by Skip Fields, the crew coach, and I joined up as soon as I graduated, in 1956. In those days, joining the agency was like entering the priesthood. It was a mission, a calling. It was the height of the cold war, and what could be more glamorous and attractive than serving your country, in secret. I did my junior officer training and drew the Clandestine Services. After a couple of years at headquarters, I was sent overseas and I put in some time as a case officer, running agents in Western Europe. Berlin and Vienna, mostly. I did well, and in February 1963, when the agency set up the Domestic Operations Division, I was brought home and assigned to it as a branch chief. I wasn't too happy to be back in Washington. But the division was only a block from the White House, and Towny Black pointed out that I'd be 'close to the power.' Two years later, I was named head of the division. That's how I got involved in the operation I want to tell you about."

"What was Towny Black at that time?" Senator Owens interrupted.

"In 1965, he was the assistant deputy director for Plans."

"Under Trilby Gates?"

"Exactly."

Goodman was almost lost in the pillows of the old sofa across from the fireplace, where Owens in the rocker and Travers in an armchair sat facing each other. Goodman leaned forward. "They changed the name from Plans to Operations in 1973, Senator, the same year that Black succeeded Trilby Gates as the DDO."

Valerie came in with the tea, in brown stoneware mugs that she had made. Only Ben refused a cup.

"At any rate," Travers resumed, "it was in 1965, while I was head of the Domestic Operations Division, that 381 pounds of weapons-grade uranium disappeared from a nuclear-processing plant in Apollo, Pennsylvania. Everybody investigated, of course. The Atomic Energy Commission, the FBI, and the agency. But nothing was ever proved. Officially, it was listed as an unexplained MUF."

"Material Unaccounted For," Goodman offered, helpfully.

"Yes. The NUFAC people, the company that operated the plant, argued that the uranium had simply gotten into the pipes and built up along the inner walls. The way your arteries harden. But then about three years ago, it leaked to the press that the agency suspected Israel had stolen the U-235 missing at Apollo and used it to build the bomb."

"At Dimona?" Owens asked.

"Yes, in the Negev, at Dimona. What it meant, of course, was that Israel had become the sixth country to get the bomb. At that point, the members of the nuclear club were the United States, the Soviets, Britain, France, China, and Israel. India was seventh, in 1974. A couple of years ago, South Africa exploded a device and became number eight."

"And there will be more," Owens said gloomily.

"Of course. Pakistan, Brazil, Taiwan. Any number can play."

"One of the CIA's jobs is to keep close tabs on proliferation," Owens observed.

"Sure, it's a priority intelligence target. In fact, the leak about Israel and the missing uranium at Apollo was based on a National Intelligence Estimate drafted by the agency in 1968. The report reached two conclusions. One, that the Israelis had the bomb. Two, that they had built it with uranium acquired by clandestine means, i.e., at Apollo. Dick Helms took the NIE to President Johnson, and LBJ ordered it hushed up. Johnson instructed Helms: 'Don't tell anyone else, even Dean Rusk or Robert McNamara.'"

"Why did Johnson cover up?" Owens asked.

"I don't know, but I can guess," Goodman volunteered. "The last thing Lyndon Johnson would have wanted was the FBI or any other agency reopening the case and digging around Apollo. Can you imagine what would have happened if word somehow leaked during the 1968 election that Israel had stolen uranium in the United States, right out from under the government's nose, and used it to build nuclear bombs? If that had become known, and LBJ denounced Israel for the theft, Hubert would lose the Jewish vote. Boom. And worse, the big campaign contributions from New York, Detroit, and Los Angeles. If he *failed* to denounce Israel, the right wing would jump on him. Nixon beat Humphrey anyway, but not by all that much—half a million votes. The Israeli bomb story, if it had gotten out, would have guaranteed Nixon's victory."

"Something like that was probably involved," Travers agreed. "I don't know all the political ramifications. I'm a clandestine operator by trade. I do know that all kinds of hell broke loose inside the government when the story leaked out ten years later, in 1978."

"How did it surface?" Owens asked.

"Initially through one man, a low-level investigator at the Nuclear Regulatory Commission. You have to keep the bureaucratic structure clearly in mind. When the AEC was abolished in 1975, it was split in two. Control over civilian production of uranium and plutonium, and over nuclear power plants, went to the NRC. So did safeguards against theft of nuclear materials by terrorists or organized crime, or anybody else. The manufacture and security of nuclear weapons—atomic and hydrogen bombs, and tactical weapons, too—was placed under what became DOE, the Department of Energy. The NRC investigator had been poking into the MUF at Apollo when he suddenly discovered that there was a whole bunch of files about the case in his own agency classified so high that he couldn't even get in the same room with them. His superiors told him to cool it and find something else to do. But he was a bulldog; he wouldn't let go. He tried to get some of the NRC commissioners interested. The political appointees. He didn't have much luck. Finally, he went to a couple of committees on the Hill. On the House side. The committees investigated, but the staff director of the NRC blandly assured the congressmen that there was 'no evidence' of a diversion at Apollo by Israel or anyone else. The National Security Council even got into the act. They couldn't find any stolen uranium, either. The White House said it never happened."

"Yes," said Owens. "I seem to remember Jody Powell saying that."

"But by this time, there were a number of reporters and environmental groups digging around at the edges of the story. That's when it was disclosed that the CIA had told the president a decade earlier, in 1968, that Israel stole the uranium in Pennsylvania and used it to build the bomb. The agency didn't get around to briefing the NRC about its conclusions until early in 1976. That's what was in those superclassified secret files. So the NRC knew, all right, at least by 1976. Well, the House committees were furious. They felt they had been lied to by the NRC. It was lovely. The NRC took all the heat, and we were home free."

"What happened to the poor NRC investigator who started it all?" Valerie asked.

"The usual," Travers replied. "He was transferred to the nuclear power plants division and assigned to a five-year study on licensing standards."

Barry Owens was rocking back and forth slowly. "Well, Mr. Travers, I'm familiar with the general outlines of the story. But you didn't bring us all the way across the pond, I hope, to tell us something that's never been proven. That CIA merely *suspected* a diversion to Israel."

"That's just the point, Senator. You see, the National Intelligence Estimate in 1968, Helms's report to the president, the whole thing was a joke. The agency pointed the finger at Israel to cover its own tracks. We *knew* Israel had received the uranium from Apollo."

"How did you know?"

"Because we stole it for them."

There was a long moment of silence which Owens broke by asking softly: "Do you mind if Mr. Goodman takes some notes?"

"Not if you can keep them secure."

"We can." Ben had taken a small spiral notebook and a felt pen from his jacket pocket. He flipped open the notebook and began writing furiously.

Travers sketched in the details. "The Plans Directorate mounted the op in 1965. Towny Black was in charge."

"Who was the field agent?" Owens was sitting on the edge of his rocker, now, leaning forward intently.

"Frank DiMario. Currently the deputy director of Operations."

"What was the operational goal?"

"To provide Israel secretly with enough special nuclear material for six atomic bombs. The agency felt our whole strategy in the Middle East depended on it."

"Did the president know?"

Travers hesitated. "I'm not sure. There are gaps in my knowledge. Johnson was distracted by the war in Vietnam, naturally. It's possible we never told him. Until 1968, at least, when we spoon-fed him the sanitized version. Of course, it's also quite possible that the analysts on the intelligence side of the house who prepared the national estimate for the President didn't know they were reporting on a DDO operation."

"Jesus," Goodman said. His felt pen was flying across the page. For a moment, it was the only sound in the room.

"How did you do it?" Owens asked at last.

"It was very simple, really. DiMario and his agents posed as mafiosi. They paid the NUFAC workers, with our operational funds, to take the stuff out in small amounts over a period of several months."

"How?"

"Under their clothing, in jocks double-lined with brass."

"You're kidding."

"I've never been more serious."

Owens was looking skeptical. "Wouldn't their bodies have been subject to dangerous radiation?"

"Yeah," Goodman interjected, "wouldn't the men be afraid their balls would fall off?"

"They knew better than that. They worked with the material eight hours a day in their jobs, after all. High-enriched uranium does not need to be shielded. You can hold it in your hands. It won't go critical unless you put too much of it together at one time."

"What does the metal look like?" Valerie asked curiously.

"It's grayish-green. At NUFAC, it was pressed into pellets no bigger than your thumbnail. So it was easily concealed. And not dangerous to smuggle out. The tables show that ninety-three percent enriched uranium becomes critical in a bare sphere of fifty kilos. Depending on what you put it in, the critical mass can be much lower—if you wrap it in steel, for example. But nobody in their right mind would ever try to walk out with a large amount. Aside from the risk of criticality, the stuff is too heavy. They would take out a kilo at a time, at the most."

"All right," Owens said, "but how would they get past the Geiger counters at the portals?"

"That's why we wrapped it in brass," Travers explained. "Just in case. But the fact is there were no Geiger counters. In 1965, security was almost nil at the civilian atomic plants. The uranium was so valuable that, in those days, the AEC relied on the profit motive for security. If anything was missing, the company had to reimburse the government. So the assumption was the companies would keep a close watch. In retrospect, it sounds crazy, but that's the way it worked."

"Or didn't work," Goodman said.

"How did the stuff get from western Pennsylvania to Dimona?" Owens asked.

"A Mossad agent in their embassy in Washington had a 'sister' in Fox Chapel. That was the drop. There were regular pickups."

"And from Washington?"

Travers shrugged. "Probably by diplomatic pouch to Tel Aviv. That would have been the simplest way."

"How long did the operation go on?"

"Again, I'm not sure. I was only in on the beginning. I had a disagreement with Towny Black and I was transferred out of the operation and sent back overseas."

"What kind of a disagreement?"

"One of the workers got scared. Threatened to go to the Bureau. DiMario had him tortured. For various reasons I opposed it." Travers carefully avoided mentioning O'Donnell's role as the parish priest. He was not sure whether Owens might be Catholic, and he was taking no chance of offending him.

Goodman had been doing some calculating. "You said 381 pounds of enriched uranium disappeared from Apollo. How much do you need for a bomb?"

"About ten kilos. That's twenty-two pounds."

"Okay," Goodman pressed on. "You claim the agency stole enough for six bombs and gave it to Israel. That would be, uh, sixty kilos, or 132 pounds."

Owens, seeing where Goodman was heading, bored in with the obvious question. "You said 381 pounds of weapons-grade uranium vanished from Apollo. Mossad got 132 pounds. What happened to the rest?"

Travers felt tired. It was midafternoon. He suddenly thought of himself as a giant marlin about to be pulled into the boat. Like all fish, he had taken the hook voluntarily, but now he summoned his strength and surged off at an angle, away from Owens, fighting.

"I'm not sure," he said.

Goodman had been totaling up the numbers. "If my figures are right, there are still 249 pounds unaccounted for. Enough for almost a dozen more bombs."

"Yes," Travers confirmed. "About a dozen."

Owens was reeling in fast. "You must have some idea of what happened to the rest."

"As I say, Towny Black pulled me off the operation."

"But you have your suspicions. That's why we're here, isn't it?"

"Yes."

Owens sat back, his voice gentler. "Mr. Travers, let's see if we can't focus in on this thing a little more sharply. Let's go back to the very beginning. You say you were in charge of the Domestic Operations Division in 1965. A covert operation was launched inside the United States. DiMario was running the agents in the field. What was the operation called?"

Travers hesitated. He took a deep breath. "With all due respect, Senator, I'm not sure you have a need to know that. As a matter of fact, it might even be dangerous for you to know. Some of the people who were witting in this operation seem to have had a short life span."

Barry Owens smiled. He was, Valerie thought, extraordinarily handsome. His chiseled features were displayed in profile from where she sat on the couch, next to Ben Goodman.

The senator and Travers had come to a crossroads. Everyone in the room sensed that. Owens chose his words carefully: "Okay. The code name is secret. The fact that we are meeting here today is a secret, too. And must remain one. As a station chief, you are not authorized by the agency to have direct dealings with the Senate Select Committee on Intelligence. As chairman of the CIA subcommittee I am not, by the rule book, supposed to deal with anyone below the level of Graham Black, the director of Central Intelligence, or his designees. What we are both doing is irregular, to say the least. You took the first step by contacting us through Valerie, and I commend you for it—although I have a great many questions to ask. But having taken that step, there can be no turning back. We'll need the full story, with nothing left out. No sanitized versions."

"I think what the senator is saying," Goodman added tersely, "is that you've burned your bridges."

Travers looked at Valerie for a moment. "They're right," her eyes said.

"Well," Travers resumed with a resigned expression, "in for a dime, in for a dollar. The name of the operation, Senator, was Spectrum."

Owens' taut, muscular body relaxed. "All right," he said, "who chose the code name?"

"As far as I know, Towny Black. I suspect, although I don't know, that he named it somewhat whimsically, because the instrument that nuclear physicists use to differentiate among uranium isotopes is a mass spectrometer." Travers warmed to his subject. "The spectrum of visible light is made up of seven colors. But if you've ever looked closely at a rainbow you know there are usually only four you can easily distinguish— blue, green, yellow, and red. The operation had four phases, matching those colors of the spectrum. The part I've described, the acquisition of the high-enriched uranium by clandestine means and its transfer to Israel was only the first phase. It was called Phase Blue."

"What were the other phases?" Owens was taking the lead in the questioning. Goodman continued to write rapidly in his little notebook.

"As I say, I participated only in Phase Blue. But over the years, I've been asking questions. Trilby Gates wouldn't talk much about it. But I got a few pieces of the mosaic from Putney Barnes, his assistant. Black himself has dropped certain hints. Then, in 1969, when I was back from Rome briefly on home leave, I got a fleeting look at the file. It was very closely held, of course. You couldn't punch it up on Intellofax. That's the data bank readout in which our files normally appear. You sit in front of a computer in a secure area and the files come up on a screen. Green letters on a black background. But thousands of agency officers are cleared for Intellofax. The Spectrum file was never put in the computer. It was kept separately, in a small safe in Trilby Gates's office."

"Then how were you able to see it?"

Travers smiled. "You might say it was a one-time op, in and out. I picked a day that I knew Gates was away. I knew his secretary fairly well. I just walked in, late in the day, around five o'clock, and asked to see the file. She checked the access list, and I was still on it from Phase Blue. We're efficient but not infallible; someone had forgotten to cross my name off the list. I was still cleared for Spectrum. She put me in a conference room alone, and I raced through it. Ten minutes, that's all I dared. Then I gave her back the file and waltzed out. Of course, I was praying she wouldn't mention my visit to Trilby."

"Describe the file."

"Four folders, varying in thickness. One for each phase. I flipped through the Phase Blue file very quickly, thinking I already knew what was in it. That was my first surprise."

Travers broke off. "Val, do you think you can find that open bottle of J&B in the kitchen? Our guests might like a drink. I know I would."

Both Owens and Goodman accepted a Scotch and water, Travers took his on the rocks.

He continued his narrative.

"On the other hand, perhaps I shouldn't have been surprised, now that I think back on a conversation I had with Towny Black just before I went to Rome. We talked in July of 1965. At that time, DiMario and his people had pulled seventy-five pounds of uranium out of Apollo. The target was 132 pounds. The Mossad agent in Washington was driving to Pittsburgh every two weeks for the pickups. So, if everything went according to schedule, the operation should have ended around the end of October."

"And," Owens asked, "it didn't?"

"That's right," Travers responded. "Phase Blue went on for another six months, until April of 1966."

Goodman looked pleased with himself. "That explains what happened to the other 249 pounds."

"It doesn't," Travers corrected him. "The files clearly indicated that the Mossad courier made his last trip to Pittsburgh on October 28, 1965. The Israelis got their quota— enough for six bombs, and that's all. But Black and DiMario kept on siphoning weapons-grade uranium out of Apollo for another six months."

Owens was sipping his drink, but he did not take his eyes off Travers. "Where did it go?" he asked.

"I can answer that by explaining Phase Green. Apparently, it began in the spring of 1966. At that point in the file, there is a lot of paper from the Central Cover Staff. But the bottom line is that CCS set up a dummy Army unit, the 758th Special Operations Tactical Group. That in itself was not unusual. By mutual agreement we use the Army for cover all the time. Check out one of our officers who has moved from the Clandestine Services into a job outside the government. Typically, his bio will show his background and education, and later on perhaps positions in industry, a university, or the foundations. But there will be a gap for the years when he was in the agency. Very often, to cover those years, it will say something like: 'civilian employee, Department of the Army, 1959-64.' Or it might list him as a retired Foreign Service Reserve Officer. We use that, a lot, too. I'm listed here in London, for example, as a political attaché, R-3 rank. At any rate, when the agency sets up a dummy military unit, normally it's strictly for cover purposes, to be listed on stationery or in a building lobby. When I ran the Domestic Operations Division, for example, it was set up that way. We called ourselves the Joint Operations Group, SD7753. But the unit set up for Phase Green was different."

"How so?"

"It became operational. I'm flipping pages like crazy in this little conference room where Gates's secretary had put me. My hair stood on end when I came to that part. The file showed that on November 14, 1965, the CIA, using official

Pentagon forms—which the Technical Services Division had undoubtedly fabricated—requisitioned twelve Honest John tactical nuclear rockets for the 758th Special Operations Tac Group. Normally, weapons-procurement requests would have been routed through the AEC, and the order for production of a dozen W31 nuclear warheads would have been added to the president's stockpile memorandum. But that would have set off all sorts of alarm bells inside the government; too many people would have seen the paperwork. So what the agency did was to fake the AEC approvals as well—TSD again—and send the whole package of paper directly to Amarillo. It looked in every respect like a routine production order to Pantex."

"My God," said Owens.

Pantex. Owens had seen it once, when he toured the vast installation in Texas with a small group of senators who had responsibilities in the national security area. There, along Route 60, amid the green fields of winter wheat, the World War II complex sprawled over ten thousand acres. It looked like an old industrial plant sitting in the middle of nowhere, twenty-three miles northeast of Amarillo in the Texas panhandle. But it wasn't. Pantex was America's atomic-bomb factory. The innocent-looking buildings in the middle of the dead-flat wheat fields had turned out more than twenty-five thousand nuclear warheads. Enough to destroy the planet several times over.

Travers continued, "As you know, Senator, nuclear weapons are manufactured in the United States like automobiles. Production is dispersed. The big oil companies, Exxon, Atlantic Richfield, and others, dig the uranium out of the ground in the Southwest. Most of the weapons are designed at Los Alamos and at the Lawrence Livermore Laboratory in California. The Sandia labs in Albuquerque do the really futuristic stuff, the advanced-design nuclear weapons. Bomb parts are made in half-a-dozen widely scattered locations. Union Carbide makes uranium bomb parts at the Y-12 plant in Oak Ridge, as well as deuterium components for the hydrogen bomb. Bendix makes the electrical circuits in Kansas City. Monsanto manufactures detonators at the Mound plant in Dayton. General Electric makes electronic parts in Pinellas, Florida. Of course there's Savannah River, South Carolina, and Rocky Flats, Colorado; they make plutonium bombs. Both kinds of fission bombs—uranium and plutonium—are also used as the triggers for hydrogen bombs. But everything goes to Pantex for final assembly."

"I know. I've been through the plant," Owens said grimly. "But you haven't explained how the nukes ordered from Pantex tie in with the rest of the missing uranium at Apollo. The 249 pounds that never got to Israel."

"The answer was in the files. Every two weeks, beginning in October 1965, DiMario's team shipped just under twenty pounds of high-enriched uranium from Apollo to Pantex. They used perfect copies of NUFAC containers, so it looked as though they were regular shipments. It went on for six months, until Phase Blue was buttoned up in April."

Owens looked perplexed. "But why? Why go to all the trouble to steal the stuff and then turn it right back to the government?"

"It puzzled me, at first," Travers replied. "But then I understood. It was brilliant, diabolical really. Never underestimate Towny Black. You see, it had to be done that way. When the Pentagon wants to add to its supply of nuclear weapons, it tells the Department of Energy—in those days it was the AEC, of course, DOE didn't exist—and the department's Albuquerque Operations Office sends out the production orders to Pantex. But at the same time, DOE issues a matching order to the uranium-fabricating plants. Otherwise, the plants wouldn't know how much to produce. The agency was shipping the stolen uranium from Apollo to Pantex in precisely the amounts needed to fill the orders from the dummy Army unit for twelve tactical nukes. In that way, you see, the AEC auditors, their material-accounting and control people, would not notice any shortage or discrepancy in the amount of uranium being shipped to Pantex and the number of warheads shipped *from* Pantex. It was like a tube of toothpaste. The amount going into the tube was the same as the amount squeezed out."

They had talked all afternoon. The sun was going down over the meadow now, and even the red glowing embers in the hearth could not warm the room. The cottage was cold.

Travers 'had grown weary from talking, and Senator Barry Owens seemed drained by what he had heard. To Valerie, he suddenly looked older.

"If I understand you correctly, Mr. Travers," Owens said slowly, "your agency now has somewhere in its possession and under its control twelve atomic weapons. What you are saying is that the CIA has become the world's ninth nuclear power."

"Or," said Travers, "Towny Black has."

Chapter 9

It was Saturday night, and the Italian restaurant in Soho was crowded, hot, noisy, and not very good, except for the *stracciatella*. Owens was disappointed, especially since they had waited in line on the sidewalk for half an hour. Goodman, letting go after the tension of the afternoon, drank too much Chianti.

A swarthy waiter brought their dessert. He had been hustling them through the meal—the owner liked a fast turnover on the tables—and now he slapped down a check, although they had not asked for one.

Goodman left his *zabaglione* almost untouched. "I feel a little queasy," he complained. "I think I overdid the red wine."

Owens laughed. "Jews can't drink, Ben. Give it up." It was a standard joke between them. Owens could drink a good deal, and not show it. His drinking had not become a problem, but Ben worried about it. If the press, particularly the Georgetown columnists, should begin to mention it, the stories would not help Owens' political image as the clean-cut junior senator from Colorado. And Goodman's own future, as he never forgot, was tied to that of Barry Owens.

They paid the check and took a cab back to their rooms in Gloucester Place. In the taxi, as in the crowded restaurant, they did not dare to talk about the chilling story they had heard only a few hours before in the cottage. In the privacy of their rooms, however, Owens and Goodman mapped their strategy for the next day. It had been agreed that they would return to Essex in the morning; Robert and Valerie were staying overnight at the cottage.

"What do you think now, Ben?" Owens asked, probing. "Do you still suspect the whole thing may be a setup?"

"I don't know," Goodman replied cautiously. "I think we have to listen to the rest of his story and then test him. Pepper him with as many questions as we can think of. Try to trip him up, catch him in a contradiction."

"If we believe him, there's one question that has priority."

"What's that?" The wine had fogged Ben's brain.

"We've got to try to find out where the missiles are now."

The next morning, the two men were up early, Goodman with some difficulty. After a breakfast of bacon and eggs in the shabbily-genteel downstairs dining room, they drove out to Stapleford Tawney, arriving at the cottage just after nine o'clock. Saturday's blue skies had turned gray and it was drizzling lightly when Valerie unbolted the heavy wooden door and let them in.

"Come and sit by the fire," she said. "It's the only cure for our ghastly English weather."

The senator joined Travers by the hearth. "I didn't sleep very well last night after hearing your story," he confessed.

"I understand," Travers replied. "I've been living with it for a long time."

Owens leaned back in his chair. "You'd best tell us the rest." His voice sounded tired.

Travers was having a second cup of coffee after breakfast. He held the cup between his hands so that it warmed them. "There isn't much more to tell," he said. "In Phase Yellow, the missiles were moved to a secret underground storage point. The storage area is referred to in several documents as Site Orange. As far as I know, the rockets are still there and still operational."

"Where is Site Orange?"

"I wish I knew. Somewhere in the Washington area, I suspect. Out in the Maryland or Virginia countryside."

"What makes you think that?"

"Logic. The cover Army unit had an address in Arlington, actually an agency building, of course. It's a huge, rambling place, normally used as a garage and auto-repair shop. The missiles would have been transported there from Pantex under guard, in an AEC convoy, and signed over to the cover Army unit. Black would have had to move them out of Arlington pretty fast. But my guess is that he would not have wanted them moved very far."

"Why not?"

"The longer the move, the greater the risk of detection and exposure. We had our own army, navy, and air force at the Bay of Pigs, but normally, the agency isn't supposed to be moving military hardware around. Especially nuclear rockets. Somebody might get curious."

Ben Goodman was still a little hung over from Soho. His whole body felt shaky. He made a mental note to go easy on the wine next time. Valerie offered their visitors coffee, and Ben was working on his second black cup when he spoke. "There were *four* colors. What was Phase Red?"

Travers looked grim. "The file was explicit. Phase Red is the code for the deployment or actual use of the agency's nuclear weapons."

The silence was broken by Owens. "But *why?* Why did the agency want nuclear weapons?"

"From what I've learned the company had two objectives," Travers said. "First, by acquiring our own atomic weapons, we could covertly give nuclear arms to friendly countries without White House approval. Not just uranium, like we gave the Israelis, but actual weapons. We'd have the capability to conduct covert operations of the most powerful kind— using nuclear warheads—despite any restrictions that might be placed on covert ops by the president or Congress."

"But there was no talk of restricting covert operations back in 1965," Owens said. "The agency was riding high."

"I think that even back then, to give the devil his due, Towny Black could see what was coming. We'd been through the Bay of Pigs, after all. And what Black foresaw happened. During the 1970s, the exposures of CIA led to a great hue and cry against covert operations. For a while, Congress forced us to report to eight congressional committees on each covert action. Rather than share our secrets, and risk having them leak, we cut way back on covert operations all around the world."

"Or so the agency says," Owens interjected.

"Okay, we're still running some under the table. You must suspect that, and I imagine the president knows it. But we have cut back. So, Spectrum gives the company some powerful options. With what Towny Black's got stashed away at Site Orange, the agency could run one hell of a covert operation."

"An incredibly dangerous one," Owens snapped. "A covert operation that could trigger a nuclear war."

"I'm not defending the agency's rationale," Travers said quickly, "just explaining it."

The senator seemed somewhat mollified.

"There was a second reason," Travers continued. "The proliferation problem. A lot of smaller countries are scrambling for nuclear arms. Hell, Quaddafi in Libya even sent an envoy to China a few years ago to try to buy one. Suppose another Idi Amin somehow got the bomb and threatened his neighbors? The agency could neutralize him. We could arm the nation he was bullying. And not necessarily without presidential approval. Officially, the United States might not want to get involved in a third-world nuclear confrontation. But there might come a time when a president would want to move covertly in that kind of a situation, without even telling the Joint Chiefs of Staff. If so, the agency would be ready."

Senator Owens put his coffee cup down on the little table next to his rocker. "Frankly, Ben and I are still somewhat skeptical. For the moment, we've reserved judgment on whether to accept your story. I told you yesterday that I had a lot of questions. Perhaps your answers will help."

"Shoot." Travers appeared confident.

Owens smiled. He had been an assistant district attorney in Denver. He enjoyed interrogating witnesses at committee hearings and considered himself pretty good at it. "You claim that Israel built the bomb with 132 pounds of uranium that the agency stole at Apollo in Phase Blue and gave to Mossad."

"Yes."

"But a few years ago, Israeli intelligence hijacked a whole shipload of uranium. They got tons of the stuff. Why would they have bothered with the relatively small amount provided by Operation Spectrum?"

Travers appeared unruffled. "Mossad did hijack a ship, the *Scheersberg A,* but that was in 1968, two years *after* Phase Blue. Actually, it wasn't so much a hijacking as a diversion. Israel bought the uranium in Belgium through cutouts in West Germany and Milan. They loaded two hundred tons of yellowcake on the *Scheersberg A* in Antwerp. The freighter was supposed to be sailing under a Liberian flag for Genoa but it never got there. Several weeks later, the ship reappeared with a new captain and a new crew. The cargo had vanished. The uranium went to Dimona. But, as I say, that was 1968."

"So there's no way that the *Scheersberg A* uranium could have been used as Israel's initial ticket of admission to the nuclear club?"

"That's right. Besides, Spectrum provided Israel with enriched uranium that could go directly into nuclear weapons. The yellowcake that Mossad hijacked was milled ore, only one step removed from the mine. The Israelis would still have had to enrich it to make bombs."

"Did they know how?" Valerie asked.

"Interesting question," Travers said. "We think so. It's not a simple process. When uranium is mined, it's mostly U-238. Less than one percent is the fissionable U-235. The isotopes have to be separated to sift out the U-238. What you're left with is the enriched, bomb-grade uranium—about ninety percent U-235."

"Could they do that at Dimona?" Owens asked.

"Yes. There are several ways to manage the separation, all of them complex and expensive. The United States uses the gaseous diffusion method. The uranium is converted to gas and forced through thousands of membranes to extract the U-235. There are only three gaseous diffusion plants in the entire country and each one cost several billion dollars. Israel probably used a cheaper technique—centrifuge."

"But that cuts two ways," Owens persisted. "Why would Israel hijack a ship and go through a complicated enrichment process if they already had bomb-grade material from the agency?"

Senator Owens, Travers realized, was nobody's fool. He had turned Travers' argument around and was using it against him. "The answer is Dimona," he said. "The Israelis built their nuclear complex out there in the desert so that their atomic-weapons program would be self-sufficient. They were glad to get the uranium we gave them in 1965. But they couldn't afford to base a national policy on Towny Black's goodwill. The French provided most of the equipment for the reactor at Dimona. But they didn't provide much uranium to fuel it. So Mossad went out and got more, by hijacking the ship."

Goodman asked, "Some of the hijacked uranium was enriched to make weapons and some was used to fuel the reactor?"

"Right. Uranium used in reactor fuel only has to be enriched to three percent. But plutonium is obtained from the spent reactor fuel through reprocessing. And, of course, bombs can also be made from plutonium. So a reactor like the one at Dimona can insure a steady supply of weapons. The agency's scientific experts estimate that Dimona has produced enough plutonium by now for approximately thirty nuclear bombs."

Owens tried a new tack. "If the company's initial purpose, at least, was to arm Israel, why engage in a high-risk domestic operation? Why didn't the CIA first try to persuade the president to give nuclear weapons to Israel, secretly, if need be?"

"You probably understand how the agency thinks as well as anyone on the Hill, Senator. The basic rule is to do nothing openly, even within our own government, if it can be done covertly."

"The clandestine mentality."

"Exactly. And, as you know, the philosophy of the DCIs since Allen Dulles has been to 'insulate the president.' The less the man in the Oval Office knows, the better off he is. Then we can run the operation, the president can say he didn't know, and everybody's happy. Even the Forty Committee was set up that way inside the White House."

Owens smiled. "The Forty Committee was strictly window dressing."

"Of course. It was supposed to approve all covert operations. But it was just a circuit-breaker to protect the president. The result was that we had a free hand. That's the beauty of it. We can rationalize everything as a way to insulate the president. But it also allows us to do as we please. Have I answered your question?"

"I think so." It occurred to Senator Owens that deliberate ambiguity was an important policy tool of the agency. Few people seemed to understand that. "And I suppose," Owens added, "that any president who gave nuclear arms to Israel would be taking an enormous political risk. It would be a lot easier for the agency to do it."

"And plausibly deniable—if anyone found out."

It was Goodman's turn. "Okay," he said, "but given the objective of Phase Blue, why didn't the agency pilfer a few nuclear rockets from a military base in this country or abroad and give them directly to Israel? The finished product, so to speak?"

"Out of the question," Travers retorted. "Nukes are much too well protected at military installations. Short of an Entebbe-style commando raid, you couldn't get near them."

"They're more vulnerable when they're being transported, aren't they?" Goodman countered.

"Not much. I think some consideration was given to an in-transit hijacking operation in the very early planning stages of Spectrum, but it was quickly rejected. We ran into SECOM."

"What's that?" Owens inquired.

"It's the code name for the Department of Energy comm

net in Albuquerque. In those days the AEC ran it, of course. When nuclear weapons or materials are moved, they go out in transport convoys, with armed-escort vehicles. The escorts have rifles, grenades, and machine guns. Nowadays they even have M-16s that fire gallium arsenide laser beams for targeting. The convoys are in continuous communication with SECOM. They call in every half hour and their position is plotted on a map by a computer."

"They could still be hijacked, couldn't they?" Goodman asked.

"It would be very difficult. The trailer trucks are unmarked, and the escort vehicles look like ordinary campers, so there isn't much to attract attention on the highways. The trucks are steel-plated and especially designed to withstand penetration by any means—drills, explosives, or blowtorches —for one hour. The cabs are constructed to protect the drivers; you can't gain access to them. The trucks can withstand a head-on collision at sixty miles an hour and a nineteen-hundred-degree fire for half an hour. If anyone *did* get in, there are sprays, chemical foams, and other James Bond stuff that are automatically touched off by sensors. An intruder would be zapped. Also, the drivers can push a button that locks the wheels so the tractor-trailer can't be towed away if it is hijacked."

"You've convinced me," Goodman said. "I'm not going to try it."

"It convinced us, too. On top of all the physical obstacles, we would have been fighting off EACT, the government's secret Emergency Action Coordinating Team. It blasts off the minute there's any sign of trouble involving nuclear weapons. If somehow we did penetrate the trucks, we would still have to elude NEST, the Nuclear Emergency Search Team. If anything *is* stolen from fixed sites or the convoys, NEST has the job of finding it fast. They have airborne and surface sensors to detect uranium and plutonium."

Owens was impressed. Travers seemed to have done his homework. If the committee was being set up, he decided, it was certainly being done expertly. But then, the thought also occurred to him, that's exactly how the CIA would do it.

"All right," Owens said. "You make a good case. But I want to know more about you. You're a professional intelligence officer in charge of a major station, which means you're making fifty-seven thousand dollars a year, plus perks. You have everything to lose and nothing to gain by going outside the agency and coming to us. You're risking your career. I'd like to know why."

Travers chose his words carefully. "I suppose Watergate had something to do with it. It shook up a lot of us in the agency. Up to then, we always thought that if we got in trouble for breaking the law, someone up the line would fix the traffic ticket. Then we saw the president forced to resign and his top assistants marching off to jail. Over a *burglary*. Well, we'd done a lot worse than that. Suddenly, we realized how vulnerable we were."

Goodman snorted. "A lot of your colleagues in the agency seem to think that the only lesson of Watergate was not to get caught."

"It cut much deeper for me. I watched the company cover up for Nixon and lie about our own ties to the Plumbers. I began to think about all the things the agency had covered up. We'd been breaking the law and lying about it for thirty years—everything from opening mail to plotting murder. I guess it was during Watergate that I began to think it had to stop."

"But when did you make a personal decision to do something about it?" Owens asked.

"Not right away," Travers admitted. "There was so much going on. After Watergate there was the Rockefeller Report, the Church Committee, and the Pike investigation. I think that period was the real turning point for me. It all came tumbling out. We had hired the Mafia to try to kill Castro; we targeted Lumumba, Trujillo, Duvalier, and Sukarno. We plotted against Diem and Allende, and they both died in coups. Hell, we even set up an Executive Action unit to kill people."

"But you knew about the assassination plots," Owens said accusingly. "You were high up enough to know."

"Yes, I knew. There were some things I knew and some

things I didn't. I think Valerie has already made that clear to Ben. I didn't know we were spying on the peace movement. Operation Chaos was strictly Angus Maclaren's show. They were literally operating out of the basement in Langley, totally compartmented. The drug-testing and mind-control experiments were run by the Technical Services Division. The LSD freaks, the hypnotists, and the brainwashers were running loose in safe houses in San Francisco and Greenwich Village. They weren't in my car pool. Oh, I knew we were opening mail and wiretapping. I reaped some of the benefits of that in my own operations, and it was damn helpful."

"But now you've suddenly got religion," Goodman said drily.

"Look, what I knew or didn't know isn't really very important. What is important is that after the congressional investigations, the American people knew. The agency was exposed. For all of our Ivy League, Old Boy pretensions, we were shown to be a bunch of killers, lawbreakers, footpads, wiretappers, and mad scientists. In my view, anyone who thinks that anything could ever be the same again *after* those disclosures is smoking Santa Marta gold."

"The fact is," Owens reminded him, "the people have forgotten. Sure, in the presidential campaign, Thurlow Anderson got some mileage out of the CIA issue by promising to reform the agency, sort of. He said he favored a charter to keep the agency strong but curb the abuses. Then what did he do after he was elected? Turned around and named Towny Black the DCI."

"I think the president felt he had to put in a career man or risk losing the loyalty of the agency, after what we'd been through. The investigations were necessary, I believe that. But it's also true that they lowered our morale and damaged our ability to collect intelligence."

Owens reacted angrily. "I don't buy the part about morale at all. The agency can't have it both ways. You can't break the law, operate out of control, and then turn around and complain about low morale when you're caught. That's like a cathouse complaining that police raids are giving the place a bad reputation."

Goodman laughed, and Travers looked uncomfortable. "The point is," Travers said, "that the company must be forced to obey the law. That seems simple enough. And as long as Site Orange exists, we're breaking the law. That's why I'm blowing the whistle on Spectrum. I don't know any other way to put it."

"If I have it right," Goodman said, "you want the agency to turn into Snow White, reform itself, confess its worst secret, and start fresh, with a clean slate. And you're acting from the purest of motives. But there may be a simpler explanation. You don't like Towny Black."

"It's true. I don't like him at all. But our differences aren't just personal, they're philosophical. I no longer believe in a higher morality that permits the company to break the law in the name of national security. Towny Black does."

Senator Owens got up, walked to the window, and looked out at the rain, which had grown heavier, turning the fields an even darker shade of green. After a moment, he faced Travers.

"The disclosures you're talking about took place six years ago. Why has it taken you so long to come forward?"

Travers had expected the question. "It's been a cumulative process. A man doesn't change overnight, if he changes at all. Maybe we don't really change. We just come to see things differently. Our vision becomes sharper. And I haven't been totally silent. For some time now, I've been arguing my views inside the agency."

Owens nodded. "We're aware of that. We know that you and Black have been skirmishing."

"Until now, I haven't dared to put my head above the water. You saw what they did to Bill Colby for cooperating even a little with the Church Committee. The agency pilloried him. They even whispered that he was the Soviet mole. The one who Angus Maclaren claimed has been burrowing away all these years at Langley."

Owens left the window and returned to his chair by the fireside. "Then why have you chosen to go public? Chief of the London station is a prestigious position. You could continue to make your voice heard inside the agency."

"I have prestige but no power. Towny Black saw to that. He's kept me far from Langley. My efforts to reform the company from within haven't worked."

"I thought you'd built up a certain following," Owens said.

"Oh, there are a number of younger officers in the Clandestine Services who look to me as their leader. They know my views, and they agree with me. But we're scattered around—some at headquarters, some overseas. There's no cohesion."

"So you came to us." Owens' face did not reveal whether he accepted Travers' explanation. The chiseled features, the blue eyes were expressionless. "You realize, of course, that you aren't just risking your own career. You're placing the future of the CIA in jeopardy."

Travers was silent.

"You see that, don't you?" Owens asked. "In the past, it's true, there have been some horrendous disclosures about the agency. But now you're coming forward with the most damaging secret of all. Nuclear weapons. What if the agency dropped a little acid on innocent Americans, or tried to poison Fidel? By comparison, your story makes the drug tests, the domestic spying, and the assassination plots seem like a cub scout picnic."

"I realize I may damage the company," Travers replied slowly. "I know it sounds obvious, but damn it all, I believe that from the very beginning the agency's fundamental problem has been a confusion of ends and means. It's got to stop. We can't go on breaking the law and violating the Constitution because we think, or pretend to think, we're saving the country. We'll end up destroying it."

"And now you have the means," Valerie said quietly.

Senator Owens looked at her thoughtfully. She was, he decided, a woman whose extraordinary beauty was matched by her intelligence. He had not seen that, at first.

Valerie asked, "If Robert's story becomes public, Senator, what will happen to the agency?"

"The CIA was badly tarnished by all the revelations. It's regained a lot of power, but there are proposals floating around Washington—some have been introduced in Congress —to ban all covert operations, or split up the CIA into two parts. The president is backing the milder reforms, to carry out his campaign promises. There's no real support, though, even for Anderson's watered-down bill. A lot of people feel the agency's been criticized enough, that it should be left alone to do its job. Even unleashed. But if the American people find out that the CIA stole uranium and has nuclear weapons hidden away somewhere, the picture could change overnight. There could easily be a move to abolish the agency." He turned to Travers. "You may end up reforming it right out of existence."

"I don't want that to happen," Travers insisted, "but I'm willing to take the chance. There's a lot more at stake here than what happens to the agency. Towny Black has nuclear weapons. The time may come when he'll use them in a covert operation. As you pointed out, Senator, he could trigger a nuclear war."

Owens nodded. "The risks are enormous."

"I also realize the personal consequences," Travers said. "Once I go public, my career in the agency will probably be over."

"There are other risks you've hinted at," Owens said.

"Yes," Goodman joined in, "you implied yesterday—and Valerie told me in Washington—that there has been a cover-up inside the agency, people killed."

Travers backed off. "I don't know that for sure," he said cautiously. "But I think it's happened. Three senior agency officers who were fully witting during Operation Spectrum have died under ambiguous circumstances. Trilby Gates, who was the DDO during the operation, was first."

"I thought he collapsed on his tennis court in McLean," Goodman interjected.

"He did," Travers replied. "And the death certificate listed a heart attack as the cause. But it was signed by an agency doctor. And the symptoms were not inconsistent with shellfish-toxin poisoning."

Owens looked skeptical. "You're saying that a person poisoned with shellfish toxin might appear to have had a heart attack? Are you sure of that?"

"Positive. The toxin is incredibly lethal. It attacks the cardiovascular, respiratory, and nervous systems simultaneously. Death results in seconds. Even with an autopsy, and there wasn't one, there would be no way to tell that Gates had died of any cause other than that officially listed—cardiac arrest."

"Who was he playing tennis with?" Valerie asked mildly.

"Towny Black. It was a Saturday morning. Gates had invited him over."

"You said the toxin causes death in seconds," Goodman cut in. "How could it have been administered on a tennis court, in broad daylight?"

"TSD is resourceful. My theory is that Black could have provided a new can of balls for Trilby after they had played a set. One of the tennis balls could have been prepared with a pin protruding perhaps a sixteenth of an inch. Gates would never have noticed anything. The stuff is so lethal it only takes a tiny scratch and you're dead. I understand that Gates was just starting to serve the second set, when he collapsed."

Goodman was shaking his head. "But you can't prove it was murder."

"No."

"Who else has died?" Owens asked.

"Putney Barnes, Gates's deputy. He disappeared two years ago while scuba diving off the Spanish Mediterranean coast with his mistress."

"Where did it happen?"

"Somewhere around Torremolinos, on the Costa del Sol. He vanished without a trace. Accidental drowning, we were told. 'You know Putney, always taking risks. Always looking for new conquests, on the ski slopes, underwater, or between the sheets.' That was the talk in the agency. But a couple of days later, the girl disappeared without a trace. She's never been seen or heard from since."

"Tell them your suspicions about Angus," Valerie said.

Travers nodded. "It's been almost six months since Angus Maclaren was killed in an automobile accident on the George Washington Parkway near headquarters. He had been working late at the agency, and was driving home at night. His car plunged over an embankment into the Potomac. I'm sure you remember the story, *The Washington Post* put it on page one."

"Yes," said Owens, "but I had no reason to assume it was anything more than an accident."

"Again, I can't prove anything. But I think the steering wheel was coated with an incapacitating drug or poison that was absorbed through the skin. Maclaren was an experienced driver, alone in the car, nothing to distract him. The road wasn't icy or wet. He'd driven that stretch of the parkway a thousand times. Yet he suddenly goes sailing off the embankment like Chitty Chitty Bang Bang."

Owens appeared unpersuaded. "Why would Maclaren have been cut in on Spectrum in the first place? He was in charge of counterintelligence."

"He had been," Travers agreed, "until he got fired during the shakeup over Operation Chaos. But we quietly kept him on as a consultant, and he still had an office at headquarters. The press didn't know that. We called Angus the Gray Ghost, he was so thin. His hobby was raising prize-winning orchids. He chain-smoked cigarettes, even in his greenhouse. When he was chief of counterintelligence, he thought the Soviets had a mole under every rock in Langley. If you listened to Angus, you'd think they were digging up the whole garden. I never believed it. He'd become paranoid on the subject. As far as Spectrum is concerned, the reason he was witting is logical. For complicated reasons, going back to 1948, Maclaren handled the Israeli account for us. And Phase Blue was a joint operation with Mossad. Angus would never have stood for being cut out of the rest of the operation. And the director wouldn't have dared to try. Maclaren knew too much. He had wiretaps all over the place and a file on everybody. The files were the source of his power."

"Yeah," said Goodman, "he was the J. Edgar Hoover of the CIA."

"The bottom line," Owens summed up, "is that you suspect that Trilby Gates, Putney Barnes, and Angus Maclaren were all murdered because they shared the secret of Operation Spectrum."

"Yes—and I may be next."

"That's another reason you're coming to us." It was less a question than a statement.

"Yes."

Owens looked unconvinced. "You say you may be in danger. But why hasn't Black moved against you before now?"

"He must not know I've seen the Spectrum file. But he might find out at any time."

"So you want to go public, with our help."

"Right. I want the truth out. And I figure that if I surface and make my charges public through the committee, the exposure in the news media will give me a degree of protection."

"There are other ways to handle the problem," Owens said. "We could give you a new identity. Relocate you. The Justice Department does it for some of their informers."

Travers winced at the word. "That might work against the Mafia, but it won't do any good with the agency. You can't just give me a new name and ship me off to run a pizza joint in San Diego. If Towny Black wants to find me, he can."

"I suppose you're right. Going public gives you the most protection. But how many others may be in danger? Who else knew about Spectrum?"

"There were possibly two dozen people in the agency who knew something about one phase or another. But they're in no danger. The operation was highly compartmented on a need-to-know basis. The Phase Green people who handled the paperwork with Pantex, for example, would not have known anything about Phase Yellow, and so on. And the code name itself was very tightly held. That's why I hesitated even to say it in this room."

"Who knew it?"

"Towny Black. Frank DiMario. But they're as close as two snakes in a basket. Gates, Barnes, and Maclaren. And me."

Owens shook his head. "It's not very much to go on," he said. "The fact is that you haven't a shred of proof. Either that Spectrum ever took place or that any of the deaths were from other than natural causes or accidents."

Goodman sounded a similar note. "Basically, you're asking us to take your whole story on faith. When it comes to CIA, we don't take anything on faith anymore. You guys have given faith a bad name. Do you have any documents? Any kind of proof?"

Until this moment, Travers had not fully realized just how weak his position was. The Senate was not so different from the agency. Owens was demanding facts, evidence, documents. And Travers had little more to offer than a story. "There's one thing I can show you," he said. "It isn't very much."

Travers disappeared into the bedroom. He reached into the closet and pulled out an attaché case. The rich brown leather and shiny brass fittings seemed oddly out of place in the rustic cottage. Travers swiftly worked the combination lock, unsnapped the clasps, and opened the case. He took a Swiss Army knife from his pocket, and worked the blade gently along a slit in the lining. In a moment, a whole section came free. He reached in and removed a sheet of blue paper.

He rejoined the others and handed the document to Owens. The senator examined it. The words "Central Intelligence Agency" did not appear anywhere on the letter-sized sheet. But Owens had seen enough CIA documents to know that the agency preferred blank paper for all but official correspondence. At the top and bottom of the sheet, the classification TOP SECRET-ALPHA had been rubber-stamped in capital letters. The words "Spectrum/Phase Blue" had been typed in the center of the page. In the upper-right-hand corner were someone's initials, in ink. Owens thought he could make out the letters "TG," but he was not sure. The page had at one time been folded in three parts; the creases were still visible.

"It's the classification cover sheet for Phase Blue," Travers explained. "I removed it when I read the file. I folded it up, put it inside my jacket pocket, and walked out with it. The inked initials belonged to Trilby Gates."

"And that's all you have?"

"Yes. No other souvenirs."

Owens looked disappointed. "I'm afraid that by itself, it proves nothing." He handed the sheet to Ben Goodman, who studied it and shrugged. "If the committee were to investigate your charges," Owens said, "we would want to obtain the entire file as our first order of business."

Travers chuckled. "You'll never see it," he said. "If it still exists, Black will destroy it at the first hint of any congressional investigation. Just the way Helms got rid of most of the files on the drug-testing, the mind-control experiments, and Watergate. The minute you lift a finger, the Spectrum file will end up in the Pit, if it hasn't already."

"The Pit?" Owens raised his eyebrows in a quizzical expression.

"That's the destruction area in the basement at Langley where we burn, shred, and pulverize whatever we don't want to see the light of day. A few years back, the agency was dumping so much top-secret pulp into the Potomac that we were cited for water pollution. Now we take it out to West Virginia and sell it for landfill."

"You're assuming," Owens protested, "that Black would somehow find out about a committee decision to investigate him even before he received a subpoena for the files."

"We'd hear," Travers said. "The intelligence committee staffs are infiltrated. On both the Senate and House side. You don't really think the agency would let Congress establish oversight committees on CIA and not penetrate you?"

"We've heard rumors," Owens said defensively, "but as far as we know, our people are all loyal."

"Don't bet on it. And it isn't just the intelligence committees. The agency has a whole network of people on the Hill. There are eight former CIA agents who are members of Congress right now, including one senator. I'm not going to name them. We have literally dozens of staff aides and secretaries in Congress who either work for us full time, or report to us on a free-lance basis when they have something interesting. We don't pay them much, but over a year's time, it's often enough to take care of the summer cottage at Rehoboth. Or a shopping spree at Neiman-Marcus."

Owens stood again and paced up and down in front of the fireplace. The rain had increased and was beating a staccato on the cottage roof.

"I don't know," he said, finally. "Your story has convincing elements, yet we're not wholly convinced. You can't really prove that any of this happened. When I ask for proof, you come up with one piece of paper that could mean anything, or nothing. When I say we need the files, you say they've either been destroyed or they will be." He paused. "Right now, I don't have enough to go to the full committee. Or for that matter, even to my subcommittee." The senator stopped pacing and sat down. He took a long sip of Scotch and stared at the rain streaming down the window in rivulets.

Travers felt that Owens was on the verge of slipping away from him. He had taken a terrible chance on this man. For two days he had bared agency secrets to an outsider, violating every security rule in the book, jeopardizing his own position. Now it seemed as though it might all be for naught.

Owens sensed Travers' alarm. "Look," he said, "the first hurdle you have to cross is to convince us. You've come very close, but we need more."

Travers listened to the rain tattooing on the roof. "There is a way to get what you want," he said softly. "If we were to run an operation against the agency. Against Towny Black."

"That," said Owens, "is what I was hoping you would say."

Goodman exploded. "Senator, I hope you realize what we're getting into. The odds against anything like that succeeding are a million to one, and the risks are enormous. You're taking on the whole goddamn CIA."

"What I had in mind," Owens said calmly, ignoring Ben, "is something that might shake Black up. Cause him to panic, and possibly make a mistake. And at the same time give the committee the evidence it needs."

Valerie came over and sat on the raised hearth to be closer to Robert. She reached up and touched his hand lightly.

Travers felt exultant. Perhaps it was Owens, after all, who had been hooked and brought into the boat, not he. He did not have much time to savor the thought.

"What might shake Black up the most," Owens was saying, "would be somehow to let him know the truth. That you are getting ready to go public."

"Yeah," said Ben with a piratical grin. "I like that idea." He realized that Owens had set his course. In that case, he calculated, it was far better to have Travers walk the plank, and for the moment, to keep the committee well in the background.

For precisely the same reasons, Travers was alarmed. He knew that at some point, his charges would have to become public. It would be a wrenching change for someone whose name had never, up to now, appeared in print. When it came, there would be the white glare of publicity, the network cameras, the reporters hounding him. In one way, he would welcome the notoriety for the protection it would offer. But emotionally he was not ready for it yet. Travers' deeply ingrained instinct for secrecy, the anonymity he had cultivated in a lifetime as a clandestine operator, could not be shed like a chrysalis in one afternoon.

Owens was drumming his fingers on the arm of his rocker. "From what you've told us," he continued, "you are the only person left inside the agency, other than Black and DiMario, who knows the code name Spectrum and what it means."

"I'm not positive, but I think that's true."

"What I want you to do is send Black a letter. Don't sign it. Don't mail it from London. Let's not make it too easy for him. The letter will consist of only one word: 'Spectrum.' If I'm correct, Black will surmise that it had to come from you. He'll read it as a threat to reveal the secret. He'll *have* to react. He'll have to do something. He may call you back from London, for example, and confront you directly. In that case, you might be able to get him on tape with a concealed recorder."

"Yes," Travers retorted drily. "There are a lot of things he might do. He might even have me killed."

"If your suspicions about Gates, Barnes, and Maclaren are correct, you're already in danger," Owens countered. "You said so yourself."

"Suppose I agree to your plan," Travers said, "what will the committee do in return?"

"If you can get Black on tape making incriminating statements about Spectrum, or if he tries to have you liquidated, the committee will accept that as proof of your story. I give you my word on that. We will open a full-scale Senate investigation of your charges. We won't stop until the story of Operation Spectrum is laid out before the American people in televised public hearings. That's the deal I'm offering."

"A congressional investigation in exchange for my life? That doesn't sound like a very good bargain."

"We don't want you killed, Mr. Travers. You're our key

witness. You're our only source of information about Spectrum at this point. If we ever reach the stage of public hearings, we will need you to testify."

"Black is a dangerous and clever man. He will do anything to prevent the secret of Spectrum from being revealed. And he has the full resources of the agency at his disposal. If I do send the letter, as you propose, there's a good chance it will trigger an attempt to have me assassinated. How can you be sure it won't succeed?"

"We can't. Basically, you're on your own. You'll have to rely on your own skills, your knowledge of Black the man, and the agency's methods, to outwit any attempt on your life."

"Then it's no deal," Travers said. "Not unless your committee is prepared to provide full operational support for me. I won't run a covert operation without backup. In this case, I can hardly ask the agency to provide it. So you'll have to."

Owens glanced over at Goodman. "I don't suppose that's impossible, is it, Ben?"

"No, sir. Depending on what he has in mind."

Travers' thoughts were racing ahead. If he could enlist the power and prestige of the United States Senate, there was just a chance that he could win. He would take the gamble.

"Since 1974," Travers said, "the agency has been required by law to notify your committee of any new covert operation."

"That's correct," Owens agreed.

"Okay. As chairman of the Intelligence subcommittee, I want you to approach the National Security Agency. Remind them of your responsibility over covert action. Ask them secretly to monitor CIA cable traffic for the next six months on the pretext that the committee wants to check on compliance by the agency in reporting covert operations."

Goodman was gnawing nervously on an unlit cigar. "You're hoping that way we can pick up the traces if Towny Black dispatches an agency hit man to kill you?"

"Yes. It would give me some warning. And it would provide part of the proof you need."

"We can approach NSA," Senator Owens said doubtfully,

"but it's a pretty wild card. What makes you think that Admiral Hughes will agree?"

"He'll jump at the chance. The rivalry between the two agencies is very strong. You'll be offering an officially approved assignment to put their big ear right into Langley. They'll be breaking out the champagne in Fort Meade the minute you leave. Take my word for it."

"All your traffic is enciphered. I realize that code-breaking is NSA's business, but will they be able to read your cables?"

Travers laughed. "NSA provides all the codes and computers that the agency uses. We have our own cryptanalysts, of course, and a whole set of special procedures for communications security. On-line encryption for just about everything. But NSA provides all the hardware. They'll read us loud and clear."

"We'll try it," Owens promised. "But in the meantime we have to move ahead on other fronts. You have to try to find out the location of Site Orange. Use your resources, work from the inside. If you can pinpoint the location, we can try to verify it from our end. But even after you've convinced us, we'll need to find those missiles, or there's no way to convince the public that your story is true."

"I'll do my best," Travers promised.

"And you'll send the letter to Black?"

"Yes."

"Fine. Give us about two weeks. If NSA goes along, we'll let you know immediately. We'll communicate through Valerie. Ben will write her a note containing the word 'retriever.' You still own a golden, don't you, Ben?" Goodman nodded. "We'll have to make special arrangements within the committee if what you say about agency penetration of our staff is correct. We can't afford a leak. Only Ben and I, Ben's assistant, Howard Radner, and my personal secretary, Karla Warren, will know about any of this."

"Good," Travers said. "The tighter the better."

Owens got up. "I think that about wraps it up for now. We're with you, but we need proof before we can go any further. We'll help you in any way we can."

Travers shook hands with the young senator and with Ben

Goodman. "There's one thing more that perhaps I should tell you," he said. "It's partly speculation on my part, so I hesitate to mention it."

"Go ahead," Owens said. "I want to know everything."

"Well," Travers replied, "you've talked about President Anderson's campaign promises to reform the agency, and the various proposals floating around Washington to split us up. You've predicted that if my story becomes public, there might even be demands for more drastic action against the CIA."

"I think that's a realistic appraisal on my part."

"I told you that Phase Red is the designation for the deployment or use of the agency's weapons. It may also mean something else, something so sensitive that it isn't even spelled out in the Spectrum file."

"What's that?"

"There might come a time when the agency was in so much trouble that a president might want to abolish it. From reading between the lines, I'm convinced that the final phase of Spectrum is a fail-safe device, designed to prevent that from ever happening."

"How?" Senator Owens was staring at Travers.

"I believe that Phase Red is a euphemism for the director's use, or threat to use, the nuclear missiles for political purposes. To blackmail the president of the United States."

Chapter 10

Holly Corcoran answered the director's buzzer. She moved quickly across the thick carpet to his desk, her young body, red dress, and blond hair flowing in one lithe motion. She wore her Malibu smile and carried a steno pad in her right hand.

"Yes, sir?"

Someday, Graham Black resolved as he looked at her, he would have Holly Corcoran. Perhaps she would consider it an honor to be laid by the director of Central Intelligence. But not today. "I want to see Bill Harrington right away. Find out if he's in the building, and get him up here."

"Before the staff meeting?"

The director checked his watch. It was 7:45 A.M. He had forty-five minutes until the rescheduled staff meeting, enough time to meet with Harrington if he could be found. "Yes," he confirmed, "before the meeting. Don't list him in my appointment book. And you needn't mention it to Evan Younger."

Holly's light-green eyes widened. "I'd already forgotten it," she said, flashing another wide smile. But Holly was surprised. There was very little that Evan Younger, the director's staff assistant, was not privy to. His small office was right next to Towny Black's, and opened on the secretarial area, where Holly had her desk. He had a clear view of any visitors. However, she could easily bring Harrington in through the conference room adjoining the rear of the DCI's office. That way, no one would see him, not even Rick Alesi, the dark-haired, pale-faced hood from the Office of Security who presided over the glass booth in the outer office.

The director automatically focused on Holly's clockwork rear as she went out the door. Someday, he thought. He reached distractedly for the leather pouch containing his Dunhill's London mixture. He opened it and removed a pinch of the rich, dark tobacco, savoring the aroma. He filled and lit his pipe, the favorite root briar he had bought on a trip to London several years earlier, and settled back to reflect on what needed to be said to Harrington.

Holly understood what a summons to Bill Harrington meant. It meant, or could easily mean, that someone, somewhere in the world, was going to get killed. She found that exciting, a thought she would never admit to anyone. There were times when Holly missed the easy life in California, hopping into a van on a clear day and heading for the beach and the surf, but it was mornings like this that made her job with the agency interesting. If she had stayed in Los Angeles, she reflected, she would probably be deep into the singles rat-race at the Marina in Venice, and working her tail off by day in a boring secretarial job for the Bank of America. Or Arco. But this morning, she was hunting up a professional killer for her government at the request of America's top spy, her boss. And, even more delicious, she was to keep it secret from everyone, even from his principal assistant. She liked that. She opened a desk drawer and took out a yellow telephone directory. The words TOP SECRET were printed in black letters on the cover and on each page. She turned to the E's, and her eye moved quickly down the coded symbols on the left-hand side of the page until she came to EA. "Let your fingers do the walking," she murmured. She dialed a four-digit extension.

"This is Holly in the director's office," she said crisply, confident of the magical effect the words would have. Inside the agency, when the director was calling, other telephone conversations were abruptly ended to accept the DCI's call. Only the phrase "the White House is calling" could have a more galvanizing effect.

In every branch but EA, apparently. The secretary who answered did not seem particularly impressed. "Mr. Harrington is away from his desk," she said in a bored tone. "He just stepped out for a moment."

"Well, put on your roller skates and go after him," Holly snapped. "The director wants to see him immediately."

Harrington's secretary grimaced at the phone. Then she dialed the south cafeteria, the agency's classified dining room. The covert operators always ate there, knowing that they would not be recognized, since no outsiders were permitted to enter. Visitors from the Defense Intelligence Agency, the NSA, or other government agencies, even officials with top secret clearance, were shepherded to the overt cafeteria. Harrington's secretary knew he was having coffee; nothing stronger was served in either dining room. She also knew that he had probably had a couple of Campari and sodas before coming in. Harrington started his drinking day off slowly. By lunchtime he was out of the building, downing martinis at the Shanghai on Lee Highway. In the evenings, at home, he usually switched to Rémy Martin.

A uniformed security guard at the cafeteria entrance got Harrington to the phone.

"Yeah?" he grunted.

"God is not dead," his secretary informed him. "He's alive and well on the seventh floor and he wants you up there right away."

Harrington grunted again, hung up, and headed for the elevators at a fast clip. A laminated ID badge with his color photograph jiggled from the beaded metal chain around his neck. He was a huge, bullet-headed man, well over six feet tall and two hundred fifty pounds. Despite his enormous bulk, and a characteristic, ducklike walk, Harrington moved with surprising agility. As he punched the elevator button he wondered what lay behind the summons from the director.

It had been almost ten months since Towny Black had called him in, and that, he recalled sourly, was to ream him out for the death of a Soviet diplomat who had been mugged and shot in Central Park. Ambassador Kalugin had lodged a vigorous, albeit secret, protest with the State Department over what he called "the murderous activities of certain uncontrolled hooligan elements of U.S. intelligence." Foggy Bottom had just as vigorously rejected the protest after Secretary of State Jordan Bancroft had checked with Towny Black, who assured him that "the fellas" weren't involved.

The director had not found it necessary to share his own doubts with the secretary of state. New York's finest had logged it as just another robbery and homicide in the Ramble, a thickly wooded and particularly hazardous area of Central Park, but Black thought it might be something else. Harrington, looking innocent, had denied it. "Fucking Sovs," he had told Black. "They send in their KGB legals under UN cover and don't even brief them on what a dangerous place the big city is. They're so damn dumb they wander around Central Park at night. No wonder they get mugged and killed." The director had not appeared entirely convinced. "See that there are no more accidents in the park," he snapped.

So what was it this time? Harrington wondered. Perhaps Black was really going to shut down Executive Action. The agency had already assured Congress that it had been done. Only it hadn't. Somehow, Executive Action always survived. There were enough people on the covert side of the house who insisted that the agency "maintain the option."

Trilby Gates had created the Executive Action unit in 1961 to plan and carry out assassinations. He had been customarily vague in briefing the Kennedy White House, leaving the impression that the agency simply wanted an untargeted "capability" for murder. Gates had not mentioned that his directorate was already targeting specific individuals and that EA, under Harrington, had actually become operational. Later, during the uproar over CIA assassinations, the DCI had falsely informed the Church Committee that the Executive Action unit had been dismantled.

Harrington got out on the seventh floor and turned right, heading down the long corridor to the director's office. He passed the conference room used by the National Foreign Intelligence Board, the interagency unit that prepared crucial intelligence estimates for the president. Holly Corcoran was waiting for him in the hall outside the director's office.

"He's expecting you," she said. She pushed open the door that led from the hall to the DCI's conference room, which was known as the French Room for reasons long since forgotten. Holly showed Harrington into Towny Black's office. She left immediately, and the two men were alone.

"Sit down, Bill."

The director was leaning back in his executive chair, enveloped in a cloud of smoke. Harrington ponderously settled his bulk into a chair across from the director.

Black unobtrusively touched the fountain pen resting in his desk set to make sure it was securely in its holder. When loosened or removed, it activated the taping system. In the French Room, a button under the table served the same purpose. Once the pen was dislodged or the button pushed, the tapes began to roll in a special recording room seven floors below. They were routinely transcribed each week. The transcripts, marked "DCI-Eyes Only" were hand-delivered in sealed envelopes to Rick Alesi in his glass booth. For this meeting, however, Towny Black wanted no tapes and no transcripts.

Harrington wondered whether the taping system was on. He figured, correctly, that it wasn't. Harrington grinned, showing his gold teeth.

"What have I done now, Mr. Director? Whenever I'm called to the seventh floor, I always think, 'Holy shit, it's the woodshed for Bill again.'" He let go a deep-throated fat man's laugh.

"I don't know, Bill, you tell me. What *have* you done?" Black's laughter blended with Harrington's.

"Not damn near enough," the big man replied. "We've been sitting downstairs rereading old copies of *Penthouse* and waiting for the fire bell. Every once in a while I get out my broom and whisk the cobwebs off the ceiling."

"Well, in your line of work, you can't expect to keep busy every day."

"It would sure help with the population explosion." Harrington's laugh boomed out again.

Black joined in, although less enthusiastically this time. He studied the big, red-haired man across from him. Harrington flaunted a crew cut that would have done justice to a Marine recruit; the styles of the moment meant nothing to him. His skin was fair and almost as red as his hair. His large round face was blotchy and freckled. For a big man, he had unusually small eyes, like those of some ferretlike animal,

Black thought, but his nose, which showed the effects of his heavy drinking, was disproportionately large. He wore a double-knit gray suit, a nondescript blue tie, somewhat food-stained, and a white, short-sleeved shirt that left his hairy wrists bare under his jacket. He sat motionless, like a round-eye Buddha, his coat unbuttoned. But the folds of fat on his belly did not conceal the bulge under his left arm. Black knew it was the shoulder holster for the revolver that Harrington always carried. He did not know that in the small of his back Harrington also had a .38 Special in a holster strapped to his belt.

Once, Black remembered, Harrington had even packed a gun into the Oval Office for a meeting with President Kennedy, a fan of Ian Fleming, who had asked to meet "the American James Bond." Kennedy must have been greatly disappointed, Black thought. Harrington, mountainous and unkempt, was about as far as one could get from the suave image of James Bond. But like the fictional 007, he was licensed to kill.

Harrington, to be sure, had missed his most notorious target. The botulinum capsules he had turned over to the Mafia for use against Fidel Castro had never been slipped into the Cuban leader's arroz con pollo. Harrington blamed both Johnny Rosselli and the Cuban exile who had claimed to have a contact in the restaurant where Castro usually ate.

Usually, however, Harrington did not miss. In the course of his agency career, Black reflected, Harrington had probably killed twenty men and at least one woman, a GRU agent in Madrid. Harrington was Number One on the KGB's most wanted list, having murdered a dozen of their agents on three continents. He used guns, knives, and less conventional weapons, including a long ice pick. He had, he once told Black, borrowed the latter idea from Pittsburgh Phil Strauss, a hit man for the old Murder, Inc. The technique was interesting. Harrington would enter a movie theater and seat himself directly behind his victim. Halfway through the film, using a sharp blow with the heel of his hand, he would plunge the ice pick through the seat in front of him and into the target's body. Then he would slip away. There was seldom any blood visible because the point of the weapon was so fine and the puncture wounds so deep. Usually, it was not until the movie ended and the theater was emptying out that anyone would notice the lone patron who sat motionless, staring glassy-eyed at the blank screen.

Harrington had used this method to murder a Czech intelligence officer in Rome, and a wizened, little East German double agent in Berlin who had apparently forgotten which side he was working for. To Harrington, killing was his profession; he thought no more of the taking of a human life than he would of squashing a bug. Despite his heavy drinking, his ham hands were steady and his legendary marksmanship unimpaired.

Bill Harrington was not a man whom Graham Townsend Black would invite into his living room or to lunch at the Metropolitan Club. Even as Black's guest, Harrington might have had trouble getting past the ancient black man who wore an organ grinder's monkey costume and traditionally guarded the front door of the club.

The director fished a metal reamer from his pocket and used it to empty his pipe bowl into the ashtray on his desk. "Bill," he asked casually, "how well do you know Robert Travers?"

"Never met him," Harrington replied. "I had nothing to do with Domestic Ops when he ran the division, and our paths never crossed overseas. Well, almost never. He was pointed out to me once by Bill Bradford in a restaurant on the Via Veneto. So I know what he looks like, but that's all. I hear he's become a real crybaby. A goddamn reformer, taking shots at you from the London station."

"Worse than that." Black looked grave. He removed his glasses, leaned back and studied the acoustical tile in the ceiling, trying to remember which one concealed the microphone. He had forgotten.

"How do you mean?" Harrington looked interested.

"You recall when Bill Colby was toadying up to the Church Committee a few years ago. Around that time, Angus Maclaren started floating the rumor that a KGB mole had penetrated the agency, at a high level. Soon after, Colby fired

Maclaren. Well Angus even whispered around town that Colby himself might be the mole. That was ridiculous, of course; Maclaren just wanted revenge."

"That's what I always figured. The old cock-sucker—may he rest in peace—just wanted to get even with Colby."

"Yes." A lot of the mole talk, Black reminded Harrington, had started with the interrogation of Yuri Novchenko, the Russian defector whom the KGB had floated out in Geneva just after the Kennedy assassination. Novchenko assured the CIA that he had personally handled the center's file on Lee Harvey Oswald and could vouch for the fact that the president's assassin had no connection with Soviet intelligence. Maclaren had refused to accept Novchenko's bona fides. Particularly when the defector had cast doubt on information provided by an earlier KGB turncoat, Anatoli Dolnytsin. It was Dolnytsin, who had defected to the West in 1961, who first suggested to the agency that a high-level Soviet mole had penetrated Langley.

"Angus never believed Novchenko," Black ruminated. "He put the poor bastard through hostile interrogation. Three years in a concrete vault at Camp Peary, with a light bulb burning all night. Total isolation, no books, no cigarettes, no one to talk to. Novchenko damn near went crazy. He tried to make chess sets from the threads of his clothing. Maclaren's goons found them and took them away. But Novchenko never broke. Although, at one point, he damn near became one of your clients."

"Howzzat?" Harrington asked.

"The deputy chief of the Soviet Russia Division sent a memo to Maclaren: 'One option might be to liquidate the man.' With the SR Division making noises like that, Novchenko was almost turned over to you."

Harrington grimaced, and the corners of his mouth turned down. Black realized he was registering disappointment. "I stayed clear of the whole thing," Black added, "but personally I always thought Angus had tied himself and the agency into a pretzel. Even if Novchenko *was* a disinformation agent, it didn't begin to prove that Oswald was working for the KGB. It didn't follow." Black paused and started fussing with his pipe, tamping in fresh, moist tobacco and lighting up. He shook out the match. "But Angus was right about one thing. There is a mole."

"Jesus!" Harrington swore. "Have you found the son of a bitch?"

"Yes." Black puffed on his polished briar. "Frank DiMario came out to the house last night. He had a whole dossier from Brooks Abbot." Abbot had taken over as chief of Counterintelligence after Angus Maclaren had been fired. "Frank showed me the material. Surveillance photographs of the mole."

"Meeting with his KGB case officer?" Harrington sounded incredulous.

"No, of course not," Black said reprovingly. "They would never take that kind of chance. He was meeting with a cutout. But there are more photographs. Taken by a surveillance van. And they show the cutout on a street corner with a known KGB colonel, a top officer of the First Chief Directorate with thin diplomatic cover. It's all there, on film."

"It's Travers?"

Puff. Puff. Puff. Black let the suspense build for a full moment before he answered.

"Yes."

Harrington whistled. "So that's why you wanted to know whether he'd make me."

"Bill, you were my first choice for this assignment. But, naturally, I had to know that."

"Yeah. Naturally. What are my orders?"

"The evidence is cut and dried. I can't ignore what Frank and Brooks have brought to me. We've dreaded this for years. A KGB penetration. And now it's definite, a nightmare come true."

"The bastard." Harrington's huge hands were working, his fingers opening and closing.

"Travers will have to be neutralized, Bill." He used the same distasteful tone of voice that he might have employed in calling in the Orkin man to spray for roaches. "He has to be eliminated, removed. We have to make certain that he is no longer in a position to harm the agency."

Harrington shifted on his enormous haunches. "I think I understand the mission. But I don't want to make any mistakes. Maybe you could spell it out a little more."

Black had lapsed almost automatically into agency double-speak, the careful ambiguities with which he felt most comfortable. Harrington, he realized, was fencing, trying to get him to use words of one syllable, to share the culpability. Normally, Black would not have played. But he needed Harrington. The younger men in Executive Action, he knew, lacked seasoning. Harrington could be trusted to do the job. There were no witnesses to their conversation. And the tapes were not running. Almost involuntarily, he touched the desktop pen to make sure.

"I don't mean to be vague, Bill. The agency can't afford Robert Travers. Neither can the country. He's the mole. Kill him."

"Right. Fine." Harrington's voice was flat, devoid of emotion.

"As for the operational details, I want this held very tight. You, me, and Frank DiMario. Period."

"That's tighter than a snail's ass. What about Brooks Abbot? Mole removal is a CI concern, isn't it?"

"He'll be told the problem is being taken care of," the director said sharply. "That's all. You're to have no contact with him."

"Approach to target?"

"I've given that some thought. You'll be sent to the London station with a completely new identity. You'll have physical disguise and an alias, with full, backstopped personal documentation. You'll be going in as an officer in the Clandestine Services being rotated to London from Langley in a routine change of assignment."

"And my cover?"

"London station has two layers of cover, both housed in the embassy in Grosvenor Square—the Political Liaison Section and the Joint Reports and Research Unit. Travers is listed as head of both. You'll be assigned to JRRU cover. Get together with Frank to work out the details."

"Isn't it a little dicey to assign me to Travers' own staff?"

"There's no better place for you to be. Travers' termination has to look accidental. Once you're in London, you'll be in an excellent position to gather the preliminary operational data you need to carry out the assignment—the layout of Travers' apartment, where he eats, shops, plays, sleeps, and with whom. Where he goes on weekends. His car. His weaknesses. Does he gamble? Take drugs? Does he have a girl? Who is she? You know the drill better than I."

"I may need to put some things in his apartment."

The director understood. After killing, Harrington's main field of expertise, in which he had earned a considerable reputation, was wiretapping and bugging. It was Harrington, some believed, who had thought up the idea for the Berlin Tunnel in 1955. Posing as construction workers, building an "experimental radar station," Harrington and his men tunnelled five hundred feet under the border into East Berlin and wiretapped the central Soviet Army switchboard, including its lines to Moscow. The intelligence take was enormous and the operation went on for ten months before it was discovered. In later years, Allen Dulles often cited the Berlin Tunnel as one of the agency's most valuable coups. Harrington's career was assured.

"You'll have to go carefully on the electronics," Black advised him. "Travers' office in the embassy is routinely swept by our own Division D people. It's possible he also has them check his home. You'll have to find out before you put anything in."

"When do you want me to leave for London?"

The director hesitated. "There's one little detail that has to be taken care of first." Black looked uncomfortable. "You see, Bill," he resumed, "the Technical Services Division can do wonders with your facial appearance and documentation. But there's one thing you'll have to do."

"What?"

"You'll have to go on a crash diet and lose thirty pounds."

"Shit. I can't do it. No way."

"You've got to do it, Bill. Travers is betraying the company. This is probably the most important assignment you'll ever have."

"Jesus Christ. I'm supposed to be head of Executive

Action, and now you want me to join the fucking Weight Watchers."

The director pointed his pipe stem at Harrington, jabbing the air for emphasis. "You've got to do it. The company doctors will help you if you want their help. Or you can do it on your own. But you see the reason. At two hundred and twenty pounds, you'll just be a somewhat heavyset officer reporting for duty in the London station. At two-fifty, you'll look too damn much like Bill Harrington, no matter what we do to your hair and face. Someone might make you. Not Travers, perhaps, since he doesn't know you, but somebody else in the station. I'll tell Frank, by the way, to do a computer run on how many of our people currently assigned in London were ever stationed anywhere with you, no matter how long ago. I'll want to see the printout."

"How long do I have to make weight?"

"It'll take the Technical Services Division at least a couple of weeks to prepare your physical disguise and longer than that for the alias documentation. Frank will want to brief you thoroughly and it will take him some time to arrange the paperwork for your transfer. It has to be plugged in through the Office of Personnel so that it seems completely normal, even in-house. I don't want the deputy director for Administration coming around, asking questions. All of that will take time. So, let's say you can have six weeks, on the outside."

"All right. I'll try. Shit." Harrington groaned again.

"Once you have complete data on Travers' movements, personal habits, strengths, and weaknesses, your job is to develop an on-scene operational plan for his elimination. I'll want to know exactly where and when you plan to take him. You are not to do anything until it's approved in advance by Frank and by me. Is that clear?"

"Yes, sir."

"You'll need your own communications, naturally. We can't have Travers reading your reports. I'll arrange for a back channel from the embassy, with your own on-line link encryption. That way your messages will be coded differently from any other traffic moving out of the station to Langley. The operation will be called LS/Talpia." Black spelled the code name and Harrington committed it to memory. "All your cables should bear that slug and be directed to the DCI, eyes only."

"Check." Harrington cleared his throat. "My choice of hardware, I assume?"

Black shook his head. "No. I don't want any Bonnie-and-Clyde stuff, or poison toothbrushes."

Harrington laughed. "Yeah, we tried that on Lumumba, but it didn't work. I don't think the jig bastard ever brushed his teeth." He roared at his own joke.

"This has to look like natural causes. A heart attack. You'll be using a dart gun. The flechettes will be coated with shellfish toxin."

"Won't the darts show up in his body?"

"No. They're nondiscernible, almost microscopic. A considerable improvement on the weapon used by the Bulgarian service in London a few years ago. You remember they stabbed an exile, a BBC broadcaster named Georgi Markov, with a poison-tipped umbrella while he was waiting for a bus. But the round metal poison pellet injected by the tip had a diameter of a fifteenth of an inch. The pellet was so long, MI5 easily found it in the autopsy, embedded just under the man's skin."

Harrington did not look pleased. "I'd be happier with an ordinary gun," he grumbled.

"Sorry, Bill." It was clear from Black's tone that the subject was closed. "Right now, you'd best go down and see Jorgensen in the Technical Services Division. Have him look you over and get started on the documentation and disguise. Ask him to fit you out with the dart launcher. I'll have Holly call ahead so he's expecting you. And I'll get things rolling with Frank. There's a fair amount to be done. And, Bill?"

"Yes, sir?"

The two men had stood up and were facing each other across the director's desk. "This has to run absolutely smoothly. Nothing that can be traced back to the company. A sterile operation."

"It will be."

Harrington lumbered out through the conference room. When the door had closed, the director opened the middle drawer of his desk and removed a single sheet of blue airmail paper and the envelope with the Zurich postmark still clipped to it. He placed them both carefully in his burn bag. By nightfall, he knew, they would be fed into a great, yawning orange funnel eight floors below in the Pit. He had seen what the disintegrator did to documents. The letter and the envelope would be chopped and mashed into a dry pulp. They would be completely destroyed. LS/Talpia, he was confident, would do the same to Robert Travers.

Chapter 11

The main door of the Technical Services Division was secured by a touch-tone electronic lock. Only senior TSD staff personnel were cleared for the seven-digit combination. Harrington had to ring a buzzer.

After a moment's wait, a metal portal, not unlike a walk-up window at a bank, flapped open. Harrington shoved his plastic ID card into its jaws and the tray retracted. Another short wait and then: "You may enter." The metallic voice coming over the speaker in the wall could as easily have been a robot as a human being.

Inside the door, Harrington saw that it belonged to a middle-aged security type, a tubby, pink-faced man who looked like he was counting the days to early retirement. He peered over his glasses at Harrington, handed back the pass, and waved him on.

Harrington headed down a long corridor. The doors along the way were yellow, green, blue, red, and purple. The wall at the end of the corridor was a baby blue. Several years before, the agency's Fine Arts Commission had ordered the doors and the ends of all the hallways painted in pastel hues. Harrington did not think much of it. "Probably done by some faggot Georgetown decorator," he had grumbled. Actually, the agency had brought in a psychologist who ran a study and concluded that the original gray doors were depressing to the employees. The pastel colors were substituted as a sort of visual Muzak, designed to soothe the inner spy.

The TSD's specialized sections occupied offices on either side of the hall. He passed Explosives, where Jorgey's scientists had developed something called "Super Alice," a *plastique* that could be shaped into almost any innocent-looking object. Molded into an ashtray, for example, it could be set in a target's motel room and attached to a timer. When it went off, it would blow up the room and all of its occupants. The agency tested its explosives at Isolation Base on Harvey Point, a remote spit of land jutting from the North Carolina coast near Elizabeth City. Harrington had visited the test facility once and had watched the demonstrations with keen professional interest.

Through the glass wall of the Toxic Agents section Harrington waved to a vaguely familiar face, a woman in a white lab jacket. From inside her goldfish bowl she smiled and waved back. It was there in the rather small TSD laboratory that the agency's scientists conducted their research with various poisons, bacteriological and chemical agents, and toxins. Within the confines of the lab, Harrington knew, was probably the world's deadliest supply of chemicals, poisons, and bacteriological warfare agents. For a time, the Geneva Protocol, which the United States had finally ratified in 1974, had put a damper on the agency's research. But in the past few years things had eased up and the company had resumed its "defensive" research. Name a disease, from anthrax to psittacosis, and the CIA could supply it from its lethal inventory. The Technical Services Division stocked everything, including cobra venom (the inventory showed 8 mg) and cyanide for L-pills, which field agents carried and had the option of swallowing to avoid torture if they were captured.

Harrington passed Weapons and Ballistics, one of his own favorite haunts. He could browse for hours there among the exotic armaments, the way other people browsed in bookstores. There were guns designed to look like almost any conceivable kind of everyday object, from fountain pens to cigarette packs. One of Harrington's personal favorites was a boutonniere, a bright-yellow flower that fired a single, vicious, soft-nosed bullet from the wearer's lapel. Harrington thought it might be ideal to use against a sidewalk target, someone he might arrange to pass, perhaps, while strolling up the Champs-Elysées on a fine spring day. He was mildly disappointed that he had not yet had an opportunity to try it out.

Farther along, he passed by the wig merchants in Disguises, the engravers in Identification, the mail-openers with their tea kettles and steam ovens in Flaps and Seals, and the wiremen in Electronic Services. ES, Harrington knew, had recently developed bugs so sensitive that they could pick up a whispered conversation in a bedroom from a distance of ten miles. There was no longer any such thing as private pillow talk, Harrington knew. If the agency wanted to know someone's sexual kinks or preferences, they could easily find out. Just beyond ES section was Photography and Imagery, which handled all photographic work for the agency except overhead reconnaissance; that was the job of the National Reconnaissance Office and the National Photographic Interpretation Center. The PI section technicians could provide cameras disguised as almost anything—tiepins, wristwatches, costume jewelry, belt buckles, automobile headlights. They had even made a camera that could be concealed in a hollow tooth. To shoot, the photographer smiled instead of the subject. For an officer in the Clandestine Services who had only one eye, the Technical Services Division had constructed a miniature camera in his other, artificial eye; the "pupil" was the lens. Nothing seemed beyond the abilities of Jorgey's scientists and technicians; Harrington didn't doubt that if he wanted to take pictures through his asshole, TSD could arrange it.

He knew where he would find Jorgensen. He pushed open

a door marked R&D and entered a lab area that looked like a cross between Gepetto's workshop and backstage at Ringling Brothers. Strewn around on workbenches and tables in chaotic profusion were a weird collection of objects—hairpieces, underwater spear guns, a suitcase from which a small airplane could be fully assembled, chemical vials, makeup creams, exploding candles, sword canes, clothing, miniature tape recorders, electronic bugs, conventional weapons, including several automatic rifles, and a variety of switchblade knives that would have been the envy of a South Bronx street gang.

A thin, gray-haired man, wearing gold-rimmed spectacles and a nondescript, khaki lab coat was bending over a sink, concentrating on an eye dropper and a small plastic bottle. He did not look up immediately; but after a moment or two, he seemed satisfied with the color of the liquid and turned to his visitor.

"Ah, Harrington. I was told you would be visiting us. Here, you may be interested in this." He held up the little bottle, which Harrington could see was a common nonprescription remedy for tired eyes. "Looks ordinary," the TSD chief said in a pleased voice, "but it contains phencyclidine HCL. A nasty incapacitant. Causes disorientation. In high dosage, convulsions and death. Perhaps you'd like to slip this into the medicine cabinet of one of your targets."

"No thanks," said Harrington sardonically. "I'm not usually invited in to use the bathroom."

Jorgensen looked disappointed. "Well, I always look forward to field testing. We scientists can develop all kinds of things in the laboratory—and we do—but they don't mean much unless they work under actual operational conditions. Well, let me know if you change your mind."

"Sure," Harrington said. "I'll let you know. What I do need, Jorgey, is a dart gun and projectiles tipped with shellfish toxin. Also, physical disguise and a complete, backstopped iden."

"Darts. Yes, a good choice." Jorgensen seemed pleased. "We don't get much call for them. But I think you'll find we have a nice selection." It occurred to Harrington that Jorgey would have made a perfect clerk in a hardware store in rural Indiana. He knew the location of every item in stock and loved to gossip with his customers.

"I knew I could count on you, Jorgey."

"I'll just take you down to Weapons and Ballistics," the TSD chief said briskly. "Personally, I rather liked the sleeve gun we fitted you out with when you disposed of that unpleasant little KGB colonel in The Hague. Velnikov? Lukyanov? I can never remember names. Have you seen this?" Jorgensen walked over to a cubbyhole and extracted what looked like a conventional telephone. He unscrewed the mouthpiece and pointed to a small, black cube, no bigger than a quarter of an inch on each side.

"A transmitter?" Harrington inquired politely.

"A phase-locked loop tone decoder and miniaturized amplifier, actually. An ingenious device. I have to admit we copied it from the Israelis. They used it on Hassan Sharami, the head of the PLO in Paris. While he was out of his apartment on the rue Alésia, Mossad put a pound of RDX and a detonator under his mattress. Then they put one of these little gadgets in his telephone. They called him and when he answered the phone he heard a high-frequency electronic whine. It was the last sound he ever heard. The decoder in the mouthpiece picked up the tone and retransmitted it to the detonator. Mossad had piped a signal right into the target's bedroom and set off the explosion by remote control. His body was severed at the waist. The first known case of murder by telephone. Think of the possibilities! You could place an overseas call and liquidate someone on another continent. You would have a perfect alibi, too, since you were three thousand miles away."

Jorgey was humming a little tune as he showed Harrington around his sorcerer's stockroom.

"What the hell is that?" Harrington asked, pointing to a large spiral seashell with a spectacular pink, flaring lip, graceful whorls, and fine, unbroken points.

"*Strombus gigas*," Jorgensen replied. "A queen conch. Lovely specimen, isn't it? At one time, we had some thought of rigging it with an explosive and planting it near the Isle of

Pines at Cayo Largo, where Castro likes to skin-dive. He'd be sure to see it and swim over to it. When he touched it, it would blow up."

"Why wasn't Executive Action informed?" Harrington asked, with more than a little annoyance.

"We ran this one by Task Force W," Jorgensen explained. The Task Force, Harrington knew, had run a series of covert operations against Cuba under the rubric of Operation Mongoose. "They approved it, but we never could solve the technical problems. If we made the detonator sensitive enough, it would almost certainly have been set off by a fish or a turtle, or even the tides, before Fidel ever got down there." Jorgensen shook his head. "I always liked the idea, though."

"You never made his beard fall out, either," Harrington reminded him.

"But the concept was brilliant," Jorgensen insisted. "If it had worked, it would have completely destroyed his machismo. The Mongoose staff planned to do it while Castro was on a trip away from Cuba. They were going to dust the inside of his shoes with thallium salts when he put them outside his door overnight to be shined. In time, the thallium would have worked its way into his bloodstream and made all his hair fall out. Not only his beard. Even his pubic hair. First his mistresses would have laughed at him, and pretty soon the entire Cuban people. Imagine the Maximum Leader with no hair on his balls." Jorgensen sighed. "But it never happened. Castro canceled his trip."

As he talked, Jorgensen led his visitor through the inter-connecting series of offices and labs until they were all the way back at the other end of the division, in Toxic Agents. "If it's shellfish toxin you're going to be working with," Jorgensen said, pushing open a door, "we'd better talk to Nat."

Nat, Harrington knew, was Dr. Nathan Louis Rosen, the legendary biochemist who had been in the forefront of the CIA's research and experiments with mind-control drugs, poisons, and toxins. Rosen was on the telephone when the two men entered his cluttered, book-lined office. Still talking, he waved them into a pair of expensive, chrome-and-leather Eames chairs.

Now in his late fifties, Rosen was a lean, athletic-looking man with snow-white hair. He was muscular but not very tall. Except for the thickness of his features, he might have been handsome. He prided himself on staying in shape, and he jogged from his home in McLean to headquarters every morning, even in the rain or snow. Back in the early 1950s, the agency had become convinced that the Soviets had developed drugs that could control the human mind. How else to explain the confession of Joseph Cardinal Mindszenty when the Hungarian government put him on trial? The CIA set about trying to develop mind-control drugs of its own. Under Nat Rosen's direction, the agency plunged enthusiastically into work with LSD, testing the drug on unwitting Americans whom prostitutes lured from bars to agency safe houses on Bedford Street in Greenwich Village and Chestnut Street on San Francisco's Telegraph Hill. In the safe houses, the victims were slipped LSD in their drinks, while agency operators watched, photographed, and tape-recorded their reactions and sexual activities. It was Nat Rosen's agents as well who had trekked to the mountains above Oaxaca a few years later and brought back to Langley the fabled Mexican mushrooms from which the powerful hallucinogen psilocybin had been extracted. Harrington knew Rosen well, for the CIA scientist personally selected and gave to him the botulinum toxin that Harrington in turn had passed on to the Mafia for use against Fidel Castro. And it was under Nat Rosen's direction that a whole range of deadly substances had been stockpiled by the company. Did an agent need a little salmonella to spike a KGB officer's cocktail in Bamako? "Clear it with Nat" was the in-house motto. An abrasive and dangerous man, Rosen did not always engender affection among his colleagues, some of whom referred to him, behind his back, as "Dr. Strangelove." Rosen did not appear to mind the criticism. For a poor Jewish boy from New York, as he often liked to refer to himself, he had gone far. He occupied a senior-level headquarters position and had earned a reputation inside the agency as a brilliant and innovative scientist. Although he prepared murderous potions in his work, his life-style was simple and healthful. A strict vegetarian, he subsisted mostly on salads, yogurt, sunflower seeds, and mung beans, which he sprouted in his own cellar. He also milked his own goats. He devoted much of his leisure time to his principal hobby, birdwatching. Rosen had once complained to Harrington about duck hunters. "I don't see how anyone could harm a bird," he had declared. "They're such beautiful, fragile creatures. I couldn't bear to kill one."

When he got off the phone, Rosen greeted his visitors cordially. He was genuinely fond of Harrington, whose work for the agency so closely dovetailed with his own. Jorgensen quickly sketched in Harrington's needs.

Rosen listened approvingly. "Shellfish toxin is one of our most lethal and efficient agents," he said. "It's a pity that Francis Gary Powers never used it. We provided it to him, of course, in a silver dollar that he carried with him on his overflight."

"I thought the Russians said it was curare," Jorgensen corrected him.

"They did," Rosen replied in an amused tone. "They found the pin when they searched Powers, and they tested it on a dog and a mouse. Both died immediately. But our Soviet friends were mistaken. They confused the shellfish toxin with curare, which is extracted from certain South American plants, chiefly *Strychnos toxifera*. The effects are superficially similar, although curare victims often turn blue because their lungs are paralyzed. But take my word for it, the U-2 pilots carried shellfish toxin. The KGB was wrong."

Harrington tried to cut short the scientific debate. "Personally, Nat, I prefer conventional weapons," he said. "But my orders are to use a dart gun that fires your fancy shrimp cocktail."

"Clams and mussels," Rosen corrected him. "The toxin comes from bivalves. And you understand, of course, that there are other, equally effective means of delivery besides a dart launcher. The gun is not as easily concealed, as, say, this ball-point pen." Rosen picked up an ordinary-looking black pen from his desk and handed it to Harrington, who examined it.

"The pocket clip is the firing mechanism?"

"Yes. The chief advantage, naturally, is its size and the

element of surprise when approaching the target. Unfortunately, it fires only three darts and its range is relatively short."

Jorgensen had gone over to the credenza behind Rosen's desk. He picked up a small, fluorescent lamp. "You might consider an entirely different approach, Bill. This lamp for example."

"Aerosol?"

"Exactly. Place it in the target's office. When he switches it on, it releases a slow aerosol vapor. Shellfish toxin, or whatever you choose."

"And you might end up terminating a secretary instead of the target."

"Well, there is that risk," Jorgensen admitted.

"That's the trouble with a lot of your stuff. No warranties."

Harrington enjoyed needling the TSD chief. "Which reminds me. How are your pussycats, Jorgey?"

"The Directorate of Operations withdrew funding for that project," Jorgensen answered tersely. "I don't think it ever had a fair chance."

Three years earlier, TSD had embarked on one of its most disastrous and bizarre experiments. Jorgensen's scientists had attempted to wire a cat to serve as a living transmitter. Machines cannot easily discriminate among sounds, tune out background noises, and listen only to conversation. But one of Jorgensen's people had the idea that an ordinary household cat, if properly trained, could serve as the perfect eavesdropper. Imagine the intelligence benefits, the scientist had argued, if during the Cuban missile crisis, Khrushchev's cat had secretly been a CIA agent. Assuming, of course, that Khrushchev had a cat. For months, rumors circulated through the building that Jorgensen's people were cutting open vast quantities of cats and implanting transmitters and batteries inside them. There were stories of cats loose in the hallways and of bags of Purina and kitty litter being clandestinely delivered to the division at night. Finally, a group of cat lovers in the Employee Activities Association had protested directly to the DCI. The director made no promises, but soon thereafter, the cat funds were quietly withdrawn.

Rosen offered a small pocket-sized cylinder to Harrington. "Don't push the spray-top," he warned. "It's loaded with liquid nitrogen mustard gas."

"Lethal?"

"Oh, yes, it can be. But it's really designed more for sending a message to the opposition. If an arm or leg is sprayed, even through clothing, it will almost certainly have to be amputated. If you spray it near the eyes, even a small amount will permanently blind the target."

Harrington admired the little aerosol device. "I might like that, but not for this assignment."

"We really developed it to keep up with the Sovs. The KGB used it quite effectively at the Zagorsk monastery." Harrington recalled the case: Horst Schwirkmann, a young sweeper for the Gehlen organization, had been sent to Moscow by the Bonn government to debug the West German embassy. Visiting the monastery on his day off, he stopped to admire a gilded icon of a Russian saint. A man was kneeling by it, praying. He rose politely and stood behind Schwirkmann. Suddenly, the young electronics technician felt the ice-cold liquid on his thigh. He survived the attack, but just barely.

"We've also developed some interesting ways to transport biological or chemical agents, or toxins, into other countries," Rosen said enthusiastically. "These, for example."

He held out a handful of what appeared to be ordinary buttons from a shirt or a man's jacket.

Harrington examined one with interest. It was black and opaque.

"What is it?"

"*Bungarus candidis*. Pure venom of the blue krait, one of the world's most lethal snakes. Found in India and southeast Asia. What's remarkable about the process we've developed is that we've found a way to dehydrate and compress these agents so that the button is actually made of the lethal material. You can sew these right on your clothing and smuggle them where you will."

Harrington picked up a small, clear button and held it to the light between his thumb and forefinger. "And this one?"

"Pyrolo," Rosen said. "An incapacitant. Causes temporary amnesia. Perfect size for a shirt button, isn't it? This little bluish one is colchicine. Extracted from the *Colchicum autumnale*, or autumn crocus, a lovely but deadly purple flower. Named, by the way, for Colchis, the home of Medea, where Jason and the Argonauts stole the Golden Fleece. But that is, perhaps, of secondary interest."

"What are its effects?"

"Death by paralysis and respiratory failure. To put it simply, you stop breathing. An interesting drug. In smaller doses, it produces mutations." Rosen reached up and took from a shelf what appeared to be an ordinary plastic swizzle stick. He handed it to Harrington. "Don't let anyone mix your drinks with this little fellow," he said archly.

"What does it do?" Harrington asked. "Blow up your martini?"

"No. It releases enough bacteria into your drink to give you a severe case of brucellosis—better known as undulant fever."

"Fatal?"

"Sometimes. But you would be more likely to use it against a target whom you wished to incapacitate for several months. An unfriendly prime minister who was running for reelection, perhaps. A nice disease, because there is no preventive vaccine."

"Remind me not to hire you as a bartender," Harrington cracked.

Rosen chuckled. "If you did, I might bring this along." From his desk drawer, the white-haired biochemist produced an unusually long, thin hypodermic needle. "For introducing drugs or poisons into a bottle of wine," he said. "You inject the substance right through the unopened cork. The hole is so small it can't be detected. Neat, isn't it?"

Harrington agreed, but he was growing impatient. Rosen sensed this, because he got up and suggested they have a look at the dart gun. Jorgensen led them back to the Weapons and Ballistics section. Once there, the TSD director walked along a row of gray metal cabinets. He opened one and removed a gun. It looked not unlike a conventional .45, but, oddly, for a handgun, it had a large telescopic sight. An insulated wire ran from the rear of the barrel to the butt.

"It's really a modified .45," Jorgensen explained. "A follow-on model to the famous dart launcher that Colby waved around at the Church Committee hearings. This one is considerably more accurate."

"The launch mechanism is electrical?"

"Yes. The battery is in the handle and the circuit runs from the trigger, to the handle, to the barrel through this wire."

"Range?"

"One hundred and twenty meters," Jorgensen said, with a touch of pride.

Harrington whistled. "I wouldn't have expected that," he said. "Almost four hundred feet. I have to hand it to you, Jorgey."

"Thank you."

"Can you add a silencer?"

"It isn't really necessary, even at closer range. The action is almost silent."

"And the projectiles are actually invisible?"

"Yes. It uses a nondiscernible microbioinoculator. In layman's terms, an invisible dart. The flechettes are so tiny that the target does not feel the dart piercing his clothing or entering his skin. Because the dart is nondiscernible, it would not be found in an autopsy."

"But what about the toxin?" Harrington asked. "Wouldn't that show up in an autopsy?"

"No, it wouldn't," Jorgensen explained. "There is simply no way for a pathologist to detect it. There is no chemical test for shellfish toxin. The victim appears to have died suddenly from natural causes. It's almost the perfect weapon, from all points of view."

"Except the target's." Harrington laughed, and the folds of his enormous stomach rippled.

"Actually," Jorgensen confessed, "we did have a little difficulty at first with the darts. There was some sort of chemical reaction between the metal and the shellfish toxin. The reaction affected the stability of the dart. The gun wouldn't fire accurately."

"What did you do?"

"We switched to platinum for the flechettes. Expensive, but it solved the problem."

Harrington turned to Rosen. "How quick does the shellfish toxin kill?"

"Two or three seconds. Instantaneous, really."

"How do you get the stuff?"

"We collect the shellfish and extract the toxin ourselves. It's a rather slow and elaborate process. You've heard of the red tide, when the sea turns red and fish die. Well, that's caused by a single-celled marine organism called a dinoflagellate. Usually the *Gonyaulax catanella* species. What happens is that shellfish ingest these microorganisms for food, and become highly poisonous. A toxin, you see, is produced by a living organism. The toxin itself isn't living; it can't reproduce and it isn't communicable. Most of our supply was extracted from mussels we gathered along the Pacific Coast near San Francisco and from Alaskan butter clams, which at times are extremely toxic. I flew to Anchorage with a headquarters team and dug some of them out myself."

"How much is a lethal dose?"

"Two-tenths of a milligram," Rosen replied. "The darts are coated with precisely that amount. Our people calculate that a gram is sufficient to kill five thousand people. The agency's stockpile is eleven grams, enough to take care of fifty-five thousand persons. Of course, there aren't that many prime ministers in the world."

Jorgensen demonstrated to Harrington how the darts were loaded. "These are special cartridges. To protect the operator, each flechette is contained in a protective gelatin capsule, which dissipates on firing. So the darts present no danger to you if you handle them with caution. The telescopic sight screws off easily, like this, if you prefer to work at close range. That's about it."

Harrington thanked the TSD chief and pocketed the gun and a small plastic case containing the darts.

"For the physical disguise," Jorgensen said, "I'll take you down to see Max Gordon. He's the best in the business." Rosen bade them good-bye to return to his office. "Good hunting, Bill," he said, with a parting handshake.

As the TSD chief escorted Harrington down the hall, he

asked casually, "Where to this time, Bill? I gather it's important or I wouldn't have gotten a call from the director's office."

"Bangkok," Harrington lied. "A small problem with the Chicoms."

Jorgensen wagged his head. "Never underestimate the lure of the Golden Triangle. Even for some of our agents. I suppose the temptations are enormous, with the Thai generals getting rich on heroin and opening Swiss bank accounts. But I do object to using agency aircraft to fly the stuff in from the provinces."

Harrington smiled. "Don't worry, Jorgey. I won't even be there long enough to get laid, let alone rich. I'll just do my job and get out on the next plane. No fuss, no muss."

"And one dead Chinaman."

Harrington nodded his agreement. They entered the Disguises section. Max Gordon, the Technical Services Division's makeup wizard, was a stocky, balding man in his fifties who looked like a cloak-and-suiter from New York's garment center. Harrington could picture him standing out on Seventh Avenue at lunchtime, drinking an egg cream. In truth, Gordon had worked far from Manhattan, on a different stage. For a number of years, he had been a leading makeup man in Hollywood. Bogart, Marilyn Monroe, even the aging Gable had passed through his talented hands. Then, in 1960, he had been lured East by the agency. For Max, the unreality of both worlds was the same; only the subjects had changed.

Max had one idiosyncrasy. He was constantly dreaming up bizarre ideas for the Clandestine Services, covert operations that had no hope of being adopted. During the 1960s, before Washington had opened diplomatic relations with the People's Republic of China, Gordon had suggested that the agency airdrop millions of fortune cookies over Mainland China containing copies of the Bill of Rights in Chinese. "How else are the Chinese going to learn about freedom?" he had asked.

Jorgensen had promised to take up the idea with Trilby Gates, the DDO at the time, but of course he had no intention of doing so. Another of Gordon's zany schemes had become a legend inside the agency. "Let's drop a hundred thousand rubbers, two feet long, over the Soviet Union," he had urged Jorgensen. "Each one will be stamped 'Made in U.S.A.—Small.' When the word gets around, the Soviets will be completely demoralized."

The TSD chief tried to let Gordon down easily. Max was a fine makeup man and he didn't want to lose him. "It's brilliant," he told him. "But far too innovative for the Forty Committee. They'd never approve it."

Gordon countered that the plan was no weirder than one that the OSS had tried out during World War II at the suggestion of Eleanor Roosevelt. "The idea was that bats would be wired to incendiary bombs. The bats would be chilled to make them sleepy so they could be transported by submarine. When they were released off the coast of Japan, they would seek shelter in the eaves of Japanese houses. Since the houses were made of paper and cardboard, the island would go up in flames." Jorgensen knew Gordon was right; the OSS had actually tried out Mrs. Roosevelt's scheme in an abandoned mining town out West. They had rounded up a bunch of bats in Carlsbad Caverns and released them near the town. But the bats flew off in all directions presumably looking for the nearest cave; none of them landed on the houses.

Harrington and Jorgensen found Gordon seated on a stool at a worktable, deeply absorbed in Conley's *Plastic Reconstructive Surgery of the Face and Neck*. He wore a long white smock. He looked up and greeted Harrington: "As I live and breathe, it's Wyatt Earp! Check your gun at the door, my boy, we run a peaceful saloon down here."

"Hello, Max." Harrington did not appreciate Gordon's sense of humor.

"Bill needs a complete physical disguise for a high-level singleton mission overseas," Jorgensen explained. "We want him to look as different as possible."

"That should be an improvement." Gordon guffawed.

Wordlessly, Harrington pulled a card from his wallet and handed it to Gordon. "Your expression of criticism was greatly appreciated," it read. "Fuck you very much."

Max grinned good-naturedly and pocketed the card. "I want to try that one on my wife," he said. Then, serious, he studied Harrington for a moment. "For openers, we have to change that red hair. Much too recognizable."

"What do you have in mind?" Harrington asked.

"Wigs have been out of fashion since Watergate," Gordon replied. "They always seem to fall off at the wrong moments. I think we'll just dye your hair. Blond, to match your fair skin coloring. But you'll have to let it grow a good deal longer."

"I like it this way."

"Bill, you look like a Marine drill instructor at Parris Island. No one's worn their hair that short since the Eisenhower administration." He shook his head. "There's not much that TSD can do if the officer won't cooperate."

Harrington first looked grim, then resigned. "All right, Max. If the company wants me to look like a goddamn hippie, I'll do it. All in the line of duty, huh?"

Gordon nodded. "We'll use contact lenses to change your brown eyes to blue. And you'll need glasses. That's basic. You'd be amazed at how often people are remembered by whether or not they wear glasses. Try these." He handed Harrington a pair with heavy black frames and thick lenses that might be worn by a person with severe myopia.

Harrington put them on. "I can see fine," he said, surprised.

"They're a lovely item," Gordon explained. "They have no effect on the wearer's vision, but to anyone else they appear to be thick prescription lenses. About a minus eight. From now on, the world will think you're extremely nearsighted. We'll make up a pair that fits you."

"What else do you suggest for the face?" Jorgensen asked.

Gordon looked at Harrington from a couple of angles before replying. "A large artificial wart, I think, on the lower portion of the left cheek."

"An artificial wart?" Harrington felt a little as though he wandered into a carnival funhouse and might never get out. Jorgensen's Big Top.

"Yes," Max said. "A stick-on wart. You'd be surprised how any little physical defect of that sort draws people's attention. It's like a magnet. They pretend they don't notice, but they do. They may not remember much about you later on, but they remember the wart."

Harrington looked skeptical. All of this was new to him. On previous missions there had been no need for a disguise.

"Open your mouth," Gordon commanded. He peered in. "The gold teeth are a giveaway," he said. "They'll have to be capped. Go see Otto Kroger in Dental Services."

Harrington agreed to do so, but he flatly rejected Gordon's suggestion that he also let Kroger take an impression of the roof of his mouth to cast a speech-alteration device, a thin layer of flesh-colored plastic. "Changing your voice is important," Gordon argued. "It's not much good to alter your appearance if someone recognizes your voice."

But Harrington had heard about the devices from Andy Bowman, a fellow officer in the Clandestine Services, who had used one while operating under commercial cover as an American businessman in Istanbul. "The damn things are uncomfortable as hell," Bowman had warned, "and they make you lisp." Bowman complained to Harrington that the Turks thought he was gay.

Harrington did accept Gordon's offer of a heel-lift, a thick leather pad that was inserted in one shoe to give the wearer a slight limp.

"Let's see," Harrington said, "so far I'm going to be a nearsighted blond man with long hair, thick glasses, blue eyes, one bad leg, and a wart."

"And a beautiful Hollywood smile," Max reminded him. "Don't forget the smile."

"That's it?"

"Well," said Gordon, hesitating a bit, "we can't do much about your height, but it would help a lot if we could trim your width. But you're the only one who can do that, Bill."

"I've already got my marching orders. Thirty pounds."

Gordon looked suitably impressed. "Well," he said, "good luck. They won't recognize you down at the O. K. Corral."

Jorgensen was already steering Harrington through the door to Fred Keegan's office. Keegan was a wiry little Irishman with a thin face, small features, and rimless glasses. In another life, he might have been a successful leprechaun. When they entered his office, he was working at a slanted architect's drawing table. He was in shirtsleeves and wore an old-fashioned green eyeshade. That had been his usual costume at the Bureau of Engraving, where he had toiled for twelve years before he crossed the Potomac and made his talents available to the company at a substantial increase in salary.

Keegan, known affectionately inside TSD as "Freddie the Forger," was head of the Identification Section. His office resembled an old-fashioned newspaper morgue, with file cabinets lining every available inch of wall space. In Keegan's files were official documents, passports, visas, credit cards, birth and death certificates, business cards, and thousands of other forms of identification from virtually every country in the world. These were Keegan's models. For his expert forgeries he obtained the appropriate paper stock from the laboratories of the Directorate of Science and Technology, as well as from private and commercial sources. The labs could duplicate the special fibers, watermarks, and inks used in official documents of more than a hundred countries.

If an officer of the Clandestine Services needed a Dutch passport, or an Algerian driver's license, or a student ID from the Sorbonne, Freddie Keegan and his staff could fabricate one so skillfully that even the experts would be unable to tell it from the real thing. Keegan did not have to forge American passports. When needed by the CIA, those were routinely provided by the passport division of the Department of State. In theory, the agency's spies traveling under aliases turned in their false-name American passports when their missions were completed. In fact, the control system was loose; Harrington himself had half-a-dozen U.S. passports made out in different names.

"Bill needs a complete new iden for an important overseas mission," Jorgensen told Keegan. "The works."

"It will take a while," Keegan replied. He looked Harrington over with a professional eye. "You forget how much paper we carry around with us these days. And how many computers we're in. It's not as simple as it sounds to create a new person. Is this to be backstopped?"

"Yes," Jorgensen answered. "Fully backstopped."

The thin-faced engraver sighed. "That'll take weeks," he said. "It means applications for credit cards under the alias identity, establishing bank accounts, both checking and savings, working up a complete false vita, not to mention a driver's permit, Social Security number, credit ratings, and so on."

Keegan, Harrington knew, could easily provide a counterfeit American Express card, for example. But to produce a credit card that actually worked and could be used meant applying for one in the normal manner, but under a false name. That in turn meant creating the whole complex web of documentation that surrounded each individual in a modern, computerized society. For that reason, "backstopped" paper took much longer to create than simple "flash alias" documentation that could be shown—flashed—but never subjected to real scrutiny.

"I'll also need some pocket litter," Harrington said. "Some club memberships, a library card, photographs of a wife and children, that kind of stuff."

"Of course," said Freddie the Forger. "We'll take care of that automatically. You'll have to come back here to have your picture taken for a driver's permit. But you won't be ready for that, of course, until Max finishes working on your appearance. Is he going to see Kroger for those teeth?"

"Yes," said Jorgensen.

"Well, I don't see any major problems except time. You'll have a new name, of course, but we'll keep the same initials. We find it avoids problems with monogrammed shirts, luggage, hatbands, et cetera. By the way, what will your occupation be?"

"Unchanged," Harrington replied. "An officer in the Clandestine Services. Operating under embassy cover."

Keegan shot a sharp glance at his boss. "Rather unusual," he said.

"Don't worry about it, Freddie," Jorgensen said reassuringly. "Bill gets unusual assignments."

But in the hallway, out of earshot, the TSD chief looked worried. It was normal for an agent to use another identity when operating overseas under commercial or press cover. But this was different, and puzzling. Harrington was reporting in to a station, inside an embassy. "Bill," he said slowly,

"I sure hope the seventh floor knows what it's doing. What the heck is going on?"

"Jorgey, you don't really want to know. Okay?"

Jorgensen took a deep breath. "Okay. Max will call you when he's ready, and I'll keep Freddie working overtime." Harrington thanked the older man and took his leave. Jorgensen watched him lumber down the hall. Then he shook his head and walked slowly back to his own office. He wasn't humming anymore.

Harrington left his office a little early that afternoon. He drove along the George Washington Parkway to Key Bridge, cut over to Wilson Boulevard and pulled into the parking lot of the Safeway. Inside the store, he pushed a metal shopping cart up and down three aisles before he found what he was looking for. He picked up a small box and read the label: "Slender from Carnation." It was, the label informed him, a "hunger-satisfying diet meal in a glass." When mixed with whole milk, the label added cheerfully, four servings equaled nine hundred calories and provided 100 percent of the RDA, the recommended daily allowance of protein, vitamins, and minerals.

"Shit," Harrington said.

A little old gray-haired lady in a dark-blue straw hat was edging by and pretended she had not overheard him. She pushed her cart faster and hurried away.

Harrington, still studying the label, groaned inwardly. I wonder if you can mix it with gin? he thought. The stuff came in several flavors. Harrington decided on Dutch Chocolate. He dumped two dozen boxes in his cart with one sweep of his ham hand, cleaning off the shelf. At the checkout, the bill came to $29.76. Harrington paid in cash.

The checker, a young and friendly dark-haired girl, eyed Harrington's girth and his purchase and started to make a bantering remark. Something in his face made her change her mind. She handed him his change and said simply, "Thank you. Come again."

Harrington didn't answer. He carried the bundle to his car and drove to his red-brick apartment building, the Fairfax

South. In the hallway, he fished in his pocket for a key, but he could hear, from the Cat Stevens tape booming through the door, that Shirley was already there. She got off early two afternoons a week from her job as a manicurist in Crystal City. Harrington had never married. They had lived together for over a year. She asked no questions about his work, or his prolonged absences on trips. She called Harrington "my grizzly bear." When they made love, she usually sat on him.

Shirley was thirty-three, the daughter of a mill hand from Logan County, West Virginia. She had very black hair, wore cerise lipstick and green eyeshadow, and had almost kept her figure. She was flirtatious and earned fairly big tips from middle-aged government bureaucrats who could not afford them.

"Hello, hon," she called out. Harrington came into the living room. She was sprawled in an armchair next to the tape deck, holding a lighted cigarette in her right hand. An open can of Bud rested on the table by the chair. Cat Stevens was singing "Moonshadow."

Shirley got up and gave Harrington a quick kiss on the cheek. She took the bundle from him and they went into the kitchen. She glanced inside the bag, looked at him, and burst out laughing.

"You really gonna drink this stuff?"

He patted her on the rear end. "That's right, baby. There's gonna be less of me, but don't worry, it'll still be just as good."

Shirley giggled. "You want me to mix you a glass?"

"Tomorrow. I don't start my diet until tomorrow." Harrington lumbered over to the liquor closet. He reached in and took out the Rémy Martin.

At 1:00 A.M., in a one-bedroom efficiency in the Arlington Towers, a mile from Harrington's apartment, Holly Corcoran nuzzled her blond hair against her lover's bare shoulder. They had made love for the past two hours. Now they were naked together, resting quietly and talking.

"I know something you don't know," she said teasingly.

"Whazzat?" He was a good-looking, dark-haired man of

about thirty, and he seemed much more interested in Holly's large, soft breasts than in her secret.

"The director called in Bill Harrington today. It was supposed to be super hush-hush. I wasn't supposed to tell anyone. Not even the director's top staff assistant."

"Really?" asked Evan Younger.

She laughed. "Really."

"And he actually thought you wouldn't tell me? Is it possible he doesn't know about us?"

"I think he has his own fantasies of making it with me. So he wouldn't *want* to know about anyone else. The director is very good at not seeing what he doesn't want to see."

"Of course. That's how you get to be head of the agency. You learn not to see, and you tell the president what he wants to hear." Evan looked thoughtful. "I wonder what he had in mind for Harrington?" He shuddered. "That guy gives me the creeps." Younger had grown up in Greenwich, Connecticut, the son of a prominent investment banker in Manhattan. He had joined the agency nine years earlier, right out of Amherst. There were no Bill Harringtons in his social set.

"Me too. He's so ugly."

"Well," Evan said, "don't worry. Sooner or later, I'll find out what it's all about."

His hand was resting lightly on Holly's bare right breast.

"Let's do it again," she said suddenly.

Evan looked uncomfortable. "We just did."

"That was an hour ago." Holly had reached down and was caressing him tantalizingly with her right hand, her cool fingertips barely touching him. He felt something happening. He leaned over and kissed her full on the lips. Her mouth was soft and seeking.

He swung his body over her thighs and in a swift hard motion he penetrated her. Holly moaned with pleasure and began rotating her hips in a slow, sensuous stripteaser's grind. She was giggling and laughing and then she let out a little cry and was holding on to him tightly, whispering his name.

Afterward, Younger glanced at his watch, which he was still wearing in bed. It was almost two o'clock. "Got to get some sleep," he said thickly. "It's very late."

They lay next to each other, bodies touching. Holly started to drift off.

After a moment, she asked drowsily, "What's a Talpia?"

But Evan Younger did not reply. He was already asleep.

Chapter 12

Travers cut through Grosvenor Square, past the fountains flanking the statue of Franklin D. Roosevelt. He crossed the street and mounted the steps of the American embassy.

He passed beneath the oversized gold eagle, with its thirty-five-foot wing spread, that had so offended British taste when it first glowered over Mayfair. There had been a great fuss, but the bird still flew over the embassy, a six-story, gray-concrete structure that occupied the entire block on the west side of the square.

Travers made a point of using the front entrance. Since he was listed in the State Department's *Biographic Register* as a Foreign Service Reserve Officer, it would only have called attention to his real job if he were to be seen slipping in by a rear door.

He passed through the metal detector and up a short flight of stairs to the lobby. The uniformed Marine guard seated at the desk was busy watching the closed-circuit television monitors that covered the entrances to the embassy. He did not even look up. Travers took the elevator to the fourth floor.

"Good morning, sir." The clean-shaven young man in the dark-blue suit sat at a desk in front of a door marked "Political Liaison Section." Under his jacket, he carried a .38.

Travers returned his greeting perfunctorily and pushed through the door. Once inside, he was on his own territory. The Political Liaison Section and a companion unit, the Joint Reports and Research Unit, provided only the thinnest sort of official cover for the station because of their enormous, and thereby revealing, size. London was the company's biggest outpost and, as the Chief of Station, Travers presided over a staff of more than two hundred. Most of the American correspondents in London knew his real job in the embassy, as did several of the more knowledgeable reporters on Fleet Street, and a substantial number of foreign diplomats.

Still, the fiction was steadfastly maintained that Travers was a political officer. At diplomatic receptions and private cocktail parties, which Travers disliked and shunned whenever possible, he was always introduced as a State Department officer, even when the guests knew better. It was a universal system that suited the convenience of the world's intelligence services, all of which sent at least some of their spies abroad under embassy cover. Not only was it less expensive to house both foreign service and intelligence officers under one roof, it also provided diplomatic immunity for the spies. If they were caught doing something wrong, they were more likely to be expelled than arrested. Travers' opposite number, Sergei Nikolayevich Rumin, was listed by the Soviet embassy as a consular officer. In fact, he was chief of the KGB's London *residentura*.

Ann Ganley, Travers' petite, dark-haired secretary, was waiting at her desk. She followed him into his corner office, which overlooked the square and had a view that rivalled Ambassador Cushing's. She held out a cup of coffee—cream and sugar already in—which he accepted gratefully. Ann was the youngest sister in a large, Irish-Catholic family from Paramus, New Jersey. She had green eyes and was almost pretty, but she had never married. For years, she had cared for her elderly, ill mother until one day she was thirty-eight, and it was too late. After her mother died, Ann had gone to work for the company as a secretary in the Manhattan base. Three years later, she applied for an overseas post and was transferred to London. The agency had become the center of her life. She was fiercely loyal both to the company and to Travers.

Travers sat down and sipped the coffee. He stared over the rim of the cup at Ann, who stood dutifully by his desk. He wondered where her loyalties would lie if she were to find out that the company and Travers were no longer one and the same, that her revered boss had mounted a covert operation against the director of Central Intelligence. It would be best, he decided, not to put her to that test. A good lawyer, Travers remembered from somewhere, never asked a witness a question to which he did not himself already know the answer.

"I don't like to start your day this way," Ann said, "but there's more trouble over LS/Primrose-1 and -2. They've received a written notice to vacate the flat in sixty days when their lease expires."

"Damn." Travers drummed his fingers on the desktop. "That doesn't give us much time. Ask Lisa to come in with the file on the building owner. Get word to LS/Primrose-1 through the audio team that we're working on it, and not to worry."

"Yes, sir."

LS/Primrose-1 and LS/Primrose-2 were a retired Army colonel, Donald Russell, and his wife, Barbara, who had moved into an expensive flat in the Westview, an apartment building in Bayswater Road, three years ago. The agency often employed elderly couples to man its Observation Posts, and the Russells ran the London station's most important OP. Their carefully chosen flat faced south and overlooked the rear of the Soviet Embassy at 13 Kensington Palace Gardens. Using powerful binoculars, including some equipped for night vision, the Russells gradually came to know the face of almost every employee of the embassy. An audio-surveillance team and a photographic team also operated out of the Russells' flat. The audio technicians monitored the transmitters inside the embassy and made certain there were always fresh reels of tape in the recorders in the front bedroom, which resembled the control room of a broadcast studio. Thick blue drapes on the windows concealed the sophisticated electronic equipment from Bayswater Road and the embassy. The photographic team took stills and motion pictures of the Soviet diplomats and their visitors who often strolled in the garden to hold their conversations. Sometimes, the audio technicians were able to pick up the conversations on boom mikes, but often, street noises, the tall hedge at the back of the garden, and the trees interfered. When that happened, the reels were processed and shipped to Langley, where Russian-speaking lip-readers studied them. The lip-readers sat at projection machines and ran the films over and over again, attempting to match them up with the audio fragments and assemble a complete transcript. In time, the London station developed a fairly accurate knowledge of the jobs and personalities of most of the officials of the Soviet embassy, including the agents in Rumin's KGB *residentura*.

This intelligence was invaluable when the agency, as it sometimes did, attempted to recruit Soviet embassy employees. That had been proven in the case of Vladimir Orlov. During a conversation in the garden, Orlov, a young GRU agent and an assistant Soviet naval attaché in London, had complained to a close friend in the embassy that it was impossible to support his mistress on his low salary. A week later, a friendly American businessman approached him in a pub and began paying him for information which the American said would be useful to his company. The arrangement ended after only six months, unfortunately, when Orlov was suddenly transferred to Murmansk.

Travers' Counterintelligence staff had not succeeded in turning any senior officials of the Soviet mission, but occasionally, a chauffeur, secretary, or cleaning woman could be bought, blackmailed, or otherwise persuaded to work for Langley. The watch on the embassy had provided more than counterintelligence. Although the Soviets assumed they were bugged, and were extremely cautious in their conversations in the embassy, and even in the garden, the Russells' OP from time to time produced important positive intelligence. The Russians were only human and, occasionally, they would slip up and say something of special interest to the analysts in Grosvenor Square and Langley.

For all these reasons, the trouble that had developed over the Russells' lease was disturbing. The London station operated another OP close by from a flat on the corner of Ossington Street and Bayswater Road. It was manned by LS/Hyacinth-1 and -2, a retired American business executive and his wife in their mid-sixties, who had been recruited by the company. But that OP, while it enjoyed an excellent view of the entrance to the modern Czech embassy at the top end of Kensington Palace Gardens, was of little use in monitoring the Soviet embassy and consulate to the south.

Lisa Layton breezed in and seated herself in the soft leather chair opposite Travers. She could easily have passed, Travers thought, for a young account executive on Madison Avenue. She had grown up Republican in Westchester and graduated from Radcliffe. Her glasses, tailored suit, and coolly professional air did not conceal the fact that she was a very attractive woman. A number of her colleagues in the London station had tried, but Lisa had no difficulty fending them off. She had lived for the past year with a rich young American who worked in London for the Chase Bank. Although she did not know it, Travers had read the file on her friend and approved the liaison. So had Pat Nolan, the station's thin, sharp-featured security officer. Normally, there were no objections to an American lover. The Office of Security people preferred that the station's employees not enter into personal relationships with British citizens; Travers had not mentioned Valerie to Nolan. In no case were liaisons permitted with other foreign nationals.

Although Lisa was only twenty-eight, she was the Clandestine Services officer in charge of OPs for the London station. She supervised the elderly couples who manned them, and the audio and photographic teams as well. She did her job extremely well, if a trifle impersonally, and Travers was pleased with her performance.

"Here's the file on our mustache-twirling landlord," she said, handing a folder across the desk. "Shall we tie him to the railroad tracks?"

"You're confused," Travers replied with a smile. "That fate is usually reserved for the hapless heroine." He studied the dossier on Harry Bullock, age fifty-eight. Born in Liverpool, served in the Army as a corporal, settled in London after the war, and became a successful promoter and real-estate operator. He had got his start by buying up bombed-out houses in London on the cheap, remodeling in shoddy fashion and selling them dear. He had extensive real-estate holdings in Kensington and Southwark. He also had possible ties to the London underworld, and was believed to be the silent partner in a string of porno shops and several private nightclubs in Soho. He lived high, drove a silver Jaguar XJ12L, and snorted coke from a fourteen-karat gold tooter. Around his neck, he wore a jeweled, custom-made gold spoon said to have cost three thousand pounds. Travers stared at his picture, a black-and-white, head-and-shoulders photograph. The corrupt, hard face of Harry Bullock stared back.

"He doesn't look very nice," Travers said.

"He isn't," Lisa replied. "He has no criminal record, but you wouldn't want him for your landlord."

"I thought it was almost impossible to force a tenant out in London. What reason has he given the Russells?"

"There's a loophole in the Rent Act. If you owned a flat before 1965, you can repossess it for use by a member of your immediate family. Bullock claims he's moving in his aged mother."

"Does he have one?"

"Yes, unfortunately—even Bullock. I've checked."

"And there's no way to block it?"

"No. He can get a court order. The building manager thinks something else may be going on. You can see in the file. LS/Primrose-1 and -2 have been told confidentially by the manager that Bullock plans to remodel all the flats and turn them into deluxe leaseholds. The manager says Bullock plans to winkle the other tenants out, even if their leases aren't up, by offering them cash inducements."

"And you don't believe it?"

"No. It's not the pattern of his operations. He owns a lot of property, but he doesn't spend money upgrading it. He started off that way, but now he turns a profit by minimum maintenance and the highest possible rents. As far as we can tell, he isn't planning to convert any of his other property into fancy leaseholds. Only the building in Bayswater Road."

"So you think it's Rumin."

"Got to be. They've spotted the OP and want us out. And it's not just a harassment operation; it won't be that easy to relocate in another flat in the same area with as good a view. The Sovs were smart; their embassy backs up on Kensington Gardens. It's a completely open area with no buildings. So the Westview is by far the best location for us. There's a soccer field right behind the embassy, but we can't very well have our people running around out there in short pants. Of course, there's Kensington Palace, but we can hardly ask the Queen to let us set up an OP in the State Apartments."

Travers looked pained. "Hardly."

"We do have a couple of possibilities," she went on. "There's a row of houses alongside the Christian Science church in Palace Gardens Terrace, the next street over. From the rear of those apartments we might at least get a view of the entrance to the Soviet embassy, although not the garden. But while we're trying to arrange for a new OP, Rumin might buy himself three or six months free of visual surveillance."

"What about the audio operation?"

"That's less of a problem. The mikes will continue to function, of course, and if necessary, we can always monitor them from mobile units."

"So it's back to the bakery trucks?"

"If we have to."

"Well, we really can't let that happen. LS/Primrose has to stay where it is. What do you recommend we do about Bullock—short of the railroad tracks?"

Lisa tapped a pencil on her chin. "Buy him out, I think. Bullock obviously likes money. We could top Rumin's offer. I figure the KGB is paying him about ten thousand pounds to uproot the primroses in our garden. We could offer fifteen, on condition that he tell Rumin to take back his mink."

Travers shook his head. "I don't want to get into a pissing match with a skunk like Rumin," he said. "Bullock would be delighted to have us bidding against each other. A high-priced auction for the key to the flat. We have more money, but in the end who's to say Bullock won't take from both sides and *still* kick out the Russells?"

"There are other options." Lisa's pencil was still tapping against her chin. "Once a week, quite regularly, Rumin gets it on with a girl who works in one of Bullock's clubs, hustling the customers to buy drinks. She's probably the link, the way he got to Bullock in the first place. From what the audio people tell me he's quite a lover boy. Three or four times a night and then he sometimes wants a trip around the world." Travers never ceased to be amazed at the depth of Lisa's education. "The audio technicians have nicknamed him *'Galodniy,'*" she continued, "because he's always hungry. We could photograph them together in glorious color and threaten to show the pictures to Mrs. Rumin. A real hatchet-face with a dumpy figure whom he married right off the collective farm. I'll bet she has no sense of humor at all about Sergei's birds."

"But rather tricky if anything goes wrong," Travers said. He pondered Lisa's suggestion. Rumin was not the typical squat, beetle-browed KGB apparatchik whom the Moscow Center seemed to favor for its important posts abroad. He was fairly tall and blond, quite Western-looking, and spoke excellent, although noncolloquial, English with an American accent. Travers added, "Rumin is so glib, he could probably bluff his way out of it. He'd tell his wife the pictures were faked by the CIA."

"Then let's put pressure on Bullock directly," Lisa countered. "We can ask MI5 to lean on him a little. A drug bust, perhaps. Or close up his porno shops in Soho and yank his private club licenses. They're not real clubs, of course. Most of the 'members' join at the door. Then pass word to Bullock that his troubles would end if he dropped his real-estate development plans in Kensington."

"Good. I think Sir Edward will cooperate. I'm having lunch with him next week at White's. I'll take it up with him then."

Sir Edward Furnail, the head of MI5, the British equivalent of the FBI, was a prickly ex-Army officer with a guards' mustache who did not always cooperate with the company.

But he was a member of White's, and Travers had found that he was often at his most approachable at lunch, over a few whiskey and sodas. A fair amount of important business was accomplished between the United States and Her Majesty's government across the tables at White's. And in this instance, Travers knew, Sir Edward would have a particular reason to order the Metropolitan Police to lean on Harry Bullock. Scotland Yard was still recovering from a scandal in which some six hundred "bent" policemen had resigned or gone to jail. Several were imprisoned for taking bribes from the owners of sex shops in Soho. Sir Edward, Travers guessed, would be glad to demonstrate to his American friends that a sleazy operator like Bullock no longer could count on immunity from the police.

Lisa arose, smiling. "So we move a knight and checkmate Rumin. An end game a Russian should appreciate. Thank you, sir." She retrieved the Bullock file and left.

Travers swiveled around in his chair and looked out the window across the square at the buildings opposite. He wondered in which one the Soviets had set up *their* OP. Despite all the secrecy treasured by intelligence agencies, he sometimes pictured the company and the KGB as two enormous goldfish bowls, side by side.

He turned back and buzzed for Ann.

She came in with a batch of cables from headquarters and put them on his desk. "The overnight traffic," she said. "Nothing that requires immediate action."

"Good. I'll look at them. Meanwhile, see if you can find Dick Austin and ask him to come in."

While he waited, Travers leafed through the cables and a stack of papers in his in-basket. As chief of station, Travers was, inevitably, the administrator of a large staff, with all the dull management chores that entailed—assignments, promotions, recommendations for pay increases, vacation schedules, and expense accounts. Despite the supposed glamour of his job, he spent a large portion of his time as a glorified bookkeeper and office manager. The expense accounts were particularly troublesome in the Clandestine Services, since bizarre items were always being submitted without much way to check on their legitimacy. Years ago, one legendary agency figure, the COS in Morocco, regularly put down $4000 a year for "rental of camel." The auditors in Langley did not challenge the item until the inspector general finally paid a visit to North Africa and discovered that only the tourists used camels in Rabat.

Travers initialed the cables and papers and marked most of them "HW," which meant that Ann would route them to the deputy chief of station, Harding P. Westerfield 3d. Fortunately for Travers, most of the drone work of the station was competently handled by his deputy, a colorless, fusspot bachelor with impeccable WASP credentials and what was rumored to be the best collection of pornographic photographs in the agency. It was said to include such choice items as a Folies-Bergère chorine *soixante-neuf* with an orangutan. Westerfield, who was otherwise a stickler for the rules, kept his dirty pictures in the station's top secret safe. Travers overlooked this blatant breach of security regulations because Westerfield was so valuable to him as a paper pusher.

Even with help, Travers had a demanding job, although some of the agency's normal tasks were not required in London. Because England was America's principal ally, there was no opposition political party to spy on or finance, and no government to subvert, as was the case in so many other stations. By long-standing mutual agreement, London and Washington were pledged not to spy on or run covert operations against each other. Up to a point that agreement was respected by both sides, but there were exceptions.

Because the Brits were friends, one of the station's principal tasks was to maintain close liaison with MI6, the British secret intelligence service, as well as with MI5 on matters involving internal security and counterintelligence. Perhaps Travers' most important job was to preserve a harmonious working relationship with Sir Richard Whitworth, the head of MI6. The day-to-day liaison with Century House Travers left to Dick Austin, but he carefully cultivated a personal friendship with "C." Sir Richard, a distinguished, silver-haired intelligence professional, was listed in all his official biographies as "attached War Office." His name never appeared in print, except on the occasions when it was listed unobtrusively with hundreds of others on the Queen's Honors List. When he was knighted in 1963, the reference under KBE in the London *Times* read simply: "Whitworth, Sir Richard, for official services."

Travers envied the tight cocoon of secrecy the British were able to weave around their intelligence service. In contrast to the United States, where each day seemed to bring a new headline about the CIA, the British were able to maintain the attitude that the secret service simply did not exist. Yet exist it did, and had for four centuries. Politically and historically, C was a direct descendant of Sir Francis Walsingham, Queen Elizabeth's spymaster in the sixteenth century, who was credited with gathering the intelligence that helped Drake defeat the Spanish Armada. With four hundred years of experience, the Brits had burrowed so deep in the woodwork that MI6 was all but invisible.

Through the carefully nurtured relationship between Grosvenor Square and Century House, the agency received a considerable body of intelligence from MI6, particularly on Africa and the Middle East. In turn, the agency shared many of its own reports with MI6. Both sides, of course, despite the mutual assurances of hands across the sea, held back more than they shared. But that was to be expected.

The London station also maintained a somewhat less close relationship with Sir Edward Furnall. Within Great Britain, MI5's cooperation was essential to the station's various counterintelligence operations, for which Travers was responsible. Often, the intelligence interests of the two countries overlapped, as in the example of the Cohens, the American couple who had some years earlier operated an antiquarian bookstore on the Strand. Under that cover, they handled microdot and radio transmissions to the Moscow Center for the KGB ring that stole secrets from the Portland Naval Base near Southampton. Sir Edward's cooperation was important for another reason; in the Commonwealth countries, such as Tanzania, Ghana, Nigeria, Uganda, Singapore, and the Bahamas, MI5 still had important intelligence-collection responsibilities, a vestigial anomaly from the days when those countries were British territory and fell under the "internal" jurisdiction of MI5. As with MI6, the joint agreement between Langley and Whitehall obligated Sir Edward to share his overseas intelligence with the CIA's London station.

Aside from administration, counterintelligence, and liaison with the British services, Travers was responsible for overt collection of general economic and political intelligence on Britain, mainly the state of its economy and politics, as well as Common Market and European community developments. The London station also provided support, and often cover arrangements, for third-country operations carried out in a number of Western European nations. Travers, in short, had a full plate. All of these responsibilities, he realized, would have to be carried on in normal fashion while he ran his own clandestine operation against Towny Black.

He looked down at the square. It was a pleasant spring day, and several nannies were wheeling prams near the fountains. A few young, well-dressed mothers sat on the benches with their pre-school children. As he watched, a little blond-haired boy picked up a huge red ball, threw it to his mother, and fell down from the effort. He picked himself up off the grass, grinning.

Travers wondered whether Senator Owens had kept his promise yet to see Admiral Hughes. Without the Senate Intelligence Committee's support and the NSA intercepts, he reflected, he was a sitting duck, no safer at his desk in London than Trilby Gates had been on his own tennis court, or Angus Maclaren behind the wheel of his car. Even with the committee's aid, the risk was high.

His thoughts were interrupted by the booming voice of Dick Austin, who was standing in the doorway. "The season's hardly begun and the Red Sox are already in a losing streak." Austin shook his head sadly. Although he had become Anglicized, ten years in London had not dimmed his love for baseball, or his fanatic, if seldom rewarded, devotion to the Red Sox. He had grown up in Dedham, a suburb of Boston, and over a drink or two, he could expound for hours on the relative merits of Jimmy Foxx, Ted Williams, and Carl Yastrzemski. He was a big, breezy, dark-haired man, well over six feet tall, and in Travers' opinion, a superb officer. As Travers' deputy in charge of liaison with both MI6 and MI5, Austin had one of the most important jobs in the station. Travers relied on him heavily, and both on and off the job they were old and close friends. And, of course, it was Dick and Diana who had introduced him to Valerie.

Travers waved Austin to a chair. "Cheer up, Dick," he said, "I'm working on getting you transferred to Fenway Park."

"Very funny," Austin rejoined, gloomily. "I'm thinking of giving it all up and becoming a soccer nut like our British friends. I'll root for Liverpool."

"Don't do that," Travers said. "Stick to the Sox. You might win another pennant in ten or twenty years."

Austin grunted. He spied the stack of cables on the desk. "What joyous tidings from Langley? Do they want Section K to run an audio operation against Century House? Or maybe Frank DiMario would like us to flutter C?"

Austin's wild jokes might not be so far off the mark, Travers thought. The DDO, had not, of course, gone so far as to suggest that the station bug MI6 or administer a lie-detector test to its chief. But headquarters' suspicion of the Brits ran deep. Travers shared Austin's dislike for Section K and the distrust that lay behind it.

The section had been established inside the London station in the wake of a series of disastrous British security scandals that had opened a wide gulf of mistrust between the CIA and MI6. It had begun in 1961, when Guy Burgess and Donald Maclean, the two turncoat Foreign Office officials, narrowly escaped arrest as Soviet agents by fleeing to Moscow. In rapid succession, their defection was followed by the Portland Naval Secrets case, the arrest and later escape to the Soviet Union of George Blake, an MI6 officer who sold out a whole network of British agents in Germany, the Profumo scandal —in which Britain's war minister had shared Christine Keeler, a voluptuous call girl, with a GRU agent—and, most damaging of all, the shocking revelations about Kim Philby.

More than any other single event, it was the jolting, catastrophic news about Philby that had led to the creation of

Section K. As some had suspected, it was Philby who had warned Burgess and Maclean in time for them to escape from London. And Philby himself, all the while secretly an agent of the Center, had risen to within a hair of becoming C. Had he reached the top of MI6, it would have been the ultimate Soviet coup, the dream of all spies—to have a penetration agent running the opposition intelligence service! Travers still shuddered to think of it.

As it was, Philby had headed the Soviet branch of MI6. He had betrayed dozens of British and American operations, including an early covert action by the agency directed at Albania in 1949. Thanks to Philby, all the CIA-trained émigré agents were rolled up as soon as their small boats hit the beaches.

In the uproar at Langley that followed the Philby disclosures, there were those who urged that the traditional, two-way liaison arrangement with the Brits be cut off entirely; London could not be trusted with U.S. intelligence secrets. Fortunately, cooler heads prevailed. The moderates in the agency pointed out that the special relationship, while not without risks, benefited Langley as much as Whitehall. And Towny Black, with considerable glee, noted that when Philby had been stationed in Washington in 1950, Angus Maclaren had lunched regularly with him. Yet the renowned counterintelligence sleuth, who prided himself on his ability to detect and ensnare Soviet spies, had failed to see through Philby's mask. At a distance, Black liked to say, of two feet.

So there was no open break, but Langley had permitted the legendary Frank Wollner, one of Travers' predecessors as London station chief, to establish Section K, on condition that its existence be kept secret from the Brits at all costs. The purpose of the section was to compile a list of MI6 personnel whose backgrounds, Old Boy ties, sexual preferences, weaknesses, or other characteristics might make them unreliable from a security point of view. Burgess, Maclean, and Philby had all been at Cambridge together. It was there, in the 1930s, that they had joined Communist clubs and had been recruited as Soviet agents. They were members of the Suspect Generation, the prewar Oxbridge undergraduates who later rose to positions of power in the British government, industry, and the press. Many of those who had flirted with Communism in the universities were disillusioned by the Nazi-Soviet Pact of August 1939, and broke with their left-wing past. But others, like Philby, burrowed deeper into the woodwork of the Establishment. They were protected by their elite credentials and the ingrained but erroneous belief that men who belonged to the club would never betray it.

Perhaps, Wollner had reasoned, there were other Oxbridge men within MI6 whose Communist ties could be traced, if only one dug deep enough. Eventually, the researchers in Section K compiled an index, a card file of possible or suspected unreliables. Those on the list were considered to be potential Soviet agents, and their names were passed on to the Counterintelligence Staff at headquarters. From time to time, with Langley's approval, carefully selected items of disinformation were leaked by the London station to one of the MI6 officers on the Section K index, in the hope that it could be traced all the way to Moscow. In one such effort, slightly distorted information about the new XM-1 tank being adopted by the NATO forces in Western Europe was leaked to a contemporary of Philby's. If the man were a Soviet mole, Section K reasoned, a KGB agent in Brussels would soon be asking questions about the new tank in a way that would reveal that the cooked information had reached Moscow. But it never happened.

The final, and most sensitive, rationale for the establishment of Section K was that the personal weaknesses and skeletons turned up by the section's researchers might prove useful in recruiting a penetration agent inside MI6. Such a penetration would have been a blatant violation of the Anglo-American intelligence agreement, but in the atmosphere after Philby's defection it had seemed only prudent. In actual fact, Dick Austin had developed a source inside the senior levels of MI6, a disillusioned Old Boy who drank and talked a bit more than he should. From time to time, he passed along information of marginal value. But the joke of it was that the man's name had never appeared on Section K's lists. And it was a British journalist, not the staff of Section

K, who had uncovered Anthony Blunt, curator of the Queen's art collection; in 1979, Blunt had been revealed as "the fourth man" in the Burgess-Maclean-Philby spy case.

"Section K is a mastodon," Travers agreed. "It serves no useful purpose and it should have been declared extinct years ago."

Austin nodded and said, "But it lumbers on, crashing through the forest, and making my job twice as difficult. I'm scared to death that the Brits may find out about the section one of these days. C is no fool. He may figure out what's going on. If that happens, it will blow the whole goddamn ball game. The Brits will cut us off. The company's track record is already feeble. We seem to be the only ones who didn't know that the shah was about to be booted out of Iran, for example. If we lose MI6, in a fairly short time, our intelligence estimates all around the world will suffer. Especially in Africa."

"I've asked headquarters several times for permission to close the section down," Travers said.

"With what response?"

"My cables have not been answered."

"Bloody bastards. But if things go wrong, we'll be blamed."

"Naturally."

It was the way of the agency. Not that Travers hadn't tried. He had done more than send in the Project Termination Requests. On several trips back to Washington, he had raised the matter directly with both Towny Black and Frank Di-Mario. The British, Travers argued, had made substantial progress in tightening up their security apparatus. The present C, Sir Richard, had been head of MI5 at the time of the Philby scandal. He had been moved over to MI6 specifically to clean up the stables, and by all indications, he had done well. If anything, Travers pointed out, the shoe was on the other foot now. There had been so many leaks of U.S. intelligence secrets that it was the Brits who should distrust the agency. But Travers' arguments fell on deaf ears.

"Frank Wollner may not be around anymore," Austin observed with a trace of bitterness, "but Section K has survived nicely."

Wollner, they both knew, was a tragic figure within the agency. A tall, balding, driven man, he had been the agency's first director of covert operations and had almost single-handedly overthrown the Arbenz government in Guatemala. He had been a great favorite of Allen Dulles. But Wollner could not adjust to the post–Bay of Pigs era of caution; and much like Travers two decades later, he had been shipped off to the London station to get him out of the way. He returned to Washington, retired from the agency, and, a few years later, blew his brains out with a shotgun. His widow, Penelope, was still a doyenne of Georgetown society, a formidable and influential woman in political Washington.

"Unless Black relents, we can't actually close the section down," Travers said. "On the other hand, it doesn't have to work overtime." Travers had assigned only two secretaries and one officer to run the section under Austin. To be the section head, Travers had deliberately selected Upton Ashford Cheever, a dull-witted Philadelphia socialite who typified the agency's deadwood. Behind his back, his colleagues in the Clandestine Services referred to him as "Under A. Cheever."

Austin snorted. "Under's index cards are a laugh riot," he said. "Do you know he's listed George Olds, Sir Richard's deputy? When I asked him why, he said, 'Because his wife is a foreign national.' Well, old Under's onto something there. Poor George does have a foreign wife, and he'll never be promoted to C. But it's not because she's Dutch, it's because she's a fanatic vegetarian. She carries on boorishly at dinner parties, complaining about bits of meat getting on the string beans. Because of the missus, poor George is perpetually doomed to be number 2, the Avis of MI6."

"I know," Travers said. "I've had to sit next to her."

"That's the price you pay for being a station chief."

Travers smiled. He leaned back in his chair and gestured toward the window and the green park beyond. "It's a nice day, Dick," he said. "Why don't we take a walk?"

Austin understood. Travers had something ultrasensitive to discuss, and he detested the "tank." By the rules, that was where such conversations were supposed to take place. The tank, which resembled a streamlined railroad car on stilts, was actually a room within a room. It rested on steel legs above the floor. A speaker had been mounted on the outside, and when the tank was in use, a noisemaking tape emitted the loud, steady sound of whirring machinery. Travers had been told the cacophony had been recorded in a cotton mill in North Carolina. The tank was reputedly bug-proof and absolutely secure, but its windowless walls gave Travers claustrophobia. In addition, the air conditioning sometimes failed, and when that happened, the tank became stifling.

"Sure, Rob," Austin said. "A little promenade would be just the thing today."

They left the building, cut across the square, and turned into Duke Street. When they were well away from the embassy, Travers asked, "How about the zoo?"

"Fine with me. I have a soft spot for the penguins."

They turned into Marylebone High Street and walked in silence toward Regent's Park.

"How's Diana?" Travers asked after a while.

"Great. She spends a lot of time in the garden now that the weather's better, and she still has her pottery class. And Valerie?"

"I try to keep her happy."

"I'll bet you do."

Travers ignored the innuendo. "I'm really grateful to you and Diana. Valerie's marvelous. I'm seeing a lot of her. You're the only one who knows that, by the way."

Austin wanted to ask whether Travers was thinking of getting married again, but he didn't. If the time came, Travers would tell him.

They entered the park at York Gate. At a brisk pace, they made their way through Queen Mary's Gardens and continued north on Broad Walk. The park was in full splendor, with spring flowers everywhere, especially the daffodils and other narcissus. Dozens of people were sunning themselves in chairs that they had rented for 15 pence. When they reached the zoo, they walked along the south end to the Penguin Pool and stood watching. The sleek birds were strutting stiffly on the rocks, as though they had important business to transact with one another.

"God's headwaiters," said Austin.

Travers laughed. "And you don't even have to slip them a five-pound note."

A small boy of about seven, holding a red balloon, stared thoughtfully at the penguins and turned to his mother. "They're awfully small, aren't they?" he said disappointedly. "They look much bigger on the telly."

"Perhaps they don't eat proper meals."

The little boy's younger sister tugged at her mother's sleeve to get her attention. "Mummy," she asked, "how do penguins go to the loo?"

The mother did not reply. She took both children firmly by the hand and marched them toward the seal ponds.

Travers and Austin were alone.

"Dick," Travers said, "do you remember the Schillerplatz?"

"Yes," Austin replied quietly. "I remember."

More than twenty-five years before, when both men were young officers in the Clandestine Services, they had served together in Vienna. In the wake of the Hungarian revolt, tens of thousands of refugees had come over the border into Austria, and headquarters had relied on the Vienna station to provide intelligence from Budapest. Travers was running an agent named Kurt Brunner, who, as a businessman able to supply needed machine tools, was able to travel freely across the border to Hungary. Then Travers received a disturbing report. Although the information was of uncertain reliability, it led him to believe that Brunner might have sold his services to the puppet Kádár government. Travers sent a message through a cutout asking to see Brunner. The agent, nervous, and possibly sensing he was in trouble, proposed a night meeting in an alley behind the Schillerplatz. Despite the obvious danger, Travers had agreed. A case officer had to take risks in agent handling. Dick Austin, carrying an automatic pistol, had accompanied Travers to the meeting and covered him from a doorway in the alley. Brunner showed, acted normally, and began talking to Travers. As he did so, two KGB goons converged on them from each end of the alley. Travers had walked into a Center mousetrap. Austin stepped from the doorway. Back to back, the two Americans started firing. For a few wild moments, it was like a scene from a Grade-B western. Austin winged one of the Russians in the leg. He screamed in pain and limped back down the alley, cursing. The other ran into the street. During the shoot-out, Brunner, realizing that his career as a U.S. spy was definitely over, had bolted.

Austin had saved Travers' life, a fact that created a special bond between them. Neither had ever spoken about it, however, until this moment.

Travers said, "I'm in a dark alley again, Dick, and I need your help."

"Well, I'm a little older, and a lot heavier, but I think I can still fit in the doorway."

"Thanks."

"What's up, Rob? It sounds rather serious."

Before Travers could reply, a busload of schoolchildren swarmed around the Penguin Pool, laughing and pointing. Several of the boys puffed out their chests and started imitating the penguins' walk, which made the girls giggle uncontrollably.

The two men glanced at each other. Austin rolled his eyes, and they moved on, away from the noisy children. They headed up past the elephant pavilion toward the giant pandas. But along the way, they encountered large numbers of tourists.

"Let's go to the aviary," Travers said. "It should be quiet there."

As they walked toward the north edge of the zoo, Travers, in cautious and elliptical fashion, briefed his friend. "I'm doing some things out of channels," he said. "I believe that what I'm doing is right for the country, and ultimately, right for the company."

"I know where you stand," Austin said. "I've listened to what you've been saying about the agency. How we've got to clean up our act or lose our base of public support. I'm not as optimistic as you are that things can be changed. But if you want my help, you've got it."

"There may be some risk."

"I wouldn't mind that. It's been a while."

"You're sure?"

"Yes."

"Then I'll arrange for you to go back to Langley for about a week to do what needs to be done. I can spare you at this end for that long."

"I'll need a little cover story. What will I tell all those folks out in the woods?"

"You have a leave due anyway. Being the conscientious fellow that you are, you're combining it with a little research into a sensitive CI problem that has come up in London."

Austin laughed. "Thereby earning the gratitude of the expense account watchdogs in the DDO's office."

"Yes. Your story is that the sensitive counterintelligence problem has arisen in the person of Jean-Paul Giraud, a walk-in. Giraud is a diplomatic correspondent in London for Agence France Presse. A few weeks ago, he came to us and volunteered his services on a free-lance basis. He's married but he's keeping a mistress in a flat in Hampstead and could use some extra pounds sterling. He has good access to all the embassies, including the Eastern bloc, and is willing to send us regular reports at a reasonable price."

"Does AFP really have a reporter named Giraud here?"

"Oh yes. I've even met him. At any rate, you can say we're considering his offer. We've asked headquarters for name traces on Giraud, and we've also requested that they ask the FBI for a name check. I'll make sure we do all that before you go. Up to that point, it was a fairly routine walk-in, not of exceptional interest. But in filling us in on his biographical details, Giraud claimed to have done the same sort of work for S-deck when he was stationed in Washington for AFP in the 1960s."

Like most of the world's intelligence services, the SDECE, the French CIA, used press cover for some of its agents. Travers lapsed into silence for a moment. They were crossing the bridge over the canal, and a group of earnest German tourists, armed with cameras and guidebooks, were streaming past the other way.

He resumed when the tourists were safely out of earshot. "The sensitive part is that Giraud, in trying to impress us, said he had worked with us before, in a sense. He claimed that in Washington he had developed a source inside the agency, a secretary in the Records Division of the Directorate of Operations, then Plans. She had access to certain administrative files—logistical and support stuff. Giraud was bouncing the girl and he insists she told him some bits and pieces. Nothing very damaging, but he claims he was feeding it all to S-deck."

Austin grinned. "And naturally we have to know."

"Naturally. Giraud, the perfect French gentleman, won't reveal the name of the girl. But under some pressure, he had recalled certain specific information he allegedly received from her. If anyone asks, and they probably won't, you can explain that you need to cross-check that information against the old files of the division. It will be laborious work, but from the dates Giraud provided, in the mid-1960s, it may be possible to verify whether the alleged information is actually in our files, and perhaps even possible to identify the source. We are more interested in checking out Giraud's bona fides, of course, than in plugging a seventeen-year-old leak, but obviously if we uncover the name of the secretary, and if she still works for us, we will pass it along to Brooks Abbot for appropriate action. Of course, by now she's probably a little old blue-haired lady retired in Sarasota."

"Very nice," Austin said admiringly. "And what will I really be looking for?"

They were at the aviary, a large, tentlike structure of wire mesh supported by steel poles arranged in geometric patterns. It had been designed by Lord Snowdon. They mounted the steps to the elevated walkway that zigzagged through the aviary and strolled along, pretending to admire the birds. There were, a sign proclaimed, more than a hundred and fifty different kinds living in natural surroundings.

"What you will really be looking for, Dick, are financial records—purchasing orders, invoices, bills of sale, expense vouchers—for the period from April to about October of 1966. See if you can find any clue at all to what means of transportation was used by the company around that time to move a dozen pieces of heavy equipment from our repair garage in Arlington to somewhere outside of Washington."

"How big was the stuff being moved?"

"Very big. Probably in heavy wooden crates."

A brilliant yellow-and-red game bird skittered through the brush very close to the two men on the walkway. "A golden pheasant," Travers said. "Originally from Central China. They're bred in captivity now." Not far from the walkway, they could see sacred ibis and cattle egrets nesting in the poplar trees.

Austin asked, "Then I should probably be looking for purchase orders for trailer trucks?"

Travers checked his reply. A middle-aged woman in a wide-brimmed hat and a tweed suit was fast approaching from the opposite direction. From her sensible, flat shoes, Travers guessed she was fond of walking, perhaps a zoo regular. She stopped when she reached them. "Isn't it thrilling?" she asked, in an upper-class accent. Travers agreed that it was. The woman was almost certainly harmless, but by stopping to ask her question, she had gotten a close look at both men. He would remember if he ever saw her again.

"Not only trucks," Travers resumed when they were alone. "Look during that time period for the purchase or rental of a dozen moving vans, trailer trucks, RVs, even large buses that could have been converted to cargo carriers. Any vehicle big enough."

"Only surface vehicles? How about helicopters?"

"No. Choppers attract too much attention. This would have been a very quiet operation, with the vehicles probably moving by night."

"Anything else I should be watching for?"

"Yes. Any mention of the 758th Special Operations Tactical Group. It's one of ours, a cover Army unit. And any reference in the files to the operational code designation Phase Yellow. I doubt you'll find either in the support files that far back. At some point, and I don't know when, financial records of that sort are routinely destroyed. It's done under CSI-70-10, 'Retirement of Inactive Records.' But perhaps we'll be lucky."

Austin sighed. "In other words, there may not even be a haystack left, let alone your needle."

"That's about it." Travers stopped on the walkway and lowered his voice, although there were no other strollers nearby. "There's one more thing. We must know, if at all possible, where the crates were taken. The storage point is called Site Orange. If you find any reference to the site, or its location, it's crucially important."

"Suppose we do locate Site Orange," Austin said lightly. "What will we find there? Atomic bombs?"

"I think so," Travers replied.

"Holy shit!" Austin said, dropping his Anglophile manner. "Jesus Christ, Rob. You really are back in the alley."

An East African white-cheeked turaco strutted across a large boulder near the walkway. Travers stopped to admire its startling red-and-purple plumage. Below them, a sightseeing boat crowded with tourists glided along the canal.

"There's no guarantee of a happy ending this time, Dick," he said. "If you want to change your mind, go ahead. And I'll understand."

"I've only got one question."

"Yes?"

"What do I find out about Giraud?"

"When you get back to London, just write a short report to me saying that your search of the records revealed no documents to verify his story. You assume, therefore, that no such agency source as Giraud describes ever existed. On the basis of your report, I will decide that London station will not avail itself of Monsieur Giraud's services. I'll send a memo to Brooks Abbot, just to cover us. He'll be delighted to know there was no leak to S-deck."

"When do you want me to leave?"

"As soon as possible. This week."

They exited by the north gate into Prince Albert Road and Travers hailed a taxi. Neither man cared to walk back all the way to Grosvenor Square. The driver, a garrulous, rough type in a cap, caught Travers' American accent and assumed they were tourists.

"A fine zoo, isn't it, guv?" he asked. "Six thousand animals, thirty-six acres, finest in the world, I'd say."

"Yes," Travers replied. "Very nice."

"Did you see the gibbons? Regular acrobats, they is."

"Missed them, old boy," said Austin, wondering how to turn him off.

"Best of all," the driver persisted, "is the lions. Great beasts, they is, prowlin' about on the terraces, just like they was back home in the jungle." He shook his head. "I wouldn't want to get near one of them, I wouldn't. Not bloody likely. You muck about with anything that powerful and strong, why you'd soon get gobbled up, mate, wouldn't you?"

"Yes," Travers replied quietly. "Yes, I suppose that's exactly what could happen."

Chapter 13

Senator Barry Owens turned the wheel of his green Mustang, swung off the Baltimore-Washington Parkway at the Fort Meade exit, and said a little prayer. A lot, perhaps everything, would depend on how the next hour went.

A few hundred yards through the pine trees and he saw it; a sprawling, three-story, glass-and-steel building and a modern, nine-story annex, surrounded by a vast, asphalt parking lot. The headquarters of the National Security Agency, the most secret arm of the United States government. Compared to NSA, the CIA and the FBI were babblers. The employees joked that NSA stood for "Never say anything."

The physical surroundings were in keeping with the ultra-secrecy that enveloped the security agency. Although NSA was a unit of the Defense Department, it had its own, hidden headquarters many miles from the Pentagon. To approach the building, which was set on an eighty-two-acre site, Senator Owens had to pass through three fences that completely ringed the headquarters. The first and last fences were topped with barbed wire. The middle one, Owens knew, was electrified. Touch it and you were dead.

Armed Marine guards manned the four gatehouses. One of the Marines, crew cut, blond, and very solemn, carefully inspected Owens' identification. He placed a phone call and received some sort of confirmation. He handed the senator a plastic badge and directed him to a visitors' parking area.

It was NSA's mission, Owens knew, that explained the extraordinary secrecy surrounding everything about the place. NSA was the government's ultimate eavesdropper, the supersecret agency that listened in on the communications of other nations and attempted to break their codes. In addition, it created and protected all the codes used by agencies of the United States government.

In some two thousand listening posts scattered around the globe, and especially along the fringes of the Soviet Union, NSA's big ears sucked in the world's voice communications, radar emissions, radio transmissions, Teletype messages, and satellite broadcasts like a monster vacuum cleaner. At Fort Meade, whirring banks of the world's most sophisticated computers aided by thousands of mathematicians, electronic experts, and cryptanalysts sought to unlock the secrets spewed out by the vacuum cleaner. Twenty thousand people worked at headquarters. In some ways, Owens knew, this building was America's first line of defense. Like an animal in the night, we would hear the danger before we saw it.

Admiral Thomas Crawford Hughes, the director of this vast electronic enterprise, rose from his desk when Owens entered his office. He extended his hand and a great smile crinkled his square, weatherbeaten face.

"A great honor, Senator," he drawled in his Mississippi accent. He pronounced it "Sinatuh." "It's not that often that members of your body find the time to visit our little pea patch. Yessir, a great honor."

Owens smiled at the irony of the NSA director's welcome. Only a select few members of Congress were ever permitted inside the headquarters—those who could be trusted to champion NSA at appropriations time. Despite Owens' responsibilities as a member of the Senate Intelligence Committee, he had never been in the building before. And "Crawfish" Hughes, justifying his nickname, had moved sideways, forward, and backward to try to discourage this visit.

"It's not all that easy to get in here, Admiral," Owens said.

Crawfish Hughes chuckled. "Well, sir, we're not the FBI, that's true. No guided tours for the public. I do try to keep the bridge clear."

"You've been here three years now?" Owens asked.

"Four. And I can tell you it wasn't easy, Senator, for a Navy man to accept duty on an Army base, especially one named for General George Gordon Meade. Down in Yalobusha County, where I come from, the folks haven't forgiven him for Gettysburg. General Meade, by the way, was born in Spain; he'd have a right hard time getting a security clearance around here, I can tell you." The admiral chuckled again.

Owens laughed. He found it hard to dislike Southerners, even though their charm was so patently designed to con the rest of the world. Like most successful men from the Deep South, Admiral Hughes, Owens reflected, was protected by an impenetrable layer of corn syrup. It masked the steel. Coming from the Senate, Owens knew. Although reforms in the seniority system were gradually bringing some change, the Senate, in character and style, was still largely a Southern institution. It revered the memory of Dick Russell, Harry Byrd, and Jim Eastland. It clung to its brass spittoons. The Barry Owenses who understood the uses of television, drank Scotch instead of Bourbon and branch water, and had no taste for black-eyed peas could never really become members of the Inner Club.

"Well, I hear you're doing a fine job, Admiral," Owens said, trying a little of his own, Western charm.

"Oh, my, I appreciate that, Senator, I surely do," Crawfish responded. "But I can tell you, sir, even in four years the job has gotten much harder."

"Why so?"

"Technology, sir—that's part of it. The science of cryptology has become so advanced that even some of the smaller countries are using codes that are well nigh unbreakable. It's all done with computers nowadays, as you know, Senator, and I can't say very much about the details, but take my word for it, it's getting harder."

"Are you having any other problems?"

"Well, sir, I have to admit that you folks have added to our burden. With all the investigations and restrictions that the Congress has enacted, sometimes I feel my job is like tryin' to skin a catfish with one hand."

Owens knew what Admiral Hughes was referring to. For two decades, with the collusion of the major cable companies, NSA through its Project Shamrock was able to read millions of cablegrams that Americans sent overseas. Well into the 1970s, in Project Minaret, NSA eavesdropped on thousands of overseas telephone calls and cables flowing in and out of the United States. At the request of other federal agencies, NSA developed "watch lists" of American citizens whose calls were automatically bugged and tape-recorded. But these programs had ground to a halt when Congress began investigating the security agency. NSA still listened to overseas traffic to and from America but it was not supposed to target individuals.

"I know how you feel, Admiral," Owens said soothingly. "We expect results from the executive branch agencies, but we don't always give you the tools."

"You've hit the target amidships," Hughes replied. "I couldn't agree more."

"But we have our responsibilities, too," Owens said smoothly, "which brings me to the reason for my little visit with you today."

"Yes, indeed, Senator. You go right ahead and tell me what's on your mind. If I can help in any way, I surely will."

This was it. Owens looked somber. "As you know, Admiral, for the past several years the Central Intelligence Agency has been required by law to report to the Congress, in a timely fashion, any covert operations that it undertakes."

"And the president must find that an operation is important to national security," Hughes interjected. "Or it can't take place."

"Yes. Which creates rather a gray area. How can Congress be sure that the company is telling us everything it should? Or even telling the president? For all we know, it's pulling the wool over Thurlow Anderson's eyes. Launching all kinds of covert operations that Langley doesn't consider 'important' enough to bother the president with."

"You don't trust Towny Black, Senator?"

"Do you?"

Crawfish Hughes gave a soft, Southern chuckle. "My daddy was a farmer back home. He always told me, 'Trust everybody, but get cash for your cotton.' So I trust ole' Towny, indeed I do."

"I grew up on a farm, too. Your daddy gave you good advice. The problem, Admiral, is that gray area. We suspect that there are a number of covert operations going on that we simply haven't been told about. The agency has notified us of a few, of course. Maybe half a dozen. But how many more are there?"

"You surely do have a problem," Crawfish Hughes said slowly. He was beginning to sense where the conversation might be heading.

Senator Owens leaned forward. "We think the agency may be throwing curve balls at us, slipping operations by on the grounds that they're not 'important' enough to come under the statute. But we need to be sure."

Admiral Hughes looked sympathetic. "Watching the agency must be a little like trying to track a nuclear sub," he said. "Even with the best ASW computers and detection equipment, you can't always be sure exactly where it is and what it's up to."

"Precisely. My subcommittee has primary responsibility for the CIA—although as you know, Admiral, we also have partial jurisdiction over your own agency, and the DIA. If we're to meet our important responsibility of monitoring covert operations, we have to have some way of checking up on Langley. Some way to verify that we're really getting the full picture."

"I see." Admiral Hughes had learned, during his years of infighting in the Navy bureaucracy, always to let the other man ask for what he wanted. It put him under an even greater obligation. Never make it easy for him by anticipating the question.

"Frankly, Admiral, I'm here to try to enlist your help. You and your agency have the technology to solve our problem."

"What exactly do you have in mind, Senator?"

"We'd like you to spot-check the CIA's traffic in and out of a few selected geographic areas for the next several months. Decipher the traffic and make the plain text available to us. That way our staff—specialists with top-security clearances—can analyze the messages. The purpose would be to see whether we can pick up evidence of any covert operations going on that the committee has not been told about."

"Oh my. My my." Crawfish Hughes leaned back in his leather chair and chuckled again. He shook his head, doubtfully. "Oh my." To Owens it seemed as though the Mississippi drawl had gotten even thicker. "Senator," the NSA director said, "that's a mighty tall order. Yes indeed, mighty tall."

Admiral Hughes had risen through the ranks by following a simple precept; he always got something back for what he gave away. He knew trading off was the essence of politics, whether it be in the Navy, the Congress, or the county courthouse. Admiral Hughes was a genial, but very cagey officer who, like so many Southerners, understood politics instinctively. It could not be learned; one had to be born with it. The Crawfish was a ringknocker—an Annapolis graduate who had served under Nimitz during the battle of Midway as a young lieutenant junior grade aboard the *Hornet*. He had commanded a destroyer during the Korean War and a missile frigate in Vietnam. In between, he was assigned to shore duty in the Pentagon, first in BuShips and then in BuPers. In 1969, he was given command of the USS *Enterprise*, the nation's first nuclear aircraft carrier. By 1971 he had advanced to the rank of admiral. A few years later, he had been named director of NSA, a post always filled by a military man.

"Senator," he drawled, "I've had a good life in the Navy. The country's been mighty kind to me. But this is my last watch. I'm almost sixty-two now, and it won't be very long before I put in my papers and retire. All I want to do is go back down to the farm in Coffeeville, and do a little huntin' and fish the Tallahatchie and live out my days in peace."

"I can understand that."

"But now you come along and what you're proposing could bring me a heap of trouble. Yes, sir, a heap of trouble."

"You'd be complying with an official request from a duly authorized subcommittee of the United States Senate. To assist us in fulfilling our statutory responsibility."

"You make it sound mighty easy, Senator. But the fact is, you're asking us to listen in on a sister agency in the intelligence community, without authority from the secretary of defense or the president. Now, from a technical standpoint we could do it very easily, of course." The admiral smiled broadly. "We provided the company with all their code machines, rotors, keys, one-time tapes, and computers. Our COMSEC division designs all the cryptosystems used by every agency of the government. Not only by Langley but by State, the Bureau, and the military services. So we'd have no difficulty reading the agency's traffic. No difficulty at all."

"It would be of great assistance to the committee, Admiral."

"Well, now, I don't doubt that. I don't doubt that for a moment. It surely would. But there's a little favor I might like to ask of you, sir, if I may."

"Please do."

Hughes knew he might be sailing into rough waters. On the other hand, the bargain was there if he wanted it. So far, at least, NSA had been lucky. The Church Committee had let it off with a light tap on the wrist. The next time around, the agency might not fare so well—and Owens held the key. A congressional investigation meant leaks from the Hill and more secrets trumpeted in the press. He would agree to the trade-off. "As I understand it," the admiral said, "your subcommittee staff has been thinking for some time about holding hearings into the operations of our agency. As you know, Senator, our work is very sensitive. The less publicity we get, the happier we are."

Owens had anticipated the move. Ben Goodman and Howard Radner, the young staff assistant assigned to NSA affairs, had picked up whispers that the security agency might be turning its electronic ears on microwave-long-distance-telephone calls within the United States, in violation of the law. For some years, as the intelligence community was well aware, the Soviet Union, from its embassy in Washington, the UN mission in New York, a private mansion in Riverdale, just north of Manhattan, and the consulate in San Francisco had been eavesdropping on microwave relays, listening in to and taping hundreds of thousands of government, business, and personal conversations. The calls were then beamed to the Russian communications satellites that pass over the United States every day. Using highly sophisticated computers, programmed to scan and recognize key words of intelligence interest, the Soviets could then discard routine calls and analyze those—such as calls between government officials and defense industries—that contained the key words. Howard Radner was convinced that NSA was doing the same thing, on the pretext that it needed to see exactly what kind of take the Soviets were getting from their microwave operations. But the NSA surveillance, if it was going on, was strictly illegal. Ben Goodman and Radner had urged him to hold hearings. Owens had not decided whether to do so, but he knew that even the possibility of an investigation would give him a powerful bargaining chip with Admiral Hughes. In preparing for this meeting, Owens had already decided to sacrifice the hearings if the NSA director wanted to horse-trade.

"I understand your feelings about secrecy, Admiral. We've made no final decision on holding hearings. But if you were willing to cooperate with us on monitoring the agency's traffic, I believe our staff would be so busy analyzing the information that we would have to postpone our hearings on any other matters indefinitely. We simply wouldn't have the time."

Crawfish Hughes rocked back and forth in his executive chair for a moment, saying nothing. Then he smiled, the tanned skin around his blue eyes crinkling handsomely.

His voice was soft, and sweet. "What traffic did you have in mind, Senator?"

"Well, I realize the company's traffic is so vast we can't expect you to provide all of it. I thought we might spot-check by having a look at everything going in and out of three stations in separate areas of the world. I think New Delhi, London, and Accra." Owens had thrown in the other two stations to mask his real interest in London; but he knew that Admiral Hughes would have no way of knowing that.

"All right. Three stations for three months only. And I'll need a subpoena from the subcommittee, of course. This will not be voluntary compliance on our part."

"Understood. I'll take care of that."

"I'll also need a letter from you, Senator, giving your assurance that any sensitive materials provided by our agency in response to the subpoena will be carefully stored by the committee in safes approved for top-secret documents, and guarded at all times."

"We have those facilities, Admiral, and I'll be glad to put that assurance in writing." Senator Owens rose and extended his hand. "I'm really grateful to you, Admiral."

Crawfish Hughes came out from behind his desk and shook hands. "I'm glad to be of help to the committee, Senator, mighty glad." He paused and broke out into a grin. "And the good Lord help us if Towny Black ever finds out."

"We don't plan to tell him, Admiral," Owens said.

He bid the director good-bye, left the office, and walked rapidly down the corridor to the elevators. He wanted to get into his Mustang and drive through those barbed-wire and electrified fences and past the Marine guards just as quickly as he could.

Before Crawfish Hughes changed his mind.

Chapter 14

Frank DiMario, the deputy director for Operations of the United States Central Intelligence Agency, settled his bulk into the couch across from Towny Black's desk. From a slim leather attaché case, he removed a single folder marked TOP SECRET in red letters. He tapped the file with his index finger.

"It's all here," he said. "A complete 201 file on William Hansen. Personal background, college education, JOT records, evaluation reports from the various stations where he has served. I've even included a couple of commendations for his work in the Clandestine Services."

The director laughed appreciatively. DiMario handed him the file, and he leafed through it briefly. "Harding Westerfield will find this most impressive, I'm sure. Good work, Frank."

"Thanks. It should fly."

"How soon can we launch him to London?"

"Max Gordon down in TSD is putting a few finishing touches on his physical appearance. And Bill's still on his crash diet. I estimate about a week from now he'll be ready to go."

"Fine. You don't think the pseudonym you've chosen might be a little too close to the real thing?"

"I think it will be all right. Freddie Keegan suggested that we keep the same initials—it avoids trouble with mono-grammed shirts, luggage, that sort of thing."

"Yes, of course."

Black studied the big man on the couch opposite. He was heavier than in the old days, his dark hair now flecked with gray. The hawk nose, swarthy face, and massive frame made

DiMario, even in his fifties, a powerful, menacing figure. It amused Towny Black to think that the head of clandestine operations for the United States government looked increasingly like a *capo di tutti capi,* a Mafia Godfather. DiMario, he reflected, would have fit right in with the patrons at his father's old restaurant on Mulberry Street.

But the director trusted DiMario as he trusted no one else in the agency. The DDO, it was true, had not gone to the right schools, and he did not belong to the right clubs. But, instinctively, Black had known from the beginning that he and DiMario shared the same values: in covert operations and clandestine collection, whatever worked was right, whatever did not work was wrong. It was a simple formula that avoided moral dilemmas and ethical, emotional, or religious baggage that tended to interfere with effective tradecraft.

He not only trusted Frank DiMario, he needed him. Together, they shared the secret of Spectrum, and together they would eliminate the man who foolishly threatened to rake up the past. Only DiMario, the brilliant mechanic, Black knew, was capable of threading his way through the maze of internal paper, of creating a national Clandestine Services officer and inserting him into the London station, fully backstopped and totally plausible. Only DiMario knew the levers to pull, the buttons to push, so that the vast bureaucratic machine that was the CIA would change William Harrington into William Hansen without blinking. Without even knowing. It was no simple task; all along the line, in the Office of Personnel, the DDO Records Division, and the Directorate of Administration bureaus, files on William Hansen had to be created and quietly placed in the proper places. The ragged edges, where pieces of the new identity might not have fit, were now seamless. If Robert Travers or anyone else inside the agency checked on William Hansen, the records would attest to the indisputable fact that he existed. DiMario had even remembered to plant the supposed record of Hansen's polygraph tests in his 201 file, since all company officers were given a lie-detector test, or "fluttered" before being hired, and every five years thereafter. The polygraph reports showed that Hansen admitted to a drinking problem, which Black considered a nice touch. In all, it was a virtuoso performance by DiMario, and the director was pleased.

DiMario lit a Schimmelpenninck. He still smoked cigars, but over the years they had gotten smaller as he grew larger. "Will you be needing to see Bill before he goes?"

Black coughed delicately. He preferred to keep as much distance between himself and Harrington as was possible. "Ah, no," he said. "I've already had a chat with him and assume you will have briefed him fully before he leaves."

"Yes. He's primed and ready. He's memorized all the details of his new identity. He can talk convincingly about his previous posts, his family, even his childhood."

"Are the communications squared away?"

"Yes. I've worked out the back-channel relay, completely compartmented from the rest of the London station's traffic. It wasn't easy, but it's arranged, and secure. All messages will bear the LS/Talpia slug, as you directed. Travers won't see them."

"Well done." The director removed his glasses and rubbed the bridge of his nose with his fingertips. He fiddled for a moment with an unlit pipe. "Frank?"

"Yes?"

"What do you estimate are the chances of success for this operation?"

"High. Very high. There's no reason to think that Harrington will fail to carry out the mission. He's motivated and completely ready." DiMario grinned. "And he usually doesn't miss."

"It's important that Travers accept this as a routine personnel transfer."

"I've given a good deal of thought to that. There are currently three vacancies on the Clandestine Services staff in London. There's a fair amount of normal turnover in the station, since it's so big. Two other officers on routine reassignment will be posted to London at the same time. LS/Talpia will piggyback with them. It's all been cleared with the Office of Personnel and the deputy director for Administration."

"But they're unwitting, of course."

"Of course."

Black put his glasses back on. With his white hair and even features, he looked every inch the chairman of the board. "Frank, I've been turning this thing over in my mind, and I'm afraid there's one loose end that needs to be tied up."

DiMario looked both wary and puzzled. "I can't think of any."

The director filled his pipe slowly, rummaged for a match, found one, and struck it. Black was like a fine actor, DiMario thought. He used his pipe as a stage prop, for effect. The DCI blew a puff of white smoke into the air. "Frank, tell me this. What happens to William Hansen after he completes his mission?"

DiMario shrugged. "He will send back a code word, Goldpot. As in what you find at the end of the rainbow. I selected it myself; it seemed appropriate under the circumstances."

"And then what?"

"We bring him back, give him a medal, and maybe a little pay increase. He resumes his own identity."

The director shook his head. "Frank, we can't do that. Harrington is expendable. Just like Powers and the rest of the U-2 pilots. Don't you see? If we bring William Harrington back, he's a loose cannon on the deck. He'll drink, and he may talk. But if William Hansen should disappear, who will mourn him? He never existed in the first place. And you and I can close the Spectrum file for good."

DiMario understood the reference to the U-2. He had never forgotten the meeting he had attended as a young company officer in the mid-1950s, when the supersecret U-2 program was just becoming operational. Trilby Gates presided. The others were Gates's deputy, Putney Barnes, Angus Maclaren, Towny Black, and Reeves Mason and Courtney Forbes, both senior officers in the Clandestine Services assigned to the overflight program.

The cover story had already been approved; the CIA pilots would ostensibly be civilians under contract to Lockheed, flying "weather research" aircraft for NASA. The U-2's were about to be launched over the Soviet Union to photograph missile sites and other defense installations. Gates had called the meeting to consider a sensitive and delicate question, which he euphemistically referred to as "the time-lag problem." Each of the U-2 planes, he explained, had built into it a destructor unit containing a three-pound charge of powerful cyclonite explosive. In the event of trouble over the Soviet Union, the pilots were instructed to activate a timing device and bail out. After that, they were told, the plane would blow up.

"The problem, gentlemen," Trilby Gates had purred, "is to decide just how long a time lag there should be, if any, once the destruct button is pushed." Gates, with support from Putney Barnes, argued that the program was so vital to the nation's security that no evidence must be allowed to fall into Soviet hands; if a U-2 ran into difficulty, the pilot should be destroyed along with the aircraft. He did not put it in those words, however. He simply said, "I believe that from an operational standpoint there should be no time lag between the time the destruct button is pushed and the explosion occurs."

Courtney Forbes professed to be shocked. "These pilots are our own people," he objected "They are Americans, and company employees. They're risking their lives to gather intelligence for their country. Do we have the moral right to—to sacrifice them in this manner?"

"From a technical and legal point of view," Trilby Gates countered, "we will not be responsible for their deaths. They will push the button themselves. They will commit the act that results in their own destruction. The timing device will simply fail to function as the pilots were told it would. But we can hardly be held responsible for their voluntary decision to push the button."

The problem was not an easy one. The men sitting around the table were graduates of the nation's best preparatory schools—Groton, St. Paul's, Exeter. As DiMario sensed, if he did not actually know, they had sat in chapel at those schools and been exhorted to live by noble moral and religious precepts. But the world, they had soon learned, did not live by those rules. The United States was faced with an evil, implacable enemy. Intelligence work required men who could make tough, pragmatic decisions. So the graduates of St. Grottlesex adopted a double standard. With the confidence bred of their elite social class, they came to believe that their morality could be set aside in the higher interest of the state. Yet, what they had heard in the school chapels was deeply ingrained in their collective memory. It could not so easily be shed. The men in the room were uncomfortable.

It was Towny Black who had come up with the perfect solution to the moral dilemma. "Since we're telling the pilots there will be a time lag," he said, "there should be one. But let it be about two seconds." Trilby Gates broke into a broad smile and the others nodded. It was a brilliant solution, everyone agreed: not enough time to permit the pilots to live, but enough to salve the consciences of the men around the table.

And so, Allen Dulles had assured President Eisenhower that in the event of a mishap over the Soviet Union, both the plane and the pilot would be destroyed. Eisenhower had not inquired too closely into why this would happen. But the agency had overlooked the human factor. A number of the U-2 pilots began to worry about the delicate timing device in the destruct mechanism. What good would it do to destroy the plane, the fliers reasoned, if a live pilot came floating down inside Soviet territory? In the event, Francis Gary Powers never pushed the button; he testified that he couldn't reach it.

All of this, DiMario remembered. "I understand what you're saying," he said. "But do we really need to go down that road with Harrington? He won't know what he's done. As far as he knows, he will have liquidated a mole and removed a dangerous threat to the agency and the country. He'll think of himself as a hero."

"That's just the problem. He'll be so puffed up over it, he may start to talk about it. And if he ever compares notes with Brooks Abbot, for example, he'll discover that Travers was not a mole. That there is no mole."

"At least none whose identity we know." DiMario snuffed out his little cigar in an ashtray by the couch. "I suppose," he said finally, "it would be tidier to terminate LS/Talpia once he has served our purpose. Tidier and safer. But how would you propose to do it?"

"We wouldn't," Towny Black replied with a tight little smile. "We'd let the KGB do it for us."

The two-second solution again, DiMario thought, not without a touch of admiration. Not all of the company's senior executives shared DiMario's loyalty toward Graham Townsend Black, but even the director's bureaucratic enemies admired his brilliant tradecraft.

DiMario said, "Pavlov would love to get his hands on Bill Harrington. They have more than one old score to settle." General Yevgeny Vladimirovich Pavlov was the head of the First Department of the Komitet Gosudarstvennoye Bezopasnosti, the KGB. The First Department handled clandestine operations against the United States; it came under the KGB's First Chief Directorate, which ran all foreign operations.

"I don't doubt it," the director replied. "He's liquidated a dozen of their men, including one with the rank of colonel, in The Hague. Velnikov, I believe. There was also a woman in Madrid, but she was GRU."

"There might be a problem getting Bill to stay put long enough to send him down the tube," DiMario said. "His operational pattern is to leave the scene of a hit immediately. On the first plane out."

"I know that. But in this case I want you to instruct him in advance to sit tight wherever he is when he messages us that his mission is completed."

"It's unusual. He might get twitchy."

"Tell him that this mission is so important we'll need to fly in a verification team. The CI people will want positive, on-site confirmation that the target has been eliminated. That's how important it is. Tell him we'll have the verification team standing by, so he won't be delayed for very long."

"That should work."

"What I need from you, Frank, is a plan for the actual approach to the oppo. It has to be plausible to the Center."

"I don't see any insurmountable problems. In fact, if we handle it right, we might be able to kill two birds with one stone."

"How so?"

"We can pull the string on Bill and float a double agent on

the Center. Betraying Harrington will prove the double's bona fides beyond any shadow of a doubt."

"Who would you use?"

"Gunnar Borg, I think. He's a low-level access agent who's been performing some chores for the Stockholm station. Al Rossi is his case officer. Borg is good; back in the late sixties and early seventies he infiltrated the Vietnam deserters who had fled to Sweden. He posed as a sympathetic left-winger and helped the Americans find housing. About eight months ago, the Soviets approached Borg in a cold-pitch recruitment. Walked right up to him on the Strandvagen. Borg played along. Since then, Rossi has been building him with chickenfeed to pass to Alexei Rogov, the KGB *resident* in Stockholm. We want Rogov to think he's doubled Borg. But Rogov is nervous; he won't ask Gunnar for much and handles him very cautiously. Rogov is getting close to retirement age, and has visions of a cottage in Sochi. He probably doesn't want to take any risks."

Black nodded. "But if Borg fingers William Harrington, Rogov won't dare to sit on it. He'll have to report Borg's information to the Center, and General Pavlov will be licking his chops."

"I think so."

"We don't know at this point exactly where Harrington/ Hansen is going to carry out the termination. It might take place outside London or even on the Continent, if Travers happens to be on a trip. Borg will have to have a plausible explanation of how he knows where Harrington can be found."

"That shouldn't be too difficult. The number three KGB agent in Stockholm, under Rogov, is one Pavel Komarov. Six years ago, a KGB officer in Tokyo tried to come over to us. Darren Murphy was handling him. There was a scuffle on the street, and Murphy was shot dead. We now know it was Komarov who did it. Only his name in Tokyo wasn't Komarov. It was Korovin."

Black gently tapped the ashes out of his pipe into the ashtray on his desk. "So Harrington's been assigned to neutralize Komarov. To even the score."

"Yes. Borg can tell the Soviets that he is to meet Harrington, who is using the pseudonym William Hansen, somewhere outside of Stockholm to brief him on the target. Borg will say he is to bring out surveillance photos with him. Also, since he has been inside the Soviet embassy, and has met Komarov, he can provide a first-hand description."

"That sounds fine, Frank. LS/Talpia has been instructed to get our advance approval of the time, place, and details before he completes his mission. Once we have that information, everything will come together."

"Right," DiMario replied. "Through the Stockholm station, we'll provide Borg with Harrington's exact location and a description of his new physical appearance, since it will have changed considerably from whatever the KGB has in its files. Once we get LS/Talpia's coded message that his mission has been carried out, we signal Borg to go to Rogov. Meanwhile, Harrington is sitting still in his hotel room or apartment waiting for the verification team to fly in."

"Only the knock on the door won't be from the verification team." Black permitted himself a smile.

But DiMario appeared worried. He was scowling, which made his dark, hawk's face even more sinister. "Suppose they don't kill him on the spot? Suppose they kidnap him and take him back to Moscow? Once they get Harrington in those basement rooms on Dzerzhinsky Street he'll talk. He'll be a gold mine for their CI division."

Black shook his leonine head. "He won't have that much to give away, even if he does break under their pressure. A lot of dead operations, like the Berlin Tunnel. For the last two decades, Bill's been confined to Executive Action. The Soviets already know who he's killed; they hardly need his confirmation."

"Bill will deny he was to meet Borg or liquidate Komarov."

"But they won't necessarily believe him. He may also say that he terminated Travers because he was their mole. And the Soviets *know* that isn't true. No, Frank, once they've raked over a few old coals and have wrung him out, they'll kill him, slowly and surely. Given Bill's weight, they'll probably decide to starve him. General Pavlov likes to select appropriate forms of death for his victims."

"Those bastards," DiMario spat. "They really are inhuman."

"But in this case, they're doing our work for us." The director looked at his watch. "I'm going to have to break this off, Frank," he said. "I've got a meeting with the Africa Division in a few minutes. The president is still fussing over Angola."

"Before I go, you may want to look over these computer runs on our personnel in the London station." DiMario reached into the attaché case. "You wanted a list of anyone in the station who had ever worked with Harrington."

"What did you come up with?"

"There are only two. A secretary, Kathleen Grant, who was stationed with him in Berlin, and Ken Varney, who briefed him in The Hague before he liquidated Velnikov."

"Transfer them."

"Where to?"

"I don't care, so long as it's far away from London. Send one to Rangoon and the other to Jakarta.

"All right. I'll take care of it."

There were two loud clicks in the quiet room as DiMario snapped the latches shut on his attaché case.

"Oh, and Frank?"

"Yes?"

The director smiled warmly. "Tell Bill good luck from me."

Chapter 15

It was seven in the morning, and Valerie had slipped into the shower ahead of him. Travers did not mind; he lay in bed, enjoying the coolness of the sheets against his naked body. It was mid-June, and the past few days had been unseasonably hot for London, but after the chill, wet winter he welcomed the change.

Valerie had spent the night at his flat on Bryanston Square. The Division D sweepers from the station went over the apartment once a week for bugs. So far they said they hadn't found any, but Travers sometimes wondered whether they had dropped any in. He trusted Pat Nolan, up to a point, but one could never be sure.

Travers felt rested and relaxed. Val had cooked a steak, and he had uncorked a bottle of Beaune. After dinner by candlelight, they had sat together in the living room, listening to Vivaldi string concertos on the stereo and talking quietly. Around midnight, they had gone to bed and made love. Valerie had been very passionate and free.

The shower was still running, and Travers threw off the sheet and stole into the bathroom. He silently slid open the glass door to the shower stall and stepped in. Valerie was covered with white soapsuds and had her back turned. She looked marvelous. He grabbed her around the waist from behind and pressed against her body.

Valerie squealed and twisted around in his arms. "You nasty spook," she said, laughing. "Sneaking up on me like that isn't fair. Besides, this is a private shower, for women only."

"Sorry," said Travers, "I didn't see you."

Valerie giggled and pushed against him. They were facing each other, their bodies slippery from the soap. Travers suddenly ducked his head under the stream of water and kissed her breast. He slid his tongue back and forth against the nipple.

Val looked down at Robert's loins. "Well, good morning to you, too," she said, touching him lightly.

"Have you ever made love in a shower?" he asked.

"No, but it looks like I'm about to."

"Yes." Travers penetrated her and they held on to each other tightly, swaying slightly under the warm, flowing water. Valerie placed her lips against his and kissed him languidly, her mouth soft and welcoming.

Afterward, they had dried each other with Robert's huge, blue bath towels, and Valerie had cooked sausage and scrambled eggs. He put on a lightweight suit, a blue shirt, and a silk challis tie. He had a second cup of coffee and kissed her good-bye.

The sun was up as he drove the short distance to the embassy, and it felt like another warm day. He arrived at the office early but Ann Ganley was already there.

"You look very nice this morning, Mr. Travers," she said.

"I feel good, too," he said. "Had a restful night, a nice shower, and a big breakfast." He didn't see the need to tell Ann any more than that.

"Lisa Layton wants to see you, and I've scheduled Harding Westerfield for ten o'clock. He's bringing in the three new staff officers to introduce them to you. You're lunching with Dick Austin at noon if his plane gets in on time. The cables and mail are in the basket. Coffee this morning?"

"No thanks, Ann. I've already had two cups. Tell Lisa to come on in."

Travers began reading the incoming cables. After a few moments, Lisa entered and seated herself opposite his desk, legs crossed, cool and poised as usual. But Travers read the hint of trouble in her face.

"How are we coming with Primrose-1 and -2?" he asked.

"I'm not sure," she replied hesitantly. "Special Branch raided Bullock's clubs last week and tramped around at great length in three of his porno shops, which should be very bad for business."

"I know. Sir Edward notified me last week that the Yard was ready to move. It took a while because he had to clear it with the Home Secretary."

"After the raids, I had one of our street agents place an anonymous phone call to Bullock. The caller made it clear that his difficulties would be over if he dropped his real-estate plans in Bayswater Road."

"And?"

"Well, it's been a week. But the eviction notice for the OP hasn't been withdrawn."

"Rumin must really be squeezing him."

"Shall we place another phone call to Bullock? Tell him the raids were only the beginning?"

"Yes, let's try that. Keep the pressure on him. And keep me informed."

"Yes, sir." Then Lisa was gone, but, Travers noticed, a trace of her perfume lingered pleasantly in the room.

He returned to the in-basket. There was a report from the Records Division of the Directorate of Operations, replying to the request for name traces on Jean-Paul Giraud. There was very little in the files. Subject was a correspondent for Agence France Presse, the report said, and resided on Wellington Road in St. John's Wood. The names of his wife, Marie-Françoise, and of their two children, Jacques and Georgette, were also given. The rest of the printout listed a series of lunches Giraud had apparently had in London with Soviet, Czech, and other Eastern European diplomats. These were based upon MI5 contact reports, shared by the Brits with Grosvenor Square, routinely forwarded by the station to Langley, and now played back across the Atlantic by the magic of Intellofax.

Travers chuckled at the FBI report. The Bureau had sent Langley a name trace on Jean-Paul Giraud, a pastry chef employed at the Rive Gauche restaurant in Washington. Also a Jean Giraud, MNU, Bureau jargon for Middle Name Unknown, who was believed to be a card-carrying member of the French Communist Party, and who had written to his aunt in Passaic, New Jersey, in September 1958. The letter had been opened, read, and photographed by the Bureau but contained no information of intelligence interest.

He put the name traces in a folder and placed it in the file drawer of his desk. He would hold them for Dick Austin. He continued leafing through the morning's cables. Tweedy Bird, a staff assistant to Arthur Wilcox, the deputy to the director for National Intelligence, was requesting that the station ask MI6 for biographical intelligence on Agrippa Kimbundu, an emerging, young opposition leader in Angola. Travers noted that it was the fourth request in the past month for intelligence dealing with Angola. He assumed, correctly, that Towny Black was feeling the heat from the National Security Council and President Anderson.

The White House feared that Angola, with fifteen thousand Cuban troops and strong Soviet support, was a tinderbox that might blow at any time. There were rumors of plans for another Angolan invasion of Zaire. President Anderson worried that if war engulfed southwest Africa, it could quickly turn into a great power confrontation. The NSC was pressuring Langley for daily, even hourly intelligence reports from Africa. Despite the complete failure of the agency's covert operation in Angola in 1975, the Directorate of Operations, Travers had heard, was proposing to rearm Joseph Mugawe, the same leader who had been defeated by the MPLA six years before. Travers considered the plan insane. He routed the message to Dick Austin.

He shoved the paperwork aside and took a few moments to read through the London *Times*. Normally he liked to do that at home, but he had been otherwise occupied this morning. *The New York Times* and *The Washington Post* were flown in daily but did not arrive at the embassy until late in the afternoon.

Travers had scarcely finished the paper when Ann Ganley popped in to announce that Westerfield and the three transfers from Langley were waiting in the anteroom. She discreetly placed their 201 files on Travers' desk.

He was pleased that headquarters had finally filled the three slots, which had been vacant for several months. It seemed to take personnel forever to rotate people into the station when vacancies occurred. He would keep the meetings as short as possible. Travers did not like ceremony.

Westerfield escorted a somewhat plump, round-faced woman into the office. "Mary Jo Farmer," he said.

"Sit down," Travers said pleasantly, "and welcome aboard. This is a busy shop, as you may have heard, so we're glad to have you here. London is expensive, the food is almost as bad as you've been led to believe, and the weather's terrible. But I'm very nice to work for, as Mr. Westerfield will tell you."

"Oh, yes," Westerfield rejoined solemnly, "Mr. Travers is a very fine COS."

The new recruit smiled nervously. Travers studied the woman. She wore glasses and looked rather like a librarian from the midwest. He opened her 201 file and saw that she was thirty-seven, unmarried, and her previous post had been Tokyo.

"What sort of work were you doing in Tokyo?" he asked.

"I specialized in the Yamaguchi," she replied. "Their largest criminal organization. I was running an agent codenamed Flower Card, who was tight with Kazuo Taoka, their don."

"Taoka was shot, wasn't he?"

"Yes, but he lived. There was a lot of killing going on between the Yamaguchi and a rival gang, the Matsuda. That's when Taoka was shot. But thanks to Flower Card, we knew what was happening."

"And your operational interest?"

"It ran in several directions. We were closely tracking Yoshio Kodama, the overlord of the Yamaguchi's Tokyo operation. He handled the bribes for Lockheed. As you know, we have a particular interest in Lockheed because of the U-2."

"What else?"

"Kodama founded the Zen-Ai-Kaigi, the biggest rightwing paramilitary force in Japan. They've got ten thousand members and they're armed. They're extremely dangerous, of course, but they also represent the strongest anti-Communist force in Japan. We have good lines into them through KS/Teahouse-1, an agent on their executive committee, whom I also ran. And we had Kodama under audio surveillance."

Travers was impressed and once more reflected on how much like the Army the allegedly sophisticated agency was—transferring someone with so much expertise to a new and unfamiliar post. Under the plain-Jane exterior, she was obviously a crackerjack agent. "Harding," he said, "I think we have just the thing for Miss Farmer. Why don't we assign her to track the SAS hit squads? Right now we have almost no coverage, and it's heating up."

"That would be excellent, sir," Westerfield replied.

"The SAS?" Mary Jo asked.

"Special Air Services," Travers said. "They're our British cousins' version of the Green Berets. They were a crack commando outfit in World War Two, and they're still around, based in Hereford. There's evidence that they're engaged in covert operations. We think they've assassinated IRA leaders in Ulster and several Soviet-backed Arabs in the Persian Gulf."

"Do we have anyone inside?"

"No. That's the problem. A number of ex-SAS men have been recruited as mercenaries in Africa. They're supposedly independent but we think they have close ties to the commando unit. One hit team of mercenaries recently tried to assassinate the president of Togo. The president had personally shot his predecessor to death, which is an interesting way to handle the problem of succession. Anyway, the hit team tried to infiltrate over the border from Ghana, but when they got there the police were waiting. We think that MI6 tipped off the Togolese. We also think that the SAS had approved the mission, informally. It's pretty clear that the Foreign Office and the military are at loggerheads over the mercenary question. Whitehall wants it stopped, and the military thinks it's useful. I need someone who can target and penetrate the SAS and insert an agent or two who can monitor the situation for us."

"And since MI6 is feuding with the SAS, I suppose they can't help us on this one."

"You see the problem exactly. If there are hit teams dispatched to Africa from Britain, we have to be able to identify them at this end, and know who they are and who they're working for. Otherwise, our stations in Africa won't know what they're dealing with."

"I'll do my best with it, sir."

Travers arose. "I'm sure you will." They shook hands and Westerfield saw her out.

He was back in a moment with a slight, blond young man.

"This is Philip Moffet, sir. He has recently transferred over to us from the Intelligence side. This is, ah, his first posting in the Clandestine Services."

"I see." Travers' voice hardly concealed his annoyance. Personnel was obviously doing a number on him. First they had transferred two of his staff back to headquarters on very short notice. Now they were sending an inexperienced, young analyst for on-the-job training in covert work at a major station like London. Why didn't they break him in someplace like Bujumbura or Mbabane, for chrissakes? He stared at the pale-skinned young man sitting opposite. He looked at his 201 file and noticed that Moffet's work as an analyst had mainly been for the Western Hemisphere Division, covering Latin America. It would be small help in London, unless he proved knowledgeable about the intelligence officers operating from the Cuban mission in Kensington Court.

"I'm terribly excited to be here, Mr. Travers," Moffet volunteered. "I know I don't have any covert experience, but I did take a refresher course at the Farm before they transferred me. In paramilitary skills, clandestine collection, and basic tradecraft."

Something about his inflection and appearance bothered Travers. He had a queasy feeling that Moffet might be spending his free time in a drag pub. He made a mental note to have him fluttered. If it were left to him, Travers would have regarded the sexual preferences of his staff members as their own business, but it was company policy not to employ gay men or women, on the assumption that they were subject to blackmail. He was reasonably sure, however, that at least a few homosexuals had slipped past the polygraphs and had made it into the agency's closet. Perhaps Moffet was one. Travers decided to assign him to Section K, at least until he could be polygraphed. It would keep Moffet inside the station, where his inexperience could do the least harm. And it would allow him to make use of his training as a researcher.

"Well, we're glad to have you with us," Travers said unenthusiastically. "Harding, why don't we start Mr. Moffet in Section K? I think Upton Cheever could use a little help."

"Oh, yes, sir. I'm sure the section would welcome any assistance. Right now, they're working on the class lists for Trinity and Kings at Cambridge. But they're only up to 1936."

"Fine, fine." Travers glanced down at the last folder. "Send in William Hansen."

Westerfield shepherded Moffet out the door and returned with an impressively large man, well over six feet, heavyset, and brawny.

"Have a seat," Travers said.

"Thank you, sir."

The voice was deep, and confident. From the name, the modishly long blond hair, and blue eyes, Travers assumed that the new officer was of Scandinavian descent. The file showed his guess was undoubtedly correct; Hansen had grown up on a farm near St. Cloud, Minnesota. The newcomer wore thick glasses with black frames. Travers noticed his complexion was blotchy and his appearance marred by a large wart on the left side of his face.

"I see your last post was Moscow."

"Yes, sir. I'll miss the Stolichnaya, but that's all." He laughed.

Travers, fingering the 201 file, noted that Hansen, when fluttered the last time two years earlier, had admitted to a drinking problem. He wondered if London was becoming a dumping ground for Personnel's problems. On the other hand, Hansen looked competent and tough, and Travers noticed he had received two commendations. He also noticed that he had very powerful hands.

"I see you spent about six months back at headquarters before they sent you here."

"Yes, sir. I was awaiting reassignment. They had me shuffling papers in the Soviet Russia Division."

"How did you spend your time in Moscow?"

"Mostly countersurveillance. We used two of the women

officers in the station to service the dead drops. I'd tag along about a hundred feet behind. The women seemed to attract less attention. Unfortunately one of them was caught. Nina Jarvis. The KGB kicked her out with a lot of noise."

"And shot the agent she was running, as I recall."

"Yeah. It was a bad show all around. Nina was out on a bridge over the Moskva, the one connecting the Luzhniki sports palace with Lenin Hills, when they grabbed her. I barely got away myself. She was heading for a dead drop behind a loose stone in the bridge wall. Unfortunately, she was carrying a milk carton containing a miniature camera, gold, and two ampuls of poison. The Sovs uncorked a barrage of publicity. They had a field day with the poison. They claimed she had given some to the agent before, and that he had used it to murder someone."

"Who nailed her? Pavlov's people?"

"No. Mironov's. He's in charge of the American Department of the Second Chief Directorate. They handle all the counterintelligence activity directed at our station, the Canadians, and the Latinos. They have a separate department for the Brits and Europe, and another for Asia."

"I see your tour in Moscow was three years. Were you working on anything else?"

"Yeah. I helped to get us a sample of Harmalin. It's a speech-inducing drug developed by the Sovs, very exotic, and it was a high-priority target for the station. Apparently the boys in TSD wanted it very badly."

"Is it anything like scopolamine?"

"Yes, but much more powerful. The Gestapo used it as a truth serum during World War Two. The Nazis learned about it when they occupied the Crimea in 1943. They sent a botanist down to study the Nikita Gardens and discovered the Russians were growing *Peganum harmala*. The Soviets had produced the drug by combining the flower's extract with *Anabasis aphylla*, a plant found only in Tashkent, in the foothills of the Tien Shan mountains."

"How did you get it?"

"I had an asset who'd been a doctor in the gulag, where they'd used it on some of their dissidents. What he saw in the camps made him sick. He turned over a few milligrams to us in a brush contact in Leningrad. I used our Air Force attaché, sheep-dipped, wearing civilian clothes."

"Very nice."

"Headquarters thought so." Hansen smiled. Travers noticed he had excellent teeth.

"London may seem tame by comparison," Travers said. "However, I may have an interesting project to start you off. We're having a little trouble over one of our OP's. It may reach a point where we'll want someone to pay a visit on a man named Harry Bullock. Harding, take Mr. Hansen over to see Lisa Layton and have her brief him." Travers arose. "If you need anything, or have any questions, Mr. Westerfield will be glad to help. Or come and see me."

"Thank you, sir. I appreciate that." The two men headed out the door. Hansen was the last to leave, and Travers noticed that he favored his left foot.

Travers returned to the pile of incoming cables. He finally dug out, signed off on a number of messages to Langley, and fielded a couple of telephone calls, including one from his insurance agent, who reminded him that the premium on his automobile policy was overdue. He promised to get a check in the mail. He asked Ann Ganley to call Sir Edward Furnall's secretary and set up a lunch date for later in the week; Travers had a feeling that he would really have to work on Sir Edward to get him to unleash Special Branch on Harry Bullock a second time. If another raid didn't work, there was always William Hansen, who looked tough enough to get the message across. But he wanted to keep the station in the background if he possibly could; Hansen would be a last resort.

Travers looked at his watch. The morning had flown by and it was almost noon. Ann Ganley roused him on the intercom. "Mr. Austin called over an hour ago. His flight from Dulles was on time and he's coming in on the underground from Heathrow."

"Great. Thanks, Ann."

It was only about ten minutes later that he heard Dick's booming voice greeting Ann Ganley. In a moment, he appeared, bounding energetically across the room and pumping Travers' hand.

"Hey, Rob, I see you managed to keep the place running without me. I thought sure you'd be closed down by now."

"Well, the fact is I haven't been working too hard. Diana and I have been hitting all the nightclubs and discos while you were away."

"Well, don't tell Val," Austin countered.

Travers asked quietly, "How'd you do?"

"Mezzo mezzo." Austin wobbled his hand sideways. "I'll fill you in at lunch."

They walked out of the embassy together. Travers suggested they go to the Red Lion, a pub on Waverton Street. A number of MI5 men frequented the spot, but the tables were far enough apart so that they could talk.

"Saw your friend Frank DiMario," Austin said as they strolled along Carlos Place, past the Connaught. "Bumped into him in the hall while I was on my way to the Records Division."

"What did he say?"

"Seemed quite surprised to see me. He asked after you, but mostly he wanted to know why I was in from London. I told him I was back on home leave, and was combining it with some CI work in the files."

"Did he let it go at that?"

"No. He was friendly enough, but insisted on knowing exactly what I was doing. So I had to run him through the whole Giraud thing."

"Did he buy it?"

"He seemed to."

"Good." They were at the pub. It was crowded, but Travers knew the manager, who gave them a corner table. Austin ordered a beer, and Travers asked for Bass ale.

"What did you find?" Travers asked.

"At first nothing," Austin replied. "I spent three days in the division. They couldn't believe I wanted records from 1966. It took them almost all of the first day to dig out the right boxes. Some of them had to be brought in from a warehouse in Falls Church. Finally, they had everything laid out for me. About twenty boxes, most of them dusty, stacked on a big table."

The waiter brought their drinks and took their lunch order.

Austin chose the steak and kidney pie and Travers ordered the roast beef, rare.

"It was slow going," Austin continued. "Although I learned more than I wanted to know about our purchasing practices. Most of what I looked at were records of the Covert Procurement Branch for 1966. Some of it really was procurement. Did you know we provided 'female companions' for King Hussein?"

"Yes, I've heard that."

"Only the best hundred-dollar-a-night stuff from the East Side of Manhattan. The girls were flown into Amman for the weekend, turned their trick, and through the modern miracle of jet travel, were on their way back to Sutton Place by Monday morning. It's all in the financial records, down to the last dinar—"

Austin broke off while the waiter put lunch on the table.

"All right, Dick," Travers said. "I didn't send you to headquarters to investigate the sex life of His Hashemite Majesty. Did you find any trucks?"

"I'm coming to that. Most of the purchasing orders are attached to sterility codes. There seemed to be two kinds. One is not traceable to the United States government. The other kind is not traceable to the agency."

"Westerfield's really into sterility codes. All of our electronic equipment for the Listening Posts was purchased that way."

"Well, I zeroed in on those records, figuring what we wanted would have to have been a sterile procurement. A lot of it was operational gifts by station chiefs to foreign presidents and cabinet ministers, especially in Africa and Asia. Everything from liquor to air-conditioned Cadillacs. Also a lot of requisitions to furnish safe houses overseas. Some of them even have crystalware and sterling silver."

"I know. They're not all as grubby as the ones we have in London. What about the trucks?"

"There were a fair lot of cars, vans, and other vehicles purchased on sterility codes. For use in surveillance, I suppose, and routine agency business. Also several replacements for those little Blue Bird buses that shuttle between the agency installations in Langley and Washington."

"But nothing big enough?"

"Not until the third day, when I got down to the last couple of boxes. Then I found something really odd."

"What?"

"In September 1966, using a sterility code traceable to the government, but not to the agency, the company purchased twelve intercity U.S. mail trucks. Tractor-trailers, each thirty-five feet long, manufactured by International Harvester."

Travers leaned forward across the table.

"Where were they delivered?" he asked.

"Well, that's the funny thing. The procurement order was set up so that it looked like the Post Office was buying the trucks. But the bill of lading showed that the trucks never got to the Post Office Department."

"Where did they go?"

"Arlington, Virginia."

Travers broke into a grin. "Hell, Dick, you've done it. You've found the trucks. It's got to be."

"I hope so. That's the good news. The bad news is that there was absolutely no record of where they went from there. And no reference anywhere to Site Orange."

"I didn't really think there would be. But you've done well. It may turn out to be very useful information. Thanks, Dick."

"Cheers, Rob." Austin raised his glass. "Glad to be of help. Maybe you'll even tell me what it's all about."

"In time. Not now."

"All right. Your show."

"The traces on Giraud came in. I'm holding them for you. When you get squared away, write me a report on your stint in the Records Division. Then I'll send a memo to Brooks Abbot, concluding that there was no leak, and that Giraud is puffing. I think I'll even send a copy to Frank DiMario."

"That would be a good idea."

They split the check, and walked back toward Grosvenor Square. It was hot, as Travers had suspected the day would be. "Personnel finally filled the three slots," he said. "Harding brought them by this morning."

"Who'd we get?"

"A woman who looks top-flight, a cowboy named Hansen

with a drinking problem, and one Phillip Moffet, whom I'm assigning to you for Section K."

"Oh?" Austin raised his eyebrows. "I thought you wanted to downhold on the size of the section, since old Under's managing so well."

"I do. But Moffet looks like he might end up as a drag queen at the Green Man. I'm going to ask Harding to have him fluttered. Then we'll see. Also, he has no covert experience. Until now, he's worked as an analyst."

"Well, thanks a lot."

"Don't mention it."

"What about the woman?" Austin asked.

"Her name's Farmer. I'm going to have her track the SAS mercenary squads. We've needed someone to do it."

They were approaching the embassy. Travers, looking up, noticed that the American eagle was covered with pigeon droppings as usual. Ambassador Cushing had given orders that the eagle be hosed off once a week. But it was an uneven struggle; the pigeons were winning.

"What are you going to do with the cowboy?" Austin asked.

"I may ask him to help Lisa Layton out. We're having a little problem with one of the OP's. After that, I don't know."

"What's his background?"

"Moscow, Paris, Mexico City. Mostly CI and street work. He looks like he's good at it."

"Funny I've never run across him."

"Well, we're a big company. But if you'd ever met him, you'd remember him. He's a big, blond man with a limp."

Chapter 16

On Saturday morning, Travers was up early. He made coffee and toast, threw a shaving kit and a few articles of clothing into a small leather bag, and walked downstairs. On the table in the front hall, he left a note for Mrs. Wilson, the grandmotherly lady who lived on the ground floor and looked after the flats, asking her to take in his mail and newspapers and saying he would be back Monday.

He had parked his Triumph TR7 around the corner in George Street. It was only seven-thirty and there was no one else in the square. Travers liked the early-morning feel of a sleepy Saturday. No nannies, schoolchildren, dogs, or commuters hurrying by, just a quiet London street, all to himself.

Since it was a splendid June day, he drove with the top down. He was ahead of the weekend traffic, as he had planned, and in less than an hour, he was in Stapleford Tawney. He turned in at the Sheffields' farm and drove down the long country lane toward the cottage.

He drove rapidly, by habit and because Valerie was there. She had gone out to the cottage in midweek to work on her pottery. Travers had promised to join her for the weekend. He had hoped to drive out on Friday afternoon, but his work had kept him at the office. He had stayed at his desk until 10:00 P.M., pouching a number of Field Information Reports back to Langley. The FIRs were the raw intelligence reports compiled by the station, and although he did not have to, he liked to read and initial all of them before the bag was sealed and sent down to the couriers. The FIRs tended to pile up toward the end of the week.

The more important reports, and those of immediate significance, were cabled to Langley in messages known as Intels. Travers' Intels were signed J. Wesley Brindel, the pseudonym that the company had given him years before when he had completed his junior officer training. For security reasons, it was required that all agency communications be signed in pseudonym.

As he bumped along the dirt lane through the green fields, he thought of his lunch with Dick Austin earlier in the week. He would have liked to have taken him fully into his confidence, but for Dick's own sake he had not. Austin understood by now that they were on the trail of nuclear missiles, but Travers had not briefed him on the full picture. Spectrum was too dangerous a secret to share with a friend. He worried enough as it was about Valerie's involvement and her physical safety. He did not want to jeopardize the lives of Dick and Diana as well.

He came to the end of the lane. The narrow road broadened there, enough for cars to turn around at the bottom of the hill below the cottage. He parked next to Valerie's white Marina, grabbed his leather bag, and loped up the path to the cottage.

Valerie had heard the car, and she was waiting outside the front door in clay-spattered blue jeans and an old cotton blouse. She gave him a quick kiss, but held her hands out away from his body.

"Hello, darling," she said. "I'm full of clay so I mustn't get it all over your shirt. I missed you last night."

"Had to work late," he said. "The usual Friday crunch. But I'm worth waiting for, right?" He kissed her, careful to avoid the clay.

"No," she said. "You're a conceited spy and you haven't even shaved this morning. Furthermore, you molest innocent girls in the shower." She kissed him again, lightly. "And I love you. God, I love you, Rob."

"I love you, too." He hugged her, felt the warmth of her body, and inhaled the sweet scent of her cologne.

"Even though you're conceited, would you like some coffee?"

"Even though I'm not conceited, I'd like some."

They went inside. Valerie brought the coffee from the stove and they sat at the kitchen table drinking it from mugs that she had made, happy to be alone together. As Travers had grown older, he had learned to treasure good moments like this. The warm feeling of being together after a short separation. Twenty years earlier, he would not have appreciated the moment. But twenty years ago, he realized, he would not have been sitting in a cottage in Essex with a beautiful younger woman with whom he was deeply in love. He would have been in his apartment on the Sandgasse in Vienna, and Margaret would have been complaining about the other wives in the station.

"How did the week go?" Valerie asked.

"Not fast enough."

"Did Dick Austin get back?"

"He did, and he may have come up with something important. There seems a good chance that the missiles were moved in U.S. mail trucks."

"How will that help?"

"Well, Ben Goodman is trying to locate Site Orange. He's checking suburbs, towns, farms, and villages around Washington, following several leads. It's barely possible he'll run into someone who will remember seeing a convoy of mail trucks."

They finished the coffee and moved into the living room of the cottage, at one end of which Valerie had set up her workshop. She mixed her own clay and stored it in airtight containers. She removed a batch and sat down at the wedging table to knead it. She cut a ball of clay in half with a copper wire, slammed one half hard against the other, and repeated the whole process for ten minutes.

"How long has it been since I mailed the letter from Zurich?" she asked as she pounded the clay.

"Over six weeks."

"And no reaction at all from your Mr. Black?"

"Nothing. Not a blip on the screen. It's as though we dropped the letter into the Grand Canyon. Why do you have to beat up the clay that much?"

"To get the air bubbles out. You can't make pottery with air bubbles. It explodes in the kiln."

"Ah, I see." Travers could not help himself; he soaked up information even when he was not working. It had become automatic, a reflex action. Sometimes Travers worried that he was in danger of becoming a human sponge.

Valerie moved over to the kick-wheel, sat down and carefully centered a ball of clay on the wheel. "But you think he will react?"

"I think so."

The wheel was spinning rapidly. Valerie opened the clay, making a hole in the top of the ball with her thumbs. She deftly pulled up and molded the clay, bracing one hand against the other to steady them, using her left thumb as a bridge. Travers watched her. A bowl was taking shape before his eyes, so quickly that it almost seemed a feat of magic. He was always amazed at how swiftly Valerie could produce a fully formed piece on the wheel.

"What's it going to be?" he asked.

"Just a bowl. To match the pitchers and cups that are drying over there. When do you think something . . . might happen?"

"There's no way to tell."

"But no sign of anything yet?"

"Nothing." He watched her fingers moving delicately back and forth. "Why do you have to work so quickly when the wheel is turning?"

"If you overwork the clay it collapses, or tears. It's like anything else. People. Feelings."

Only a few minutes had passed, but the piece was finished. Valerie cut the bowl off the wheel with a thin strand of wire stretched tightly between her hands. She set it on a shelf to dry. "Do you really think he'll try to have you killed?"

"I don't know. It's very possible."

"And yet if he doesn't try, the committee won't believe you."

"That's about it."

She shook her head. "Why didn't you go into some other line of work, Rob?"

"I wasn't smart enough."

Valerie laughed. But she was frightened all the same. "It's

like a cat-and-mouse game," she said. "And we're the mouse."

Travers tried to reassure her. "Dick Austin's information may help. I want you to write to Ben Goodman. Tell him we think the packages may have been moved in mail trucks."

"All right."

It had been arranged that Valerie and Ben would communicate by letter. Ben's letters were addressed to Valerie's flat in Chelsea. Valerie wrote to Goodman at his home address in Cleveland Park, on Newark Street. There would be no reason for the agency to intercept their mail unless the link between Travers, Valerie, and Goodman had somehow been traced by headquarters, which Travers doubted.

Val worked at her kick-wheel for the rest of the morning. Travers went out and chopped some wood for the fireplace. At noon, Valerie packed a lunch and they went for a long walk across the meadows that sloped gently downward from the back of the cottage. They picnicked in the shade of a willow tree on the bank of a narrow stream.

Valerie had brought some hard-boiled eggs, cold chicken, and a bottle of Chablis. She produced two glasses from the wicker basket and Travers poured a little for both of them.

"Sometimes I have days," he said, "when I wonder whether I have any right to do what I'm doing."

"As much right as the company has to overthrow governments, assassinate people, and lie to your Congress."

"It isn't that. Life is a series of choices. Politically, morally, I believe in the choices I've made. The agency is corrupt, and I'm fighting it."

"Then why the doubts?"

"I wonder if I have the right to endanger your life. If they come after me, you might be with me when it happens."

"I wouldn't want to be anywhere else." She leaned over and kissed him on the lips.

"You're sure of that?"

"Yes. That's *my* choice."

"There's Dick Austin, too. He knows a certain amount now, and I may have put him in jeopardy."

"But surely you told him there was a risk?"

"Of course."

"Then he has made his choice, too. Rob, do what you must do. Don't take on the burden of the whole world. You can't take care of everyone. You can't be responsible for everyone. People are responsible for their own acts."

"It's not that simple. I've asked agents to do things that have placed them in great danger. Some of them have been rolled up and killed. Who was responsible for that?"

Only the birds, chirping in the willows, answered him. But then Valerie said, "My father was in Special Operations Executive during the war. He was part of Operation North Pole. That was the Germans' name for it. We parachuted fifty-four Dutch agents back into occupied Holland. The German direction-finding was too good. The Abwehr found the transmitters and captured them all. Then they used the captured radios to lure in more agents, and bombers as well, for air drops of supplies and weapons. They called it a *Funkspiel*, a 'wireless game.' Most of the bombers were shot down after they had made their drops. Only five of the agents survived. Forty-seven were shot without trial at Mauthausen. My father has never talked about it to me. But my mother told me about the pain that he felt when he found out the truth."

"Then you do understand."

"Yes. Of course."

Travers said, "My father would have cheered what I'm doing. He was fiercely independent. He always told me to follow my own star." Stewart Richardson Travers was a successful businessman who had turned a small machine shop into a large and successful tool company near Boston. The family lived in Manchester in a big frame house set high over the water above a rocky cove. Some of the most prominent families in Massachusetts were their neighbors. The Fricks had a summer place in Prides Crossing, and the Cabots, the Lodges, the Coolidges, and the Hunnewells all spent time on the North Shore. But Stewart Travers, despite his success, was never fully accepted by Boston society. He was seldom invited to dine in the great houses of his Brahmin neighbors. For one thing, he was an Australian, who had come to the States in his late teens, aboard a merchant ship. It was all right to have arrived in Massachusetts on a ship, Stewart discovered, provided it was the *Mayflower*. For another thing, he was an unconventional man who acted as his conscience commanded. He had shocked his fellow members of the exclusive Myopia Hunt Club—it had been eccentrically named by its founder, an ophthalmologist—by proposing a black attorney as a member. The president of the club acidly suggested that Stewart's friend apply for work as a caddy. Stewart punched the club president in the jaw and was asked to resign. It had occurred to Robert that because his father had not been accepted by the Cabots and the Lodges, he had become an iconoclast at least in part to live up to their opinion of him. To some extent, he had become what others already thought he was.

"You loved him, didn't you?"

"Yes. He taught me so many things. He taught me how to sail. We had a Herreshoff 12. It was gaff-rigged, with a short mast and a one-ton keel, so it was very stable. By the time I was twelve, I knew every cove between Beverly and Gloucester. He never once told me to be careful; he just assumed I would be. I felt very free. There are beaches along the North Shore that you can get to only by boat. I would take a lunch, anchor offshore and go skinny-dipping. Once, when I was a little older, I sailed to the Isles of Shoals. There's a church on one of the islands. You're in the middle of nowhere, out of sight of the mainland, but you wake up in the morning to the sound of church bells."

"It must have been lovely."

"It was a good time for me. In the summers, we went to Nantucket."

"And your mother?"

"She would have been happier if she had had something to do besides taking care of the family. She was a brilliant woman with no outlet for her creative talents. Before her marriage, she had just begun to gain recognition as a pianist."

"And she didn't keep it up?"

"No. She practiced, and I loved to listen to her. But she gave no more recitals."

"That's a great pity."

"Yes."

Travers lay down in the grass, and rested his head in

Valerie's lap. He looked up and watched the white, puffy clouds race across the blue sky.

Valerie traced the outline of his eyebrows with her finger. "Why did you leave Margaret? You've never said."

"She left me, actually. I've never said because there isn't much to say."

Valerie leaned over and kissed him. "Darling," she said.

"It was fairly predictable, really. I married a year out of Yale. She was beautiful, but from a rather conventional background. Her father was a banker in Philadelphia. They were very Main Line. I was posted overseas after my JOT training, to Berlin and then Vienna, and Margaret didn't like it. Everything was foreign. She complained about waiting in line at the butcher, the baker, and the candlestick maker. She was bored with the other embassy wives. She felt they were below her socially, and most of them were. And she said I never talked about my work, which was true. It's a fairly common complaint in the agency; the husband gets deeper and deeper into his clandestine work, goes off on unexplained trips, and keeps appointments at eleven o'clock at night. The wife naturally begins to imagine all sorts of things, sometimes with good reason. A guy sent off on a trip to Paris with liberal operational funds may forget he has a wife back in Vienna. The girls at the Crazy Horse look pretty sensational."

"So it wasn't all that easy for Margaret?"

"I suppose not. No wife likes her husband to have secrets from her. There was a lot I couldn't share."

"When did things begin to fall apart?"

"We were sent back to Washington for a while, and things improved slightly. When I was running the Domestic Operations Division. But then we went to Rome, for reasons you know about, and Margaret went wild. She was spending money on decorating, dinner parties, and clothes, as though she had invented La Dolce Vita all by herself. An agency salary in those days didn't go very far. We weren't getting along at all. We argued bitterly about money, and about my work."

"And that's when she left you, in Rome?"

"Yep. Took the children and flew right back to her mother in Bryn Mawr. The divorce came through in 1973."

"How often do you see the children?"

"Not often enough. They're great kids. Melissa is twenty-one and has a job in a book-publishing house in New York. Jack is sixteen and a junior at Deerfield Academy. He's a track star, and very handsome. Believe it or not, they write to me often."

"I'd love to meet them."

"Oh, they'd like you, I know it. Especially Jack would. You might have to watch out for him."

"It's in the genes, I suppose." Valerie laughed. But secretly, she was very pleased. In part because of the nature of his work, Travers was a very private man. It was the first time that he had really opened up and talked much about his family.

They sat by the stream a while longer, and finished the bottle of wine. Then Valerie said, "Let's go back. I want to fire the kiln."

Grumbling a little, Travers got up. "I was just settling down for the afternoon," he said. They packed up the picnic basket and strolled back toward the cottage at a leisurely pace.

"It's odd," Valerie said. "I have absolutely no sense of danger here, although I know I should. It's so idyllic."

"No one will find us here."

"I hope not."

Back at the cottage, Valerie returned to her worktable and prepared her pots for the kiln. Travers settled down near the fireplace with a paperback novel. From the shelves, Valerie took down several pieces of bisque ware that had already been fired once and were ready for the second, glaze firing. She began preparing the glaze in a bucket. She was using Leach Clear Glaze and slowly added water to the powder. Carefully, she dipped the chalk-dry pots in the glaze, then set each piece on a wooden table. She had waxed the bottom of the pieces to keep the glaze off so they would not stick to the shelves of the kiln.

She worked most of the afternoon. Then she came over and perched on the arm of Robert's chair. He looked up from his book. "Will you help me stack the kiln?" she asked.

"Sure. Provided that, afterward, you'll stop working and have a drink."

"Deal."

Travers helped her carry the pieces out back to the shed and Valerie carefully placed them inside the kiln. They had to make several trips. They carried bowls, pitchers, vases, cups, and plates. Valerie put them inside the bricks, making sure that the pieces did not touch each other. Then she turned on the kiln.

"How long will you leave the pieces in?"

"Until tomorrow afternoon. I'll get up early and turn off the kiln. But it will have to cool most of the day before we can take the pots out."

"I think your ceramics are very beautiful. They remind me of you."

"You're sweet to say so."

"No, I mean it."

It was getting dark and rather chilly in the cottage, so Travers built a fire. They sat by it on big pillows, and Valerie opened a bottle of Soave.

"It's been a perfect day," Valerie said.

"Yes. But I'm getting hungry."

"C'mon then. I've got something good for supper." They went into the kitchen and Val unwrapped a package of veal that she had bought in Ongar, a nearby village, the day before.

"You fix the salad," Travers said, "and I'll make veal piccata. My favorite dish." He sliced the veal into very thin strips and laid them out between sheets of wax paper. He went outside to the shed and came back with a narrow length of board, which he used to pound the meat to make it even thinner. He seasoned the veal with salt and pepper and lightly brushed it with flour. Then he heated some butter in a big skillet and browned the slices for a couple of minutes on each side. He put the meat on a platter, squeezed almost all the juice from a lemon into the pan, added some chopped parsley, and then poured the sauce over the meat.

Valerie was impressed. "Where did you learn to do that?" she asked admiringly.

"In Rome, a long time ago. From Mario Catucci, the one-eyed owner of a trattoria on the Via Chiavari."

"It looks fabulous. Let's eat by the fire. It's gloomy in the kitchen."

They settled back on the pillows by the fire and ate their dinner. The Soave was just right with the veal, and Travers, looking at Valerie by the firelight, and having drunk a lot of wine, wondered what he had done to be so lucky, to have spent this day with this woman.

Travers poured half a glass of wine after dinner and stared into the fire. "You know it's ironic," he said.

"What is, darling?"

"For me to be dangled. That's what the committee is doing with me, you know. I've dangled enough agents in my time. Put them out as bait and exposed them to danger. But now *I'm* the one who's being dangled."

Val giggled. "It sounds awfully sexy. All that talk about dangling."

"Don't tell me you've been lonely out here all by yourself."

Valerie did not reply but unzipped him. "I adore making love by the fire," she said in a low voice. She reached in and touched him.

Travers took her wrist and gently pulled her hand away. He sat up and put his finger to his lips.

Then Valerie heard it, too, the muffled sound of an approaching car. The crackling of the fire and their conversation had drowned out the noise until now.

"Who could it be?" she asked. "I wasn't expecting the Sheffields."

Travers sprang up, dashed into the kitchen and turned off the light. Now the only light in the cottage came from the fire. He took Valerie's hand and led her quickly into the bedroom. "Stay down," he ordered. He peered out the window. In the darkness, he could only see the headlights of the car, nothing else. Whoever it was had stopped at the bottom of the hill.

"It must be someone who's lost their way," Valerie whispered. "No one comes down this lane. And no one knows we're here."

"It isn't a stray," Travers said tensely. "He's turned off the engine and the headlights. But he hasn't opened the car door. He's just sitting there."

"Perhaps it's just a couple of teenagers come to neck."

"No. They wouldn't park so close to the two cars."

"Well, let's just wait a few minutes. Perhaps they'll go away."

They waited in the darkness of the bedroom but heard no sound. Five minutes went by. Valerie reached up and found Travers' hand. "I'm scared," she said quietly.

"Stay down."

"What are we going to do?"

"I don't like playing possum. I'd rather know what we're up against. I'm going out to have a look."

Travers considered the terrain. On one side of the path leading down to the car there was only grassy, open meadow. It would provide no cover. But there were bushes and heavy undergrowth along the other side of the path. "I'm going out the back door and down through the bushes parallel to the path. There's an old streambed in there and I can follow it down. If I hear anyone coming up the hill, I'll cut over and intercept them. When I get to the bottom, I'll work my way through the copse and try to come out behind the car. I want to get a closer look at it—and at the driver."

Valerie grasped his hand again. Her own hand was ice-cold. "Rob, for God's sake, be careful."

"Don't worry. Lock the door behind me. Then get back in here. Stay on the floor and don't go in the other room. I don't think anyone will get by me and up to the cottage, but there's always a chance they will. Whatever you do, don't put yourself between the fireplace and the window. You'll make too good a target."

"All right, Rob. I'll do as you say. Come back as soon as you can."

"I will." He paused. "Valerie, if anything happens to me, stay inside. Don't come out."

He plunged into a thicket behind the cottage and began working his way down the hill, through the undergrowth. He ripped his shirt on a thorny vine. Sharp branches tore at his face and arms. It was a dark night. The moon and stars were intermittently covered by clouds, but he had not dared to take a flashlight for fear of being seen by whoever waited below. It was slow going. He had to feel and fight his way through the bushes and he stumbled several times. His pace picked up considerably when he hit the old streambed, but as he got closer to the bottom he had to slow down again to avoid making noise.

He calculated that he was about thirty feet to the side of the path. He worked his way carefully through the dense thicket that bordered the lane. If he had figured the distance correctly, he would come out at the road about ten feet behind the car.

Travers was not sure what he would do then. He had not expected trouble here; his automatic was back at his flat in Bryanston Square. But he hoped at least to get close enough to the car to try to read the license plate, determine the make, and catch a glimpse of the driver. If the intruder was out of the car, he might be able to get close enough to jump him.

Travers stopped dead. A few feet ahead he could dimly see an open space; he had come to the lane. He crouched down and inched forward the last few feet. He had guessed correctly; looming ahead in the darkness was the car. It looked like a Mercedes, but in the blackness he could not be sure. Its lights were off and there was no way to tell if the driver was still sitting behind the wheel. The rear license plate had been smeared with mud.

Still crouching, Travers crept forward, closer to the car. As he did, he stepped on a small branch. It cracked noisily. Travers swore under his breath. Instantly, the engine roared to life. The car swung around sharply, power steering screeching, and the headlights blazed on. Travers dove for cover. He wasn't fast enough; for a second he was caught in the full glare of the beams, like a jacked deer. There was the sharp crack of a gun, and Travers felt a searing pain as he hit the ground. The bullet had missed, but his right leg had been gashed by the sharp rocks along the edge of the road. He kept his face down and his body flattened against the ground as the car peeled out and roared down the lane out of sight.

In the cottage, Valerie heard the shot and saw the car race

away, the red taillights receding rapidly into the distance. With the car gone, she decided it was safe to disregard Robert's instructions. She grabbed a flashlight, unbolted the front door, and ran down the path.

"Rob!" she shouted. "Rob! Where are you?"

"Over here, Val," he answered.

She found him propped up on one elbow by the side of the lane.

"Are you all right? I heard a shot."

"I'm okay. The bullet was well over my head. It wasn't meant to hit me. Just to keep me pinned down while our visitor made his getaway."

"Oh my God, look at you."

Travers' face and hands were cut and scratched and his clothing torn from the bushes. His leg was bleeding freely from a three-inch gash. Valerie ripped a strip of cloth from Travers' shirt, which was already torn, and tied it around the wound.

"I'm really okay." Painfully, he got to his feet.

"Robert, who was it? What was he doing?"

"I don't know who it was. I couldn't get a look at him. I think the car was a black Mercedes, but I couldn't read the plate. As to what he was doing, he was casing the cottage. He didn't come to kill me. This time."

"But how did he find us here? No one knows I've rented the place from the Sheffields. I'm sure I wasn't followed. You've taught me to check the rearview mirror."

"I wasn't tailed, either. Traffic was light coming out. I would have noticed. So there must be some other explanation."

"But what?"

Travers limped over to his TR7. He raised the hood. "Shine the light over here," he ordered.

Valerie did, and Travers searched around the carburetor and the engine. He ran his fingers along the sides of the battery. Suddenly he stopped. He reached down swiftly under the battery and ripped out a tiny black cube, no bigger than a thumbnail, with two tiny strands of wire trailing from the bottom.

"The answer to the mystery," he said. "A transmitter, powered off the car battery whether or not the engine is running. It broadcasts a signal to a directional indicator, probably mounted right on his dash. All he had to do was follow the beeps to our doorstep. Better than a road map."

"But when did he put the bug in?"

"Almost anytime. I usually park on the street near my flat. It could have been dropped in at night. It only takes a minute or two to install."

Valerie was shivering. "Let's go back to the cottage. I'll fix up your leg."

"I'm okay."

They made their way back up the path, Travers moving painfully. Valerie sat Robert down by the fire and went into the bathroom. She returned with some cotton and a bottle of alcohol. He winced as she cleaned out the wound on his leg and bandaged it.

"Will he come back?" she asked.

"Not tonight. But this means you really shouldn't come out here by yourself anymore. I'm sorry about that. I know how much you love the place."

"It's all right."

"We can still come together on the weekends. But I'd better bring a gun."

"It won't be the same, now."

"No."

"It's frightening, being stalked," Valerie said. "There's no way to know where or when he'll turn up again."

"You'll have to be careful at your flat from now on, I'm afraid. He'll have seen your license plate, and he'll be able to trace it to your address."

Valerie huddled by the fire to keep warm. "So now they know about us."

"Yes."

"I think I resent that part the most. Our love has been secret, and very private. Now they've taken that away."

Travers did not reply. He went into the kitchen and brought back a bottle of brandy and two glasses. He poured them each a slug.

"What you said when we were sitting under the willow

trees, about not wanting to be anywhere else when the danger came. Do you still mean it?"

"Yes." She kissed him.

"When you write to Ben," Travers said, "tell him what happened. Tell him it's begun."

"Yes," she said. "I'll tell him."

"And he'd best write to you from now on at the shop in King's Road that sells your pottery. Send him the address. Your flat's no good anymore."

They sat by the fire, sipping the brandy, and after a while they took off their clothes and made love on the pillows by the hearth. But Robert's leg ached, and he was distracted. He drifted off to sleep thinking of the black Mercedes.

In the morning, Valerie was up early to inspect the kiln. She peered through a small hole in the door. The cones she had placed inside to measure the temperature had melted, so she turned the gas jets off.

Later in the morning, they took a long walk together. After lunch they stayed close by the cottage, waiting for the kiln to cool. Late in the afternoon Valerie decided it could be opened. It was the moment she liked best. The first glimpse of the finished stoneware when she opened the door to the firing chamber. Most of the pots had turned out well. There was a fine network of cracks on two of the bowls; Valerie assumed the crazing had been caused by uneven temperatures in the kiln. But on the whole, she was pleased with the lot.

Toward evening, they left to drive back into London. Robert suggested dinner at his place, but Val said she had to go back to straighten up her flat. "It's an awful mess. I haven't been there since Wednesday. And I think I'll take a bath and wash the clay out of my hair."

"All right. I'll follow you into town. But call me when you get home."

"I will, darling." They embraced by the cars. "Take care, Rob. Please take care."

"Don't worry." He kissed her gently. He watched her drive off a short distance in the Marina, then started up the TR7. He wondered whether his visitor from the night before might still be somewhere in the vicinity, hoping to pick up the signal from under the hood. He took some grim satisfaction from knowing that whoever it was would be wondering by now whether the device had malfunctioned or had been discovered and ripped out.

The Sunday traffic was heavy going into the city, but he managed to stay behind Valerie. On Baker Street he waved good-bye and she waved back. He parked in Bryanston Square and got his bag out of the car. As he approached the front door, he saw Mrs. Wilson peering out from behind a curtain of her ground-floor flat. She intercepted him in the hall, in a highly agitated state.

"Oh, Mr. Travers, I do hope I did the right thing. He said he was from the embassy, a very official-looking gentleman, and he showed me a card that said 'United States of America, Department of State.' He insisted on going to your flat, and he said it was very important official business, so Mr. Travers, I let him in. He stayed for about half an hour and then he left. I do hope it was all right."

Travers cursed inwardly, but he smiled. There was no point in getting Mrs. Wilson even more upset. "I'm sure you did the right thing, Mrs. Wilson. Could you describe the man?"

"Well, I suppose you would say he was on the short side, very dark-haired and thin, with sharp features. He was an Irish gentleman from the looks of him."

Pat Nolan. Travers wondered what had brought the station's security officer to his flat, unannounced, on a weekend. He would find out in the morning. He also wondered, as he went up the stairs, whether it had any connection with the man in the black Mercedes.

He fished for his key and opened the door. The flat looked untouched. Nothing was out of place. Not a book or a paper. Whatever Nolan had done, he had done professionally.

He checked the bedroom, living room, kitchen, and bath, but there was nothing to be seen. He was helping himself to a beer from the fridge when the telephone rang.

"Hello, darling, I'm home, safe and sound."

"Good. Thanks for remembering to call."

"I've got some news. A letter from Uncle Ben."

"What's he have to say?"

"He says his retriever has had puppies."

Chapter 17

Pat Nolan tried to hide his embarrassment with a shrug and a grin. He was a New York Irishman, that special breed, who had found he could soft-shoe his way through life, relying on his charm if he missed a step.

Travers was not amused. He had called Nolan into his office, and for once, it was the security man who was being grilled. "What the hell is going on, Pat?" Travers demanded. "If it was a training exercise, you fellas can damn well practice your break-ins somewhere else."

"It wasn't a break-in," Nolan protested, looking wounded. "We had the landlady's approval."

"I know that," Travers said drily. "You want some kind of medal for conning a sixty-five-year-old woman? What were you doing in the flat?"

"It was a panty raid," Nolan said. "Nothing to get excited about. Headquarters has ordered ferret searches by the security officers in all stations. Residential targets, from the COS on down."

"What the hell for?"

"Ever since the manual for the Keyhole-Eleven was sold to the Sovs, OS has been goosey. Big Bird was our most effective reconnaissance satellite. You remember what happened when the case came to trial; we had to admit that thirteen other copies were missing and unaccounted for. Well, it was worse than that. A couple of months ago, we discovered the number of missing manuals was actually much higher."

"And that's your justification for the flash raids?"

Nolan shrugged. "Too many people are breaking the rules and taking stuff home to read at night. Sometimes I think this place is a lending library. By the way, we didn't find anything in your flat."

"There wasn't anything to find." At least not now, Travers thought; he had given the top-secret cover sheet for Operation Spectrum to Barry Owens.

"Aw, I know that, Rob. I was just doing my job." The Irish smile again.

Travers was silent for a moment. "Look, Pat," he said, "I spent the weekend in the country. Someone followed me out there and took a shot at me. Could there have been any connection with your visit to my flat?"

For once, Nolan didn't smile. "It wasn't us. My God, Rob, we did a little bag job on your flat, under orders. But the company wouldn't target one of its own station chiefs. Come on."

"I thought perhaps my visitor in the country was there to make sure I didn't return to London unexpectedly and surprise you in my flat."

"No, I swear we had nothing to do with it. Maybe it was one of Rumin's goons."

"Maybe."

Travers opened the top drawer of his desk, and removed a small object. He handed it to Nolan. "This is how they found me."

The security man stared at the little black cube. His face had turned white.

"What's the matter?" Travers needled. "Haven't you ever seen a transmitter before?"

"Of course. Hundreds."

"Then what's the problem?"

"This one looks like one of ours."

Howard Radner closed the front door of the red-brick, federal-style town house in Georgetown that he shared with three other young lawyers, two men and a woman. The woman was his roommate. Attaché case in hand, he walked up 30th Street to the corner. He stopped in Morgan's for a copy of *The Washington Post* and then headed for the P Street bridge.

It was hot and humid, a typical late-June day in Washington, and by the time Radner had reached the bridge, his shirt was damp. He removed his jacket and slung it over his shoulder. Once he was on an air-conditioned subway car, he knew, it would be cool.

At twenty-eight, Howie Radner was doing nicely. His father owned a dry-cleaning store in Bensonhurst, a mixed Jewish and Italian neighborhood in Brooklyn, but Radner, a brilliant student, had made it across the East River. He had graduated near the top of his class at Columbia Law School and landed a job with Cravath, Swaine & Moore, one of the great WASP law firms in the canyons of Lower Manhattan. Norm Fine, one of his classmates at Columbia, had gone to work for Senator Javits in Washington. A few months later, he had telephoned Radner to tell him about an opening on Senator Owens' committee staff. Radner flew to Washington for an interview with the senator and was hired on the spot.

For the past year, he had lived in the house in Georgetown with Julie Cahn, an attractive Radcliffe and Harvard Law School graduate who worked for a public-interest law firm on L Street. He preferred having a beautiful housemate to fighting the singles scene at Clyde's or prowling the meat rack at the Greenery. His job was stimulating, he got along well with his boss, Ben Goodman, and Julie was no more interested in marriage at this point than he was. She was content to have what she called a meaningful relationship.

He took the escalator down into the Metro station at Dupont Circle, bought a fare card from the machine, and rode the Red Line to Union Station. It was only a short walk from the station to the Capitol and the committee offices in the New Senate Office Building.

Linda, the plump secretary from Silver Spring who loved cats, came jiggling into his office before he had even hung up his jacket on the coat stand. "Ben wants to see you the minute you come in," she said. "And you're in."

Radner made his way around the corner to Goodman's cluttered cubicle and found Ben. He was sitting at his desk, cigar in hand, poring over what looked like a pile of teletype printouts.

"Howie, my friend," Ben said, waving his cigar in the air, "we have good news this morning. The Crawfish has come across. The first batch of cables came in by special courier from Fort Meade a few minutes ago."

"Terrific!" Radner was excited.

"I want you to go over them. I'm not going to have the time once this stuff starts to flood in. You become the resident expert on the agency's Intels. You can set aside the cables to or from New Delhi and Accra, of course. We're only interested in traffic in and out of the London station."

"You want me to drop everything else? I've been deep into microwaves, preparing for the NSA hearings."

Ben took the cigar out of his mouth. "There aren't going to be any NSA hearings."

It was the first Radner had heard. But he thought he understood. "The admiral drives a hard bargain."

Goodman scowled. "Let's just say that the senator has other priorities right now. It's not for you to wonder why, Howie."

Radner picked up the pile of printouts and tucked them under his arm. As he walked out, Goodman said, "Let me know the second you find anything."

Back in his office, Radner closed the door, sat down and began plowing through the traffic. It was an exciting feeling. Not too many other kids from Bensonhurst were sitting in Washington in a United States Senate office reading the CIA's top-secret cables. He wished he could tell his father. But on second thought, he realized that Morris Radner might not approve. ("Howard, what you're doing, this is right, this is proper? I didn't raise my boy to be a sneaker!")

He wished even more that he could tell Julie. But she accepted the fact that there were certain aspects of his work that he could not share with her. A friend of his, a young public-interest lawyer, had played one of the Nixon Watergate tapes at a Georgetown cocktail party and gotten into trouble over it. Radner, working on the Intelligence Committee, had learned to be discreet.

If the assignment to read the Intels was exciting, the

substance of many of the cables proved a good deal less so. In one long message, Harding Westerfield complained to the Directorate of Administration that the London station's allowance for office supplies was too low. The station had been forced to buy a cheap brand of felt pen, one of which had leaked through a pocket and ruined his shirt, an expensive striped broadcloth from Turnbull & Asser. The auditors in the Directorate of Administration messaged back tartly that the supply budget could not be increased and that, furthermore, headquarters would not pay for the shirt.

There was a report from MI6, relayed to Langley by J. Wesley Brindel, which Radner assumed, correctly, to be Travers' pseudonym. The British report presented new evidence in support of a 1978 MI6 analysis of Soviet military strategy.

In the earlier report, the Soviet president had been quoted as saying that détente was a stratagem to allow the Soviets to build up their forces until the world balance of power shifted in Moscow's favor by 1985. According to MI6, the Soviet leader confided these thoughts to a meeting of East European Communist leaders in Prague. But the CIA had not accepted the Century House analysis. In a covering Intel, Travers reminded Langley that the agency's own sources at the Prague meeting had denied that the Soviet president ever made the statement. "C is still flailing a dead horse," Travers messaged.

Radner scanned with interest another report from London addressed to the DCI and Brooks Abbot, the director of Counterintelligence, detailing the difficulties that the station was having with LS/Primrose-1 and -2, and the remedial steps being taken by Phyllis R. Quigg. Radner had no way of knowing that this was the agency pseudonym of Lisa Layton.

There were several cables back and forth between the London station and the DDO about a fleet of Boeing 707 jetliners that had been sold by Israel, through a Mossad laundry in Zurich, to Uganda Airlines. On their run between Kampala and Europe, the planes refueled at a military airport in Bengazi. The real purpose of the arrangement was to collect overflight intelligence on Libya, and the reports were shared by Mossad, MI6, and the CIA. The operation was called Triple Play. But the original deal had been made with Idi Amin, who got the planes at a cut-rate price, and the present government in Uganda had notified Whitehall that it wished to discontinue the arrangement. London station was instructed to ask MI6 to request that the Foreign Office place pressure on Kampala to honor the original commitment.

There were reams of traffic, back and forth, dealing with Angola, including a series of messages from Aaron Davidow, the director of the NSC, asking for updated information about the political situation in that country. Davidow also queried London about the logistical problems that might be encountered in secretly airlifting arms to Joseph Mugawe in Zaire for use in Angola. When Davidow had worked for the Church Committee, Radner knew, he had been a vocal critic of covert operations. Not anymore.

But it was a series of personnel transfers in the London station that caught Radner's eye. Kathleen Grant, a secretary in the Joint Reports and Research Unit, and Ken Varney, a case officer in the Political Liaison Section, were being rotated back to headquarters for reassignment. Three new officers in the Clandestine Services were being transferred to London: Mary Jo Farmer, Philip Moffet, and William Hansen.

Radner wrote the three names down on a yellow pad. Then he took a break. He stepped out into the corridor and walked down to the coffee machine, made himself a cup, and added some nondairy creamer, which he loathed. The coffee tasted like the cardboard cup in which it came; it was better than nothing, but just barely. He went back into his office and stared at the yellow pad. He reached for a thick directory on his bookshelf, the *Biographic Register of the Department of State*. It was an old and somewhat dog-eared copy; for the past few years, under pressure from the agency, the State Department had classified the publication.

Radner knew the reason. Frequently, although not always, clandestine officers were listed under diplomatic cover in the *Biographic Register*. He found the woman. Mary Jo Farmer's last post was Tokyo, where she had been a political attaché in the U.S. embassy with a rank of R-5. Before that she had served in Manila and Kuala Lumpur. She had been born in Terre Haute, Indiana, on May 6, 1944, and had graduated from Northwestern University.

He could not find a listing for either Philip Moffet or William Hansen. He reached behind him for a slimmer State Department pamphlet, entitled *Foreign Service List*. It, too, was an old copy; for the same reasons the publication had been discontinued in 1976. Once again, he found an entry for Ms. Farmer in the Tokyo embassy, but drew a blank on both Moffet and Hansen.

Radner picked up the telephone and dialed the Congressional Research Service of the Library of Congress. Outsiders had little understanding of what the service could provide for a member of Congress or a staff assistant. At the touch of a computer button, detailed information on literally any subject was available—databank printouts, background reports, bibliographical lists, abstracts, microfilms, newspaper clippings. Radner reached a Mrs. Moore, a specialist in the Government Division. He asked for a search of the two missing names in all the available back issues of both the *Biographic Register* and the *Foreign Service List*. He was told it would take a couple of hours. She promised to call back.

Next, he called the Social Security Administration. A secretary put him through to Martin O'Rourke, the director of the congressional relations staff. They had met recently, at a reception for Senator Kerwin of Iowa.

"Howard Radner on the Senate Intelligence Committee, Marty. You remember me, I'm with Senator Owens."

"Sure, Howie. What's up? You planning an early retirement?"

"Would that I could. No, I was wondering if I were to give you a name, whether you could match it to a number and tell me anything about the person. It's official business, of course."

"Negative, Howie. Wish I could help. A few years ago we could sometimes do it for a friend. But with the Privacy Act and all that, the answer has to be no. Sorry. I'll try to be more help next time."

"That's okay, Marty. Thanks." Radner hung up and

thought a moment. Then he dialed the Social Security Administration's headquarters in Baltimore and asked for Cindy Blair in Program Operations. Cindy was a stacked blonde from Laurel, Maryland. He had picked her up one night at the Apple Tree two years ago, and dated her for several months until their ardor had cooled and they had each, amicably, moved on.

"Howie!" Cindy sounded genuinely pleased to hear from him. "Howie, how *are* you? It's been months, years. Have you been appointed to the Supreme Court yet?"

"No," Howie replied, "but I'm definitely in the running. Listen, Cindy, can you do me a fantastic favor? I'll remember you in my will. I'll even buy you a drink at the Apple Tree."

"Oh, no, this is where I came in. What kind of a favor, Howie?"

"It's a small thing, really. The senator wants to check out a couple of guys who work for the government. Philip Moffet and William Hansen." He spelled the names. "We'd like to do it sort of unofficially and quietly, you know, without going through a lot of red tape. So I thought of you. Can you do it, darling?"

She sounded doubtful. "We're not supposed to, you know. I could get in trouble for something like that. You say it's for the senator?"

"Right, Barry Owens. He asked me personally to take care of it for him."

"Let me see what I can do and I'll call you back. But I might hold you to that offer of a drink. I just broke up with my boyfriend. It might do my ego good to see you again."

"Thanks, Cindy, you're terrific."

Radner hung up with a self-satisfied smile. He wondered how far he might have to go in the line of duty with Cindy. Well, Julie was very understanding about the things in his work that he couldn't tell her. And that would certainly be one of them.

Next, Radner dialed Sam Carr, the congressional-relations man for the Internal Revenue Service. Sam was an old gray fox, a Hill veteran who had survived half-a-dozen IRS commissioners. He knew everybody.

"Sam? It's Howard Radner with the Senate Intelligence Committee."

"We haven't done anything. Honest."

They both laughed. "It's not like that, Sam. Not this time anyway. I'm checking out some CIA people for Senator Owens' subcommittee. I don't want anything from their returns, like financial information. Just whether they filed, their addresses, marital status, and occupation. That's all. Can you do that?"

"Theoretically, no. Actually, yes. I'm delighted to help you investigate those *momzers*. Do you know we're still trying to untangle their foundation fronts? They created so many goddamn headaches for the service that for six months I was having nothing but aspirin for lunch. The commissioner was up testifying to the House Banking Committee so often that we thought we might as well move his office to the Rayburn Building."

Radner thanked Sam and passed on the two names. Carr wrote them down and promised to call back.

It was past noon. Ben Goodman stuck his head in the door. "How about some lunch, Howie? You can tell me how you're enjoying reading other people's mail."

They walked over to the Monocle in the broiling sun. It was only two blocks to the restaurant, but by the time they got there they were grateful for the air conditioning. They sat down at the bar to have a drink and wait for their table.

Ben had a beer on tap and Radner ordered a gin and tonic.

"So what does it look like?" Ben asked.

"Some of the stuff's incredibly dull. They're like any other bureaucracy. Everyone's creating paper trails to cover their ass. But some of it was pretty fascinating."

"Did you find any gold among the pebbles?"

"I don't think so. But there was some sort of personnel shake-up recently, including three transfers into the London station. I have calls in to a few people to check out the names. Just to see what we can find out about them."

"For Chrissakes, Howie, I didn't ask you to play Woodward and Bernstein. I just wanted you to *read* the stuff."

"It's not going to do any harm. Just a few routine checks."

Goodman was rapidly losing his temper. "It might get piped back to the agency. You never know who's working for them. That would be the last thing we want."

"I hadn't really thought of that," Radner admitted. "But don't worry, it will be all right. I played it very low-key."

"Okay, okay. But from now on, check with me before you do any more investigating. Travers warned us. He said they have people all over the Hill."

"Sure, Ben. They recruited me right out of Columbia Law School. Hadn't I ever mentioned it?"

"Fuck you, Howie." But the joke had broken the tension. Ben was grinning.

The hostess, a pretty girl with long red hair and a low-cut dress, led them to a table. Over lunch, Radner filled Goodman in further on the traffic he had read that morning.

They ordered iced coffee and Ben mixed in sugar and a lot of cream. He watched it swirl, making a marbled pattern in the glass. "I've started looking for Site Orange," Goodman confided.

"How?"

"For openers, I've asked the Pentagon for a list of all military bases within a twenty-five-mile radius of Washington."

"Why twenty-five miles?"

"The maximum range of the Honest John rocket is twenty-three miles," Goodman explained. "If Travers is right about Phase Red, Towny Black would probably have kept the missiles within range of the capital."

"How can the Pentagon help us?"

"I'm hoping the 758th Special Operations Tactical Group will turn up on the list."

"It's not very likely that the unit still exists under that name. Or, if it does, that the Pentagon would even know about it, let alone list it."

"I know it's a long shot. But I figured it was worth starting out that way."

"Have you gotten the list yet?"

"Not yet."

They walked back to the Dirksen Building in the relentless heat. By the time Radner reached his office, his shirt was soaked through. He took off his tie and hung it up next to his jacket.

Linda had left a pink telephone-message slip on his desk to call Mrs. Moore at the Library of Congress. He dialed the number.

"Mr. Radner? I'm sorry it took so long, but I checked both publications going back to 1952. There's no listing for Mr. Moffet or Mr. Hansen."

"Well, I appreciate your looking."

"Have you tried calling the State Department? They must have a record of their former employees."

"That's a really good idea, Mrs. Moore. I'll do that."

Radner hung up. He fiddled with his pencil for a moment. There was a variety of possible explanations, he knew, for the fact that the two names were not listed. For one thing, the directories were out-of-date. And not all of the agency's officers were sent to foreign posts under State Department cover. The two could have served overseas under commercial cover or some other kind of nonofficial cover. Or perhaps both were young officers being posted abroad by the company for the first time.

Ben came in with the final page proofs of the subcommittee's recent hearings on a proposal to make public the total size of the intelligence community's budget. "Check these over in your spare time," Goodman said. "They have to go back to the Government Printing Office by Friday."

Radner started reading the proofs. The proposal was a hardy perennial, always defeated in one branch of Congress or the other. Towny Black had testified that merely revealing the total size of the intelligence budget would permit the KGB to make all sorts of sinister inferences about specific operations. Neither Black nor anyone else had ever explained how this remarkable feat could be accomplished, but the senators, complaisant as always before incantations of national security, had voted to bottle up the bill in committee.

He was interrupted by the telephone. It was Sam Carr.

"Howard? You didn't get this from us, of course, but I have the name checks you wanted."

"That's great, Sam."

"Philip Moffet is twenty-nine. He lives in Old Town,

Alexandria, on South Lee Street. He's filed returns for the past eight years. I can't help you on Hansen. We have no record of him."

"What?"

"Well, the trouble is I'm not really sure we have no record of him. There's nothing on file at the regional headquarters in Philadelphia. But to be positive, we'd have to do a national name check. The problem is that the computer is down in Martinsburg. Anyone who files a federal-income-tax return is in this big computer out in West Virginia. We call it the Martinsburg Monster. But the damn thing is being over-hauled. It'll be two or three weeks before it's back on line and I can get you an answer."

"Let me know, Sam, will you?"

"Sure, Howard. Sorry about the foul-up."

"No problem. We're in no hurry, Sam. Just call me when it comes in."

"Will do."

It was almost five o'clock when Cindy Blair called back. "Hi, Howie," she said. "I've checked out the information you wanted." She lowered her voice. "But I don't think we should talk over the phone."

"I understand. Are you doing anything tonight? We could get together."

"Fantastic, Howie. I'll just zip home and change and then I can meet you downtown."

"Well, I'm stuck working late at the office. But I could see you a little later on. Say nine o'clock at Tramp's?"

"I'll be there." Cindy clicked off.

Howard had promised to take Julie to dinner. They could go somewhere close by in Georgetown. Then he could drop her off at home, make an excuse, and meet Cindy at the disco on Wisconsin Avenue.

Radner took the Metro back to Dupont Circle and walked home. He had time for a shower and a change of clothes before dinner. They went to La Ruche, a little French restaurant south of M Street, that was one of their favorites. During dinner, Julie talked animatedly about the legal proj-ect she was working on.

"We're representing a group of women who want to ban herbicides that are causing spontaneous abortions and mutations. We're in the federal courts. It's a dynamite issue."

"But you're taking on the big chemical companies."

"We think we'll win. Howie, do you know that out in Oregon, the Forest Service was spraying perfectly good deciduous trees with Agent Orange and killing them so that only the evergreens would be left?"

"Why were they doing that?"

"Because some bureaucrat decided that it was tidier to have only one kind of tree growing in each forest."

"It sounds insane. The trees were doing fine for billions of years before the government came along and decided how they should grow."

"Exactly. And the herbicides get into the food chain and cause abortions. First they try to defoliate Vietnam, and now they're defoliating pregnant women in Oregon."

He walked Julie home after dinner and told her he had to go back up to the Hill for a staff meeting that Senator Owens had called on the intelligence budget. He gave her a little peck on the cheek. "Don't wait up," he said. "It may run pretty late."

Cindy was waiting by the entrance to Tramp's. She was wearing white stretch jeans and a dark-blue silk blouse belted at the waist. She looked terrific. There was a line, but they did not have to wait long to get inside.

The disco was crowded with well-dressed, beautiful people, mostly young, although Radner spotted a couple of aging congressmen with what looked like secretaries from the Hill. The music was deafening and the lights were pulsating, casting yellow, red, and blue shadows on the dancers and the mirrors, and on the blow-ups of Charlie Chaplin on the walls. Radner would not have picked it as a place to talk, but Cindy liked to disco.

They fought their way to the bar and Howard had to squeeze past a voluptuous blonde who seemed to be wearing nothing but a fish net. Cindy ordered a Margarita and Radner asked for an Amaretto. They found a table and Cindy took his hand.

"It's terrific to see you, Howie," she said, moving her fingers lightly against his palm.

Radner felt himself turned on by the touch of her hand. The top of Cindy's blouse was unbuttoned and he was staring at her terrific cleavage, trying not to be too obvious, but looking all the same. She was not wearing a bra.

"It's great to see you, too, Cindy. You're looking fabulous." He meant it.

"Hey, thanks, Howie. Do you like my hair this way? I let it grow longer since I saw you last."

"Yeah, I like it. I like it all." He rested his hand on her arm. "And it was really great of you to help me out today."

"Okay, but if I get caught and transferred to Butte, Montana, you and your senator have to go to bat for me."

"Don't worry. What did you find?"

"Your friend Moffet has worked for the spooks for eight years. He's twenty-nine. No spouse. Lives in Alexandria."

It was hard to talk above the din of the music and Cindy had her mouth next to Howard's ear. He didn't mind.

"What about Hansen?"

Cindy touched her tongue to Howard's ear and kissed it. Howard decided he wanted to fuck her. Cindy was very good in bed. He had forgotten all about his meaningful relationship with Julie Cahn.

"Like, that's the weird part," Cindy said.

"What is?"

"According to our records, Hansen is fifty-eight and applied for his first Social Security number six weeks ago."

"That's crazy, Cindy. Nobody goes to work for the first time at age fifty-eight."

"Maybe he's a millionaire who's fallen on hard times. I want to dance, Howie."

They joined the other wildly gyrating couples on the crowded dance floor. It was hot and dark, and the music and the flashing light surrounded them completely. Radner felt as though he and Cindy were suspended together in some giant womb, a warm, flowing liquid of color and sound.

Suddenly Cindy stopped dancing and was pressing her pelvis against him. Her hair was soft and smelled good. "You're turning me on, Howard," she whispered, "just like you always do." He let his right hand slip down to her buttocks.

It was a long drive to Cindy's apartment in Laurel, Radner knew, and he would have some explaining to do in the morning. But, what the hell, he thought, he was on official business for the Select Committee on Intelligence of the United States Senate. *Ask not what your country can do for you, but what you can do for your country.*

"C'mon, Cindy," he said. "I'm taking you home."

Chapter 18

Harrington had taken a service flat in Aubrey Walk, near Holland Park. As "William Hansen," he had paid the landlady three months' rent in advance. The furnished flat was small and overly expensive. He didn't care, since it was the company's money; DiMario had given him a generous operational allowance for LS/Talpia.

He had deliberately chosen a flat close to Notting Hill Gate, a busy high street crowded with small family-owned shops, restaurants, and cinemas. The location insured that there would be people in the area at night, as well as by day. The mixed residential and commercial neighborhood suited Harrington's purposes; it was the kind of place where a man coming and going at odd hours would not attract unusual attention.

At 9:45 A.M. on Thursday he slipped a Minox camera into the pocket of his suit jacket. Carrying a black attaché case, he locked the door behind him and went out. He turned into Campden Hill Road and walked up to the Notting Hill Underground Station.

A few moments later he was on a Central Line train rumbling east. He got off at Marble Arch and took the escalator up to the street. He turned into Great Cumberland Place and walked north to Bryanston Square.

The quiet, residential square formed a long rectangle with a private garden in the center enclosed by a wrought-iron fence. The gates were kept locked, although the residents had keys. Strolling along the west side of the square, Harrington had a clear view of Travers' flat across the way.

For several mornings and three consecutive nights, he had patiently studied the house from a car parked across the square. He saw who came and went and what lights in the windows went on and off. From the pattern of comings and goings, he was able to deduce who lived on each floor. He looked at his watch, and waited.

At precisely 10:30 A.M., as she did on every Monday and Thursday morning, a white-haired woman emerged from the front door and carefully maneuvered a little metal shopping cart down the steps to the sidewalk. She walked south to George Street and turned in the direction of Edgware Road. He waited until she had disappeared from view, then strolled three-quarters of the way around the square. He smiled at a young mother pushing a pram, and she smiled back. There was no one else on the street.

He walked up to the door from which the old woman had emerged four minutes earlier. From his pocket, he removed a thin, flexible strip of plastic, about six inches long. He looked to the right and left. The sidewalk was empty, except for the woman pushing the pram, who was now half a block away walking north, with her back toward him. With a swift, practiced motion, he inserted the shim between the door and the jamb. The latch gave way easily, and he pushed in the door. From the mail lying on the polished wooden table in the front hall, he was able to match names to the faces and facts he already knew. Mrs. Flora Wilson was the elderly woman out shopping for groceries. She lived on the ground floor. Mr. Geoffrey Dawkins occupied the flat above. And Robert Travers had the top floor.

Harrington lumbered up the stairs as rapidly as he could. A dog barked loudly as he passed the first-floor landing. He glanced at his watch. He would have at least forty minutes before Mrs. Wilson returned from her marketing.

Outside Travers' door, he crouched down and examined the lock. He was not happy with what he saw. It was a dead bolt, which meant it could normally be opened only with a key, or from the inside by a thumb latch. Unlike the front door, it could not be shimmed with his plastic strip.

Harrington studied the lock. It was a Union, a standard, British-make pin-tumbler type with a rim cylinder that was surface-mounted on the door. To open it, a paracentric key was inserted in the plug, the inner cylinder that turned the tailpiece of the lock to retract the bolt. Inside the lock, Harrington knew, were five hollow shafts, each containing a spring, a driver pin below it, and finally, a pointed bottom pin. The pins varied in length. The proper key, cut to compensate for these variations, would lift the bottom pins exactly to the shear-line so that the plug was free to turn. It was a simple yet ingenious mechanism, and the basis of most of the locks on most of the doors in the world.

Kneeling in front of the door, Harrington opened the attaché case and removed a tension wrench. The wrench was a deceptively plain-looking instrument, a very thin, flat band of Swedish blue-tempered steel, angled at one end. Next, he took out a diamond pick, so named for the shape of the point. This, too, was a thin, bluish band of tempered steel.

The two little tools were all Harrington needed. He inserted the wrench in the keyhole. He twisted it to the right, to create turning pressure on the plug, then felt for the tumblers with the pick. He was seeking the one that had the most spring tension. He found it, and pushed it up gently. It stayed up, because the plug, under pressure of the wrench, had turned ever so slightly. It was the imperfections in the machining of a lock that made it possible to pick most of them, he knew; if the plug did not turn a thousandth of an inch, the pins would drop back down.

Within a few seconds, Harrington had pushed up four more pins. But the plug would not turn. Harrington tried repeatedly, pressing on the tension wrench until his thumb and forefinger went white. Still the plug refused to move. He realized that he must have pushed one of the pins up beyond the shear-line, but he could not tell which one. There was nothing to do but release all the tumblers and start over again.

He tried four more times, but always with the same result. One of the pins kept jamming in the upper portion of the cylinder. The lock would not yield.

He cursed his luck and checked his watch; six minutes had gone by since he had entered the house. He would have to impression a key. It was a noisy and laborious process, and it meant he would have to spend more time in the hall, where he might be discovered. On the other hand, a key would provide him with a quick means of entry if he ever wanted to return to the flat.

From a ring of key blanks for standard British locks, he selected a Union blank and inserted it into the keyhole. He turned the key slightly to the right as far as he could. Then he took a pair of pliers from the attaché case and gripped the key with it. He yanked the pliers sharply to the right. The movement made a screeching noise that echoed through the landing. On the first floor, the dog started barking furiously. Harrington swore under his breath. He turned the key to the left and jerked the pliers hard in that direction. Then up, then down, repeating the process until he had yanked the key in all four directions. He removed the key and smiled. There were five little marks along the top, indicating the spacing of the tumblers. Harrington took a file from his case and gently started filing down the key where the marks were. After several minutes, he reinserted the key and repeated the blows with the pliers in all four directions. Wherever the marks appeared, he filed some more, repeating the whole procedure until, finally, the pins were no longer marking the key. He inserted it in the lock. It wouldn't turn.

Harrington swore again. He pulled the key out and smoothed two of the notches that appeared to be a little rough. He reinserted the key in the lock, jiggled it, and this time the plug turned. He looked at his watch. It had taken him twenty-one minutes to impression the key. He donned a pair of thin blue surgical gloves and opened the door. He gathered up his tools, put them in the case, snapped it shut, and entered the flat.

He closed the door behind him, locked it from the inside, and stepped into the living room. He removed the Minox from his jacket pocket and photographed the room from several angles. He did the same in the bedroom, kitchen, and bath.

He took a letter-size pad from the attaché case, and using a pencil, drew a sketch of the layout of the flat. There was no rear exit, which surprised him a little; apparently they did not believe in fire escapes in London.

He looked at his watch again. Eight minutes left. He searched each room, quickly and professionally, careful to disturb nothing. In the top drawer of Travers' wardrobe he found a Walther PPK automatic. He racked back the slide part way to see if it was loaded, saw that it was, and carefully replaced the gun in its original position.

In the bathroom, he opened the medicine cabinet and examined its contents. There were half a bottle of sleeping pills, some aspirin, a box of Alka-Seltzer, toothpaste, a Wilkinson razor, and a tube of shaving cream. He shut the cabinet and moved swiftly to the front door. He picked up his case, let himself out, and locked the door with the key. Then he peeled off his rubber gloves, stuffed them in his pocket and walked down the stairs.

He stepped out into the square and walked south, back toward Marble Arch. Two minutes after he had disappeared from view, Mrs. Wilson, her shopping cart laden with groceries, arrived back at her front door.

Harrington crossed Oxford Street and walked down Park Lane, across the street from Hyde Park. He turned in at Upper Brook Street and headed for the embassy. He walked up the front steps and into the entrance to the lobby. As he had expected, the metal detector squealed when he passed through it, responding to all the hardware in his attaché case. He smiled, showed his ID card to the uniformed guard at the desk, and was waved through.

He rode the elevator to the fourth floor. In his office, Harrington locked the door, hung up his jacket, and sat down at his desk. He opened the attaché case, and removed the sketch he had made of Travers' flat.

He wished Shirley were with him in London instead of

trimming fingernails in Crystal City. Well, he would see her soon enough. Harrington did not plan on staying in England more than another few weeks at most. He figured it would take him about that long to draft an operational plan, obtain headquarters' approval, and complete the mission.

From his desk drawer, Harrington removed a sheet of white paper. He picked up a pencil and slowly composed a long message:

DIRECTOR EYES ONLY
INTEL
SUPDATA LS/TALPIA after initial investigation of target.
Date: July 2, 1981
Subject: Approach to target.
Country: UK
Source Description: LS/TALPIA
Text: Insertion in station accomplished without difficulty. Have been assigned by COS to assist Phyllis R. QUIGG in neutralizing Sov threat to OP-LP operated by LS/PRIMROSE-1 and PRIMROSE-2.

Target spent weekend in cottage near Romford, Essex. Two cars were parked below cottage. One, GB license BKF321G, is registered in the name of Valerie R. KERR, 16 Margaretta Terrace, Chelsea. Occupation not determined. Other vehicle registered in target's name. Cottage is not, repeat not, suitable for operational purposes. It is located on a hill top, approximately 120 meters above parking area, making an unobserved approach to target extremely difficult. An attempt at termination from the parking area itself would be feasible only if the target presented himself in the open, and would have a poor chance of success. Although the assigned weapon has an effective range of 120 meters, accuracy is doubtful at that distance, as with any weapon near the outer limits of range. Also, probably presence of the female, KERR, is undesirable, as she might witness termination. Should this occur at whatever location is finally selected, it might require her termination as well, if you approve. Please advise.

Target resides in London at Number 14 Bryanston Square in flat on second floor of building, which is the top floor. Other residents are Mrs. Flora WILSON, who occupies ground-floor flat, and Mr. Geoffrey DAWKINS, who lives in flat on first floor. Entry gained to target's flat this morning. Photographic surveillance conducted and films and sketch will be pouched to you soonest.

No attempt was made to establish an audio operation, since it has been determined from station sources that the target's flat is swept by Division D staff once a week, and there is a consequent high risk that any transmitter for whole-room surveillance, or even a more limited telephone tap, would be discovered and removed.

Flat occupied by target consists of four rooms: living room, bedroom, kitchen, and bathroom. Search of apartment revealed no classified documents, evidence of drug use, or other items of interest except for .380 Walther PPK automatic in top dresser drawer of target's bedroom. Weapon was loaded and there were two extra magazines under a shirt next to it.

The flat is also unsuitable for approach to target. Chain on inside of door will not permit surprise entry if in place, as would be likely at night. Even if surprise entry could be gained there might be time for target to obtain and use firearm, which, regardless of outcome, would nullify purpose of mission. In addition, there is definite risk that WILSON or DAWKINS might witness arrival or departure of this officer, which could create doubt that target died of natural causes, even if termination attempt should succeed. Target's office is also obviously unsuitable since secretary or other personnel are present at almost all times.

It is proposed, therefore, to approach and eliminate target on the street within next ten days at a place and time to be chosen at my discretion depending on opportunity and movement of target. Request your approval for this operational plan earliest. LS/TALPIA. End Intel. 12:39 P.M.

* * *

Harrington folded the message, placed it in an envelope, and walked down the corridor to the code and communications room. An armed Marine guard carefully checked his plastic ID badge before permitting him to enter. The room was a busy and noisy place, with six operators seated at a bank of Teletype machines that were clattering away with incoming and outgoing messages. In another section of the room, three code clerks sat before a computer terminal, monitoring the traffic to make sure that the link-encryption system was working smoothly. The day of the code clerk laboriously deciphering a message from Washington by hand was long since gone; the traffic was encrypted on-line, and passed between the communications room of the embassy and the cable registry in Langley in code. But the cables emerged from the Teletypes in plain text, automatically decoded as they spewed from the machines.

Harrington scanned the faces of the Teletype operators and then walked over to one of them, a gray-haired woman with steel-rimmed spectacles. She had a cigarette going in an ashtray next to her machine.

"You're Betty McCann, aren't you?"

She looked up at the big man towering over her. "For longer than I care to remember. What can I do for you?"

Harrington handed her the cable text. "Some special traffic."

Her trained eyes flicked across the page. She spotted the LS/Talpia slug immediately. "I've been expecting you, Mr. Hansen," she said. "I've got special instructions on how to handle this. Will you be having a lot more?"

"Not a lot."

When Harrington had left, she punched out a series of numerals on the machine that cut it away from the regular volume of traffic moving across the Atlantic to headquarters and plugged it into a special, back-channel relay with separate encryption. When she had finished sending the message, she gathered up the original and the Teletype copy. Instead of throwing them in the wire basket to be filed with copies of all the other outgoing Intels, she put them in the burn bag next to her machine. Her orders, from Frank DiMario himself, were to keep no originals of any LS/Talpia traffic in the code room. It was a highly unusual procedure, but after working for the company for almost thirty years, Betty McCann no longer considered anything about the place very unusual. She punched her machine, did as she was told, and kept out of trouble.

That evening, Harrington returned to his furnished flat in Aubrey Walk, poured himself a slug of brandy and set it down on the kitchen table. He waddled into the bedroom, got down on all fours, and grunting, reached under the bed. He pulled out a canvas suitcase. He put it on top of the bed, unzipped it, and carefully removed a brown leather case. He took the case out to the kitchen and placed it on the table. He drank the brandy, then poured himself another. It was lonely as hell being in London without Shirley. He got up, turned on the radio, and fiddled with the dial for a moment until he got some rock music. That helped.

He went back to the table and opened the leather case. From it, he removed the specially modified .45 automatic that Nat Rosen had given to him at headquarters eight weeks earlier in the laboratories of the Technical Services Division. He mounted the Bushnell telescopic sight and adjusted it. He had already sighted it in at a hundred meters at the firing range at Langley. He had shot several test rounds, adjusting the elevation knob of the scope until he was satisfied that the gun was dead on at that distance. Most automatics were accurate only up to fifty meters; but with this gun, and with the scope, Harrington was confident he could hit a target up to twice that distance. Beyond that, he would make no guarantees.

He left untouched in the leather case a sniperscope, which would permit him to hit a target in total darkness, and a pair of special goggles for night vision. He walked over to the window. Standing a few feet back so that he could not be seen from the street, he pointed the gun in the direction of Holland Park. He aimed at a chimney on a distant rooftop. The scope brought it in close and sharp in the crosshairs; he could almost reach out and touch the bricks. He checked the elevation and windage knobs. When he was satisfied, he returned to the table.

He held up the gun and admired it. It was an ingenious mechanism. TSD had taken a standard .45 ACP automatic frame and completely redesigned it. Their technical wizards had machined a new barrel to reduce the bore to .17 caliber. The gun worked on compressed air, with pneumatic action and an electronic trigger for enhanced accuracy. A small battery in the grip powered a solenoid that released the hammer. The result was a sophisticated air pistol with a velocity much higher than anything commercially available. Yet it was recoilless and almost silent.

Harrington opened a small plastic box that had been strapped into a compartment in the larger leather case. From the box, he gingerly removed seven special cartridges, tiny plastic sabots each gripping a clear gelatin capsule. He held one of the plastic casings up to the light between his large thumb and forefinger, but he could not make out the microscopic flechette that he knew was somewhere inside.

He loaded the sabots into a magazine and shoved the clip into the gun. When he touched the trigger the top cartridge would be propelled forward with enormous power and precision. The sabot would fall away and the soft protective gelatin would vaporize, leaving the microscopic projectile, stabilized by invisible fins, speeding toward its target. Harrington pushed down the safety, and placed the gun back into its specially fitted compartment in the leather case.

Although at headquarters he had argued for a conventional gun, over the past weeks he had come to like the exotic weapon. He admired the way it looked, the cold metal resting against the purple velvet lining of the gun case. To Harrington, it was a thing of beauty, as well as an essential tool of his particular profession.

He closed the case, put on his jacket, and went out, locking the front door behind him. He walked a few blocks to Costas, a Greek restaurant in Hillgate Street, and took a table in the patio. He ordered the souvalaki and a carafe of retsina. He was hungry, but he ate mechanically, his mind on the task that awaited him. He looked at his watch. It was almost eight o'clock. He was waiting for dark.

Harrington paid his check and walked back toward Holland Park and the flat. He went upstairs, retrieved the leather case and checked his watch again. It was eight-thirty; time to leave. He walked down to the street and unlocked the garage door. The black Mercedes he had hired the previous weekend had been turned in and replaced with a dark-blue BMW. Harrington squeezed behind the wheel and placed the gun case on the front seat beside him.

He drove along Notting Hill Gate and Bayswater Road to the end of Hyde Park, then turned up toward Bryanston Square. He parked along the garden on the west side of the square, across from Travers' flat and about fifty feet to the south. He rested the gun case on his knees and rolled down the window. From his vantage point, he had a clear view of Travers' front door across the square, at about a forty-five-degree angle.

Harrington scanned the street. It was empty. He removed the gun from the case and looked through the telescopic sight. He would not need the sniperscope or the night goggles; it was dark, but the street lamps provided ample light. The door of Travers' building came sharply into focus in the crosshairs. He would have to shoot through the palings of the wrought-iron fence, but that should not be difficult since they were spaced well apart. He estimated the range at just over sixty meters. He turned the elevation knob on the scope several notches to compensate for the shorter distance to the target.

Again he looked at his watch; it was 8:57 and the street was still empty. He waited, the dart gun resting on his lap.

At precisely 9:00 P.M., the door across the square opened and Geoffrey Dawkins emerged with Gladstone, his Great Dane, on a thick leather leash. The dog heeled and then sat obediently, as Dawkins turned and tried the door to make sure it had locked behind him. The Great Dane was an enormous creature, but well trained. Dawkins had got him from a kennel in Sussex four years earlier and raised him from a puppy. He was the bachelor banker's closest companion, and as Harrington had already observed from previous surveillance, Dawkins, a man of meticulous habits, walked him every night at nine.

Across the square, Harrington gripped the gun in a two-hand hold and peered through the scope. Dawkins and the dog, heeling on his left side, were walking north toward

Montagu Place. Harrington moved the gun slowly, tracking them in the crosshairs. It would have been easier to hit the dog in the body, but he could not resist aiming at the great, proud head. Gently, Harrington squeezed the trigger. There was a low noise, a sort of "phut," that could be heard only by Harrington in the car.

The great beast fell over, the microscopic flechette embedded in its jaw. The dog sprawled on the sidewalk, its huge tongue drooping lifelessly between the fearsome teeth, the enormous body completely limp. The only sound on the street was the little cry uttered by Dawkins as the dog collapsed. The banker was down on his knees, his ear against the Great Dane's chest, listening in vain for a heartbeat.

Across the square, the BMW started up and eased quietly away from the curb. Dawkins was still on his knees. He was sobbing, and calling out the dog's name, as the car drove off.

Harrington was pleased. Rosen and Jorgensen had assured him that the gun was accurate, but he wanted to be sure. He did not like working with any weapon until he had tested it first under conditions as close to operational as possible. Unless headquarters raised some chicken-shit objection to the location, he would repeat tonight's dry run against the actual target at the earliest opportunity. Just as he had been ordered to do, he would kill the mole.

Chapter 19

At eight-thirty the next morning, Travers was leaving for the embassy when he encountered Geoffrey Dawkins on the stairs.

The short, gray-haired banker was meticulously dressed as usual, in a dark Savile Row suit, but he was obviously distraught. His eyes were bloodshot, and though he was shaven, he looked haggard, as if he had not slept.

"Have you heard?" he asked Travers. He shook his head mournfully. "A great tragedy, a great loss. He was so young. He had so many good years ahead of him."

Travers started. For a fleeting moment he thought the prime minister might have died during the night. But it couldn't be; the station's watch officer would have called him if that had happened.

"I'm terribly sorry," Travers said cautiously. "I hadn't heard the news." He still wondered what Dawkins was talking about.

"He just collapsed on the pavement. Practically in front of the house. I was taking him for his usual walk and suddenly—" Dawkins could not continue. He wiped away a tear. "Poor Gladstone," he said. "I had to ring up the veterinary hospital to have them come and take him away. I couldn't budge him by myself. He was enormous, you know."

"I'm terribly sorry," Travers repeated. Dawkins lived alone, he knew, and the dog was the closest thing he had to a family.

"It was so sudden," he said. "So unexpected."

"You have my sympathy," Travers murmured. "Let me know if there is anything I can do."

"Yes, yes. Thank you," the banker said distractedly. "It was his heart, they said. It just gave out."

At the embassy, Ann Ganley came in to go over Travers' schedule for the coming week. "Sir Richard Whitworth wants to have lunch at the Garrick on Tuesday," she said.

"Did he say why?"

"No clues. It was his snooty confidential secretary, Miss Streatley, the one who always sounds like she's calling direct from Buckingham Palace."

"Don't get your Irish up. Call her back and say I'd be delighted. He can set the time."

"Will you want to bring Dick Austin along?"

"No, but tell Dick I'll brief him after the lunch. And ask him if he has any idea of what's on C's mind."

"Will do."

"Did you get the theater tickets?"

"Yes, for Thursday night. They're in your basket."

"Fine." Travers planned to take Valerie to a drawing-room comedy at the Globe that had gotten good reviews. After last weekend, he felt they could both use a laugh or two.

"Did you get the memo from Lisa Layton? She asked me to make sure you saw it."

"I've read it." The news was not good; despite more harassment of Harry Bullock's enterprises by Special Branch, which Travers had deftly arranged over several whiskey and sodas with Sir Edward Furnall, the eviction notice for the Russells had not been withdrawn. "Better ask Bill Hansen to come in," Travers said. "He's the new boy, the big blond fellow."

"Yes, I've been chatting with him."

"What about?"

"Oh, the theater, museums, what to do in London. He seems lonely."

"Well, I'm about to give him something to do. Perhaps that will take his mind off my secretary."

The biographical information on Agrippa Kimbundu, the young Angolan leader, had come in from C, via Dick Austin, and while he waited for Hansen, Travers drafted a covering Intel for Arthur Wilcox, the deputy for National Intelligence.

He had just finished when Hansen came limping in. "You wanted to see me, sir?" the big man asked.

"Yes, Bill, please sit down."

"Thank you."

"Getting along in London all right?"

"Yes, sir. Nice town, a little expensive. But anything beats Moscow."

"I can believe that. Bill, I assume that by now Lisa has put you in the picture on the problem we're having with LS/Primrose-1 and -2?"

"Yes, sir, she has."

"Well, Harry Bullock hasn't cracked. Lisa is damn good, but I think we'll need your services for the next move."

"I'll be glad to see a little action, sir. London's been pretty quiet so far."

"Well, I want you to find Bullock. Lean on him. Don't rough him up, but put a good scare into him. The station's interest can't be revealed, of course. Just tell him you have certain influential friends who want him to drop his plans. Make it clear that the police raids will continue unless he plays ball."

"Can I tell him he might have an accident if he doesn't cooperate?"

Travers hesitated. "Use your judgment. You'll have to play it by ear."

"What about physical disguise?"

"You'd better have some, just to cover us. Go see Wade Carter at our safe house on Brompton Road. He's the station's TSD officer. He can fix you up with contact lenses and a mustache, or whatever he recommends. Harding Westerfield can give you the address."

"Good. I'll take care of it for you."

Travers was impressed with Hansen. He seemed professional and businesslike, and tough enough to make Harry Bullock see the light. If the move backfired, the disguise would prevent Bullock from linking his visitor to the embassy.

On the way back to his own office, Harrington was amused

at the thought of a disguise on top of his disguise. Travers, he was pleased to note, apparently trusted him and suspected nothing. He had just reached his own desk when the telephone rang.

"Mr. Hansen? This is Betty McCann in the code room. You have some incoming traffic."

"I'll be right down."

In the code room, McCann ripped the message off the machine and handed it to Harrington. It was slugged LS/Talpia. He thanked her and went back upstairs to his office, where he closed the door and read the cable:

YOUR OPERATIONAL PLAN APPROVED IN PART. TARGET MAY BE ELIMINATED AS YOU PROPOSE BUT NOT, REPEAT NOT, AT YOUR DISCRETION. STILL REQUIRE THAT YOU CLEAR IN ADVANCE THE PRECISE TIME AND PLACE OF TERMINATION PER YOUR ORIGINAL INSTRUCTIONS. MUCH APPRECIATE YOUR FAST WORK. DIRECTOR

Harrington swore. "The bastard is keeping me on a short string," he muttered. "You'd think I'd never done this before." But he picked up a pencil and wrote out a reply.

DIRECTOR EYES ONLY
INTEL
SUPDATA LS/TALPIA, reporting on test of actual operational conditions and proposing time and date for final termination
Date: July 3, 1981
Subject: Approach to target
Country: UK
Source Description: LS/TALPIA
Text: At 2100 hours Thursday, July 2, I tested assigned weapon under circumstances closely approximating actual operational conditions. Test subject was large dog who lives in target's building. At range of 60 meters from across the square, test subject was hit in jaw on first shot. Test subject died immediately and I left scene unobserved.

From casual conversation with target's secretary, I

have learned that he plans to attend theater next Thursday evening. Per your 7/3 I propose to carry out final termination at same location and by same means on July 9 at approximately 2200 hours, when target is expected to return from theater. Await your operational approval. LS/TALPIA. End Intel. 10:36 A.M.

Harrington folded the message in two, walked back down to the code room and gave it to Betty McCann. She scanned it and looked up, a cigarette drooping from her lips.

"You planning to knock off some Russian, Mr. Hansen?"

Harrington put his ham hand on her shoulder and gave it a little squeeze. He would have liked to do more. "You guessed it, honey. That's exactly it."

He walked down the corridor to Harding Westerfield's office to get the address of the safe house. In a way, he thought, she's right.

Travers and Valerie had decided to spend the weekend in town. After what had happened the previous Saturday night, neither of them really wanted to go back out to the cottage right away, and besides, Travers felt he should attend the July 4 reception at the ambassador's residence on Saturday night. He arranged to meet Valerie for dinner afterward.

The reception was at Winfield House in Regent's Park. The British had given the large, neo-Georgian mansion to the United States just after World War II as a residence for the American ambassador. It had been expensively redecorated during the Nixon administration by one of Winthrop Cushing's predecessors, who had put eighteenth-century Chinese wallpaper in the drawing room. The reception was well under way by the time Travers arrived around six o'clock. The weather was balmy, and the party was being held outdoors. A huge striped tent had been set up on the lawn behind the dining room.

There were the usual assortment of foreign diplomats, crowding around the buffet table, far more interested in stuffing themselves on the shrimp and hot hors d'oeuvres than in celebrating the 205th anniversary of American independence. The guests included a number of American businessmen and other Americans living in England, several officials of the Foreign Office, half-a-dozen London-based American correspondents, a few Fleet Street publishers, a large group of fat-cat British bankers and board chairmen, and a heavy sprinkling of Ambassador Cushing's titled English friends and their wives.

Cushing, a millionaire New York businessman and heir to a steel fortune, had been one of President Thurlow Anderson's earliest and most generous political supporters. He was rewarded with the London embassy, a post which traditionally went to persons of wealth, since most career diplomats could not afford to live and entertain in London in the expected style. Cushing, Travers had observed, was never happier than when surrounded with dukes, earls, viscounts, and duchesses, and they were out in full force for the reception.

Travers squeezed up to the bar and asked for a Scotch and water. He noticed with dismay that Cushing had ordered a cheap brand for the reception, one Travers had never heard of. It looked almost chartreuse. Well, he thought, that's how the rich get rich. And stay that way.

He turned to find the smiling, blond-haired figure of Sergei Rumin standing behind him, hand extended.

"Ah, Mistair Travers, the political officer," Rumin said mockingly. "I congratulate you on your day of independence from the British." He looked around the room. "But you appear to have been recaptured by them." He nodded to the barman. "Wodka, please."·

"Hello, Sergei," Travers said. "How is the consular business these days? Doesn't it get boring sometimes, just stamping passports?"

Rumin grinned. "We should, you and I, perhaps both find more interesting work to do, yes?" Rumin spied Henry Phipps, the deputy permanent under-secretary of the Foreign Office, and made a beeline for him. "Ah, Mistair Pheeps," he said, "I have been wanting to talk to you."

Travers tried to edge away from the bar, but to his dismay found himself briefly trapped by a gushing, fiftyish bleached blonde, who identified herself as Mrs. Cliff Atkinson, the wife of the Houston oil millionaire. "Ah just think it's *so* exciting to be celebratin' the Fourth of July here in London at your be*oo*tiful residence," she said. She accompanied this pronouncement with a loud giggle and much jangling of gold bracelets.

"Yes, ma'am," Travers said. "Glad you could be with us."

He slipped away and busied himself studying the rosebushes. He tried unsuccessfully to look invisible. As chief of station, he had been invited by Ambassador Cushing, but he disliked receptions.

"Ah, Travers, glad you could make it."

He turned and was surprised to find Winthrop Cushing himself, drink in hand, wearing a broad ambassadorial smile. He was a tall, well-built but rather portly man in his early sixties who had been born to great wealth and by some shrewd investments had managed to increase it. Theoretically, the ambassador was in charge of all agencies that comprised the U.S. mission. But he had made it clear long ago that he did not want to know what the CIA station was doing, which from Travers' point of view, made him the ideal ambassador.

Cushing steered Travers off to a corner of the lawn. "There's something I want you to do, my boy," he said in his Groton accent. Any request was unusual for Cushing, and Travers wondered what was coming.

The ambassador lowered his voice. "I want you to run a covert operation," he said. "Against the pigeons."

"You're joking, sir."

"Dead serious. They're shitting on the eagle. It's supposed to be gold, and it's turning green."

"But you have it washed off fairly often, don't you?"

"Yes, but it's a stop-gap measure, not a solution. If we announce we're having the eagle electrified, or putting out poison, the press will jump on us. They'd have a field day. But you people could do it quietly. And you have the technology. I was thinking of ultrasonics, or something. A high-pitched noise that would drive off the pigeons but be inaudible to humans."

"I'll certainly look into it, sir."

"I knew I could count on you, Travers. Well, we don't want the symbol of our nation turning shit-green, do we?"

Over dinner that evening at their favorite Chinese restaurant on Lisle Street, Travers almost doubled over with laughter as he told the story to Valerie. She joined in, and Chen, their waiter, seeing his friends having such a good time, started laughing, too, as he approached their table with the dim sum. For an hour or so, Travers and Valerie were able to forget the real world and its dangers.

Valerie had invited him to spend the night at her flat. On the way, they stopped off at the pottery shop in King's Road to check the mail. It was closed, but the owner, Mary Hodges, was a close friend and had lent Valerie a key. Travers waited in the cab while she went inside. There was a letter for her, bearing Ben Goodman's return address in Washington. She stuck it in her purse and rejoined Travers.

"Anything?" he asked.

"Yes. From Newark Street."

The driver let them off at Margaretta Terrace. They went upstairs to her flat, and she poured them each a glass of cold white wine. They sat on the couch, kicked off their shoes, and put their stockinged feet up on the cocktail table.

"Better open it," Travers said. Valerie was already slitting the envelope with a metal letter opener. She read the contents quickly.

"Well?"

"He says there may be something funny about William Hansen." She looked at Travers. "He says Hansen's supposed to be fifty-eight years old and he got his first Social Security number six weeks ago. He says you should be very careful."

"Write Ben back and thank him. Tell him I already know there is something funny about William Hansen."

"How do you know?"

"He was in my office yesterday. He has a limp, you know. When he walked out he was limping on his left leg."

"So?"

"He was limping when I met him for the first time, two weeks ago. On his right leg."

Chapter 20

Travers and Valerie enjoyed a leisurely Sunday together in town. They slept late. After showers and coffee, Valerie produced a magnificent brunch—orange juice mixed with champagne, bacon, and shirred eggs. They spent the rest of the morning feeding the swans in St. James's Park.

Early in the afternoon, they strolled along the Thames to the Tate Gallery. The Turner wing was crowded with tourists, but they avoided it; Travers preferred the French Impressionists in any event. They lingered over Cézanne's Provençal landscapes and a Renoir that was Valerie's favorite.

Around five o'clock they walked back along the embankment toward Chelsea. When they had reached Cheyne Walk, Valerie stopped and put her arm around Travers.

"Hansen's been sent to kill you, hasn't he?"

"We don't know that for sure."

There was urgency in her voice. "Rob, you know he has. Why don't you leave London? Please. Don't sit here and wait for him to try."

Travers looked away from Valerie, out at the river. The reflection of the late-afternoon sun on the water made him squint. "I can't leave now. I can't do a damn thing until the committee is convinced I'm telling the truth. They're watching the traffic. If they pick up anything, I'll be warned. You know the arrangement."

"But suppose the warning is too late? My God, Rob, when we were feeding the swans this morning, I thought to myself, Suppose he just came up behind us and shot you, right there in the park?"

"I know. I thought the same thing."

"Then nowhere is safe anymore? Not even St. James's Park on a peaceful Sunday?"

Travers did not reply.

Howard Radner was having trouble concentrating on the pile of cables stacked in front of him. Julie had been acting frosty ever since he had bombed in from Laurel at five in the morning, and last night she had refused him. She hadn't even claimed a headache. Just a flat-out no. And to top it all, her mother was coming down from Great Neck on Friday afternoon. It would be a weekend full of, "So, Howard, when are you going to propose to my Julie?" and similar blunt questions. Subtlety was not Naomi Cahn's strong suit; she preferred the blunderbuss to the rapier.

Linda, the cat-loving secretary, came in and Radner was grateful for the interruption. He was having a bad Monday morning.

"Like a little coffee, Howie?"

"Love some if you're serving, Linda." He gave her a big smile. Maybe, he thought, he would be better off with a shiksa from Silver Spring. She certainly had big tits. And he bet that her mother didn't have a voice like a foghorn. On the other hand, he would probably die young, from boredom. Linda wasn't very bright.

Radner went back to reading the Intels. The coffee arrived and the phone rang at the same moment. It was Hal Bonner, a reporter for *The Washington Post*. Bonner was a young bachelor, like Radner, and they had met at several parties around Georgetown. Like a lot of younger newspapermen, Bonner suffered from the Woodward and Bernstein syndrome. He wanted to be rich and famous, instantly. Radner did not particularly like him.

"Hello, Howie, how are the spooks treating you?"

"Fine. The committee has a good working relationship with the intelligence community."

"Bullshit."

"Yeah, bullshit. What's on your mind, Hal?"

"I'm trying to track down a nutty story. That the CIA once tried to capture an African crocodile. They were supposedly going to hire a witch doctor to brew the gall bladder into a special poison. You ever run across anything like that?"

"Sounds like a croc."

"Very funny."

"Actually, the story's true. It was part of the MK/Ultra stuff. Crocodile gall bladders are supposed to have special powers. One of the agency's hot-shot case officers tried to trap a crocodile in Tanzania and recruit a witch doctor to play chef."

"Did it happen?"

"How the hell do I know? Ask Nat Rosen. I'm not into crocodiles."

"Well, here's an easier question. When are the NSA hearings going to be held?"

"I don't know anything about that."

"I thought your subcommittee had NSA as well as the agency."

"I don't know anything about any hearings. You'll have to ask the chairman."

"Well, thanks, Howie."

"Always a pleasure to hear from you, Hal."

Radner picked up his cup, but the coffee was cold. Fucking *Washington Post*. Last night he couldn't get laid, and this morning he can't even get a hot cup of coffee. What next? he thought.

The answer was not long in coming. He turned up the next cable from the London station and did a double take. The message was slugged LS/Talpia. It was Hansen's July 2 cable, reporting his surveillance of the cottage and his break-in at Travers' apartment. Radner read the text and gasped.

"Jesus Christ," he said aloud. "Holy shit." He grabbed the cable and ran as fast as he could down to Ben Goodman's office, nearly knocking Linda over en route.

Goodman was on the telephone. Radner was jumping up and down, waving the cable and signaling frantically. Goodman quickly ended the conversation and hung up.

"We've got it, Ben," Radner exclaimed. "They're tracking him! Son of a bitch, they're tracking him. Look!" He shoved the cable at Goodman.

Ben scanned it rapidly. "I'll be damned. They're really

doing it. They're really trying to kill him. 'It is proposed, therefore, to approach and eliminate target on the street within next ten days.'"

"Ben, it's got to be Hansen."

"You're not really sure of that, are you? It could be the woman—what's her name?"

"Farmer." Radner was struck by the thought. "Do you really think they'd use a woman killer?"

"Why not?" Goodman replied. "They might figure she had better access to Travers. He's supposed to be something of a stick man. Or it could be the other fellow, Moffet. Or someone we don't even know about."

"Whoever it was, he or she was in Travers' apartment. That's too close for comfort."

"Much too close," Ben agreed.

He read the message again, this time more slowly. "Whoever broke into the apartment must be the same person who took the pot-shot at Travers at the cottage ten days ago."

"Probably," Radner said.

"Okay. The message asks approval to hit Travers sometime in the next ten days. But there's no answering Intel from Langley."

"I haven't seen any."

"That gives us a little breathing space, but not much. This message is dated July second. That's four days ago. Can't NSA get this stuff to us quicker?"

"I've talked to A.J. Buford, Admiral Hughes's assistant, about that. He says it takes several days to process the stuff, unless it's priority traffic for the NSC. I was afraid to push too hard, or they'll realize what we're up to."

Goodman looked worried. "But suppose LS/Talpia sets a specific date to hit Travers, and it's approved. With a four-day lead time, it may be too late for us to warn him. As it is, we've got to get word to him right away."

"You could write to Valerie, but the mails take four or five days."

Ben shook his head. "Too long. We'll have to risk a phone call or a cable. I'll brief the senator and get his approval."

Radner looked gloomy. "The minute we use the telephone

or send a cable, NSA will pick it up. It will be routinely forwarded to Langley with all the other overseas intercepts. That could blow the whole ball game."

"We'll have to take the risk. There's such a tremendous volume of traffic flowing in to the agency every day from NSA that there's a good chance that no one will spot it. Or it could be weeks or months before they do. Even so, we'll have to use very guarded language. We can send a follow-up letter to Valerie with more details."

"Do you want me to try to draft a cable?"

"Yes. You do that while I go over to the other building and try to track down the senator. I'll call you from his office."

The Intelligence Committee's offices were in the antiseptic New Senate Office Building. For his own offices, Barry Owens, although young and modish in his style of dress, preferred the Old Senate Office Building across the street, with its smaller, but much more elegant and ornate quarters.

While Goodman went off to search for the senator, Radner returned to his office and drafted a cable to Valerie. It read: "A medical diagnosis has been received. Your friend's health in grave jeopardy, probably from viral source mentioned in last letter. Dr. Benjamin urges that he take every possible precaution and restrict walks to minimum as exercise in his present condition may not be at all beneficial."

The phone rang. It was Goodman.

"I'm with the senator now, Howie. He says to go ahead and risk a cable."

"I've penciled a draft. Should I send it?"

"No. Wait until I get back across the street. I want to read it first."

"Okay, Ben."

Goodman hung up and looked at the senator. Barry Owens was sitting at his desk in shirtsleeves, tossing paper clips at a cup.

"Cheer up, Ben," Owens said. "At least now we know that Travers was telling the truth. We haven't been set up by the company."

"Yeah," Goodman replied, fingering an unlit cigar. "But now we have a few other worries. Suppose Travers gets killed, and your role comes out. The press could turn your political future into a past, fairly quickly."

"I don't think so. We were investigating grave charges against the CIA, brought by one of their senior officials, Robert Travers. He sacrificed his life to bring the truth out into the open."

"Sure, that's one scenario. But I can think of another way the story might be played."

"Such as?"

"Covert meddling by member of Senate Intelligence Subcommittee causes death of station chief in London. Senator Barry Owens admits he did not have authorization of committee chairman for secret meetings in England with victim. CIA director G. Townsend Black vigorously denies agency link to murder of Robert Travers, implicates KGB assassins. Claims senator's visit triggered Soviet operation designed to blame CIA for agent's death."

Owens looked at him, his expression no longer unworried. "Ben," he said, "you better get your ass over to the Dirksen Building and send that cable."

Goodman got up and headed for the door, moving fast. The senator remained seated at his desk for several moments, alone in his office. He had stopped tossing paper clips.

On Tuesday, Travers kept his lunch date with C at the Garrick. He was disturbed by Radner's warning, which had reached him several hours earlier. Valerie had received the cable at seven that morning. She brought it over to his flat immediately. Although the wording was cryptic, the message was clear. Someone in his own agency, most probably William Hansen—if that was his real name—was stalking him, with orders to kill. Orders that had come from the director. Travers thought grimly that his operation against Towny Black had succeeded. But his triumph might become his epitaph.

He tried, not very successfully, to put these thoughts out of his mind as he mounted the wide stone steps of the Garrick Club, just off the Strand. The club, founded 150 years before and named for the celebrated actor David Garrick, was still a place where the theatrical, literary, and legal professions gathered. The Garrick was more convivial than the social clubs of Pall Mall; at the Garrick, the joke went, the members were expected to talk to one another.

Few of the members who talked to Sir Richard Whitworth knew that he was C, the legendary head of the British Secret Intelligence Service. As far as most knew, the distinguished Sir Richard was just another civil servant, vaguely associated with the War Office.

Travers walked through the main hall, past the bust of Henry Irving, the first British actor to be knighted. He mounted the great, carved oak stairway to the first floor, pausing halfway up to admire a portrait of Nell Gwyn.

Travers passed beneath the domed ceiling of the first-floor landing. He walked by the showcases full of jewels once worn by celebrated actresses, and other theatrical memorabilia that various members had presented to the club. Dominating the room was a large statue of Bellona, the Roman goddess of war, by Rodin.

C was waiting in his usual chair in the morning room near the marble fireplace, a tall, silver-haired figure in a dark gray suit. It was an unusually attractive room, with green velvet walls decorated with portraits of actors and actresses. There were more glass showcases, some containing the letters of David Garrick.

Sir Richard rose and shook Travers' hand. "Good to see you, Robert. Will you join me for a drink before we go downstairs? And what would you like?"

"Thank you. J and B on the rocks, with a twist of lemon, please." C signaled the waiter, who took their order and disappeared into the bar in the adjoining room.

"You're looking fit," Sir Richard said. "Been keeping up your tennis game, have you?"

"Not lately," Travers admitted. "I've been too busy."

Sir Richard raised an eyebrow, but didn't press. The waiter put the drinks down.

When he had gone, Sir Richard said, "I see that your Mr. Bullock is proving obstinate."

Travers looked mildly surprised.

"I receive the reports from MI5."

"Of course."

"Our friend Rumin has even gone so far as to complain to Henry Phipps in the Foreign Office about Special Branch's raids. Can you imagine that? He refused to answer when Henry asked why the Soviet embassy had taken an interest in the affairs of a private British citizen. Well, I thought you'd want to know."

"Yes, thanks. It confirms our assumptions about Bullock and Rumin."

"Well, cheers, old chap." C raised his glass of sherry.

It was not until they were eating lunch in the dining room that Sir Richard revealed what was really on his mind. "The PM is getting edgy about Poppy," he said. "He wants to cut the missions down to one a month. The Foreign Office will be putting in a formal request to your State Department in about a week, but I thought you'd want to give Langley a bit of advance notice."

"That's very considerate of you."

"Not at all," Sir Richard replied. "You'd do quite the same for me, I'm sure."

Polite as C was, his news was disturbing. For many years, the agency's U-2 spy planes had been flying from bases in Britain and elsewhere on British territory. More recently, the operation, code-named Poppy, had used the SR-71, the more sophisticated follow-on to the U-2. But the Brits had become increasingly nervous about spy flights from their soil. During the 1973 Middle East war the issue had come close to causing an open break between the two allies. Prime Minister Edward Heath had refused Langley permission to use the British air base in Akrotiri, Cyprus, for U-2 flights over the battlefields.

The breach was healed, and once-a-week reconnaissance missions resumed from British territory. Now Whitehall was clearly trying to chip away at the arrangement, by limiting the flights to one a month.

"It comes at a rather bad time," Travers said. "We haven't had our bases in Iran for two years now. We're relying heavily on the spy flights to track the Soviet missile program."

"I understand that," Sir Richard said. "In our meetings

with the Foreign Office I've argued against any limitations, but I'm outnumbered. Henry Phipps has been waffling, and I'm afraid he'll do whatever the Foreign Secretary wants. The principal argument is that you have the satellites so you don't really need the spy flights."

"The satellites only do half the job," Travers said. To monitor the Soviet missile tests, the United States had four Rhyolite satellites twenty-two thousand miles in space in synchronous orbit. Matching the speed of the earth, they appeared to be stationary overhead. The satellites' infrared sensors could quickly spot a missile blast-off inside the Soviet Union.

"The Rhyolites are fine to detect the tests," Travers said. "But they don't give us the telemetry." The United States got its best intelligence about Soviet missile capabilities from telemetry, the enormous volume of information radioed back to earth by a rocket during its flight. All of this electronic intelligence was taped, stored in computers, and compared with data from subsequent test flights. There was so much interference with radio signals in outer space, however, that the telemetry had to be picked up from ground stations or reconnaissance flights.

In the past, to zero in on Soviet telemetry, Langley had relied heavily on its two electronic eavesdropping bases in Iran, at Kabkan on the Soviet border and at Behshahr, on the Caspian sea near Tehran. At both bases, antennas sprouting from domed buildings listened for signals from the Soviet missile tests at Tyuratam, eighty miles east of the Aral Sea. But when the shah had been overthrown two years before, the CIA had lost its bases in Iran.

"I wish I could help," Sir Richard said sympathetically, "but once Whitehall digs in its heels on something like this, they don't listen to us very much, I'm afraid."

They had finished their dessert and coffee, and Travers thanked C for the lunch. Sir Richard escorted his guest out to the main hall. They were near the thick glass doors that led to Garrick Street when Sir Richard, almost as an afterthought, said: "By the way, Robert, there's some rather odd traffic coming out of your embassy."

"What do you mean?"

"Well, you know that our listening station at Cheltenham monitors everything going in or out of the British Isles."

Travers nodded. He was well aware of Cheltenham, the British equivalent of NSA.

"Normally," Sir Richard continued, "traffic from Grosvenor Square is relayed through your naval communications center at Edzell, Scotland."

"Right." From the Edzell center, Travers knew, CIA traffic was beamed across the Atlantic to New York, then south along the eastern seaboard to Gambrills, Maryland, near Fort Meade. From there the circuit ran through a main switching station in Arlington, Virginia, and on into Langley headquarters.

Sir Richard spoke very quietly. "In the past few days, Cheltenham has been picking up a signal from your embassy that goes through your Air Force base at Mildenhall. Most unusual. We can't read the content, of course, it's all encrypted. But I thought you might want to know."

"I appreciate it very much."

"Well, in our sort of work, we do have to help one another, don't we?"

Chapter 21

On the afternoon of Thursday, July 9, two days after Travers' lunch with C, Howard Radner was at his desk in the New Senate Office Building, sipping a Coke and studying a series of messages that had Ping-Ponged between Langley and London the previous week.

The London station was requesting Provisional Operational Approval to recruit LS/Houndsditch-1, a chauffeur in the Czech embassy. He had been approached as he finished his lunch at The Ark, a restaurant in Palace Gardens Terrace, just behind the embassy.

At first the chauffeur had seemed uninterested and brusque, but his manner softened when he was shown a picture of his nephew, Jan Sokol, who had escaped from Bratislava during the 1948 Soviet takeover of Czechoslovakia, and who was now living in Manhattan at Second Avenue and Seventy-ninth Street. He became quite animated when shown the photograph, and agreed to a second meeting in St. Paul's Cathedral.

The request for the Provisional Operational Approval had been greeted with a number of questions from Langley, among them whether the chauffeur would really be able to provide enough information beyond that already being obtained through LS/Hyacinth-1 and -2, the couple who operated the OP at the south end of Ossington Street, catty-corner from the Czech embassy.

Radner suspected that the chauffeur had already been recruited, and that the request for the Provisional Operational Approval was coming after the fact. Over a beer at Clyde's several months earlier, one of his contacts in the agency had admitted to him that a really cool case officer recruited an agent first, and only then asked for the POA. "If you go by the book and ask for approval first," the CIA man had explained, "you might find that you can't recruit the agent after all. That doesn't look good on your fitness report."

Working his way through the mountain of cables, Radner was constantly astonished at the amount of bureaucratic paper that seemed to be required of the London station. In one message, the DDO's staff assistant, Wellington Lloyd, chided Westerfield for falling behind on the station's Field Periodic Reviews. Every three months, Radner knew, all CIA stations were required to fill out an eight-page form for each project and each agent under their control.

Another Intel caught Radner's eye. It was a request by Travers to the Office of Security that a polygraph operator be flown to London to flutter Philip Moffet. He wondered why. He was also puzzled, and somewhat annoyed. Through

Valerie, by mail and now by cable, they had warned Travers about William Hansen. Yet it was Moffet who seemed to be under some sort of suspicion.

"I'll never understand these people," he muttered.

The phone rang. "Hel-lo, Howie." It was Cindy Blair's unmistakable lilt. Her voice could make him horny even over the goddamn telephone. And she knew it.

"Cindy! Hey, it's good to hear your voice."

"I was hoping you'd call me, Howie. When are you going to take me dancing again? I had a great time at Tramp's."

"Uh, well, Cindy, honey, I'm up to my neck in a sea of paper these days. Underwater, really. The senator's on my back. But I'll call you soon, honest."

"For sure?"

"For sure."

Howard hung up, perspiring. Julie had finally relented last night, but she was still watching him like a hawk. She had pointedly told him about an incident in her family. "My mother likes to put up preserves, jellies and jams, every summer," she had said. "A few years ago, my father went gaga over his secretary. My mother told him, 'If I ever catch you playing around, I'll cut off your pecker, pickle it, and put it in a jar.' It was a joke, of course, but my father was never so sure it was a joke. I don't think he ever dared to play grab-ass with the secretary after that. Or with anyone else." Howard laughed loudly at the story, but he got the message.

He came to the next cable in the pile. His hand stopped, the Coke can suspended in midair, halfway to his lips.

He looked quickly at his watch. Four-thirty. He tore down to Goodman's office.

Ben wasn't there.

Linda was jiggling by, and Radner grabbed her by the arm and screamed at her. "Where the hell is he? For God sakes, answer me!"

Linda stared at him, wide-eyed. His face was red and contorted. She thought he looked like a demon.

She could hardly speak. She managed to point toward the lobby. "M-men's room, I think," she stammered.

Without replying, Radner ran down the hall and burst

through the door to the reception area. Spotting two wire-service reporters waiting on the leather couch for Davis Spencer, the committee's press secretary, Radner slowed to a dignified, if jerky, walk, then broke into a run again as soon as he had rounded the partition and was out of sight. Trying not to slip on the marble floor, he dashed into the men's room, nearly colliding with Goodman, who was just coming out the door.

"Ben, this is it!" Radner whispered hoarsely. "Get back in your office. We can't talk here."

In Goodman's office, Radner shoved the cable in front of him. "They shot the fucking dog," he said. "And they're going to shoot Travers—tonight. We've got to stop them, Ben."

Goodman's cigar had gone out, but he didn't bother to relight it. "What time is it in London?"

"Nine thirty-five. It's five hours later."

Goodman picked up the phone and dialed Extension 2244. "Karla? Ben. This is an emergency. I need to know where the senator is."

"He's on the floor. They're debating the health-insurance bill."

"Call him immediately and tell him to meet us in the President's Room. Howard and I are on our way over."
Goodman and Radner, exercising great self-control, walked at a normal pace past the two wire-service men, who were still sitting outside the door. As soon as they had rounded the corner, however, they streaked for the stairway and scrambled down one level to the basement. They burst into the almost-deserted staff cafeteria and ran through the narrow, green-tiled connecting passageway that led to the public cafeteria. They kept on going, past the south bank of elevators, to the subway that linked the Senate office buildings with the Capitol. One of the small, open cars was waiting at the platform, and they hopped on. After what seemed to Radner an interminable wait, but was actually only a minute, the operator started up the car. Ben nervously felt inside the breast pocket of his jacket to make sure the Intel was there.

At the Capitol, they bounded up the escalator, took the

elevator to the second floor, and ran down the wide marble corridor to the west side of the Senate chamber. They nodded to the pages who guarded the lobby and turned left into the ornate, chandeliered President's Room, just off the Senate floor. Barry Owens was already there, waiting for them.

The small, square room, with its elaborately patterned tile floor, red velvet drapes, and rococo, gilt mirror was decorated in the nineteenth-century bordello style so favored by the Senate. The three men huddled in thick leather armchairs in the corner by the window. They kept their voices low; there were two other senators in the room, conferring with visitors. "We've got a problem," Ben murmured. He handed the senator the copy of the CIA cable.

They waited while he read it. "Right now, it's nine-fifty P.M. in London," Radner volunteered.

"What time do you go to the theater in London?" Owens asked.

"A lot of them have seven-thirty curtains," Ben replied.

"So figure two hours, he might get out around nine-thirty," Owens said. "Where does Travers live?"

"Bryanston Square, just a couple of blocks from where we stayed. Most of the theaters are around Aldwych, St. Martin's Lane, and Shaftesbury Avenue. None of them are very far from Travers' flat."

"So he'd probably be getting home about ten o'clock. Which is when they have him targeted."

Radner tensely checked his watch. "That's about eight minutes from now."

"We could try to call the embassy," Ben said.

Owens shook his head. "I doubt they would know what theater he's at. Even if he's still there."

"His secretary might know," Radner said.

"We don't even know her name," Goodman said gloomily. "And if you call the embassy and ask for the home number of the secretary to the CIA station chief, you're not going to get it."

"We could call Scotland Yard," Radner suggested. "They might be able to cordon off the square."

"It would take me one minute to get to a phone in the

lobby," Owens calculated. "And at least three or four minutes to place a call to Scotland Yard, assuming the overseas circuits are not tied up, and allowing time to get the number from Information. Another minute to explain myself. That would leave Scotland Yard about one minute to do anything, even if they believed my story, which is not very likely." Owens shook his head. "We've run out of time."

"Damn," Goodman said.

Owens thought for a moment. "This message is dated July third. It says, 'Await your operational approval.' We haven't seen an answer from Langley yet, have we?"

"No," Radner replied. "So far, I haven't seen any cables from headquarters addressed to LS/Talpia. But there's a lot more traffic on my desk that I haven't gone through. I stopped as soon as I saw this."

"You did the right thing," Owens assured him. "But now you better get back to your office and keep scanning the traffic. There's just a chance that Hansen, or whoever LS/Talpia is, hasn't gotten the green light from Langley. Let us know the minute you find anything. Or if you don't. We'll be in my office."

As soon as Radner had left, Goodman said, "Senator, maybe we should call Scotland Yard. Suppose the play has an eight-o'clock curtain, or he goes to dinner after the theater and doesn't get home until later in the evening? There might still be time to stop it."

They were leaving the reception room, heading back to the senator's office. In the corridor, Owens put his arm on Goodman's shoulder. "Ben, I don't want to risk a call."

"Senator, do you know what you're saying?" Goodman thought he knew Owens pretty well, but he was surprised.

"Yes."

"You're sure?"

"I'm sure. At this point, we don't even know that Langley has approved LS/Talpia's proposal. The minute we pick up the phone, the agency will know what's going on. The cable we sent on Monday was a risk, but it was cryptic. They may not spot it. This is different. They'll know."

"But if there's a chance to stop it?"

Owens looked at his watch. It read 5:05. "It's probably too late. Ben, think it through. If Travers is dead, it's all over. We'll have to call off the investigation. We can't proceed without him. But if he's dead and the company finds out that we've been conspiring with him, that's another situation entirely. They can use that knowledge to embarrass the committee, even blame us for his death. They'll leak it to put me in the worst possible light. They can destroy us. You said it yourself."

"But they won't. Not as long as we have the cables."

Owens rubbed his chin. "Maybe. It does give us leverage. The two cables from London are damning. If Radner comes up with the missing piece, an Intel from Langley giving operational approval, that will clinch it. Then you find Site Orange, and we can hold our hearings. Go public."

"If Travers lives through the night."

"That's the risk we have to take. Travers has known the risk from the beginning. And there's a chance that headquarters hasn't approved. Or that something went wrong."

"There's always a chance."

"Ben, I want you to fly to London. Travers may be dead, but let's go on the assumption that he survives. Tell him we're persuaded his story is true. Our operation has worked. What he needs to do now is to get out of London and lie low until we're ready to call him as a witness."

"He may refuse to leave."

"He's got to go into hiding. Don't take no for an answer."

They arrived back at Owens' office. Karla Warren was waiting with a message. "Call Howard Radner right away," she told the senator.

Owens picked up the phone and dialed Radner himself. It was faster than going through a secretary.

"Howard? Barry Owens. What is it?"

"I've got more, Senator. Two things. A reply from Langley to LS/Talpia's first cable. It's dated last Friday and it gives general authorization for his proposal, but says they reserve the right to approve the time and place."

"What else?"

"A short cable from headquarters dated Saturday. It's obviously a reply to LS/Talpia's proposal to kill Travers on

July ninth. Tonight. It says: 'Your operational plan of July third is approved. Director.' "

Owens hung up. "Karla," he said, "I want you to get Ben on a plane to London."

"When?"

"Now. Tonight."

The dark-blue BMW nosed into Bryanston Square at 9:45 P.M. and parked along the west side of the garden. As he had during the dry run the previous week, Harrington rolled down the window and placed the brown leather gun case on his knees.

The square was almost deserted, except for one or two dogwalkers near the north end. He removed the dart gun from the case. He checked to make sure the sabots containing the capsules were loaded and in place. Then he looked through the telescopic sight and focused the crosshairs on Travers' front door. He would be shooting at an angle again, northeast across the square. He checked the range; seventy-two meters, slightly more than last time, since he had parked farther south, but still well within the gun's effective range.

In a few moments, if all went well, the lethal poison brewed inside the body of a clam or mussel in the Pacific Ocean, some six thousand miles from London, would be propelled at high speed into the body of Robert Travers. It would paralyze his respiratory, cardiovascular, nervous, and muscle systems. Within a second or two, he would die.

There was nothing to do now but wait. Harrington lit a cigarette. He took a deep drag, but after a few more puffs he put it out. He wanted to have his hands free. He checked his watch: 9:55.

Twenty minutes earlier, a little more than a mile away, Travers and Valerie had emerged from the Globe. They had enjoyed the play, one of those light comedies in which people kept popping in and out of bedrooms, with split-second escapes by adulterous spouses, unexpected twists of plot, and some good lines.

"See what you've escaped by not getting married again," Valerie said as they hailed a cab.

"Marriage isn't always that hilarious," Travers said.

In the taxi, he took Valerie's hand in his. He leaned over and kissed her on the neck, breathing in her perfume. She had her legs crossed, and her skirt was riding well above her knees. She looked sexy as hell.

"I know what's on your mind," Valerie said. She laughed.

"How can you tell?"

"I just can. Besides, in your case, I have a fifty-fifty chance of being right, no matter when I say it."

"Well, you can't blame me for thinking about sex. We've been watching nothing else for the past two hours."

In truth, Travers was thinking about how much he wanted things to stay the same between them. He did not want to lose Valerie, but he was not prepared to commit himself. The banter in the front of the theater reminded him that their future was something he had pushed into some inner recess of his mind. After the divorce, he had vowed he would never marry again. Yet, right at that moment, riding with her in the taxi with Valerie's hand resting softly in his, it seemed less impossible. He had never felt closer to a woman. Perhaps, he thought, they could have a happy life together.

They were in Bryanston Square. Travers paid the driver and helped Valerie out. The cab moved off and they walked across the sidewalk to the front door. He fumbled in his pocket for the key.

Across the square, Harrington sighted through the scope, his massive forearms braced against the car door, the barrel protruding only slightly through the rolled-down window. Valerie was standing almost directly behind Travers, blocking the line of fire.

Harrington cursed: "Fucking limey cunt, get the hell out of the way."

Travers had the key in the lock and the door open. Harrington was beside himself. He would only have another second.

At that instant, Travers took the key from the lock and stepped aside to let Valerie pass in front of him through the door. Now Harrington had a clear shot. The crosshairs were targeted on Travers' head. The darts were supposed to penetrate even heavy clothing, but Harrington had decided to go for the head. It was surer. He was aiming at Travers' right temple.

The keys slipped from Travers' hand and he ducked down to retrieve them as seventy-two meters away William Harrington squeezed the trigger of the dart gun, breathing the word "Now!" between his clenched teeth.

The flechette passed six inches over Travers' head and embedded itself noiselessly in the wooden door. In the split second that it took Harrington to realize what had happened, Travers had stepped inside. Through the crosshairs, Harrington saw the door closing.

Harrington raged at his bad luck, pounding the side of the car door with his large fist. "You son of a bitch," he said. "You bastard. I'll get you next time."

He started up the car and peeled out more noisily than necessary. The director would not be pleased.

Travers and Valerie were mounting the stairs. As they reached the first-floor landing, Valerie said, "That's odd, darling. Gladstone isn't barking at us tonight."

"He died last week."

"Oh, the poor dear. He was such a sweet dog. His owner must be heartbroken."

"He is."

They had a nightcap and went into the bedroom. Travers took his clothes off while Valerie went into the bathroom. He watched her undress when she came out. The sight of her naked body excited him, as always. She came to bed and caressed him, not that he needed it.

"Kiss me there," he said suddenly. She obeyed. She was up on her knees above him, kissing him, licking him, running her tongue gently up and down and around and then taking him fully in her mouth, and he was caressing her all the while from behind.

After a few moments, he pulled her down and entered her roughly. They were both very passionate and they came together. Afterward, they lay quietly together for a long time, bodies touching, Valerie's head on his shoulder. He thought about their love. Their physical intimacy was an important part of it, something they both wanted very much and needed. But there was something else. Before he had met Valerie, Travers realized, he had been pretending. Going through the motions of living. He did his work, he ran the station and did it well, but something was missing. There was an emptiness inside him. Now he felt alive again, for the first time in years. That was it; their love was a celebration of life.

He did not then know, of course, how close he had come to death.

Chapter 22

Travers was jolted awake by the persistent ringing of the telephone. He groped for the instrument and grunted a sleepy "Hello?"

The connection was bad and the caller sounded far away. "This is your uncle. I'm in London. I've got to see you."

Although only half awake, Travers recognized Goodman's voice.

"You shouldn't have called me here."

"I couldn't reach your friend. She wasn't home."

"That's odd." Travers looked at Valerie who was naked and propped up on one elbow, watching him. He silently mouthed the word "Ben."

He shoved a pillow behind his back and sat up. "Where are you now?"

"At Heathrow. I just got in. I didn't sleep very much on the plane, so I'm a little punchy."

"Okay, have some breakfast and a lot of coffee. You've got time to kill so don't hurry. Then take the underground to Russell Square. The Piccadilly Line is the only one that goes from Heathrow, so there's no way you can get on the wrong train."

"Where should we meet?"

"The British Museum, but it doesn't open until ten. When you come up out of the tube, you'll be in Bloomsbury. If you want to, you can wander over to Gordon Square and see where Virginia Woolf and her friends lived. Or Tavistock Square, where Dickens wrote *A Tale of Two Cities*. By then it will be ten. Walk down to Great Russell Street and go in the front entrance to the museum. You'll be in a big entrance hall. You'll see a stairway on the left. Take it to the upper floor and work your way over to the Egyptian Galleries on the north side of the museum. I'll meet you in Room Sixty, by the mummies, at five minutes past ten."

"I'll be there."

Valerie was laughing when he hung up. "By the *mummies*. Will you be wearing your cloak and dagger? Really, darling, sometimes you do act like a spy."

"I thought it would be appropriate. The company is trying to embalm me."

Valerie's smile faded. "It must be awfully serious if Ben flew all the way here to see you."

"I expect so."

"Can I come?"

"Hell, no. In case you don't know, you're my cut-out to the committee and Goodman. The three of us can't be seen together. I'm taking a big chance meeting with him. But I don't expect Hansen spends a lot of time hanging around the British Museum."

"Then take me along."

"No."

The subject was closed. They got up and made toast, eggs, and coffee. "I'll be having lunch with Mary Hodges at the Chelsea Potter," Valerie told him. "I'm trying to get her to carry more of my pieces at her shop. She'll bring along any mail that's come in for me. After that, I'll be back at my flat. Let me know what happens."

"I will."

They got ready to leave. Valerie said, "During the night, in your sleep, you rolled over to my side and were holding on to me. Do you remember?"

"No," Travers said. "I don't remember."

Goodman didn't look much better than the mummies, Travers thought. He had bags under his eyes from lack of sleep, his pock-marked features were sagging, and his suit was badly rumpled. To top it off, he smelled like a stale cigar that someone had left in an ashtray overnight.

"Hello, Ben." Travers extended a hand. "You're looking great," he lied.

"I feel terrible," Goodman said. "I don't like airplanes. Where'd the Brits steal all these mummies?"

"The fruits of empire," Travers said. "Archaeology is a fancy name for grave-robbing. At least the Egyptians will tell you that. Look at this one. Some of these fellows were pickled as far back as forty-five hundred B.C."

Goodman glanced around. The museum had just opened, and the gallery was empty. "I'm afraid I have bad news," he half-whispered. "The senator wanted me to tell you in person."

"I figured it was pretty important to bring you to London."

"We tried to warn you with the cable. There's no longer any question. Someone in the station, code-named LS/Talpia, is trying to kill you. We assume it's Hansen, although we're not positive. Last week, he killed a dog outside your house."

"Gladstone. I should have realized." Travers wondered if he were slowing down. It had never occurred to him to make the connection. Poor Dawkins, he would never know the agency had killed his dog.

Ben was still whispering. "You don't know how glad I was to hear your voice this morning when you answered the phone. Last night, you were targeted."

"How do you know?" Travers' voice was flat, unemotional.

"Did you go to the theater?"

"Yes." How the hell did Hansen know that? *Ann.* Of course. She had been chatting with him, thinking he was lonely. She must have mentioned they had theater tickets.

Goodman mopped his brow with a handkerchief. "He was

waiting for you, across the square, when you got home. By now, you should be dead."

"Either he was called off at the last minute, or he missed."

"Did you hear anything?"

"No. But he would have used a silencer. Or it could have been a dart gun. They're silent."

"Jesus."

"The code name, Ben. Did you say it was LS/Talpia?"

"Yes."

Travers pondered the information for a moment. "The LS is a digraph for London. We use it for all our operations here. But Talpia is curious."

"Does it mean anything?"

"Yes, it's an animal. The phylum is Chordata, the family is Talpidae. Of course—the common name for the species is a mole!"

"A mole?"

"Yes. It makes sense. Don't you see, Ben, Hansen—and that's probably not his real name—or whoever is tracking me needed to be given a reason to assassinate the chief of the London station. So they must have told him I'm a mole. A Soviet agent."

A well-dressed Scandinavian couple came into the gallery. The woman was blonde, and Travers noted, had a sensational figure. She stopped to admire a mummified cat.

Travers pointed to one of the Canopic jars. "They used these to hold the entrails of the dead," he said. "The jars were entombed with the mummies."

They walked into the next gallery. It was empty. They stood in front of the papyri of the Books of the Dead.

There was urgency in Goodman's voice. "The senator is persuaded your story is true. We've seen enough on the intercepts to believe you. Our concern now is for your safety. He wants you to leave London immediately and disappear for a while."

"I can't just leave. I've got a station to run. A staff of two hundred people."

"You're no use to us dead."

"Look, even if I agreed to go, the chief of the London

station can't just vanish. The press would be on it within a week."

"Then take a vacation. It's summertime. No one will think that's unusual."

Travers swiftly considered his options. If Hansen had tried to kill him last night, he would certainly try again. Perhaps next time he would not miss. Owens was right. "Okay," he said. "I can take a few weeks' vacation without arousing a lot of talk. If that's what the senator wants, I'll do it."

Ben looked relieved. "In the meantime, I'll be turning over every rock in Maryland and Virginia to find Site Orange. Radner will help me."

"We can communicate through an accommodation address." Travers took a pen from his pocket and wrote out the information on a small slip of paper. "It's listed as a theatrical booking agency on the Strand," he said. "Dick Austin will pick up any messages and relay them to you."

"Can he be trusted?"

"Completely."

"If we can locate Site Orange, we'll bring you back and have hearings soon after Labor Day."

"It won't be that simple, Ben."

"Why not?"

"Hansen will try to track me down when I leave London. The company has stations and bases everywhere, and close liaison with the security services of almost every nation in the world. He'll be on my trail no matter where I go."

"Can't you use another name, cover your traces somehow?"

"I have two or three operational passports in different names. But the pseudonyms and the numbers are stored in a computer at headquarters. They can retrieve them very quickly and teletype them around the world."

"You're a professional. You can elude them."

"I can try. But there's something else, Ben. The minute I leave London, you lose your NSA intercepts. If Hansen messages Langley from another station, you won't receive the copies."

"Unless you go to New Delhi or Accra."

"Those are hardly choice places for a white, male American to fade into the woodwork. No, I'll likely stick to the Continent. Western Europe is full of tourists this time of year, and I can blend in with the scenery. With luck, I may be able to slip between the cracks."

Goodman stuck out his hand. "Then I wish you luck." His voice was husky. He paused, then added, "I'll see you in Washington."

"So long, Ben."

Goodman left first. He turned for a moment in the door and looked back. Travers was standing alone in the gallery among the funerary boats, the tomb paintings, and the ancient papyri with their centuries-old messages of death.

Valerie was back at Margaretta Terrace after lunch, watering the plants in her flat, when she heard the key in the front door. It was Travers. She did not normally expect him in the middle of the afternoon.

"Hello, darling," she said. "You frightened me just now. For a second I thought it might be—"

"I'm sorry," he said. "I didn't want to use the phone."

"It's all right now." She smiled, and brushed a strand of hair back from her eyes. "What did Ben say?"

"That it's time for me to disappear." He filled her in on his meeting with Goodman.

"I'm glad you agreed," she said when he had finished. "It will be safer away from London. When shall we leave?"

"I'll be going alone."

"I want to come with you, Rob."

"I can't let you. Hansen will be on my trail. It would be dangerous for you, and I can travel faster alone."

"A couple attracts less attention than a man traveling by himself. We can go to small villages, out-of-the-way places where a single man would arouse comment. But a couple would seem perfectly ordinary."

"I'll be going alone," he repeated. He put his hands on her shoulders. "Cheer up. It's only for a few weeks."

She looked resigned. "When will you go?"

"Tomorrow. I told Ann Ganley that I've decided to leave on Monday for a three-week holiday. I asked her to get me a plane ticket to Lisbon. I told her I was driving down to the

Algarve and planned to spend my time loafing in a little fishing village near Albufeira."

"Where will you really go?"

"France, I think. Perhaps Switzerland. I know some villages in the Jura where I don't think even Hansen will find me."

"Stay with me tonight."

"I will. But I have to go back to the embassy first and clean up my desk, talk to Harding Westerfield, and arrange for things to keep running while I'm gone. And pick up my plane ticket."

"We'll have dinner here. I'll get a steak."

"See you around six, then." He kissed her lightly and was gone.

That night, they did not talk about his leaving, or where he would go. It was as if by not facing it, it would seem less wrenching, less final. When they went to bed, they made love fiercely, saying little. After breakfast, he kissed her and left, as though it were any other morning after they had spent the night together. Neither of them wanted to say the word "good-bye."

Travers took a taxi to his place and packed a bag, remembering to put in his .380 Walther PPK and the two extra magazines. He stopped at Mrs. Wilson's flat to tell her that he would be gone for a few weeks on holiday. She hoped he would have a good time and promised to look after the mail.

He let himself out the front door, walked up to Montagu Place and around the corner to where he had parked the TR7. Valerie was sitting in the passenger seat.

Travers reached in for her shoulder bag, put it with his in the boot, and slid behind the wheel. "I should have known," he said.

"We talked about it under the willow trees," Valerie replied. "I told you then that I wanted to share the danger. To be with you."

"It was different then. We were talking about something that might happen. An abstraction. It's real now."

"My feelings are the same."

Travers' answer was to turn the key in the ignition. "All right," he said. "If that's what you want."

"It's what I want."

Travers swung south toward the Thames. He crossed over at Vauxhall Bridge and headed southeast into Kent. It was midmorning and there was a fair amount of traffic by the time they picked up M20 near Farningham.

"Where are we going?" Valerie asked.

"To Folkestone," he said. "There's a Sealink boat that leaves tonight for Ostend. I plan to buy two tickets."

"What time do we sail?"

"The boat leaves at seven. We won't be on it."

"Oh. Then what do we do?"

"You'll see."

Despite the traffic, they reached the coast in two and a half hours, in time for lunch on the terrace of a restaurant overlooking the Channel. They inhaled the clean sea air and enjoyed the sight of the water sparkling in the sunlight.

The waiter brought them each a glass of wine. When he had gone, Travers said, "There are two ways that most people leave England. By air, or cross-Channel on the Sealink ferries or the Hovercraft. So, we must do neither."

"Then we'll stay right here in England? Hide in the north country, perhaps?"

"No, I've thought of that. It's too risky. MI5 is efficient. Hansen, if he is LS/Talpia, is acting for Towny Black. I have to assume he can enlist the full resources of the agency. That means that in any country we travel in, it's quite possible that the security forces, the local police, and the agency stations will all be on the lookout for us."

"Then how do we slip through the holes in the net?"

"Airports and major railheads are always closely watched, but there are other ways to travel. Do you remember where I grew up?"

Valerie smiled. She understood now. After Travers paid the check, they walked down to the waterfront and spent an hour wandering along the docks. It was midafternoon when Travers found what he wanted—the *Annabel,* a thirty-one-foot sloop berthed next to a hand-lettered sign that said "Available for charter—enquire at the Rose and Crown."

They doubled back to the dockside pub that they had passed a few moments earlier. The barman declined to provide the name of the owner but made a telephone call, which soon produced a ruddy-faced, bearded man of about thirty-five who introduced himself as John Campbell.

"I'm George Sinclair," Travers said, shaking hands. "I understand you have a Nicholson Thirty-one that might be available for charter."

"For the right person," Campbell replied. "She's a beauty. Normally, I'd be sailing her myself. But I've got a chance to crew an ocean racer in Cowes Week, so I thought I might just charter the sloop. To the right sort of person, you know."

"Well, we'd like to have her for about three weeks. My friend and I"—Travers smiled at Valerie—"are planning to sail around the Channel Islands and visit friends in Saint Helier. I'm a good sailor," he added reassuringly.

"I see." The captain thought he understood well enough. The rich American had found himself a young bird and planned to go on a bit of a cruise. They'd probably spend most of their time below decks.

"Well, I'm not in the charter business in a regular way," Campbell hedged. "I'm an estate agent, you see. My uncle owns the business. But I think I can judge a man, and I trust you." He lowered his voice. "If you leave your car with me as a deposit, I'll let you have her for two-fifty a week, no papers, cash in advance. No sense turning it all over to Inland Revenue, is there?" Campbell laughed heartily.

"You've got a deal," Travers said. Campbell winked at the barman and accompanied Travers and Valerie back to the *Annabel*. "You won't find a better cruiser than the Nick Thirty-one," Campbell said. "She's got a Yanmar two-QM twenty-two horsepower diesel, a two-ton lead keel, and Lewmar winches throughout. I keep her in Dover, normally. Just visiting today."

Travers checked over the hull, the engine, the stern gear, and the rigging and pronounced himself satisfied. It was a beautiful boat in fine condition. He paid Campbell in cash and they shook hands.

"I'll bring the car back in an hour," Travers said.

Campbell nodded and wished them a good holiday. "Enjoy yourself in Jersey, miss," he said.

Valerie smiled. "I'm sure we will, Mr. Campbell."

After Campbell had left, they walked back to where they

had parked the Triumph and drove to the Sealink terminal. Travers bought two passenger tickets to Ostend. The fare came to a little over seventeen pounds. They were required to show their passports, and Travers used his true-name passport, although he had the three others with him.

"Will you be taking a vehicle?" the woman behind the ticket window asked.

"No," Travers replied. "We'll be spending most of our time in Brussels and Amsterdam, and we expect to travel by rail."

When they left the terminal, Travers drove away from the harbor to Dover Road until he found a grocery store. "We'll need an awful lot of provisions for three weeks," Valerie said as they got out of the car. "Is the galley big enough to store it all?"

"We only need food for three days," Travers said. "We won't be on the *Annabel* any longer than that."

"Then why did you pay for three weeks?"

"So the owner won't report his boat missing before then. While Hansen and the agency are looking for us on the coast of Portugal or in Belgium we'll be in France."

"Where can we land?"

"Not in Calais. It's crawling with immigration, customs, and police, because a lot of the ferries and the Hovercraft go there. And the big ports like Le Havre and Cherbourg are watched. But there are dozens of little harbors along the Normandy coast where we can put in with no difficulty."

"Won't someone ask to see our passports?"

"It's a risk, but unlikely. In the summertime, there are hundreds of boats sailing along the coast every day. It would be a hopeless job for the French authorities to keep track of them all. Besides, most people don't expect a fugitive to arrive in a thirty-one-foot sloop."

"Will it be rough going across?" Valerie asked. "The Channel can be very nasty."

"If the weather holds, no worse than rounding Cape Ann to Rockport," Travers said. "We do have to be careful to cross the shipping lanes at right angles. That's the only tricky part. The shore controllers will have us on radar all the way across."

They bought their provisions, drove back to the docks, and

loaded them aboard the sloop. Then Travers drove the car back to the pub. He parked, gave the keys to Campbell, and walked back to the *Annabel*.

Toward evening a brisk wind came up from the northwest. Travers was pleased; it meant clear skies and good visibility. They sailed at dusk, as the harbor lights were winking on.

He set a course almost due southeast for Cap Gris-Nez so that they would cross the Channel at its narrowest point. The wind was fair and steady on the starboard quarter, and the sloop, heeling slightly, bowled easily across the waves for France.

The stars came out and a bright moon, and Travers uncorked a bottle of dry white wine while Valerie took the tiller. He went down the ladder for a moment and came back up with two glasses. He poured the wine and raised his glass in a toast. "To our disappearance," he said.

Valerie touched her glass to his. Sitting there in the cockpit under the stars, huddled against Travers for warmth, watching the full draw of the sails in the wind, Valerie had no sense that they were running from danger. For a while, at least, she forgot to be afraid.

At dawn, the wind still held fair as the coast of France greeted them, dark and light shades of green rising out of the blue water. Travers had taken the helm most of the night, but Valerie stood watch for a few hours before first light so that he could get some sleep.

They had hauled in sail and were moving due south now, running down the coast, away from the chalky cliffs of Cap Gris-Nez. Valerie made coffee. Travers pointed off the port bow. "The spires of Boulogne, the Haute Ville."

Valerie nodded. "It's not my favorite city. Caesar and his legions sailed from there when he defeated us."

"Well, cheer up. Napoleon tried the same thing and never left port."

The weather continued fair and the wind steady as they sailed south, past Le Touquet along the coast of Picardy. They were making about four knots. Travers seemed in no hurry, and it was Monday before they reached Dieppe and turned west along the Normandy coast. There were many other boats in the water now, as they sailed along past Pourville, Varengeville-sur-Mer, Sainte-Marguerite, and Saint-Valery-en-Caux, to the cliffs of Fécamp.

"When do we get back on dry land?"

"Tomorrow."

On Tuesday, a strong offshore breeze came up. Bucking the headwind, Travers tacked past Le Havre, and put in at Honfleur. The sun was dancing on the blue water, and the ancient fishing port, nestled against a hill on the estuary of the Seine, was breathtaking in its beauty.

"No wonder the Impressionists painted it," Valerie said. "It's incredible."

"They started here," Travers said. "Boudin was from Honfleur. In time they all came—Corot, Monet, Dufy. You can see why."

Travers came about, dropped his sails, and motored the *Annabel* through the canal and into the rectangular-shaped old harbor. Valerie admired the houses lining the quay. They found a spot to moor near Saint Catherine's church. At a signal from Travers, Valerie jumped off the deck onto the quay, caught the bow line he threw to her, and secured it to an iron ring. Travers followed, and made fast the stern and spring lines. Then they climbed back aboard and furled the mainsail and the jib.

Valerie was edgy. "Won't there be someone from the port or customs, asking to see our passports?" she asked.

"No. Look around."

Valerie did, and she was puzzled. It was the middle of the summer, the height of the tourist season in Normandy, and yet the port seemed almost deserted. There were very few people in sight.

Travers grinned, enjoying her bewilderment. "It's Bastille Day," he said. "The commandant du port and just about everyone else is marching in the parade down the rue de la République. We won't be bothered."

They strolled along the quay and found an *auberge* overlooking the harbor that was open for business. "I'm starving," Valerie said.

They sat down at an outdoor table. Travers ordered white wine and *fruits de mer*—the crab, shrimp, and mussels so plentiful along the Normandy coast. Between the fish and the meat course, the waitress automatically brought them Calvados. "It's supposed to fill *'le trou Normand,'*" Travers said, "the hole in the meal."

"It's awfully strong." Valerie grimaced after drinking a little.

"Not if you're weaned on it. In Normandy, they get their children to go to sleep by spiking their bottle with Calvados."

Valerie laughed. "It's lovely here. And I feel quite safe. As though no one will ever find us."

"He may."

"Nonsense. I'll bet he's far away. Probably poking around Lisbon or Brussels at this very moment."

"Perhaps."

Travers paid the check and stood up. "Come on. For dessert, we'll go to the market."

People had begun drifting back from the parade, and the market in the village square behind the church was bustling. Farmers' wives from the surrounding countryside sat in folding chairs along the sides of the square, selling *fraises des bois,* wild strawberries, and thick, ivory-colored cream, which they dispensed from big aluminum jugs. Women from the village came with glass jars. Travers and Valerie watched as the vendors filled them with *crème fraîche* from the metal jugs, covering the jars with wax paper and a rubber band.

"We're out of luck," Valerie said. "We don't have a jar."

"Don't worry." Travers picked out a farm woman with a friendly face and negotiated a package deal. For ten extra francs, she threw in a jar with the strawberries and cream. They wandered along the marketplace past other farm women selling squashes, leeks, peaches, melons, and cheese. Then they walked back to the quay and sat by the edge of the Vieux Bassin to eat their strawberries and cream. They were within sight of the *Annabel,* but Travers noted that no one was paying the slightest attention to the sloop in the midst of the crowded harbor.

"We'll sleep on the boat tonight," Travers said. "If we stay at a hotel, they might want to see our passports."

"And tomorrow?"

"In the morning we'll find a way to get to Paris."

"What are you going to do about the boat? Just leave it?"

"Don't worry. After it's been there a few weeks, the harbor master will notice it, get in touch with the British, and it will be returned."

"I wish we could stay here."

"We have to keep moving. It's best."

When they had finished their strawberries, they walked over to the *Annabel.* Aware of the tidal drops, Travers moved the sloop away from the quay a few feet and moored alongside a pontoon. Then they climbed the Côte de Grâce and admired the sweeping view across the Seine to Le Havre. They visited the peaceful little chapel beneath the trees. Late in the afternoon, they walked down to the rue Haute, past homes in which wealthy shipbuilders had once lived. They found a little restaurant in the Old Quarter for dinner. Afterward, they headed back to the harbor. It was getting dark, and as they walked along the rue des Capucins in the half-light, Valerie thought for a moment that she caught a fleeting glimpse of a heavyset blond man in a doorway.

She squeezed Travers' arm in alarm. "Take it easy," he said. "You're just a little jumpy. If he comes, it won't be this soon. He would need more time to pick up our traces."

They boarded the sloop. They were both tired and soon went below to their bunks. There was a light breeze from the Channel and the *Annabel* rocked gently at her mooring. Valerie was drifting off to sleep. She thought again of the man she thought she had seen in the street and shivered. She listened in the darkness, all her senses alert, but she could hear nothing except the murmur of distant voices speaking French and the steady lapping of the water against the hull.

Chapter 23

In the morning, they were up early and had coffee and croissants in a little café near the old marketplace. There was only one other patron, a short, dark-haired man in his forties. From his calloused hands, cap, and blue work clothes, Valerie judged him a farmer.

He seemed a friendly man, and Travers' French was good enough to allow him to strike up a conversation. After a moment, he turned back to Valerie. "He's taking cheeses to market in Rouen. He'd be glad to give us a lift if we don't mind riding in the back with the cheeses. It's an open truck."

Valerie smiled at the man. *"Merci, monsieur,"* she said. *"Vous êtes très gentil."*

To Travers she said, "A *cheese* truck. A bit of a comedown from the *Annabel*."

"It's the only way to travel."

They paid their checks, the farmer refusing Travers' offer to pick up his. The truck, ancient but serviceable, was parked outside the café. The farmer lowered the tailgate and motioned them aboard. They scrambled up into the truck and settled down among the Camembert and Pont-l'Evêque.

Valerie wrinkled her nose. "Whew. Something's *very* strong."

"It's the Livarot. They make it from milk that's aged."

"You ought to tell your Pentagon about it. It would make an absolutely marvelous secret weapon."

They bounced along in the truck, enjoying the lush scenery of the Risle valley. Miles of apple orchards stretched out on both sides of the road. North of Pont-Audemer, the truck swung on to the main highway and headed due east.

"He's taking the quickest route to market," Travers said.

"C'est la vie," said Valerie, who did not at all mind the shortest route. It meant less time among the cheeses.

Before long, the truck left the main highway and sped north toward the river and Rouen. The driver let them off at the place du Vieux Marché, near the spot where Joan of Arc had been burned alive more than five centuries before. A modern glass-and-concrete church had been built on the square in her memory. But it was still a marketplace, as well; in the stalls around the new church, vendors were selling fish, meat, vegetables, and flowers of all kinds. They hopped down and the farmer waved good-bye, after politely refusing Travers' offer to pay for the gas. The Americans had been in Normandy before, he reminded Travers, and they had paid enough on the beaches. *Ça c'est sûr.*

They thanked him and Valerie blew him a kiss, earning a huge grin in return. "He was a nice man," she said.

"Yes. Let's hope he forgets us."

"There's not much chance anyone would find him, is there?" Valerie sounded somewhat anxious.

"Not much."

They walked along the rue du Gros Horloge, pausing to admire the great clock and then passing through the archway below it. They stopped for lunch at a little café nearby. They sat at a sidewalk table and sipped cold white wine.

Travers said, "It's ironic that Rouen has so many monuments to Joan of Arc."

"I suppose it's their way of making amends."

"The legend is that when they burned her at the stake, the fire could not destroy her heart, so they threw it in the Seine."

Valerie shuddered. "I'm not sure the world has made much progress in five centuries."

"How do you mean?"

"Well, in your own way, you're a heretic within the agency. So they're trying to kill you."

Travers took a sip of wine. "And Towny Black is Bishop Cauchon? It's an interesting analogy. Gene McCarthy once compared the agency to a monastic order, in which the whole ritual of secrecy becomes the end."

"I think he was right. You've taken the vows. So did my father."

After lunch they explored the cathedral. They spent most of the time outside, admiring the west façade, the great towers, and the three magnificent doorways. Travers was checking his watch. "We'd better start for the station. The Paris train leaves at four forty-eight."

At the station, Travers bought their tickets. The train was a few minutes late, but they were soon aboard, watching the French countryside slip by.

"Where will we stay tonight?" Valerie asked.

"We can't risk a hotel. The passport problem again."

"You have passports under other names."

"Yes, but you don't. And they know my alias names. They can bring them up on the Intellofax screen at headquarters in seconds."

"Then what can we do?"

"When we get to Paris, I'll make a phone call."

They were pulling in to the Gare Saint-Lazare. As they walked through the vast station toward the street, Travers checked the terminal with a practiced eye. Two men in gray suits, whom he assumed to be French plainclothes detectives, lounged near the information kiosk. One pretended to read *Le Monde*. The other studied his large shoes. Both appeared utterly uninterested in Travers or Valerie.

When they had stepped out into the street, Valerie said impulsively, "Let's walk to Montmartre and climb to the Sacré-Coeur." It was near sunset; she knew the view would be spectacular.

"I should make my phone call," Travers said doubtfully.

"Later. Come on." She took his hand and led him along. They worked their way through the narrow streets to the base of the hill. Ignoring the funicular, they walked up the endless steps to the top and turned to look out at all of Paris spread before them. As they watched, the lights of the city began to come on.

The sky was pink, and even in the gathering dusk they

could see the blue and orange awnings below, bright dabs of color against the gray buildings, and winding among them, long ribbons of dark green formed by the chestnut trees along the avenues.

Valerie put her arm around Travers' waist. "It was worth the climb, wasn't it?"

"Yes. It's incredible." He nuzzled her hair. "And you, my darling, smell like Camembert."

"You *are* beastly. You have no romance in your soul. Paris has put on her diamond tiara for us, and you tell me I smell like a cheese."

"It's true. But you're still very beautiful." He kissed her on the cheek, laughing.

"Mmmm."

"I'd best find a telephone."

They walked toward the place du Tertre. Travers went into a *tabac,* bought a *jeton,* and descended the stairs to a pay phone.

He dialed a local number. The ring sounded far away, as though he might have been telephoning the moon instead of a number only a few miles away. But when it was answered, a man's voice came through strong and clear.

"Hello."

"Tom Brandon, please."

"Rob! How are you? Where are you?"

"I'm in Paris. Can you put me up for a few days? It's all rather sudden. I can explain when I see you."

"No problem."

"I've got a friend with me, a woman."

"Better yet. Ask her if she's got a sister."

"No sister. We'll be there in half an hour."

"I'll tell the concierge to expect you. And I'll be waiting for you both."

"Thanks, Tom."

Tom Brandon had been a classmate of Travers' at Yale. He was a lawyer with the Paris office of Bartley, White, Crenshaw & Underwood, a New York law firm with a blue-chip list of international corporate clients. They had remained close friends over the years, and it was a special relationship.

Brandon was aware that Travers worked for the agency. But in all the years they had known each other, he had never asked Travers a single question about what he did.

Although Brandon was from Michigan originally, he had lived in Paris so long that he regarded it as home. He had been married and divorced and now lived alone in an expensive apartment on the boulevard Suchet, overlooking the Bois.

Travers hailed a taxi. As they drove along the boulevard de Courcelles toward the Etoile, Travers filled Valerie in on Tom Brandon. "You'll really like him," he said. "I trust him completely."

"I didn't know you trusted anyone completely."

"I trust you. Dick Austin. And Tom."

Brandon was waiting with a bucket of ice cubes and a bottle of Dewar's. "You two look like you could use a drink and a shower," he said.

"Things *were* a little rustic on the way here," Valerie said, with a laugh. "And we didn't bring too many clean clothes. Just these little shoulder bags."

"Well, Rob's about my size if he needs anything. And you'd look good in one of my button-down shirts."

Valerie laughed. "I might take you up on that."

"Great." He poured the drinks and they settled in the living room. Brandon had the gift of putting people immediately at ease, and Valerie felt relaxed.

"I feel we've reached a safe port in storm," she said. Brandon raised his eyebrows but said nothing. He was an attractive man, Valerie thought, tall, although slightly shorter than Travers, with a thatch of straight, sandy hair that gave him a boyish look even in his mid-forties. He had light freckles on his face and long arms and legs that he tended to drape over whatever chair he sat in. The gangly, 4-H club appearance was deceptive, Valerie realized; the multinationals did not retain farm boys to handle their legal problems.

"This is really great of you, Tom," Travers said, "to take care of us on such short notice."

"My pleasure. Breaks up the bachelor routine."

"One thing, Tom." Travers took a sip of Scotch. "I'm having a little misunderstanding with my employer. So we're not really here, if anyone asks. You haven't seen us or heard from us."

"Fine and dandy. Let me know if there's anything I can do to help."

"I might ask you to rent a car in your name. We'll be pushing on in a couple of days."

"Stay as long as you like. I'll take care of the car whenever you give me the word."

"Thanks, Tom."

"You'd do the same for me." He paused. "Tell you what, I'll cook us a steak while you two are getting washed up. You'll be in the guest room. It's got a king-size bed, a nice view of the Bois, and a big bath. Better than the Plaza-Athénée and you can't beat the price."

Valerie got up. "I'll shower first. It takes me longer to dry my hair."

When she had left the room, Brandon raised his glass. "Congratulations," he said. "She's lovely."

"We're very happy together."

"Good. That's really good." His face turned somber. "Rob, the trouble you're having. It sounds serious."

"It is."

"And there's no way I can help?"

"You are helping, right now." He glanced around the room, with its lavish modern furnishings and high windows. "A luxury safe house on the Bois. What more could I ask?"

"Well, if you do need more."

"Thanks, Tom. For now, just the car. Perhaps you could see to it tomorrow."

"No problem. I'll leave the office a little early, rent the car, and drive it here."

"Great. Then we'll take off the next day."

Valerie reappeared looking scrubbed and relaxed in a white terry-cloth robe. "Shower's free," she said. "I stole your robe, Tom. Now I'd like to borrow that shirt you offered."

Brandon ducked into the bedroom and returned with a blue striped oxford, which he handed to Valerie. "It will look better on you than on me, I'm sure, even if it is a bit large."

While Valerie dried her hair with a blower and Travers

showered, Brandon busied himself in the kitchen with the steak. It was cooked the way Travers and Valerie both liked, medium-rare, and Brandon produced a bottle of Clos-Vougeot to go with it. "One of the fringe benefits of living in France," he said as he poured the wine.

"To fringe benefits," Travers said as he lifted his glass.

"To both of you."

The dinner went well. Valerie felt that she was welcomed into the friendship of the two men, not excluded from it, even when the talk turned to gossip about old friends from Yale. She liked Brandon, and she could see why Rob did. He was an Ivy League lawyer but not the least bit stuffy. She was impressed by what he did not ask. He did not ask anything about the company, or why the chief of the London station was in Paris incognito, or what sort of trouble they were in. That kind of friendship, Valerie realized, was a rare gift. A friendship that did not question, but accepted the friend as he was.

After dinner, Tom produced a bottle of *marc*. There was good talk, about Paris, and London, and President Anderson's political future. Travers even indulged in what was, for him, a rare luxury; he smoked a small H. Upmann cigar offered by Brandon.

It had been a long day, and suddenly both Valerie and Travers were very tired. They excused themselves and got ready for bed. Brandon switched on the stereo. "I'm not quite ready to turn in yet. I think I'll listen to records for a while." In the guest room, Travers turned off the light and Valerie stood by the window for a long time, looking out at the darkened Bois. The voice of Yves Montand, singing a love song, drifted in from the living room.

"What are you thinking?" he asked.

"Nothing," she said.

"You have to be thinking of something. Our minds won't let us not think. Even for an instant."

"I was just wondering."

"What?"

"When this is over, what will happen to us. I don't suppose we'll be in London again."

"We might. The important thing is we'll be together." He

came over to the window and cradled her face in his hands. "It doesn't matter where. We'll be together."

She searched for his eyes in the darkness. "Are you sure?"

"Just as sure as you were under the willow trees." They held each other then for a long time but neither of them spoke.

The morning sunlight was streaming in the room when Travers gently shook Valerie awake. "We have the whole day to spend in Paris," he said. "I want to show you some of my favorite places. Then, tonight, we'll take Tom to dinner somewhere on the Left Bank and in the morning we'll push on by car."

Brandon left for work after breakfast, and Valerie and Travers set off for the park. At the rue Louis-Boilly, he led her on a slight detour, down the block to the Musée Marmottan. "I want you to see the Monets," he said. Most of the paintings in the museum were the gift of the artist's son; there were landscapes and water lilies, and a portrait of Monet by Renoir.

Afterward, they walked through the Bois to the Bagatelle and admired the flowers. They sat on a hill overlooking the rose garden, and sunned themselves and talked. Then they made their way to the Pré Catelan and had lunch. Travers hailed a cab to take them to the Jeu de Paume, where they spent the middle of the afternoon.

Valerie was fascinated by Monet's studies of the Rouen Cathedral, more than twenty paintings showing the west façade at different times of day and in different seasons of the year. "I can hardly believe we were looking at the same doors twenty-four hours ago," she whispered.

Travers smiled, happy that Valerie was enjoying herself. "The Jeu de Paume is my favorite," Travers said. "It's spacious and cheerful and full of light. The Louvre is gloomy by comparison."

They left the museum and cut through the Tuileries to the Seine. Valerie thought of when she had last walked through the garden. It was less than four months ago but it seemed much longer. They strolled along the quay, hand in hand. Travers said, "This is obligatory for lovers in Paris."

"I like it, all the same."

They came to the pont du Carrousel and stopped halfway across to admire the Ile de la Cité, its prow of green, and the spires of Notre Dame.

"I've always thought that the view from this bridge was the most beautiful sight in the world," Travers said quietly.

"I'm glad you told me. I want to know all the places you consider beautiful. And I want to see them all."

"One day."

It was getting late and they returned to the apartment by cab. Tom was already there.

"I've hired the car," he said. "A snappy gray Peugeot. It's parked downstairs."

"Thanks, Tom," Travers said. "The least I can do is take us all out to dinner."

"Terrific." Brandon hesitated for a second. "But let's take my car. I know how to wind through the back streets. We might save a little time."

"Fine with me." Travers figured he would have enough driving to do the next day. They cut over to the Left Bank in Brandon's Citroën, and dined at the Pantagruel on the rue de l'Exposition. They ordered the turbot.

They were enjoying the meal, but Brandon seemed a little fidgety. Travers sensed that something was wrong. Over coffee, Brandon confided what was troubling him.

"I didn't want to say anything at the apartment," he said. "No sense ruining your meal."

"But?"

"I got a call today from a man who said he was with the Paris branch of the Yale alumni association. He was asking about old classmates and friends who might be living over here. Said they're putting together a directory. He asked about you."

Travers asked tensely, "What did you tell him?"

Brandon smiled his 4-H club smile. "Said I hadn't seen hide nor hair of you for six years."

"Good."

"I also asked him for his phone number. He gave it to me. When I tried to call him back I got a bakery in Montparnasse. The woman had never heard of *le* Yale."

"You did all right."

"There's more, unfortunately."

"What?"

"When I left my office to go to the car-rental place, I had a feeling I was followed. I didn't see anybody. But when I drove the Peugeot home, I checked in the rearview mirror. I was definitely being tailed. By a dark-blue BMW."

"Did you get a look at the driver?"

"It was hard to see his face. You know how the light reflects off a windshield, and it's darker inside the car. But he was big, I could tell that much. And he was wearing dark glasses."

"Could you tell anything else?"

Brandon shook his head. "Nothing really. Except that his hair was blond."

Chapter 24

Ben Goodman was scowling at the document on his desk. When he was angry, his dark, pock-marked face became even darker. He had been puffing hard on his cigar, and his face was surrounded by smoke, giving him at the moment the appearance of a small, fire-breathing dragon.

"The goddamn Pentagon," he said. "They take three weeks to get this list to us, and then it's screwed up." He slapped the document down on the desk.

Howard Radner looked sympathetic. "You can't expect too much from them. Their budget is only a hundred and eighty billion dollars."

"I didn't really think we'd find the 758th Special Operations Tac Group on here. But they don't even list Andrews Air Force Base. They include some broom closet the Army has in Alexandria, but they leave out a whole goddamn Air Force base."

"We could ask them to redo the list."

Goodman shook his head. "Time is running out. Travers is moving around Europe somewhere. We have to assume that Hansen is close on his trail, probably with support from all stations. We've got to find Site Orange and go public with hearings while we've still got a live witness."

"Still no word from Travers?"

"No. Dick Austin's watching the mail drop. Nothing's come in. We just have to pray he's okay."

"What do we do now?"

"You tell me, Howie. You're the ace investigator around here."

"I dunno. I don't know how you go about finding a secret missile base. Especially when the Pentagon may not even know it exists."

Goodman puffed on his cigar. He no longer looked angry, just thoughtful. "Get me a map," he said.

Radner left, walked down to his office, and rummaged in his desk with no luck. He went out in the corridor to Linda's desk. She was taking a coffee break, relaxing under a large B. Kliban poster of a cat in a tuxedo. "Hey, Linda," Radner said, "you got any local maps?"

She poked around in a bottom drawer and came up with a Triple A map for the National Capital Chesapeake Bay Area. She handed it to Radner with a smile. "If you want anything else, just let me know."

"Uh, thanks, Linda."

Goodman tacked the map up on the wall of his office with four blue pushpins. "Maybe if we look at this long enough, we can figure out where we would hide nuclear missiles if *we* were the agency."

"Well, it's worth trying, I suppose." Radner's voice lacked conviction.

Goodman did not reply. From a desk drawer, he removed a compass. He checked the scale of the map. One inch equaled 4.7 miles. He punched out some numbers on a desktop calculator. "Four and seven-eighths inches will be just a hair under twenty-three miles." Goodman measured out that distance between the two compass points. Then he stuck the sharp point into the map at the White House and drew a circle.

"That's interesting," Radner said. "Twenty-three miles doesn't really take us very far out of Washington."

"No, not far. But from any point within that circle, an Honest John rocket could be launched and hit the White House. If the president happened to be home, he'd be dead. So would a lot of other people."

Radner was examining the map. "On the north, the line goes through a point just below Columbia, Maryland. On the west, smack through Dulles International Airport, right between the north-south runways. On the south, the line crosses the Potomac at Occoquan Bay and runs right through the Naval Proving Grounds at Indian Head. On the east it almost reaches the Chesapeake."

"Okay," said Goodman, "let me check the map against our list. Just to see what military bases fall inside the circle."

Goodman glanced over the typed list again. He did not waste much time on the installations in Washington itself. "Bolling Air Force Base, the Washington Navy Yard, Fort McNair, the Naval Security Station," he read off. "And across the river, Fort Myer. But we don't need to worry about them. They're too well-known, too visible."

"And too close," Radner said.

"What do you mean?"

"That circle you drew represents the maximum range of the Honest John. But the *minimum* range is five miles. You couldn't hit the White House from any of the points you just mentioned. They're too close."

"How the hell did you know that?" Goodman was impressed.

"Been doing some homework," Radner replied, pleased with himself. "The Honest John is a free-flight, solid-propellant field-artillery rocket. Usually referred to as a missile. Free flight means it isn't guided. It follows a trajectory, like a cannonball. It has no inertial guidance, the way an ICBM has."

"What else did you find out?"

"The Honest John has been operational since the early 1950s. It's the oldest battlefield missile the government has. It's being phased out now, and replaced by Lance, which does have inertial guidance. In fact, the only Honest John battery left is in Korea."

"Except for Site Orange."

"Yeah."

Goodman lit a fresh cigar. "Well, it may be old, but it's still a nuke. And deadly."

"Extremely. It's not a strategic weapon, of course. It isn't meant to take out a whole city, like Minuteman. It's a tac missile, for use against targets like troops, tank concentrations, or POL dumps."

"What kind of fuel does it use?"

"Solid propellant. It's a brittle compound that comes in little, amber-colored three-inch squares. The agency would have no trouble at all storing the fuel."

"And the warheads?"

"Conventional or nuclear. The conventional warhead has fifteen hundred pounds of TNT. The nuclear warhead is designated the W31. Travers told us that."

"How big is the damn thing?"

"The warhead is nine feet long, and a little fatter than the rest of the missile. The overall length of the missile, including the warhead, is twenty-four point eight feet. Diameter, thirty inches. Weight, forty-five hundred pounds. That doesn't include the truck-mounted launcher."

"Well, all right, Howie. At least now we know what we're looking for."

"But not where to look."

"Let's check the rest of these bases on the Pentagon list, for what it's worth. Inside the circle, there's Cameron Station, Fort Belvoir, most of the Naval Proving Grounds, the Naval Radio Receiving Station near Clinton, Maryland, and our friends up at Fort Meade. And, of course, Andrews Air Force Base and the Naval Surface Weapons Center in White Oak. All these installations are pretty big, and well-known. Hell, I've heard of most of them myself. There's nothing here that looks suspicious—perhaps the 758th under a new name. So, the Pentagon list adds up to nothing. Zilch."

Radner paced back and forth in front of the map.

"Look, Ben," he said. "We've both known from the beginning that the chances are the Defense Department doesn't even know about the dummy CIA unit. And if they don't know about it, they can't list it. Even if there was a dummy unit that they *did* know about they probably wouldn't list it. The agency and the Army have played footsie for years."

"Then what do you suggest?"

"Why don't we take the opposite approach? Let's try to find a military installation that *isn't* on the Pentagon list. Something that people in the local area might know about but the Defense Department doesn't."

Goodman looked interested. "Okay, how?"

Radner studied the map again. "There aren't many counties involved. In Maryland, there's Montgomery, Howard, Anne Arundel, Prince Georges, and on the south, a tiny slice of Calvert and Charles. In Virginia, Fairfax, Arlington, a corner of Loudoun, and a small chunk of Prince William. Ten counties in all. Got a *Congressional Directory?*"

Goodman took one from his desk and handed it to his young assistant.

Radner riffled through the book. "From the maps in the back, we can tell what congressional districts the counties are in. There won't be as many districts as there are counties, of course, because the rural districts take in a lot of counties."

"What are you getting at?" Ben asked impatiently.

Radner was still counting. "Okay, in Maryland, the counties we want fall into the First, Fourth, Fifth, Sixth, and Eighth districts. In Virginia, the Eighth and the Tenth. That's seven districts in all." He flipped to the biographical section in the front of the directory. "This will give us the names of the congressmen. All we have to do is call the representative or a staff member for each district and ask them to tick off how many military installations they have in the counties inside our circle. It's only seven phone calls."

"Okay," Goodman said. "It's worth a try. I'll take the first three districts in Maryland. You take the rest, and Virginia. Check back with me here when you're done."

Radner went off, and Goodman sat down at his desk. He decided to begin with Maryland's First Congressional District. It was Republican country, a sprawling, enormous district that took in the Maryland tidewater counties below Washington and all of Maryland's Eastern Shore, stretching down to Crisfield and Tangier Sound, in the heart of the Chesapeake Bay's crab industry. It had been represented for years by Congressman Harley Beall, a chicken farmer from Denton. Goodman had never been fond of the people on the Eastern Shore. Insulated and suspicious, they seemed to him to have pinched faces and pinched souls. Socially, economically, and geographically, they were cut off from the rest of the country by the Chesapeake and the Delaware bays. To Goodman the result was an area that had all of the provincialism of New England, and none of the charm. Like most residents of Washington, he knew Denton mainly as a speed trap, one of a string of nondescript towns in which it was wise to slow down on the way to Rehoboth or Ocean City.

He picked up the phone and dialed Congressman Beall's office. He got a young woman who identified herself as Mary Lou Mills. No, the congressman was not in. "Look, Mary Lou," Goodman said smoothly, "I don't really need to talk to the congressman. I'll bet you could help me. Are you from the District?"

"Sure am," she said. "From Easton."

"Okay. My name is Ben Goodman. I'm with Senator Owens." He carefully avoided mentioning the Intelligence Committee. He did not want her ears to prick up. "The senator is doing a little survey of military installations in each congressional district. We're interested in trying to stop some of these base closings."

"Oh my," Mary Lou said. "I'd be glad to help with that. It's just terrible the way the Pentagon's been shutting down so many bases."

"Well, for the moment, I'm just interested in what you have in Charles and Calvert counties."

"Just those two? Well, let's see . . ." She thought a moment. "You know, I don't believe we have anything just there. There's the Patuxent air test center at Cedar Point. But that's in St. Mary's County."

"You're sure? No other military-type bases that you know about?"

"I'm sure."

"Well, thanks anyway."

"Call us again if we can be of any help."

"I will, Mary Lou. Thank you."

Goodman hung up. He went down the list, calling the three other congressional offices in turn. The results were the same. Either the staff members said there were no military installations in the areas he asked about or the bases were already on the Pentagon list.

Radner came back in the office. From the expression on his face, Goodman could see that he had fared no better.

"It's a dry well," Radner said glumly. "Nobody I talked to knows of any base that isn't on the list. You do any good?"

"Nope."

"So much for my bright idea." Radner sounded completely deflated.

"It was a good idea, Howie. It just hasn't worked."

"But why not? It must mean that Site Orange is hidden so far off the beaten path that no one knows about it, even local people."

Goodman shook his head. "It's hard to believe that someone wouldn't know. You can't hide a dozen twenty-five-foot missiles in a cow barn."

Radner walked over to the map on the wall and studied it again. "Or it could mean, Ben, that Site Orange isn't inside the circle. That we've been looking in the wrong place."

"That's not possible," Goodman argued.

"Look, Ben, we've been assuming all along that Black would stash his missiles within range of Washington."

"They wouldn't be much use anywhere else. Especially if Travers is right about Phase Red."

"But the missiles are mobile. The launchers are normally mounted on five-ton trucks. Suppose the agency set up Site Orange a little farther away from Washington. But not too far. Black would figure he could always move the missiles within range if he ever wanted to."

Goodman leaned back in his chair. "Howard, my boy, you're smart. Remind me if I ever get in trouble to hire you as my lawyer."

"That's a deal." Radner jabbed a finger at the map. "Why don't we try widening the circle. Let's go out to, say, fifty miles."

Goodman rechecked the map scale, took the compass and discovered it would not spread far enough. With a ruler, he measured ten and five-eighth inches due east from the White House, and made a little dot with a red pencil. He repeated the process seven times, swinging his ruler in a complete circle around the capital. Then he drew the circumference, connecting the dots freehand. He stepped back and admired his work. "There," he said. "That doesn't look bad."

"You see?" Radner said. "It gets us away from the suburbs and really out into the country. Where it would be a lot easier to hide missiles."

Ben agreed. He studied the map. "Now the circle runs on the north through Westminster, on the east across the Chesapeake to Oxford, on the south to the Rappahannock and Fredericksburg, and on the west through Upperville and a tiny slice of West Virginia around Harper's Ferry."

Radner flipped open the *Congressional Directory* to the maps section again. "Okay, in Maryland, we have to add two more congressional districts on our list. The Second and Third. In Virginia, the First and the Seventh. In West Virginia, only one, the Second. That's five more districts to check, plus the original seven. An even dozen."

"All right," Goodman said. "I'll take the first six districts in Maryland, and you do the others. Check back when you're done."

"Right."

Goodman called the three new Maryland districts first. They stretched almost to the Pennsylvania border on the north, and to the Blue Ridge mountains on the west.

He was able to talk directly with Ted Bailey, the congressman from the Sixth District, which was mostly in the Maryland panhandle, the narrow strip along the state's northern border that included Frederick, Hagerstown, and Cumberland. Bailey mentioned Fort Detrick, in Frederick, where the

Army and the CIA had conducted joint experiments in bacteriological warfare, and Fort Ritchie, near Sabillasville, where the president had his secret underground command post deep inside a mountain. In the event of a nuclear attack, Thurlow Anderson would be whisked there by helicopter. Ritchie was somewhat north of the fifty-mile perimeter. And both installations were well-known, at least in the Sixth District.

"Are there any other installations up there, Congressman?" Goodman asked. "Even small ones?"

"Sorry, Ben, that's it." Bailey gave a deep laugh. "And I would sure know if there were."

"All right, thanks, Congressman."

"Give my best to Senator Owens."

"I'll do that."

An aide in the office of Congresswoman Marjorie Hollis from Baltimore County, Spiro Agnew's old stamping grounds, knew of no bases in the district. Leroy Williams, the legislative assistant to Mitchell Jones, Baltimore's black congressman, mentioned only one, Fort Holabird.

Goodman ground out his cigar. Radner's idea made sense, but it was slow going. He decided to recheck the three districts he had called earlier, this time asking about installations inside the wider circle.

He dialed Congressman Beall's office again and asked for Mary Lou Mills. "Hi," he said, "it's Ben Goodman again in Senator Owens' office. You remember I asked you a little while ago about bases in Charles or Calvert counties?"

"I surely do. Would you like some more information?"

"Well, yes. What I'd like you to do, Mary Lou, is go right across the bay now and tell me about anything you've got in your other counties—Kent, Queen Annes, Talbot, and Dorchester." The counties ran north to south along the eastern edge of the Chesapeake, an area of endless coves, inlets, rivers, marshlands, and creeks. Between the estuaries of five rivers on the Eastern Shore were lacy fingers of land jutting out into the Chesapeake Bay. They formed an intricate network of snug harbors, well-known and much loved by weekend sailors from Annapolis.

"Let me think, Mr. Goodman."

"Take your time, Mary Lou." Goodman tried to sound his most avuncular.

"Well, there's the Edgewood Arsenal. The Army has that. And the Aberdeen Proving Ground, where they test weapons. But they're both on the other side of the bay up in Harford County."

And both too well-known, Goodman thought. "Anything else?" he asked. "Anything at all?"

"I don't think so. I'm from Easton, like I said, and I think there's a little radar station down on James Island. But that's all I can think of."

"Where's James Island?"

"South of Oxford. Off the mouth of the Little Choptank. But it's just a little itty-bitty place."

"Well, thanks, Mary Lou."

"Anytime."

It was only after he had hung up that a faint bell went off in Goodman's mind. The Choptank River. What was the connection? He was trying to remember something, but he couldn't. His thoughts were interrupted by the arrival of Howard Radner.

"Nothing, Ben," Radner said. "The Marine Corps air station at Quantico. And the Army Security Agency installation at Vint Hill Farms, near Warrenton. It's a code-breaking outfit. Both well-known and sure to be listed. You do any better?"

"No," Goodman replied gloomily. "Except there's something about the Choptank. Wait, Howie—I remember now. Christ, that's where the CIA hid Francis Gary Powers when they got him back."

"After they traded him for Abel?"

"Yeah. They flew him back and kept him in some sort of mansion they owned in Talbot County, on the Choptank. It was called Ashford Farms. They interrogated Powers for twenty-three days before they let the Armed Services Committee have a whack at him. I think they had a whole complex of buildings along the Choptank, south of St. Michaels. And a hell of a lot of land, maybe a hundred acres."

"Who mentioned the Choptank?"

"A girl who works for Congressman Beall. She happens to

be from around there, and she mentioned a radar station on some little island off the mouth of the Choptank."

"What's it called?"

"James Island."

Radner scanned the map. "Here it is, James Island. In the Chesapeake, about fourteen miles west of Cambridge."

"Find Linda," Goodman ordered.

Radner ducked out into the hall, and in a moment came back with the secretary in tow.

"Get me NORAD in Colorado Springs," Goodman barked. "Ask for the colonel in charge of public information."

Linda wore a bovine expression. "Do you know Mr. Norad's first name, sir?"

"The North American Air Defense Command, for God sakes!" Goodman snapped.

"Yes, sir."

She disappeared. The two men waited in silence. After three minutes, the buzzer on Goodman's phone signaled that his call was ready.

"Senator Goodman? Colonel Riley here, sir."

"No, no. I'm not a senator. I work for a senator, Barry Owens."

"I'm sorry, sir. I must have misunderstood the young lady. What can we do for you, sir?"

"Colonel, I just have a few questions. Would NORAD be the only military command to operate radars in this country?"

"Yes, sir. If you're talking about land-based radar. We're responsible for the air defense and ballistic-missile warning for the continental United States. For aircraft warning, we have a string of fifty sites around the perimeter of the United States. These are your standard, rotating disc-type radar."

"What are the locations along the East Coast?"

"Well, there's Montauk, Long Island; Gibbsboro and Atlantic City, New Jersey, Cape Charles, Virginia; Roanoke Rapids, North Carolina, and quite a few others. The list is fairly long, sir."

"Colonel, do you have an air-defense radar on James Island, in the Chesapeake Bay?"

"I'd have to check that, sir. I can bring it up on the computer if it's there, sir. I'll have to put you on hold."

There was a click and Goodman waited. He put his hand over the mouthpiece. "He's checking it out," he told Radner.

There was a four-minute wait during which Goodman impatiently drummed his fingers on his desktop. Then he heard another click in the receiver, and a dial tone.

"Fuck!" Goodman exploded. "How the hell do they expect to protect us against a Soviet nuclear attack if they can't even work a hold button?"

"He'll probably call right back."

"No. Tell Linda to get him first. I don't want him calling in and finding out I'm with the Intelligence Committee. He may be an agency fink in Air Force blue, for all we know."

Radner went out to give Linda the message and came back. In a moment, Goodman was reconnected.

"Mr. Goodman, sir? Colonel Riley here again. I'm sorry we got cut off. I have the data you want now, sir."

"Yes?"

"Negative, sir. Someone must have given you wrong information. There is no radar base on James Island."

Chapter 25

Travers' internal alarm clock awoke him at 4:00 A.M. Gently, he shook Valerie.

"Reveille," he whispered. "Getting up time. Come on."

Under his repeated prodding and cajoling, Valerie finally opened her eyes. With great effort she looked toward the window.

"Still dark out," she protested. She tried to roll over on her right side, but Travers pulled her back.

"That's just the point. I want to leave before dawn. He won't expect us to take off this early."

The mention of their pursuer was like a bucket of cold water. Valerie sat up. "What about Tom?"

"I told him last night we might leave before he woke up. He'll understand."

Valerie, fully awake now, padded barefoot into the kitchen. She made coffee and put some croissants in the oven, taking care to move quietly so as not to awaken Brandon. They ate breakfast, packed their small shoulder bags, and were on their way in the Peugeot before the first light of dawn.

There was not much traffic on the boulevard Périphérique at that hour and they were soon heading south along the Autoroute du Sud in the early-morning mists.

"How did he find us?" Valerie asked.

They were speeding past Orly. Travers had been checking the rearview mirror at three-minute intervals. He saw nothing suspicious.

"Any number of ways. They could have discovered fairly quickly that I wasn't on a Lisbon flight, or the boat to Ostend. They could have found the TR7. They may have checked along the waterfront and discovered that a couple answering our description chartered the *Annabel.*"

"But we could have sailed anywhere."

"If Hansen has the cooperation of the French DST, which we don't know for sure, they might have found the sloop at Honfleur. Sooner or later someone will wonder where the owner is."

"And they found the cheese farmer, too? It doesn't seem possible. Even if they did, our trail would end in Rouen."

"My hunch is that they didn't do it that way."

"Then how?"

Travers pulled out into the fast lane to pass a gasoline truck. "My guess is that Hansen asked them to check my soft file at Langley."

"You'll have to translate that."

"There are two sets of files at headquarters. And in our stations, too. One set is official. They're tightly controlled, highly classified, and subject to the usual physical-security controls, locked safes and the rest."

"And the other set?"

"Those are the so-called 'soft' files. Officially, they don't exist. So they're not subject to being released under the Freedom of Information Act, or subpoenaed by Congress or the courts. They're kept in special safes. They contain a lot of personal information. About friends, lovers, habits, vices, interests. If a division chief finds out that one of his case officers is screwing around with somebody else's wife, or snorting coke, he may not report it to the Office of Security. He may just drop it in the officer's soft file, for future reference."

"How would your file lead them to Brandon?"

"Tom is one of my oldest and closest friends. We were at Yale together. We've kept in touch, and every once in a while when I get over to Paris, we've gone out on the town, sometimes with dates. The Paris station may have noted his name for my soft file."

"But how could they be sure you'd come here? You must have other friends on the Continent."

"Very few. Most of the friends we had on my tours in Vienna and Berlin were fellow case officers. They've long since been rotated to other stations, or back to Langley. Or they've left the company. So Brandon was a good bet. My guess is that Hansen didn't follow us to Paris."

"He waited for us to come to him."

"Exactly. He probably staked out Tom's apartment and the Bartley, White offices on the avenue Montaigne. But maybe he missed us Wednesday night. Yesterday, he saw Tom rent a car, something out of his usual pattern of activity, so he followed him home. He was probably watching when we came back from the pont du Carrousel."

Valerie shuddered. "But he's not following us now."

Travers checked the rearview mirror again. "No. But he knows the number of our license plate. The police may be looking for us."

"Do you think they are?"

"I'm not sure. It all depends on whether headquarters asked any foreign intelligence services for help in finding us."

Near Fontainebleau, Travers left the main highway and headed east for Sens. "Why this way?" Valerie asked.

"I'm going to take the old Route Six through Burgundy. Most people in a hurry stay on the Autoroute du Sud. It's much faster. But if you're running, the best thing to do is act like you're not. We'll motor through the medieval towns of Burgundy, like all the other tourists."

They drove at a leisurely pace through Joigny, Auxerre, and Avallon. Then Travers cut east. But before reaching Dijon, he left the highway and turned south on a little back road that paralleled the Ouche. The countryside was beautiful.

"It's so peaceful," Valerie said. "Let's stop for a little while."

Travers pulled over and they sat on a grassy slope by the river. There was no wind and the Ouche looked like a mirror, reflecting the tall poplar trees on the opposite bank. Cows grazed in the meadow across the stream, and a young farmer carrying a switch for the cattle walked slowly along a path by the river.

"We're really in the wine country now," Travers said. "Gevrey-Chambertin, Clos-Vougeot, Pommard, Nuits-Saint Georges—they're all within a few kilometers of where we're sitting."

"If we had time, we could taste them all," Valerie said, laughing.

Travers looked at his watch. "If we had time. But we've got a long way to go. Let's push on."

They climbed back into the Peugeot. Travers followed the river for another fifteen kilometers to Bligny-sur-Ouche, then turned southeast to Beaune. He pulled into the boulevard Clemenceau and they stopped for lunch at the sidewalk restaurant of the Hôtel de la Poste. They ordered a light meal—the trout, a green salad, and a half bottle of Meursault.

By one o'clock they were on their way south again. There

was quite a bit of traffic on the road now. At Chalon-sur-Saône, Travers turned due east. Valerie looked at him with an amused smile.

"No one will ever accuse you of being garrulous. Where are we going?"

"The Jura. We're going to cross the Swiss border. But we have to change our appearance a little bit first."

Soon they were climbing from the valley of the Saône, across the rolling foothills and vineyards and up into the mountains. They drove to Morez, in the steep valley of the Bienne, and Travers parked on a side street. "End of the line," he said. "We'll leave the car here."

"Now what?"

"We find a camping store." They explored the main street until Travers found what he was looking for. "This will do." They went in. A bell tinkled on the door of the little shop. Travers bought a pair of low, sturdy walking shoes for each of them and two green knapsacks. "The, how do you say, hiking boots are better for the mountains, *m'sieu*," the woman owner insisted in passable English.

"These will do," Travers said. "We are not going far."

"As you wish, *m'sieu*."

"*Merci, madame.*"

When they were out of the store, Travers said, "The trouble with boots is that you have to break them in for weeks. We can use the shoes today. They'll be a little stiff, but okay."

They returned to the car, opened up the trunk and repacked the contents of their shoulder bags into the two knapsacks. Then they changed their shoes.

"We're about eleven kilometers from the Swiss border," Travers explained. "We're going to cross it without showing our passports. Our new outfits will help."

"How do you plan to get us across?"

"Just over the border on the Swiss side is la Dôle, one of the higher peaks in the Jura. It's a popular tourist attraction. In the summer a lot of people from Geneva come out and picnic in the foothills or climb the mountain. We'll try to join them."

They walked back to the main street. Near the town hall, they found a local bus, already crowded with passengers, preparing to leave for la Cure, a tiny village on the border. From Morez, the bus climbed seventeen hundred feet along the winding, mountainous road to Switzerland. In la Cure, the bus stopped at the French customs checkpoint and the passengers piled out, Travers and Valerie with them.

Across the barrier, they could see the Swiss customs post. Between the two barriers, the tradesmen of la Cure were doing a brisk business in tax-free cigarettes, cigars, and liquor. "The border slices the town in two," Travers said. "It zigzags crazily and runs right through the Hôtel Franco-Suisse. You can't go from one floor to the other without passing through Switzerland. But the dining room is in France."

Travers got out his camera and took several pictures of Valerie. Then, like two happy tourists, they explored the little village. As soon as they were out of sight of the checkpoint, however, they cut south and rejoined the road to Gex that ran along the border on the French side. They hiked three kilometers south of la Cure and came to a bend in the road with a pine forest on one side and an open meadow on the other. Above them towered the Dôle.

There was no one else in sight and no fence along the border. They left the road and cut quickly across the open meadow to the base of the mountain. "Welcome to Switzerland," said Travers.

Although, for the Jura, the Dôle was a fairly tall peak, it was only a little over a mile high and an easy climb to the top. It was a bright, sunny day, but there was a light breeze, and it was cool walking through the shaded pines. There were several other hikers at the summit. The sun sparkled off Lac Léman below and they had a spectacular panorama of the Alps on one side and the Jura on the other. To the southeast, they had a clear view of Mont Blanc. Farther to the left they could see the crests of the Valais and the Matterhorn. Although it was midsummer, there were blankets of snow on the higher peaks, which glistened white in the sunlight, in sharp contrast to the dark-green larches and firs in the valleys.

"A lot of days," Travers said, "Geneva is socked in by fog. But you can come up here above the clouds and still enjoy the sunshine. That's one reason it's so popular."

After resting from their climb, they took the chair lift down to Saint-Cergue, the closest town on the Swiss side of the border. They joined a group of children who were crowding around a puppet show on the main street. A tall, thin American and his wife were taking pictures.

"C'mon, Jane," the American said. "Let me get a shot of you with the puppets in the background."

"It would be nice to be like them, wouldn't it?" asked Valerie. "Ordinary people on vacation. Innocents. Not running from anything or anyone."

"I don't know," Travers answered. "I've never lived a normal life. I've never been like anyone else."

"You've paid a high price to be what you are."

"Yes and no. I like the sense of being different."

From the village, they took an ancient little train that wound its way two thousand feet down to the lake and the lovely town of Nyon. It was late afternoon by now, and growing chilly, so they caught the train to Geneva. In fourteen minutes, they were pulling into the Gare Cornavin.

"We'll spend the night in Geneva," Travers said.

"At a hotel? They'll want to see our passports."

"Not in Switzerland. We'll be asked to fill in the numbers of our passports when we register. But they won't bother to look at them."

"So we can make a big show of pulling them out, and checking the numbers. And then write down the wrong numbers."

"You're learning fast. The next time we do this, I won't have anything to teach you."

"I hope there is no next time."

They walked a short way to the rue de Neuchâtel and checked in at the Byron. As Travers had predicted, the desk clerk had no interest in seeing their passports. Travers filled in false numbers and registered as Mr. and Mrs. Richard Miller. Because of the traffic, most hotels in Geneva were noisy. Travers asked for and got a quiet room in the back. It cost 90 Swiss francs, but after their long day of driving, hiking, and train riding, they would both want a good night's sleep.

They showered and afterward had dinner at a fancy restaurant on the Quai Gustave-Ador, overlooking the lake and the Jet d'Eau. It was a clear night and the fountain sprayed five hundred feet into the air, shimmering in the lights against the dark background of the lake.

Valerie raised a glass of wine with a wicked smile. "John Calvin would be spinning in his grave," she said. "Here we are in his town, on the run from the authorities, drinking in public, and living in sin."

"You seem to be enjoying it."

"We're together."

"But what you said in Paris, by the window in Tom's apartment. It's still on your mind, isn't it?"

Valerie rubbed her finger around the rim of the wineglass. "I've never thought of living anywhere but England. Of being away from my friends, my family, and my roots. It's all a little strange, and frightening. I suppose—I suppose I never thought that falling in love with you would take me on a journey."

Travers tried to make his voice sound reassuring. "We might be back in England one day. When this is all over."

She smiled. "It doesn't matter. You're what matters. You and me. Us."

He smiled back and raised his glass. "To us, then."

"To us."

The next day, they breakfasted on brioches, butter, and Hero jam in little foil cups. They checked out of the hotel in midmorning, and spent the day walking along the quays and exploring the city. In the afternoon, they returned to the Gare Cornavin. Travers bought tickets to Lausanne and booked a first-class sleeping compartment on the Simplon Express, from Lausanne to Milan.

He paid no particular attention to the short man in the gray suit and black-rimmed glasses, carrying a dark-brown attaché case, who stood in line behind him. If he noticed him at all, Travers assumed he was a Swiss-German businessman, returning home to Zurich.

Valerie and Travers were walking out of the station when

the man hurried over to a pay phone and dialed a six-digit local number.

He spoke rapidly in a low voice. *"Die händ Billet für Lausanne und der Simplon Express kauft."* He hung up, glanced around, and walked quickly out of the station.

They caught the last train from Geneva, just before midnight. Travers and Valerie were the only passengers in their compartment. "We'll have twenty-three minutes to board the Simplon Express in Lausanne," he said. In almost any other country, Travers knew, that might be cutting things a little close. But not in Switzerland. The crack express had left Paris at 10:00 P.M. and was even now racing across France for the Swiss border. It would leave Lausanne at forty-seven minutes after midnight; they would climb into their berths and get off at dawn in Milan.

"They'll check our passports at the Italian border, won't they?" Valerie asked.

"Yes. But there's not much risk. SISMI, the Italian secret service, has been feuding with the agency for the past eighteen months. They bugged the bedroom of Carleton Ames, our station chief in Rome, and heard him talking to his wife about how the dumb 'wops' were incapable of counteracting the Red Brigade terrorists. A rather unflattering reference to SISMI, of course."

"So they won't route the passport lists to Langley?"

"Oh, it isn't that blatant. They won't refuse to honor their liaison commitments with us. But they'll take their sweet time about it. It could literally be months before the papers wend their way through the Italian bureaucracy to the agency."

"How lovely."

"We have one other advantage. It's clear to me now that the agency has kept the operation in-house. There's been no sign that the police in France or Switzerland were looking for us. We haven't run into any roadblocks or extra security precautions along the way. My guess is that Hansen's operating as a singleton."

"On his own?"

"Yes. With support from headquarters and the stations along the way, of course."

"What about border controls? Would he know if we had gone through customs anywhere?"

"Passport lists are routinely forwarded to headquarters by friendly countries. So he'd know. But my guess is that it doesn't go beyond that. They haven't asked for support from any foreign security service."

"Why not?"

"They don't dare. They'd have to give them my true name, as well as the possible alias documentation I'm carrying. And my name is well known to the DST and the other services on the Continent."

"Of course. You know a lot of those people, don't you?"

"Exactly. I've had to deal with them. If the agency admitted it was looking for me, it would raise too many questions that Towny Black can't afford to answer."

It was after midnight, and they were pulling into the station at Lausanne. On the hillside above them, the city was dark, except for a few lights in the center of town. But the railroad station was bustling, filled with Italian workers on their way home. They carried bread, salami, cheeses, and bottles of wine in paper bags and straw baskets. They would stay up all night, riding the second-class coaches to Milan, Venice, and Trieste.

In the crowd along the platform there were also groups of students, many carrying rucksacks or backpacks, as well as a scattering of older tourists, mostly French and German, and a few Americans.

At 12:43, the announcement came crackling over the public-address system in French, Swiss-German, and then English: "Ladies and Gentlemen, the Simplon Express from Paris for Brig, Milan, Venice, Zagreb, and Belgrade, now arriving on Track Two. Sleeping cars, couchettes, and coaches for Venice are in the rear. Coaches for Yugoslavia are forward."

A moment later, the sleek transcontinental express slid into the station. Travers spotted their dark-blue sleeping car and they climbed aboard. He showed their tickets to the porter, a gray-haired, harried man with a weasel face and deep pouches under his eyes.

"We have compartment number four," Travers said.

"Par ici, monsieur. This way." The porter motioned them ahead along the narrow corridor that ran the length of the car alongside the compartments.

They pushed open the door to number four and entered. "This is nice," Valerie said. "But who gets the upper berth?"

"I thought we might both fit into the lower," Travers said.

Valerie laughed. "I should have known."

"I can't help it. I have a thing about trains. I should have warned you."

"Oh, I don't know. It sounds like fun. Do you think the motion of the train helps?"

"We'll find out."

The train was moving out of the station. There was a knock on the door, and Travers opened it. The conductor, a thin, swarthy man in a dark-blue uniform, stepped in. Travers noticed he had a bad case of five-o'clock shadow. He also noticed the little white-on-red cross on his cap. For a moment, Travers was puzzled, but then he remembered. The train would have changed crews at Vallorbe, just over the Swiss border. A new engine would have been put on there as well, since the Swiss railways were electrified. The Swiss crew would man the train all the way to Domodossola, where the Italians would take over.

The conductor extracted a punch from an official-looking black briefcase that hung by his side from a long shoulder strap. He punched their tickets with a ceremonial flourish and returned them. *"Voilà, monsieur."*

Following along after was the porter. He announced, "I'll collect your passports now, sir, so you will not be disturbed in the middle of the night at Domodossola."

"That makes sense," Travers said. He produced his true-name diplomatic passport and handed it over, along with Valerie's.

"And when do you wish to be awakened, *monsieur?*"

"We're only going as far as Milano. Call us at five."

"Very good sir. At five then. *Merci, monsieur."*

He backed out and Travers locked the door behind him. Valerie peered out the window. She could see little in the darkness.

"We're running along the lake still," Travers said. "We'll

cut south soon, past the Dents du Midi, and east along the Rhône Valley. We should be in Brig in about an hour and a half."

Just outside of Brig, Travers knew, the train would plunge into the Simplon Tunnel, racing under the Alps for the Italian border. They would pass beneath the Wasenhorn and Monte Leone, emerge briefly into the open air at Iselle, on the Italian side, and then roar back into the tunnel for the great loop that would take them down the Val Diverdo to Domodossola.

Travers took off his tie and stretched out on the lower berth. Valerie slipped her dress off and hung it on a hook. She did not have on a slip. Travers admired her reflection in the full-length mirror on the door. Wearing her panties and bra, she climbed in the berth next to him and rested her head on his shoulder. She opened the buttons of his shirt and made light circles in his chest hair with her finger.

"Rob."

"Yes?"

"What will we do in Italy?"

"Go to ground for a while. There's a little hill town I know north of Verona. It's called San Giorgio. I don't think anyone will find us there."

"We can drink wine and eat olives and make love and be marvelously lazy."

"For a little while anyway. I'll have to get in touch with Owens through the address in London and let them know where we are."

A shadow crossed her face. "Do you have to? Is it safe?"

"Yes. Dick Austin is servicing the accommodation address." He unsnapped her bra, and slipped it off her arms.

She giggled. "So now we're about to find out if it's true about trains."

The wheels below them were clickety-clacking along the rough roadbed, and the compartment was rocking back and forth. Travers leaned over and spoke her name very softly. "Valerie." He kissed her, a long kiss that was gentle at first, then passionate. Valerie reached up and groped for the light switch. She turned it off and flipped on the night-light. Lying there together, their bodies bathed in a dim blue glow, streaking across the Valais in a locked compartment aboard the Simplon Express, Valerie felt as she had the night they sat beneath the stars in the cockpit of the *Annabel,* sailing for France. For the first time since that night, she felt completely safe.

The jolting motion of the train rocked Valerie awake. She looked at Travers, naked and sleeping peacefully next to her. She smiled and pulled the sheet up over his shoulders. After a few minutes, she got up to use the bathroom. It had become chilly in the compartment, but she did not bother to put on a robe.

Only a moment later, there was a knock on the door. Travers woke up. He looked around and realized Valerie was in the bathroom. Groggily, he checked his watch by the night-light. It was 2:27 A.M. They would be in the Simplon Tunnel. He peered out the window and confirmed his guess; nothing but blackness greeted his eyes. If they were running on time, they would be almost ten minutes into the tunnel, which meant that they had just crossed the Italian border. Perhaps it had something to do with that, although customs and immigration, he knew, were twenty minutes away, beyond the border at Domodossola.

There was another insistent rap on the door. Travers reached down for the Walther PPK in his rucksack. He racked back the slide, let it snap forward to chamber a round, and put the automatic next to his pillow. He silently flipped off the night-light. The compartment was completely dark.

"Who is it?" he asked.

"Conducteur," came the reply in a French accent. "I regret to disturb you, *monsieur,* but there is a problem concerning your ticket."

"I'm not dressed. I'll slip it under the door."

Travers tried to do so, but the carpeting on the floor of the compartment was too snug against the bottom of the metal door. The ticket would not go under. He cursed, then slipped on his shorts.

He opened the door partway, then fully, when he saw the dark-blue uniform and the black briefcase of the conductor.

"All right, come in," he grumbled, "but this is a hell of a way to run a railroad. It's almost two-thirty in the morning."

The conductor stepped into the compartment, leaving the door to the corridor slightly ajar. Travers sat down heavily on the edge of the berth, annoyed.

"I apologize again for disturbing you, *monsieur,*" the conductor said. "But we cannot account for one ticket, and the other conductor thought it was the gentleman in number four." He was a tall man. In the half-light, Travers could not see the face under the dark-blue cap.

"It's already been punched," Travers said, handing him the ticket.

"I will punch it, *monsieur.* That way we are sure." The conductor reached into the briefcase.

It was the hands. Travers caught a glimpse of the conductor's ham hands reflected in the mirror on the door in the dim light from the corridor. For a second, he froze. Then he slid his right hand along the berth toward the pillow. He felt the cold metal of the Walther and his fingers closed around the grip. It was too late. He had the sensation of watching himself in a slow-motion movie. He could see the glinting object that the big man took from his briefcase, but it was not a punch. It was an odd-looking .45 automatic and it was pointing at Travers' heart.

In the bathroom, Valerie, washing her face in the basin, heard nothing over the sound of the running water and the noise of the train. She swung open the door.

"Get back!" Travers shouted.

The big man spun his head to the right and stared, transfixed for a millisecond by what he saw: Valerie, naked, standing in the doorway, silhouetted in the bright light from the bathroom.

She reacted, finally, and leaped back. But the diversion had given Travers a chance. For a split second, Travers, still sitting on the berth, and the intruder, faced each other. The big man was lurching, swaying back and forth as the train rocked through the tunnel at eighty miles an hour. Then they both fired at the same instant.

The flechette with its deadly poison tip skimmed over

Travers' bare left shoulder, missing him by a quarter of an inch, and embedded itself harmlessly in the wall. The 9mm bullet spat from the Walther with a popping noise like a firecracker that was drowned out by the roar of the train. It caught the big man in the chest. A disbelieving expression came over his face as a red stain began to spread slowly across the front of his white shirt. He stood for what seemed a minute to Travers, but was only two or three seconds, made a gurgling noise in his throat and then toppled over, dead.

Travers turned him over on his back to be sure. Then he closed the door of the compartment, flipped on the night-light and got Valerie out of the bathroom. She had to step over the massive figure sprawled on the floor.

She grabbed Travers and hung on, digging her nails into his bare back. "My God, Rob. Are you all right?"

"Yes. He's dead."

Valerie looked down. Even in the eerie blue light she could make out the blond hair, the thick features, and the blotchy skin. His eyes had rolled upward in his head and only the whites were showing. She looked away. "I think I'm going to be sick."

She stumbled back into the bathroom and Travers heard her retching. She came back and sat on the berth, pale and sweating. Travers put his shirt around her shoulders.

"If it's any consolation, I don't feel that good myself. It's the first time I've shot a man."

She touched him. "How did you know?"

"The hands. I recognized his hands."

"How did he find us?"

"I don't know. Perhaps the Geneva base spotted us. They may have been watching the railroad station."

Travers felt a little shaky, but enormously relieved. The adrenaline was still coursing through his body, and he felt wide-awake, his mind racing ahead.

"What do we do with him?" Valerie asked, shuddering.

"We get him out of here. And off the train."

"Where's the porter?"

"Get dressed and go find out."

They both put their clothes on, and Valerie left.

Travers took the cord from his knapsack and tied Hansen's hands together in front of his stomach. Then he slipped the leather belt off the body and looped it over Hansen's wrists, passing the end through the buckle.

In a moment, Valerie returned. "The porter's sleeping in his little alcove at our end of the car."

"We'll have to try to get by him. We can't drag Hansen the other way, the full length of the car. He must weigh well over two hundred pounds."

"I hope the porter doesn't wake up. It might be hard to explain what we're doing marching around with a dead conductor."

Travers looked at his watch. "The Italian customs don't board the train until we reach Domodossola. This is probably the stretch where the porter takes his catnap. If we're quiet, we may make it."

"How much time do we have?" Valerie asked nervously.

Travers looked at his watch. It was 2:35 A.M.

"By the schedule, we don't reach Domodossola until three-forty-eight. But Italy has daylight-saving time in the summer. The Swiss don't. Which means we'll really be there at two-forty-eight, Swiss time. Thirteen minutes from now."

Valerie poked her head out the door and looked both ways. There was no one in the corridor, and the doors to all the other compartments were shut. Travers stuffed a towel inside Hansen's shirt to staunch the flow of blood. He pulled on the belt and the arms snapped up and crossed over the unseeing eyes. Hansen was lying flat on his back. With Valerie holding his legs and Travers pulling on the belt, they managed to inch the body along the corridor. But it was an enormous effort, and they were out of breath after they had gone about ten feet.

Valerie stopped, exhausted from the strain.

"Come on," Travers whispered. "Eight minutes left."

They started up again, dragging and pushing their limp burden. But it was difficult to maintain their balance. The train was curving sharply to the left, moving downgrade in a great arc. They must be past Iselle already, Travers realized; they were in the loop.

They were going by the porter now. He was nodding on his stool, eyes closed, his head thrown back against a pillow. Travers prayed that he was a heavy sleeper. They strained and pulled the body a few more feet. Travers reached behind him and opened the door at the end of the car as quietly as he could. But the roar of the train increased several decibels, and the porter stirred, muttering and shifting in his sleep.

They froze, but the porter's eyes did not open. They inched forward with their burden, heaving and struggling until they had Hansen on the little platform at the end of the car. Travers released a lever, and pulled the side door inward. A rush of cold air greeted them.

He could see the stars and moonlit clouds, so he knew they were out of the tunnel, somewhere near Varzo. They inched Hansen's body headfirst over the edge of the metal platform, and at a silent signal from Travers, they heaved it into the blackness. Travers closed the side door and they stepped back into the car. The porter was still on his stool, snoring.

They tiptoed past him and returned to their compartment. There was blood on the carpet, but Valerie managed to get most of it up with a towel. Then she washed out the towel in the basin repeatedly, until it was drained of the last traces of the blood of William Hansen. When she had finished, it was 2:48 A.M. They were coming into Domodossola.

Chapter 26

Goodman rolled down the window of his stick-shift Volvo sedan, paid the dollar-and-a-quarter toll, and headed east across the Bay Bridge. He left the window down, and the breeze from Chesapeake blew most of the cigar smoke out of the car.

He was climbing steadily, toward the twin towers of the suspension bridge that formed the highest portion of the four-mile span. The bridge arched so high above the waters of the bay, in fact, that it was said that even tough tractor-trailer drivers sometimes froze at the wheel and had to be driven across by the police. The thought amused Goodman, who enjoyed the trip over the bay. He had done it often enough, taking his family down to the beach at Lewes, Delaware, on summer vacations.

This time, however, his destination was Cambridge, a fish-and crab-packing industrial town on the south shore of the Choptank, in Dorchester County. According to the nautical chart and the maps beside him on the front seat, it was the only town of any size close to James Island.

The traffic was light in midmorning, and Goodman moved along Route 50 at a fast pace. The highway turned sharply south near Wye Mills, cutting through the middle of Talbot County, where the tidewater gentry had tolerated the CIA as a neighbor for so many years. Goodman had checked and found out that the agency had sold its safe house near St. Michaels two years earlier. He wondered if they had moved south across the river. To James Island.

The road bypassed the Victorian homes and pleasant,

tree-shaded streets of Easton. Soon, Goodman found himself crossing the Choptank on a narrow, two-lane concrete bridge that led him into Cambridge. He turned onto Maryland Avenue and crossed a smaller bridge over a creek. He could see the port area off to his right, and straight ahead, the old section of the town.

He parked on High Street, put some coins in the meter, and looked around for a place to eat lunch. He found a plain-looking restaurant called The High Spot, and had the crab cakes, washed down with cold beer. He was pleasantly surprised to find they were possibly the best he had ever had.

He took a walk after lunch to get the feel of the town, and discovered it was a much prettier place than he had expected. Cambridge was not a tourist center; Dorchester County was less fashionable than Talbot, and Cambridge was poor and largely commercial. Some thirteen thousand people lived there, about 40 percent of them black. In the early 1960s, Goodman remembered, there had been racial disturbances in Cambridge, and the governor had ordered in the national guard for six months.

He walked past the old courthouse and turned right toward the waterfront. He stood at the water's edge, looking across the channel to the port and wondering if he was on a wild-goose chase. Still, if the agency had moved its missiles onto James Island, Cambridge would be the logical jumping-off place. It was the only deep-water port in the entire area.

He returned to High Street and walked back to an old, two-story, brown-brick structure across from the restaurant. A plaque by the door identified the building as the offices of the *Banner,* which proudly advertised itself as "The Oldest Daily Newspaper on the Eastern Shore." He had telephoned ahead from Washington, and the editor, Matty Ellwood, was expecting him.

A portly man in his fifties, with a trace of a Southern accent, Ellwood greeted Ben cordially, and with some curiosity. "We don't get very many visitors from Washington," he confessed. "And we're a funny breed down here. We elect Democrats locally, and send Republicans to Congress. But then you said you knew Harley Beall."

"Well, I know who he is, of course. And I've talked to his office. In fact that's why I'm here. I work for Senator Owens. He's interested in the impact of military bases and base-closings on the local economy. Someone in Congressman Beall's office said the Army had some sort of radar station down on James Island."

Ellwood shook his head sympathetically. "I wish you luck on that one," he said. "There's something down there, all right. But it's top secret. We tried to do a story on it, sent a reporter and a photographer out. They were waved off by soldiers in green fatigues, armed with rifles. When their boat got in too close, they actually had a shot fired over their bow. They got out of there, fast. We ran a little story on the incident, and that was that. Must have been ten years ago. We haven't run anything since."

"Is there anything on the island besides the base?"

"A lot of snakes and sika deer. They're a type of Japanese deer that were introduced on the island years ago. They're about the size of a big dog, and they bark. They've spread all over the county. Some of them swam to the mainland, I guess."

"Was it ever inhabited? Before the Army moved in, I mean."

"Oh, years ago there were a few watermen out there. The Meekins family lived there around the turn of the century. But the houses are long since gone. For that matter, so's most of the island. Like all the islands in the bay, it's eroded badly. It's a lot smaller than it used to be."

Goodman opened up the nautical chart he had brought from Washington. Number 551-SC, published by the National Oceanic and Atmospheric Administration. He traced a finger downriver from Cambridge, around Cook Point, south past Trippe Bay to the Little Choptank and over to James Island. It was really two islands, the chart showed, with a short break above the south island, which was shaped a little like a dancing bear standing on its hind legs.

"When did the Army build the radar station?" Goodman asked.

The editor scratched his head. "Around 1966, near as I can

remember. Hard to say. We didn't find out about it right away."

"How did you hear about it?"

"Word of mouth, I guess. I think the first inkling we got was when a group of Boy Scouts went out for their annual picnic and were waved off. They probably talked about it to their friends. After a while, we heard about it. There's not much that goes on in Dorchester County that the *Banner* doesn't hear about, sooner or later."

Ben studied the chart. "According to this, there's only a foot of water on the east side, maybe three to six feet on the other side. Most boats can't navigate in water that shallow. How did they get their equipment in? Those radar dishes are pretty big."

Ellwood pointed to the harbor formed by the break between the north and south islands. "You've got six feet just to the west of here. That's at low tide; you can add a foot and a half at high. They probably dredged a short channel in there. A ten-foot channel would be deep enough to bring in most anything they wanted."

"I see."

"Don't know that I've been much help to you. The truth is, I don't know much about James Island. I've never been on it. It's not near to anything."

"You've been a great help. And I'd like to ask you a favor. Do you have a library, with clippings filed by subject?"

Ellwood grinned. "We can't afford anything as fancy as a librarian. We don't have any clips. But we have all the back issues on microfilm upstairs. You're welcome to look through those, long as you want."

Goodman thanked him, shook hands, and left the editor's glass-enclosed office. He walked out to the front hall, past a sign proclaiming "A Nice Day Ends with the *Banner*." He mounted the long stairway to the second floor.

A friendly, gray-haired woman in the advertising department pointed out the library, and after a few moments, and some fumbling around, Goodman figured out how to thread the microfilms through the reader. The machine was old, and he had trouble focusing it sharply. He started with January

1966. It was slow going—national and international news from the wire services mixed in with local stories, a lot of church news and social columns with headings like "Neck District News." From time to time there were interesting historical pieces, including one about Harriet Tubman, the remarkable slave who ran the Underground Railway from Dorchester County during the Civil War, traveling by night in disguise. She had been born in Bucktown, just south of Cambridge. As he wound the films, there were more and more stories about Cambridge men being drafted and sent to Vietnam, and later, stories about several who were killed or wounded there. There was a story about Watts, six months after the riots, and others about the continuing civil-rights crusade led by Dr. Martin Luther King, Jr. Lyndon Johnson was in the White House, desperately trying to convince America that it could simultaneously afford the Great Society and the war. In Ghana, Kwame Nkrumah was overthrown in February, and in March, the Supreme Court ruled that *Fanny Hill* was not obscene.

Sitting there in the offices of the little tidewater daily, Goodman relived the past. It all flipped quickly by on the blurred microfilm, like a time machine. He found no references to James Island or a radar station. But in April, he came across a fascinating local story. That month, according to a feature in the *Banner,* a movie company had come to Cambridge to shoot scenes on location. The movie was to be called "The Chesapeake Connection." It was about a ring of pot smugglers who were bringing in marijuana in small, fast power boats to various points along the bay from Mexico and South America, and about the efforts of federal narcotics agents—also in boats—to stop them. Police Chief Sonny Tilghman, with the approval of the mayor, agreed to seal off the waterfront at night so that the filming could proceed without townspeople wandering onto the set. Goodman took notes with his felt pen on a small spiral pad. There were one or two short follow-up stories later that month but they added little to the first account. He clicked off the machine and rubbed his eyes. They were weary from the strain of reading the microfilms. It was late in the afternoon.

He went back downstairs, looking for Ellwood. "Matty's gone," an attractive, middle-aged blond woman told him. "My name's Harper Todd. I'm one of the reporters."

"Ben Goodman," he said, putting out his hand.

"I know. You're the one who's interested in James Island."

"And some other things. Look, were you here in 1966?"

"I was in Cambridge. I wasn't working for the *Banner.*"

"Do you remember a movie company coming to town and shooting some scenes along the waterfront? I found a story about it."

"I remember something like that. But the one you should talk to is Sonny Tilghman. He used to be the police chief around here. Sonny would remember."

"Where is police headquarters?"

"Just a few blocks from here, beyond the Creek bridge. But you won't find him there. Sonny's retired. Lives over on Rambler Road. Little white house with green shutters and big hedge in front. He drives a rice wagon—a blue Toyota pickup."

"Thanks." Goodman walked to his car and drove back across the bridge to Rambler Road. He spotted the pickup and the house and parked his car by the hedge. A dog was barking inside as he went up the front walk and rang the bell.

A man's voice snapped: "Shuttup, Clyde." The door opened. Sonny Tilghman was a big, beefy man with a huge beer belly hanging over a thick leather belt. He eyed Goodman suspiciously.

"Chief Tilghman?"

"Shit. Been a long time since anybody's called me that. I been retired since 1972. Livin' on my pension now."

"I'd like to talk to you."

"Well, you might as well come in as stand out there." He opened the door and shooed the hound dog out of the way. Goodman walked into the living room. The blinds were drawn. The room was dank and smelled of stale beer. Several opened cans stood on a table across from the television set, which was on, tuned to a game show. Apparently, Sonny Tilghman spent most of his time these days drinking beer and watching television. If there was a Mrs. Tilghman, she was not in evidence. Clyde seemed to be the only other resident of the house.

Goodman sat down in a stuffed chair that had broken springs. "I work for Senator Owens in Washington," he explained. "I'm interested in the Army's radar station on James Island."

Tilghman yanked the flip top off another beer, and offered one to Goodman. Ben felt he was expected to be sociable, so he accepted. "Can't tell you nothin' about James Island," the burly ex-chief said. He took a drink of his beer and wiped his stubbled chin with the back of his hand. "Don't know nothin' about it, and even if I did, I couldn't tell you cause it's all secret." He guffawed, pleased with himself.

"I understand," Ben said. "But maybe you can tell me about something else. I hear that you had a movie crew in here some years ago. You sealed off the waterfront for the director. A man named Irving Jules Levitan."

Sonny chuckled. "Yeah, I remember him all right. Big, hawk-faced fella. I guess he was a Jew, too." Goodman assumed the "too" was for his benefit.

"They was supposed to be making a movie about drugs," Sonny continued. "Shit, there's no drugs coming into Dorchester by water. Maybe up in Talbot, but not in this county. I sealed off the whole waterfront for them, all right. Nobody could get in there, not even me. They tied up traffic around here for two days and two nights. Then they packed up and left. And do you know what, buddy?"

"No, what?"

"We never heard nothing more about it."

"You mean no one ever saw the movie?"

"Shit. There never was no movie. I figure those people went bust." Sonny guffawed.

"You say Levitan was a big man?"

"Yeah. Big and tall, with a hook nose. Dark hair. You'd remember him if you saw him. He was struttin' around givin' orders to everybody."

Goodman was leaning forward intensely. "Sonny, this is important. Do you remember anything else about Levitan or the movie company? Anything at all?"

"Naw, that's all there was to it. Except for the mail. I never could figure out why they were getting so much mail."

"What do you mean?"

"The trucks. There must been a dozen mail trucks, big ones, rolled into the waterfront those two nights. We had orders to let 'em through, so we did. But I never could figure it out. Unless they was usin' them for something in the movie."

Goodman stood up. He shook hands with the ex-police chief. "You've been a great help, Sonny." Clyde was barking at Ben, who edged into the hallway and quickly out the door.

"Good luck to you, Mr. Goldman," Sonny shouted after him. "Shuttup, Clyde."

It was late and Ben was tired. He had learned from the waitress at lunch that there were no motels in Cambridge proper, so he drove out onto Route 50 until he came to the Quality Inn, across from a shopping mall south of the town. He registered at the office.

"How long will you be staying?" the thin, sallow-faced man at the desk asked.

"A couple of nights, maybe longer," Ben replied.

The desk clerk handed him a key, and Goodman went back to the car. He drove along one wing of the brick-and-frame units to his room.

He let himself in and sprawled on the bed, exhausted from the drive down, the interviews, and the hours at the microfilm machine. But he rested only a couple of minutes. Then he reached for the phone and asked the operator to get him a number in Beverly Hills. He used his credit card.

In a moment, after talking his way past a couple of secretaries, he heard the unmistakable, brash voice of Al Marcus. Al had grown up with Ben in Paterson, New Jersey, and they had remained friends over the years. Marcus was now a successful agent in Hollywood, with a large home in Brentwood, a swimming pool, and a string of starlets for playmates. The whole *shmeer*, as he liked to say. He had been divorced five years earlier.

"Ben, you bum! How the hell are you? How's Judy? When are you gonna run that senator of yours for president?" Al didn't stop for any answers, that wasn't his style.

"It's great to hear your voice, Al. Listen, just a quick question. You ever hear of a director called Irving Jules Levitan? Or a movie called 'The Chesapeake Connection'?"

"Never heard of either. What are you guys investigating, skin flicks?"

"No, no. I just need to know."

"Well, he's not in Hollywood. I would have heard of him if he was. Hang on a minute, Ben baby, and I'll double-check for you." Marcus reached behind his desk into a bookcase and removed a paperback book, entitled *Directors Guild of America—Directory of Members*. He flipped through it quickly. "He's not listed, Ben. Sorry, pal."

"Thanks for checking, Al. Say hello if you ever come East."

"I will, I will. We'll go out on the town." He laughed. "Maybe I'll even fix you up. You ought to have a little fun in life, Ben." Marcus hung up.

At the Quality Inn in Cambridge, which seemed to Goodman a long way from Sunset Boulevard, Ben paced his motel room, his mind racing. It all made sense to him now. There was no Irving Jules Levitan, and no movie—Sonny Tilghman was right about that much. Frank DiMario had come to Cambridge in April 1966 using his movie set cover to seal off the port area—all of Trenton Street along the creek to the Choptank River. It was the only way to bring in the missiles away from prying eyes. They had probably loaded them onto barges and backed the mail trucks right up to them. There was a twenty-one-foot channel leading from the port to the river, and a dozen missiles could have been unloaded and on their way to the island in a couple of hours. There was a good deal of barge traffic on the river—oil and gas from Pennsylvania coming in to Cambridge, and grain and stone for road construction heading downriver to Baltimore and Norfolk. The missiles were crated and they would have been covered with tarps. They would not have attracted any particular attention as they moved down the river among the other barges plying the Choptank.

He found a matchbook, lit a cigar, and sat back in a plastic armchair. He tried to relax, but he was too keyed up. His mind kept returning to the events of the day, to the blurred microfilms and the smell of Sonny Tilghman's parlor. He saw the solid, honest face of Matty Ellwood, the county editor, and the long, curving arc of the Bay Bridge.

Ben was too excited to eat, or even to think about dinner. The CIA's sixteen-year-old secret was about to be pried open, like a Chesapeake Bay oyster. He was virtually certain now that he had found Site Orange. But he had to be sure. He sat there for a long time, doodling with a pencil on the inside of the matchbook. Then he made up his mind. In the morning, he would find a boat. He would go and have a look at James Island.

Chapter 27

TWA Flight 891 from Rome touched down at Dulles at 6:05 P.M. The landing was smooth.

The passengers debarked and the crowded mobile lounge glided slowly toward the glass-and-concrete terminal, with its soaring, futuristic lines. Travers touched Valerie's hand, but said nothing. They cleared customs quickly and rented a car.

They did not talk until they were alone in the car, heading east on the airport access road through the Virginia countryside. A summer rainstorm had broken the heat, and the air was cool.

"It feels good to be back," Travers said.

"You're supposed to be in San Giorgio. Hiding."

"I'm through running and I'm through hiding. Besides, I was getting fat on Valpolicella and polenta."

"And impossible."

Travers swung the car onto the beltway. He had contacted

the committee through the address on the Strand and had gotten the word back from Barry Owens: sit tight until we call you. Travers could not. It had been all right for a few days. The little town was beautiful, and remote, a perfect hideaway. Built on a hillside in the high Valpolicella, it could be reached only by back roads after a long, circuitous climb. It had seemed idyllic at first—the lush vineyards, the olive trees, and the old church and cloister dating from the eighth century. They had rented a rustic farmhouse and spent their time taking long walks and picnicking in the hills on salami, goat cheese, and wine. Valerie had even learned to make polenta from corn meal, mixing it with a long wooden spoon in a copper bowl called a *paiolo*. One day they climbed higher in the hills, to a place where they could see the other side, clear down the valley of the Adige.

Despite the quiet beauty of San Giorgio, Travers had become increasingly edgy, and irritable. He and Valerie had their first real argument. She accused him of being a spoiled child, incapable of accepting control by others; he always had to have his own way. He told her that sharing his love did not mean she could run his life and that she was quite free to go back to Chelsea. There were tears, then reconciliation and lovemaking. It was all right again, now, but Travers had made his decision. He would return to Washington. There was something he had to do.

He took the George Washington Memorial Parkway exit and drove south along the Potomac, past Turkey Run and the agency. In the gathering dusk, Valerie could see the spires of Georgetown University on the hill across the river. He pulled into the Key Bridge Marriott and registered at the drive-through window as "Mr. and Mrs. Charles Daniels, Charlottesville, Virginia."

They checked into a poolside unit. Travers ordered drinks and sandwiches from room service. It had been more than twenty-four hours since they left Milan for Rome to catch the flight to Dulles, and they were both tired. They turned in early.

In the morning, they had breakfast sent in—orange juice, scrambled eggs, toast, and coffee. Travers put on a shirt, tie, and a suit. He kissed Valerie. "It's a nice day," he said. "You can lounge around by the pool and relax or catch up on your sleep. I'll be back in a couple of hours."

She kissed him lightly on the lips, and brushed a strand of hair back from his forehead. "Be careful."

"I'll be all right."

He drove back up the George Washington Parkway to headquarters. A uniformed guard checked his ID card and waved him through the gate. He parked near the main entrance and walked past the statue of Nathan Hale, whose hands and feet were bound. Travers had always wondered why the agency chose as a role model a spy who was caught and hanged. He went through the glass doors into the lobby and then up a short flight of steps on the right to the badge office. His badge was on file, as he knew it would be. A short, dark-haired secretary issued it to him after casually glancing at his face to make sure it matched his picture. He signed a form, smiled, thanked her, and hung the badge, on a beaded metal chain, around his neck.

He walked back out into the lobby, thankful that no one had thought to flag his name so that the Office of Security would be alerted if he turned up in the building asking for his badge. One could almost always rely on inefficiency in any large organization, Travers knew. Up to a point.

He walked through the lobby and turned right, past the oil portraits of Allen Dulles and the other former directors, and took the elevator to the seventh floor. He walked down the long corridor toward the DCI's office. A pretty secretary in a silk blouse, her badge bouncing between two firm breasts, smiled as she passed him in the hall. He smiled back.

Toward the end of the corridor he crossed over and tried the door to the French Room. It was locked, but he had expected it would be. He continued down the hall and turned left into the director's office, striding confidently past the glass security booth in the reception room. It was 9:45 by the clock on the wall. To the right, the door to the director's dining room was ajar, and Travers could see the white linen already set with gleaming silverware and cut flowers, ready for the DCI's lunch. He was preparing to turn left toward the director's inner office when Rick Alesi bounded out of the glass booth, and with a few catlike strides, blocked his way.

"You're not on his appointments list, Mr. Travers. And no one's cleared you in this morning."

Act supremely confident when you don't belong somewhere; if you hesitate, it's all over. Bannerman, his old instructor at the Farm, had taught him that more than twenty-five years ago. Travers had practiced walking into a room past an armed guard forty times until he had got it right. Until he looked as if he *belonged.*

Travers smiled broadly. "Relax, Ricky. I just talked to him on the phone. He's expecting me. Ask Holly."

Alesi looked doubtful, but Travers had the upper hand. The security man had orders to restrain intruders physically if necessary, but he didn't want to make a fool of himself by tackling the chief of the London station in the DCI's reception room. It would be all over the building within hours, and for his zeal, he might end up pounding the pavements in Anacostia, doing background checks on potential file clerks.

Travers hardly broke stride as he headed for the director's door. Holly Corcoran was not at her desk, which meant she was either in the ladies' room or in with the DCI, taking dictation. In his side office, Evan Younger was on the phone, looking out the window, his back to the reception area. He never heard Travers glide across the thick carpet and open the door to the director's office.

He stepped inside. Towny Black was dictating a memo. He had removed his glasses, and was leaning back in his leather chair. Holly Corcoran sat near his desk, legs crossed, a steno pad on her knee. They both turned to stare at the same moment.

The director put his glasses back on, very deliberately. He showed not the slightest surprise, or fear.

"Travers. I'm afraid you're interrupting."

"I want to talk to you, Towny. Right now."

The director gazed calmly at his visitor, his sculptured features displaying no emotion. He wrote something on a piece of paper and handed it to his secretary. "All right, Holly, we'll continue this later."

She edged out of the room, wide-eyed, keeping her gaze fixed on Travers, and closed the door. As soon as she was outside the Director's office, she glanced at the note in her hand. It said, "Call OS."

Towny Black glanced at the pen on his desk to make sure it was tightly in its holder. This was one conversation that he did not want recorded. He waved Travers to a chair.

"No thanks. I prefer to stand."

"As you wish." The director smiled. "Well, Robert. I understand you've been off on vacation." Travers had to admire his poise. Black might have been routinely welcoming home a station chief from overseas.

"Let's cut the crap, Towny. Hansen was a killer. You and Frank inserted him in the London station with orders to neutralize me."

The director's eyebrows arched, and he assumed an innocent expression. "My dear boy, I don't know what you're talking about. You must be working too hard in London. Perhaps it's time to rotate you home."

"He's dead, Towny."

The director filled his pipe, tamped down the tobacco, and slowly lit it. He shook out the match. "We assumed as much. We've heard nothing from him. But we did receive inquiries from SISMI about this." He reached into a folder and pushed a document across his desk.

Travers glanced at it. It was wire copy, a one-paragraph dispatch from a news ticker: "Domodossola, Italy, July 22. The body of a railway employee, an apparent murder victim, was found today in a culvert below the tracks in the Italian Alps near the tiny village of Varzo. From papers on the body, police identified the victim as Jacques Poirier, fifty-five, an employee of the Swiss Federal Railways. He was wearing his conductor's uniform and his hands were bound together. He had apparently been shot some days earlier and thrown off a train. Italian and Swiss authorities were investigating."

Travers handed it back. "Who was he, really?"

"We've told the Italian service we know nothing about it. He wasn't one of ours."

"He was good. A real pro. I'm sorry to disappoint you."

The director sent a puff of smoke traveling toward the ceiling. "What is it you want, Robert? Frank's job? The DDO? I've always thought that's what you were really after."

"No."

"Then perhaps I've underestimated your ambition. You want to sit in my chair, is that it?"

"None of those things. Nothing for myself."

Black sighed. He leaned back, seemingly composed. "Nobody is quite that noble. It's been my experience that everyone has a personal motive. I doubt you're an exception."

"Don't judge me by your own standards."

"Then why did you send the letter? You must have had a reason."

Travers did not respond to Black's probe. His years as a covert operator had taught him to preserve the uncertainties. "My concern is for the agency, Towny. I believe in the agency."

"As I do, Robert. I've devoted my life to it."

"We've operated in a moral vacuum for thirty years. It hasn't worked. Dulles was wrong. You can't fight fire with fire."

"Don't speak to me of morality. It has no place in an intelligence service. Intelligence, Robert, is merely the extension of politics by covert means."

"But the means can't contradict the ends."

"If you believe that, you'll lose the struggle. The Soviets don't believe it. Our own government has never believed it. Hell, the American people don't believe it. Do you think for a moment that the agency could have done the things it's done over the past three decades if deep down the people didn't want us to?"

"The people didn't know. The government didn't tell them."

"They knew instinctively. They knew we were fighting a cold war and they didn't care how. Look what happened when some of our secrets did come out. After the Church Committee, did you see the people, whom you hold in such high regard, marching on Langley in protest? No. If anything, they were probably disappointed that we *didn't* kill Castro. Criticize us for our inefficiency, perhaps, but not for our morality. We share the people's morality."

"You're wrong, Towny. People are too busy in their private lives to march on Langley. But I think people in this country believe in freedom and law. If we abandon those principles in the name of defending them, we subvert the very institutions we're trying to protect. We become no different from the enemy."

Black shook his head, like a dean with a hopelessly wayward student. "Survival, Robert. That's the first principle. If we lose the battle, all your other principles won't mean very much. We won't be around to enjoy them."

"We can't uphold the law by breaking it. Watergate was a warning. We may not get another."

"The KGB would be very happy if there were more officers like you in the Clandestine Services. They'd have little to do."

"Come off it, Towny. The mole talk was for Hansen's benefit, wasn't it? Or has the paranoia around this place gotten so thick that you really believe it?"

Black puffed on his pipe. "I'm not accusing you, my dear boy. On the other hand, I don't doubt for a moment we've been penetrated. All services are. Why should we be exempt?"

"I don't appreciate the innuendo."

"I didn't ask you to come here. Why did you?"

"To tell you to your face that you, and everything you stand for, are wrong. To tell you that I know you tried to have me terminated. Just as I suspect you terminated Gates, Barnes, and Maclaren. And Putney's mistress, for that matter."

"You're wrong," Black said with a slight smile. "They died of natural causes, or in accidents."

"And I had another reason for coming. To tell you that what you fear the most is already happening. I'm going public with Spectrum."

"I wouldn't do that." Black spoke quietly, but there was all the more menace in his voice.

"It's too late, Towny. I've gone to the Senate Intelligence Committee."

"You're a damn fool. And they won't believe you. You have no proof."

"I do have proof. You provided it."

For the first time, Travers saw a flicker of apprehension in Black's eyes. A slight crack in the elegant façade.

"Me?" Black laughed.

"Hansen was the proof. Your own killer is going to bring you down, Towny."

Black seemed to recover his poise. "We have no one named Hansen. He never existed and there's nothing in our files to prove that he did. The committee is welcome to look."

"The committee knows he existed. And they have other evidence that I'm not prepared to divulge."

A look of pure hatred crossed Black's handsome face. The white hair, the clear eyes, the even features seemed to freeze into a mask of ice. Travers thought that perhaps he was seeing Graham Townsend Black for the first time.

"I'll destroy you, Travers."

"You've already tried that, and you failed." He added quickly, "You needn't press any buttons or call in your security. The committee knows that I'm here." Travers was banking on the bluff to work and it did. The director believed him.

"Nothing will happen to you here, in my office," Black said. "But we'll take care of you. And the beauty of it is that when it happens, when your time comes, Robert, you'll never know for sure that it was us."

"I'm not afraid of you, Towny. I'm doing what I must. For the agency, and for the country."

"And for yourself. I suppose you're all set to be a media hero. Perhaps a lucrative book contract. The talk shows."

"Far from it. I prefer the shadows, like you. But you took the law into your own hands when you ran Spectrum. Now there must be an accounting."

The director adopted a sorrowful tone. "There was a time when I thought you had potential in our business, Robert. How I misjudged you. You speak of law and morality. A secret agency isn't accountable to ordinary law. We're not the Department of Agriculture. We in the agency obey a higher morality. We know that our side is just, and the other side is evil. When we engage in acts that others might call evil, they are good, because it is we who are committing them. Because our ends are noble."

"What you're really saying is that you are grown men playing games. Games with no rules. That the agency can do as it pleases because the players are acting in the national interest—as you perceive it."

"Precisely." Black smiled, as though his pupil had finally understood.

Travers shook his head. "There is no higher morality, Towny. If you break the rules of a society, in time you will destroy it."

"Martin Luther King didn't think so. He followed his conscience. He obeyed a higher morality. We do the same."

"You bastard. Don't compare yourself to King. He practiced civil disobedience to fight injustice and you know it. *You're* using the power of the state to assassinate the law."

The director tapped out the ashes in his pipe, filled the bowl with a fresh pinch of Dunhill's London mixture, and lit it. He smiled. "But you've done exactly the same thing, haven't you?"

"Meaning what?"

"You've broken the rules. You violated security. You wrote a letter containing a highly secret code word and entrusted it to the ordinary mails. You went to a Senate committee with no authority to do so, in violation of agency directives. You've revealed classified information to unauthorized persons in the legislative branch in violation of the president's executive order on secrecy, and very possibly in violation of the Espionage Laws. Now you've killed a man, who, you claim, with no proof, worked for us. You've done all of these things because you believe that the ends—reform of this agency—justified the means. Well, it turns out we believe in the same things after all, the same principles. It's merely the details on which we differ."

For a moment, Travers was shaken by Black's accusation. The man seemed able to turn any argument upside down. Was the director right? Had a lifetime of covert work made him just as corrupt as Black? He could not accept that.

"It's not the same," he countered. "Perhaps I did violate the rules. But there's at least a difference in degree. Spectrum broke the law and violated the Constitution. You acquired nuclear weapons and concealed them from the president."

A buzzer on the director's desk interrupted him. Black flicked a switch and Holly's voice came over the intercom.

"You have a meeting of the National Foreign Intelligence Board at ten-fifteen, sir."

"All right, Holly." He flipped up the switch. "We'll have to continue our philosophical dialogue another time. I have to go."

Travers did not reply. He had opened the door to the French Room and was already slipping out the back way toward the seventh-floor corridor.

The director picked up his attaché case and stepped into the outer office. Holly had followed his instructions; two tough-looking officers from the Office of Security were standing by her desk. Evan Younger was with them, looking anxious.

"Ryan and Dietrich from OS," Younger said. "Are you all right, sir?"

"Fine," Black growled. He turned to the two security men, who stood expectantly, like obedient Dobermans. "Robert Travers is leaving the building," he said. "Follow him."

Chapter 28

Travers drove his rented Cutlass through the gate, waving jauntily at the guard as he passed through the chain-link fence. He swung onto the George Washington Parkway and headed south.

By habit, he checked the rearview mirror; no car had followed him out of the access road. He pushed the FM button and got WGMS. A Mozart piano concerto surrounded him.

As he sped along the river toward Rosslyn, Travers allowed himself to feel that perhaps events were finally moving his way. He had placed his head in the lion's mouth, and he hadn't been gobbled up, after all. Perhaps he would not be.

A Virginia traffic helicopter buzzed overhead, moving south along the river. The trees were lush and thick along both banks. It was too soon yet, but in another month, the leaves would begin to turn, first the dogwoods becoming a rich burgundy, then the oaks and maples, changing to yellow, orange, and red. It was good to be back in Washington, Travers thought; when summer gave way to fall, there was probably no more beautiful place in the world. Perhaps in September he and Valerie would find time to get up into the Catoctin Mountains. They would tramp in the woods, and buy fresh apples and cider. And try to stop imagining William Hansen's eyes staring sightlessly at the alpine sky.

He took the Key Bridge exit to the Marriott and parked behind their room. Valerie was just coming out of the shower when he walked in. She had wrapped herself in a white towel, and her brown hair, darker because it was wet, touched the top of her shoulders. The droplets of water clinging to her tanned skin made her face even more beautiful, Travers thought.

She came over and kissed him. He put his arms around her. He didn't mind his clothes getting damp from the towel. He kissed her gently on the neck and shoulder.

Valerie took his face in her hands. "Rob. I was so worried."

"Piece of cake. Nothing to worry about."

"You saw him?"

"Breezed right in. Just like the Fuller Brush man."

"My God, what did he say?"

"He was surprised, of course, but he's a cool son of a bitch. You would have thought he was having lunch with me at his club during most of it. Until I told him I'd gone to the committee. That seemed to shake him up a bit."

Valerie looked worried. "But now he *knows*. He'll try to stop you. You may be in even greater danger than before."

"It was something I had to do."

She rested her head on his chest. "Rob."

"I didn't tell him everything. He doesn't know about the cables."

"Have you talked to Ben?"

"I'm going out to call him now. From a phone booth. I want you to stay put. Use the pool, sun yourself, or whatever. But don't leave the motel. I'll be back as soon as I can."

Valerie gave him a mock salute. "Yes sir, captain, sir."

Travers grinned. "It's for your own good, sailor."

He drove to a gas station a few blocks away, found a phone booth, and dialed Ben Goodman.

Linda answered. "Mr. Goodman's office."

"Is Ben there?"

"Who's calling please?"

Travers hesitated. "It's personal. I'm a friend of his."

"I'm sorry, sir. Mr. Goodman is out of town. I don't know when he's expected back. We haven't heard from him."

"Okay, I'll try again."

He hung up, fished in his pocket for more change and

dialed Senator Owens' office. Karla Warren answered. He knew she was witting. "Karla? This is Robert Travers. I'm in Washington. May I speak to the senator?"

There was a slight pause. "I didn't realize you were here, sir. Please hold on a moment."

Barry Owens came on the line, surprise in his voice. There were no preliminaries. "I thought you were going to stay over there until we contacted you."

"I know. I'd had enough. I've got to see you."

"I've got a committee meeting this afternoon. But I can skip it. Where do you want to meet?"

"Be at Gravelly Point, next to National Airport, in forty-five minutes. Go north on the parkway and make a right turn into the little park just after the airport."

"Why there?"

"It's about the only place in Washington they can't bug."

Travers hung up. He headed south to the airport, drove into the terminal to turn around, and then went back up the Potomac. A short distance past the last runway, he pulled off into the parking lot near the river. A few moments later, Owens' green Mustang turned off the parkway and pulled in next to him. They got out and shook hands.

As they did, a United Airlines 727 came lumbering south along the river, landing gear lowered, flaps down, roaring in directly overhead less than a hundred feet from where they stood. The shrieking engines drowned out the senator's words, and they were hit with a blast of hot air from the jets. The plane screeched by, frighteningly close, and then touched down just beyond, on Runway 18.

"I see what you mean about this being a safe place to talk," the senator said.

"If one of those birds doesn't drop on us," Travers replied, grinning. "This place gets pretty busy toward evening. Every night, the Gravelly Point regulars come out to watch the jets land."

"Why do they do it?"

Travers shrugged. "To get their daily shot of adrenaline, I guess. They like the risk. And the noise."

An Eastern Airlines shuttle came howling in overhead.

Owens felt as though he could reach out and touch it, it was so close. The ground shook beneath their feet.

"I'm glad you're okay," Senator Owens said. "We were worried about you. That he might find you, even in San Giorgio."

"He found me all right," Travers said. "On a train, going through the Simplon Tunnel. I killed him and threw him off."

"My God!"

"I had to. He was going to kill me." Travers paused. "There's something else I have to tell you. I saw Towny Black a little while ago. At headquarters."

"That was unwise."

"I told him I had gone to the committee. He knows."

Owens was completely taken aback. After a long moment, he asked, "Why did you do it?"

"I'm tired of running and tired of hiding. I decided to face him and tell him the truth."

"You took a terrible risk, going there. And now we've lost any advantage of surprise." Owens struggled to control his anger.

"I'm the one they tried to kill, damn it!" Travers exploded. "That gives me the right to make my own decisions."

A DC-9 screamed downriver, rushing by overhead with a rumbling roar that made conversation impossible for a moment.

When the plane had landed, Owens said quietly, "I don't think I have any choice now. I'm going to the president. I'm going to tell him everything we know about Spectrum."

"Good. It's time he knew."

"We've got to warn him that the missiles may still be operational."

"Are you any closer to finding Site Orange?"

"I don't know. And now we have a new problem. Ben's disappeared."

Travers looked worried. "What happened?"

"A week ago, he got a possible lead on Site Orange. It was a long shot, of course, but Ben felt it was worth following up. He had found out about a mysterious radar installation on James Island."

"Where's that?"

"In the Chesapeake, a good way south of here. It's off the mouth of the Little Choptank River. It's not near anything, really. The charts show it's completely uninhabited. Anyway, Ben drove down to Cambridge, the closest large town. That's the last we've heard from him."

"He didn't call in?"

"No. He didn't even telephone his wife. And he hasn't called the committee."

"Then I'm going down after him. Valerie's waiting in a motel near here. I'll go pick her up and head for the Eastern Shore. It shouldn't take us more than two hours to Cambridge. I'll call you as soon as I know anything."

"Good. Here's my home number." Owens scribbled on a slip of paper. "It's unlisted." He handed it to Travers.

They said good-bye, and Travers waited until the Mustang had pulled out of the lot. As he started up his car, a huge jet roared out of the northwest straight toward him, engines shrieking. Travers thought for a moment that it was going to land right on the hood of his car, it seemed so close. The Cutlass shook from the blast as he slipped onto the parkway toward Key Bridge.

He pulled in at the motel and parked. He walked through the breezeway and along the pool. It was fairly crowded. There were several people sunning themselves on lounges, and a number of mothers with small children at the shallow end. He did not see Valerie anywhere. Perhaps she was taking a nap. He took out his key and opened the door to the room.

It was empty. Several of her clothes were scattered on the floor, along with her compact, which was open and resting upside down. The powder puff had fallen out onto the carpet.

Travers cursed. Too late, he remembered. *The traffic helicopter.* The agency had a fleet of them, with official Virginia, District of Columbia, or Maryland markings. Choppers for all occasions, which the unwary would take for police helicopters.

They had put an airborne tail on him when he left headquarters, he realized. While he was driving south along the river, feeling good about things, they were tracking him. They would have seen him pull off the parkway at Key Bridge and drive into the Marriott. They would have radioed that information to DiMario's men, in a car safely out of sight, about half a mile behind him.

When he went to make the phone call and drove to Gravelly Point, the car would have moved in. Simple and clean. No ground surveillance to alert Travers, nothing he might have spotted, no warning signals at the motel, even for his trained eye. And now they had Valerie.

Chapter 29

Only the loud ticking of the mahogany clock on the mantelpiece broke the stillness of the Oval Office. President Thurlow Anderson had turned away from his desk and was staring out through the French doors into the Rose Garden. He felt utterly alone.

He was exhausted and still shaken from his meeting with Barry Owens. It had been arranged that afternoon on short notice. The senator had contacted Aaron Davidow, the NSC director. As chairman of the CIA subcommittee, he had asked to see the president immediately on a matter "of the highest national urgency."

Now the junior senator from Colorado was gone, leaving behind a political time bomb. Ticking away like the damn clock. Thurlow Anderson was a better politician than most people gave him credit for. Instinctively, he had known from the beginning that if major trouble developed in his administration it would come from the CIA. The rogue elephant—

who was it who had called it that?—had never been tamed. His own mild reform legislation had withered on the vine and he had been forced, to conciliate his conservative supporters, to name a career man, Towny Black, as director. He disliked Black's arrogant, patrician manner, but he had appointed him anyway.

And now, goddamnit, Black and the agency were at the center of a sudden crisis that threatened to destroy his presidency. He banged his fist down hard on the arm of his chair, so hard that it hurt. Ruefully, he rubbed the base of his palm.

Thurlow Anderson's face showed the strain of office. After eight months in the presidency, the lines on the genial, handsome visage had grown deeper, the creases around the eyes more noticeable, the voice more tired. He was a tall, charismatic man in his early sixties, with a craggy face that women found attractive. But now the peaks and valleys in the face had become more pronounced. Even the press had commented: Thurlow Anderson was looking older.

One way or another, he thought, the damn job had destroyed almost every recent occupant of the White House. And now, Anderson realized gloomily, it might be his turn. Only twenty feet away, just outside the door to the hallway, four armed young men in dark suits stood by at the Secret Service command post. The glass in the windows of his office was bulletproof. More armed guards patrolled the grounds and manned the booths at every entrance to the White House. But none of that could protect him from the job itself.

Only Aaron Davidow had sat in the Oval Office with the president as Senator Owens sketched in the horrifying outlines of Operation Spectrum. Thurlow Anderson desperately wanted not to believe the story. He did not like Owens, who was young and ambitious and who wanted his job, the damn fool. But the story had the ring of truth. Owens had told it in crisp, orderly fashion, leaving out nothing. The NSA cable intercepts, copies of which Owens had left with the president, were strong, tangential evidence supporting Owens' account. Someone had tried to kill the chief of the London station. But the Senate committee had failed thus far to come up with the conclusive proof. It had not been able to locate Site Orange. The thing was ragged, messy. And dangerous as a scorpion.

It had taken Owens almost an hour to brief the president. When he left, Anderson conferred with Davidow, exploring their options.

The security adviser urged that the NSC be convened immediately. "The government is confronted with the equivalent of the Cuban missile crisis," he had argued. "You should assemble the senior national security and military and diplomatic advisers—with the exception of Towny Black, of course. You may even want to bring in the Wise Men."

The president shook his head. "This is too sensitive. We can't go outside the government." The Wise Men were a group of powerful lawyers, former diplomats, and other distinguished civilian leaders; Anderson had used them before in foreign-policy crises. It would not be possible this time.

"Then convene the NSC. But you need the best advice you can get, and you need it fast."

Thurlow Anderson brushed him aside. "If we bring in the NSC it's bound to leak. And if the CIA is excluded, Black will know immediately what's happened. If we have any chance at all to keep the lid on, we have to preserve the element of surprise."

Davidow could see that further argument was useless. "What would you like me to do, sir?"

"Call Towny Black. Get him over here to the White House right away. But don't give him any hint of what it's about. In fact, tell him it's Angola again. The president just wants to be brought up to date."

"Do you want me to sit in?"

"No. I want Black alone, here in the Oval Office."

"Shouldn't I alert the Joint Chiefs? If Senator Owens is right, the man has weapons at his disposal."

"No. Don't tell the Pentagon. Not yet. If you involve them, they'll go to a DEFCON 1 alert and the press will be all over it in an hour." He touched the red telephone on his desk. "If we need them, I can always pick up this."

"I'll call the DCI, sir."

"Do that Aaron. Do that. And pray for me."

Despite his bulk, Frank DiMario could move surprisingly fast when he wished to. He was moving very fast this afternoon, striding past Rick Alesi in the glass booth and heading for the director's office, his face grim. He did not joke with Holly Corcoran as usual, but walked straight ahead into Black's office.

The director could see from the DDO's expression that the news was not good.

"What is it, Frank? I'm on my way to the White House."

"Someone got there ahead of you. We've had a tail on Barry Owens since ten forty-five this morning. He met with Travers in a park near National Airport"—DiMario consulted a slip of paper in his hand—"for eighteen minutes. We had no audio coverage of the meeting. It was too noisy. Afterward, Owens drove back to his office and remained there for an hour. Then he drove to the White House, entering the South West gate at one P.M. He left an hour later. He's back in his office now."

"Did he see the president?"

"We don't know yet. We're checking right now with our people in the White House. But we have to assume he did."

"Where's the girl?"

"In a safe house in Rosslyn at the moment. We plan to move her out. We've notified Holly, Evan, my office and the main switchboard that if Travers phones in, the call is to come to me. I'll offer a deal—the girl in exchange for a signed statement that there is no Operation Spectrum and never was, and that he invented it to try to discredit the agency and the director."

"Good."

"What if he doesn't call?"

"I think he will. Where is he now?"

DiMario shrugged. "I don't know. Ryan and Dietrich were busy with the girl. The tail on Owens stayed with the senator after he met Travers at the airport."

The director looked annoyed. "I wanted continuous surveillance on Travers. Get on him if he surfaces anywhere.

Right now, the president is waiting for me. Davidow tried to sound casual, and he mentioned Angola. But it doesn't look good, does it, Frank?"

DiMario shook his head. Black had never seen DiMario scared, but now the big man looked frightened.

Very deliberately, the director lit his pipe and drew on it until the smoke was thick. "We're not through yet, Frank. I've anticipated this kind of problem for a long time. And we're ready for it."

"What are your orders?" DiMario seemed to take on renewed confidence from the director.

"My appointment with the president is half an hour from now, at three o'clock. If our estimate is correct and he knows the truth, he'll confront me with it. They may not let me get near a telephone. So we'll have to go to a fail-safe system. If I have *not* called you by four, activate Phase Red. It's possible I'll have trouble convincing the president we mean business. So if Anderson telephones you, confirm that we've gone to Phase Red status. Get the missiles out of Site Orange and within range of the White House. Await further orders from me."

DiMario hesitated. "It's all a bluff, of course." He looked at Black uncertainly. "I mean, you don't really expect to do anything, do you?"

"Damn it, Frank, you know the purpose of Phrase Red as well as I do. It's a deterrent, our most powerful bargaining chip. It will only work if the president believes we mean exactly what we say. So get ready to move the missiles out."

DiMario nodded. "All right. One thing—what if Travers calls in while you're across the river?"

"If he's willing to deal, telephone me at the White House. Tell them it's an emergency and the call has to be put through to me in the Oval Office. That way, we'll have two tracks going. One of them will work." He reached out and grasped DiMario's hand, a rare gesture of emotion for the director. "We're going to win, Frank."

"Magari."

Black looked at him, questioningly.

"It's just something we say." DiMario smiled for the first time. "Good luck to you, sir."

Then Black was gone, whisked from the seventh floor by the private elevator to the underground garage, where his car was waiting, engine running. "The White House," he told the driver.

They followed the parkway to Memorial Bridge, crossed the Potomac, and took 17th Street to the South West gate. Black hurried in through the basement entrance on West Executive Avenue. He turned left and took the little elevator up to the first floor. At exactly three o'clock he was ushered into the president's office.

Thurlow Anderson did not rise. Stern-faced, he motioned Black to a chair across from his desk. It was not a good sign, the director realized. Usually the president got up, came out from behind his desk, shook hands, and moved over to his rocker. The president always sat facing the fireplace between two white sofas. His guest was expected to sit on the sofa to the president's right, in part, Black believed, because Anderson's hearing was better on that side.

"Good afternoon, Mr. President," Black ventured.

"Sit down."

Black knew from the president's demeanor that this conversation was not going to be about Angola. He braced himself for what was coming.

Anderson was glowering at the CIA director, his face as dark as a thunderhead. "I want a complete report on Operation Spectrum," he snapped.

"Spectrum." The director studied the ceiling. "That was a long time ago, Mr. President. We'd be happy to provide you with a report, but we'd have to go back into the files for the details."

"You're choosing to misunderstand me, I think," the president countered. "I want a report here and now, from you. I understand you ran the operation. I'm sure you remember it well."

"It's an extremely sensitive matter, Mr. President. I'm not sure—"

"Bullshit, Towny! Let's have it. Now."

Black brushed a strand of silver hair back in place. He wore a resigned expression. "Very well. I only work for one president at a time."

"Good of you to remember that."

"Operation Spectrum, Mr. President, was a covert operation undertaken by the agency in 1965 to provide Israel with atomic weapons. It was quite successful."

"Did Lyndon Johnson approve it?"

"Implicitly, perhaps."

"What the hell does that mean?"

Black began talking in elliptical fashion. "We feel it had his tacit approval in the sense that it fell within the parameters of his policy objectives at the time. And in the sense that we certainly received no disapproval from the White House."

"He couldn't have disapproved something he didn't know about."

The director looked reproachful. "I feel that one of our jobs, Mr. President, is to keep sensitive, potentially embarrassing covert operations out of the Oval Office. To insulate the president, as it were, while working his will."

"How many operations are going on right now that I haven't been told about?"

"None, I'm sure," Black said smoothly.

"All right. I asked for a report on Spectrum. You've told me only about Phase Blue. What about the rest of it?"

Black had deliberately avoided any mention of the phases. He did not know precisely how much Travers knew, or how much detail had been passed on to the president by Barry Owens. He was fencing, moving gingerly, volunteering nothing until forced. Dancing around the room. "There were, ah, some other aspects of the operation, Mr. President. In phases Green and Yellow, we set up certain cover mechanisms through the Department of Defense, in order to preserve plausible deniability. Quite standard mechanisms, I might add." Black smiled thinly.

Thurlow Anderson looked the director in the eye, and pushed his face close to the CIA chief, much as Lyndon Johnson himself might have done. "You are a lying son of a bitch, Townsend Black. And I'm going to break you in two." The words were delivered calmly enough but with great force.

"You don't know what you're saying, Mr. President. The strain of office—"

"You let me worry about the strain of office. I'm talking

about Spectrum. After you smuggled the uranium to Israel, you kept the damn thing going, didn't you? You've got missiles, now, twelve of them, hidden away somewhere. At a location called Site Orange."

"You have no proof to back up such a preposterous charge, Mr. President. And without proof, who will believe you?" Black was gambling, correctly, that Travers and Owens had no documents to support their story.

"The chief of our London station is ready to testify to these charges. And you tried to have him killed."

"You have no proof of that, either."

"On the contrary. I have proof, here in my desk drawer."

For a moment, neither man said anything. The only sound in the room was the ticking of the clock on the mantel. Then Black said, very quietly, "What exactly is it you have in mind, Mr. President?"

"One, your resignation, in writing. Two, surrender of the nuclear missiles to the Department of Defense. Three, a public confession of Operation Spectrum by you, on television, and an apology to the American people."

Black shook his head. "You want too much, Mr. President. A resignation for personal reasons, if gracefully handled, might not be out of the question. I'm almost sixty, and I've had more than thirty years with the agency, and the OSS before that. It might not seem unusual for me to want to retire now."

"I want your resignation today, effective immediately. Before you leave the White House, I want you to set in motion the other two steps. I'll put a stenographer at your disposal. You can start dictating your statement for television."

Black flushed, his whole face pink to the white hairline. "A public accounting such as you suggest would mean the abolition of the CIA. It would trigger a tidal wave of reaction in the country. We'd be engulfed. Swept away."

"You're wrong," Anderson countered. "There'd be a tremendous outcry, of course. But when the dust had settled, there would still be a CIA. I couldn't do my job without it."

"If Spectrum is revealed publicly," Black replied, "the public will force Congress to shut us down. I'm not going to let that happen. I will never let the agency be destroyed. I'll resign, if you insist, but that's all. Nothing more."

"You leave me very little choice. If you won't take all three steps, I'll notify the networks and go to the people myself."

Black stood up, bristling with anger. "The agency protects the security of this country, Mr. President. Destroy it and you'll leave the United States defenseless. A tiger without claws in a vicious jungle. If that happens, it is you whom the people will destroy in their anger and retribution."

Anderson's voice rang out with calm authority. "Sit down, Towny." The director obeyed, still flushed. "Now listen to me," the president said. "You have broken the law and arrogated to yourself power and weapons that under the Constitution are the sole province of the Commander-in-Chief. I'm sworn to uphold the Constitution. If it means breaking up the CIA, so be it. We can rebuild and change. We can shape an intelligence agency that will operate within the law."

"Suppose we did acquire nuclear weapons," Black said. "It was only to give us the covert capability that a president might want someday. We should be commended for our foresight, not punished for our initiative. You're judging the agency by today's standards for what we did sixteen years ago, in a completely different era."

Anderson's face was grim. "That argument doesn't cut any ice with me. Sure, times change. So do policies. But one thing hasn't changed since 1789, and that's the president's oath of office. I swore eight months ago to preserve, protect, and defend the Constitution. And I intend to do exactly that."

"Mr. President, you're naïve. If you're going to have an intelligence agency, you have to be prepared to break the rules. We're not running a church picnic. Our enemies don't play by the rules."

"Oh, I know that argument. We're up against a ruthless opponent, so it's okay to deceive the people. Use the external danger to justify any damn thing. Joe McCarthy tried it, and he was destroyed. Richard Nixon tried it, and he had to resign; he was god-damned lucky he didn't end up in jail. Whatever made you think that Graham Townsend Black could get away with it?"

339

The director blanched. He had not expected the president to show this much strength. He had always tended to regard Thurlow Anderson as a genial figurehead, a weak man who would rather play golf than run the country. But he was not acting that way. The son of a bitch was wrapping himself in the Constitution. He would have to shove in all his chips.

"Mr. President," Black said slowly, "you leave me no options. I didn't want things to reach this point." He pounded his fist in his palm to emphasize each word. "I'll defend my agency against anyone who tries to destroy it. Anyone." He paused and said deliberately: "I'm targeting my missiles on the White House. They'll be aimed right at this building, until you withdraw your order that I tell the public about Spectrum."

Thurlow Anderson smiled. "You're not giving any orders to your people. About missiles or anything else. If you make a move toward the telephone, you'll be down on that blue carpet in ten seconds, with your face in the presidential seal and ten Secret Service men sitting on your Ivy League ass."

The director was unperturbed. "I've already given the orders," he said. "We had a contingency plan."

"You're bluffing."

"I'm not. Call Frank DiMario if you don't believe me."

The president buzzed Davidow on the intercom. "Aaron? Call Frank DiMario. Ask him whether he has any orders from the DCI and what they are. Call me right back."

Anderson wondered how Black could have known in advance. Was the agency bugging the president's phone? Perhaps they had infiltrated the White House staff. There had been rumors of it for years, Lord knows.

They waited for the buzzer to sound, neither man saying anything. In a moment, it did. Davidow came back on the line, his voice brittle and incredulous. "He says he does have orders, sir. To target their missiles on the White House."

The president hung up and stared at Black.

"For God sakes, Townsend, think it through. What good will it do to destroy me? You're right here in the building with me, and you're not leaving, you can be sure of that."

"Then we'll die together. I'm ready for that. But the secret of Spectrum will die with us."

"And your agency that means so much to you?"

"It will go on. Frank will take over."

Anderson shuddered. There was something Black had overlooked. In theory, only the president could launch Armageddon. But under dire circumstances, there were secret, automatic procedures for nuclear retaliation. "If you nuke the White House," the president said slowly, "SAC may think the Soviets did it and retaliate. It could touch off World War Three."

"Exactly."

The president's voice was cold. "You're insane."

"On the contrary, Mr. President. I don't fear World War Three. There are many of us in the agency and in the country, too, who believe that sooner or later a preemptive strike against the Soviet Union is in the best interests of the United States. The choice is yours. I'll win either way."

The president sighed. Black was irrational; there was no point in arguing with him. "All right, Towny," he said. "Your move. What do you want?"

The director felt back in control of the situation. He took out his pipe and lit it, without asking the president's permission, something he had not done before. "I'll strike a bargain with you, Mr. President."

"On what terms?"

"I'll agree to two of your demands. I'll resign and I'll surrender the missiles. Provided that you agree to keep the entire matter secret and persuade the Senate committee to cancel its hearings on grounds of national security."

Anderson's face darkened with anger. "No deal. The American people, just for once, are going to be told the truth." The president touched a button beneath his desk. Instantly, the door burst open. Four Secret Service men ran into the room. Clint Farrell, the lead agent, was reaching for his revolver.

"I want this man arrested," Anderson snapped. "For threatening the safety of the president." To Farrell, he added, "Hold him here in the building."

Black offered no resistance. But as he was being led away, with Farrell and another agent firmly gripping each arm, the director stopped and twisted halfway around to face the president. He glanced at the clock on the mantel. It said 4:03. He smiled broadly. "It's too late, Mr. President. The missiles are already moving toward the launch point. And I'm the only one who can stop them."

Chapter 30

Speeding along Route 50 toward the Bay Bridge, Travers could not exorcise the dark thoughts that kept edging into the corners of his mind.

Only a few hours before, everything had finally seemed to be tumbling into place. In very short order, he had surfaced, faced down the director, and forced Barry Owens' hand. For the first time, he had a sense that he was shaping events instead of responding to them. At last the president would be told about Spectrum. But his triumph had been short-lived. Valerie was gone.

The dark thoughts would not be banished, try as he would. They had kidnapped her, of course. She would not have gone with them voluntarily. Unless—he forced himself to go on with the thought—unless she had worked for them all along.

He loved her. Now that she was gone, he knew that even more. He ached to be with her. But he could not lightly discard the habits of a lifetime. He had deliberately trained himself to place his professional mind in a separate compartment from his emotions. Like a surgeon, he had learned to take a clinical approach to his work. And to the people. In running an operation, it was always essential to develop a strong, close bond with an agent in order to maintain control. But the emotions must not govern. If he allowed himself to identify with every agent he handled, he could not have been a successful case officer. The same training and experience reminded him that when something went wrong, it was necessary to review the operation from the beginning.

In spite of himself, he did so now. He thought back to how he had met Valerie. The pottery class. Diana Austin's pottery class. It had all seemed so casual. Travers checked the rearview; nothing that looked like a surveillance car was in sight.

The pottery class; his mind drifted back to that evening in Plaxtol, at the Austins' house. But, my God, that would mean that Dick Austin . . . Travers forced the thought from his mind. No damn it, not Dick. Diana, then? No, she loved Dick; but she was a strong woman who had long since made it clear she would play no operational games; she would be as discreet as his work required, but she would never become involved in it.

Trace the chain back. Always trace it back. If Valerie worked for the agency it did not necessarily mean the Austins were witting. She could have been inserted in the pottery class, knowing that Diana was enrolled. Valerie could have made a point of becoming friendly with Diana. The Austins were Travers' closest friends in London. He was a bachelor. What could be more natural than for Diana to arrange a dinner party so they could meet?

Go back another link. Could Black have enlisted C in the operation? "Yes, indeed, Townsend, good to hear from you. As a matter of fact, one of our senior officers, Kit Kerr, has a daughter who might be suitable. What's that? Yes. Very beautiful indeed."

But why then would C have warned him about the back-channel traffic through Mildenhall? To preserve his bona fides, of course, and divert Travers' mind from the very path it was now exploring. If Valerie had been working for them all along, it would explain a number of puzzles. It would explain why Hansen had picked up their traces so quickly in Paris, and again in Lausanne.

But he had been with her all the time; she would not have had a chance to alert the agency. No, not quite all the time.

She had gone to the ladies' room at the Pré Catelan and she could have called the Paris station then. They had lost Hansen by leaving Paris before dawn. Yet, the agency's killer had managed to pick up their trail somewhere in Switzerland. Again, she could have called from the powder room of the restaurant in Geneva.

"Stop it, you son of a bitch!" Travers screamed the words in the empty car. What a rotten trade he had chosen, he thought. In the last five minutes, he had just doubted the only woman he had ever really loved, his best friend in the agency, who had once saved his life, and who was jeopardizing his career for him even now, and the head of MI6, who had taken a personal and professional risk to try to warn him of possible danger. He had rewarded their trust with suspicion.

Automatically, he slowed down for a surveillance check. He moved over into the right-hand lane and looked in the rearview mirror. None of the cars behind him slowed down. All of them passed. Travers swung out again into the fast lane.

He came to the toll plaza of the Bay Bridge. He paid the toll and started across on the old, two-lane eastbound span. It had opened in 1952 at a cost of $45 million and stretched more than four miles across the bay, linking Sandy Point on the mainland with Kent Island to the east. On his left, more than four hundred feet to the north, he could see the $100-million, three-lane westbound span, which had opened in 1973. There were sailboats dotting the blue water below, moving briskly in the breeze. Off to his right, he noticed a large freighter moving slowly up the channel that ran between the suspension towers of the two spans.

Travers had always loved the smell of the bay, and the boats. It was almost like being on deck. He thought of Valerie again, this time tenderly, and of crossing the Channel that night in their Nick Thirty-one. He would think no more dark thoughts. They were dispelled by the sea breeze. He only hoped she was all right.

He was barreling past green cornfields now. Soon, he crossed Kent Narrows. He swung south, retracing the route he knew that Goodman must have taken several days before.

He checked the fuel gauge. It was getting a little low. Near Easton, he pulled into a gas station and had the tank filled. He was thirsty. He bought a Coke from the machine and wondered as he drank it how he would pick up Ben's traces in Cambridge.

He paid for the gas in cash and headed south again. In less than a quarter of an hour, he was at the Choptank. At the dock on the north shore, someone had turned an old ferryboat into a restaurant. Travers pulled into the parking lot and went inside. A bored-looking woman of about forty stood behind the cash register.

"What's the best place to stay in Cambridge?" Travers asked.

"No place," she said. "There's only the two motels and neither of them are in town. They're both out on Route Fifty. When you get across the river, don't take a right into town. Just keep going toward Salisbury. You can't miss them."

"Thanks a lot."

"Sure, mister."

Travers got back in his car and drove over the narrow bridge spanning the Choptank. He followed the highway south and in a few moments came to the Quality Inn, on the right-hand side of the road. He pulled in.

There was a thin, sallow-faced man at the desk.

"Is Ben Goodman in?" Travers asked.

The desk clerk eyed him suspiciously. "Nope. He checked in about a week ago. Number Thirty-two. Haven't seen him since. His luggage is still in the room, though. You a friend of his?"

"I work with him."

"Oh. You want to take care of his bill then?"

"I can do that. But I'd like to find him first."

"He a salesman or something? I didn't see no sample case."

"No, he's not in sales. More on the executive end of our business. We're in fish packing."

The clerk brightened. "Well, you've come to the right place. Yes, sir. Todd's Seafood and J. J. Clayton still pack a right smart lot of crabs in this town. And there's big boats coming in from Iceland with frozen tuna for the Coldwater plant."

"You seem pretty well up on it. What's your name?"

"Roy. Roy Walker."

"I'm Bill Richards." Travers extended his hand and they shook. "Roy, I'd appreciate it if you'd give me the key to Mr. Goodman's room. I'd like to look around. We're a little worried about him."

"Sure. Help yourself." He handed over the key.

Travers walked down to the room. The bed had been made up, and Ben's open canvas suitcase rested on a luggage rack next to the television. His shaving kit was in the bathroom. A tube of toothpaste and a toothbrush rested on the counter. A bathrobe, a rumpled shirt, and a tie were hanging from a rack. A pair of pajamas, a pair of blue undershorts, and two dirty socks lay on the carpet below. There were no car keys on the dresser.

From the physical evidence, and from what the desk clerk had said, Travers decided that Goodman had spent only one night in this room. He went through the suitcase quickly, but aside from clothing, some matches and a small box of cigars, he found only a slip of paper with the words "Matty Ellwood —*Banner*," and a phone number on it.

Of course. Ben had checked in with the local editor. Travers started to pick up the phone, then stopped himself. If the editor found out Goodman had disappeared, it would be a story. A story that Travers did not want. He would avoid Matty Ellwood, at least for now.

He sat down in the plastic armchair across from the television to think. Roy, the desk clerk, would hold for a while. He probably figured Ben was shacked up somewhere with a cocktail waitress and neglecting the fish business, so his partner had come after him. Travers pondered his next move. If he went to the police, or Ellwood, or tried in any way to reconstruct Ben's movements, to find out whom he had talked to, it would be all over town in no time. He picked up a matchbook and fingered it idly, opening and closing the cover with one hand.

Something caught his eye. He looked more closely. Someone had doodled in pencil on the inside of the matchbook. They had drawn a circle. Inside it were two words: "James Island."

The matchbook completed the story. Ben had come to town, already suspicious of what might be on James Island. He had spent a day talking to people, perhaps running down some leads. Whatever he had found out was enough to convince him to go to the island. Travers pocketed the matchbook and left.

He walked to his car, started it up, and drove out of the motel lot. He turned left and headed back up the highway for Cambridge. This time he drove into the town. He crossed the creek and followed High Street down to the wharf at the end, next to the Yacht Club. A grizzled waterman, his face bronzed and weatherbeaten, was unloading oysters from his workboat. A younger man on the pier was tossing them into a waiting truck.

Travers watched them for a while. From the long metal rakes lying aft, he could tell the waterman had been tonging for oysters. It was tough, grueling work, scraping the bottom of the bay since before dawn with the heavy poles, which were like huge scissors, and receiving for his bushels a fraction of what the customers in the fancy restaurants paid for their raw oysters on the half shell.

Travers struck up a conversation with the loader. After a few moments' chitchat about oysters, crabs, and the weather, Travers asked: "Do you know any place around here where I can rent a boat?"

"There's no place in Cambridge, I can tell you that," the youth replied.

"I see a lot of boats over in the marina by the Yacht Club," Travers ventured.

"Them's all private. Not for charter."

"How about your workboat here? Would you rent that?"

"Need it for tonging arsters."

"Maybe you know somebody who could help me."

"My cousin Eustace has a boat he might rent out. But most probably he won't, after what happened with the other fellow."

"What other fellow?"

"You're the second one. About a week ago, another man come down here just like you, asking about boats."

"And you sent him to Cousin Eustace?"

"Yep. He rented him a workboat he keeps on the creek. It was supposed to be just for the day. Well, he was gone for three days, and someone else brought the boat back. A Mr. Smith, he said his name was. Well, I can tell you, Eustace was madder than a Jimmy in a crab pot. Boat gone for three days, and the keel all scraped. He'd gone in too shallow somewhere."

"The man who chartered the boat, what did he look like?"

"Short fella. Smoking a cigar all the time. He musta been afraid of what Eustace would say when he saw the boat. So he sent the other fella around to return it."

"I see. So you don't think it's worth my talking to Cousin Eustace?"

"No way. Your best bet, mister, is to go down to Taylors Island. There's a marina down there. No regular boats for charter, but you might find someone who'd let you have one."

"Okay. Thanks for the information."

Travers walked back to his car and looked at a map. Taylors Island was not really an island, but a long neck of land on the bay southwest of Cambridge. And it was a good deal closer to James Island.

He cut south onto a back road and drove through a series of tiny rural communities with names like Christ's Rock, Church Creek, Woolford, and Madison. He crossed the bridge over Slaughter Creek and parked at the marina. A gnarled old man in khakis, wearing a yachting cap, seemed to be in charge. He started to give Travers the now-familiar story about no boats for charter. He seemed to change his mind, however, when Travers produced two crisp $100 bills.

"I guess I've got one I can let you have," he said. "If you can handle her."

"Don't worry," Travers said. "But I need a fast boat."

"She's fast, all right. A twenty-eight-foot Topaz with twin 255 horsepower Mercury inboards. She'll do thirty-four knots easily when you get her out in the open water."

He led Travers down the pier. The boat, the *Annie Lou,* out of Hooper Island, looked every bit as fast as the old man said. Travers took the keys from him and jumped aboard. "Thanks," he said. "I'll have her back tonight."

He put the engines in reverse and slowly backed the cabin cruiser out of the slip, then swung the bow north and headed straight up Slaughter Creek for the bay. He passed the Coast Guard station to starboard and rounded Holland Point into the mouth of the Little Choptank. He spun the wheel hard to port and followed a bearing due west for James Island. He was in deep water now, and he opened up the throttle until the boat was slapping through the waves at more than thirty knots. He watched intently for the dangerous, little red crab-pot markers; the lines could foul his propellers.

It was hazy out on the bay. The water was dark blue and moderately choppy, and the sun sparkled on the waves through the light overcast. After a few minutes, Travers cut the engine back. There, looming dead ahead through the mist, was James Island. He was startled to see how high it rose in the water. A white line of fog ran the length of the island at its base, giving it an unreal, ethereal quality.

He ran closer to the island, still moving slowly, then swung north parallel to its eastern side. The island was thickly overgrown with trees and foliage. He could see long-needle pines, maple, oak, and slender white birches. The tree line was separated from the bay only by a narrow strip of beach.

He got out his binoculars, but could make out no people or buildings through the haze. He nudged the boat in closer to shore, idling very slowly and keeping a wary eye on the depth sounder. He didn't dare get much closer than five hundred yards. The charts showed a steep drop-off around the island, with depths of only one to three feet along the eastern perimeter. The flashing red indicator on the depth sounder over the wheel showed six feet, then five, four, and three. Travers dared go no farther. The Topaz had a two-foot draft. He cut off the engines and dropped anchor.

Through the glasses he could now make out a dock and two small power boats in the little harbor formed by the break in the middle of the island. They must have dredged a channel somewhere close by, Travers realized, although it was not on the charts. In any event, he would avoid the harbor; it was the spot most likely to be guarded.

He swept his glasses to the right and to the left. No movement on shore, no one patrolling the beach. Except for the dock and the boats, there was nothing to indicate that the island was inhabited. Travers opened a chest in the cabin and pulled out an inflatable life raft and a wooden paddle.

He threw the raft over the side, holding on to the line secured to it. The line yanked out the plug on the CO_2 cartridge and the raft inflated itself. Then he eased himself over the side, balancing carefully until he was in the raft. He sat down in the well of the raft and began paddling rapidly for the beach. He figured he had at least a little time before one of the patrol boats came out of the harbor to investigate the cabin cruiser that had anchored so close to shore.

In a few moments, the raft scraped against the sandy bottom. Travers hopped out and lifted the raft out of the water. He plunged into the bushes and fought his way through the thick growth for about twenty feet. Then he covered the raft and the paddle with brush and walked back out to the beach. He put a large white stone near the point where he had entered the thicket. It would not be obvious to anyone else, but it would mark the spot for him.

Then he headed south along the tree line, toward the harbor. If a boat did show up he would hear it coming and would have plenty of time to duck into the woods, which would provide ample cover.

After he had walked about ten minutes he came to the break in the island and followed the shoreline around toward the harbor, moving more cautiously. After going a short distance he turned into the woods. He calculated that there would be a road leading from the dock inland. Whatever installation the agency had built would be in the center of the north island, protected on all sides by the thick forest, and invisible from any point in the bay.

He came to a barbed-wire fence, a sign that his guess was correct. He got down on his stomach and inched under the bottom strand, careful not to touch it in case it was electrified. It was rough going through the woods. There was no path and the brambles tore at his clothes. He was bitten about the face, arms, and legs by chiggers, which seemed to be the principal form of wildlife on James Island. The itching was painful. Once, he thought he caught a glimpse of a deer.

Travers slowed down. Up ahead, through the trees, he saw a clearing. He worked his way closer to the edge until he had a good view. Near the center of the clearing was a low, one-story barracks, apparently quarters for the crew who manned the missiles. There were two other buildings nearby. The smaller structure had an antenna on the roof that reached as high as the treetops, but no higher. That would be the communications shack. Travers assumed the larger building was a mess hall. Behind it, a volleyball net had been set up. In the center of the clearing was a large, paved helipad with a yellow circle painted around the perimeter.

What interested Travers the most was a set of narrow-gauge tracks running from the direction of the harbor, past the buildings, and into a low hillside at the far end of the clearing. He unslung the binoculars from around his neck and focused on the hill. Through the glasses, he could see that the tracks ran into a tunnel.

He studied the scene through the binoculars. A small dog, some sort of terrier, was frisking about near the volleyball court, but there was no other movement. The place looked completely deserted. He decided to risk it, and walked out into the clearing. Boldly, he followed the tracks into the tunnel. The dog saw him and ran in after him, tail wagging. The tunnel was lit by bare bulbs. The tracks led into a large storage room some fifty feet into the hill.

The room was empty, except for a series of long metal racks, stacked three rows high, four across. A giant's wine cellar, Travers thought. It was as he had suspected. The missiles had been unloaded at the harbor, brought here to their hiding place on the narrow-gauge tracks, and stored underground. And now they were gone. He was too late.

"C'mon boy," he said to the dog. He walked out of the tunnel, the terrier frisking at his heels. He made his way across the deserted missile base to the communications building. He pushed open the door. There were several telephones, all with scramblers, and a bank of sophisticated radio equipment, which he assumed had linked the base with Langley. He picked up one of the phones. There was no dial tone. He tried several others, all dead. The lines must have been cut when the base was abandoned.

He went across to the mess hall, and into the kitchen. Some of the pots on the electric stove were still warm. The camp had apparently been evacuated less than an hour before. In the barracks nearby, there were further signs of a hasty departure—clothes strewn around, shaving kits and duffel bags on the beds, olive-drab fatigues still hanging in the lockers. The crews had obviously been told to move out quickly and leave their personal belongings behind. On one bed, Travers found a half-written letter, beginning, "Dear Katherine." A quarter of the way into page two, the writer had suddenly stopped in mid-sentence.

At the far end of the barracks there was a door with a glass panel. Travers walked down and opened it. He found himself in a corridor with individual rooms on both sides—officers quarters, probably. He opened some of the doors and what he saw confirmed his guess; the rooms had beds, desks, and bookcases, and some were carpeted. Suddenly, Travers stopped dead. He strained to listen. He thought he heard a sound of crying. Perhaps a cat, abandoned like the dog when the crews moved out. He moved farther down the hall and realized the sound was coming from one of the rooms. He tried the door.

The crying abruptly stopped. A woman's voice, frightened, came through the door. "Let me out! I'm locked in."

"Val? Is that you?" Travers rattled the doorknob but it would not open. "Get back!" he shouted.

He got a running start and slammed into the door with his left shoulder. The wood splintered. He kicked hard at the door and broke it down enough to squeeze through.

Valerie, still crying, was in his arms and he was kissing her tears. "It's all right," he said over and over again. "It's all right." The room was sparsely furnished with a bare cot and a washbasin in the corner. There was no window.

"Oh, Rob, thank God. How did you find me?"

"Long story. Tell you later. Are you okay? You're not hurt?"

"I'm all right. They came right after you left. Two men. One of them had a gun. I opened the door to the motel room. I thought it was you, coming back without a key. They ordered me out of the room. I tried to fight them, but they were too strong. They took me in their car, not very far, to an apartment."

"One of the safe houses in Rosslyn. We've got several in the area."

"They didn't keep me there very long. They got a phone call and took me back down to the car. They blindfolded me. We drove a couple of miles and I heard a helicopter. We got out and I felt the blast from the rotors. Next thing I knew I was strapped in and we were going straight up. It was like riding in an elevator. We flew for maybe an hour or less and then we landed here. Where am I?"

"An island in the Chesapeake. It's called James Island. And then what happened?"

"They took me to a room, somewhere in this building, I think. They took off the blindfold. There were three men sitting at a table. I was in a chair in the center of the room facing them. They started asking me all sorts of questions. Everything about you, and where we had been, exactly, since we left London. And what happened on the train. They kept asking about that. They went over it again and again."

"Damage-assessment inquiry," Travers said tersely. "It's a standard procedure when an operation goes bad."

"I told them about our trip, and about the train. I figured they knew most of it anyway. But then they started pressing me on who warned us to leave London, and how long had we known about Hansen, and how did we find out? I wouldn't tell them about that."

"What happened then?"

"They made me strip. Right in the room, with the three of them watching me. They brought in an ugly little man named Vento, I think. They said he was an expert with a cattle prod. They said you'd remember."

"The bastards."

Valerie was crying again. "I was so frightened. Rob, what did they mean, you'd remember?"

"The worker who was tortured in Pennsylvania. Vento did it, with a cattle prod. What happened then?"

"I was naked and they started asking me more questions, with that awful little man still standing there. Then someone else came in the room, in a big hurry, and he started whispering to the man at the table, who seemed to be the one in charge. They all got up and broke off the questioning. I was told to get dressed, and they put me back in here and locked the door. After a while, I heard a lot of heavy equipment being moved and a lot of shouting but, of course, I couldn't see anything. Then everything was still. I guess that's when I started crying. I thought they'd left me here in this room to die."

"What you heard were the missiles being moved out. It means they've gone to Phase Red. We've got to get word to Owens right away so he can warn the president."

"There must be phones."

"The lines have been cut. We've got to get off the island as quick as we can and get to a phone on the mainland. Come on."

The dog was waiting outside and followed them. "We can't leave him here, Rob," Valerie said. "Let's take him with us."

"All right. Looks like we don't have much choice."

The late-afternoon sun was still warm. "My boat's anchored north of here," Travers said. "We'll follow the tracks to the loading area, then go back along the beach. It should be faster than fighting our way through the woods, the way I came. Have you seen any sign of Ben on the island?"

"Ben? No. Is he here?"

"I think they may have held him here. He's been missing for several days. He found out the island was Site Orange."

"Maybe they took him with them when they left."

"Maybe." They were at the harbor. As Travers had assumed, the tracks led right out onto the pier. They scrambled over some rocks down to the beach, and headed east along the winding shoreline.

"Owens has gone to the president," Travers explained as

they walked rapidly along the beach. "Partly because of me, partly because of Ben. The thing is moving very fast. It's busting open."

"Where do you guess they've taken the missiles?"

"Either Cambridge or to the north shore of the Choptank, around the mouth of the Tred Avon. The agency still has some installations near there. Wherever they land, the launchers will be waiting."

"Which means the missiles will be mobile."

"Exactly. The launchers are truck bodies with rails to elevate the missiles for firing. They may even be using the mail trucks to conceal the rockets. The trucks could easily have hatches on the top that roll back for launching."

"By now we're at least an hour behind them. They could be anywhere."

"No. There's only one place they can be heading after they're on the launchers. Straight up Route Fifty to the Bay Bridge. Once they're over that bridge, they only have to go a short distance and they'll be in range of the White House."

It was slow going in the sand, and at Valerie's suggestion they stopped and took off their shoes. The shoreline turned sharply, and they followed the beach into a narrow cove, well-hidden from the bay.

"Look," Travers said suddenly. "There's something up ahead." The dog was barking furiously.

She followed his gaze. About a hundred yards up the beach a dark object rested near the water's edge. "It looks like a log that drifted in," she said.

Travers broke into a trot. He knew it was not a log. But he was not prepared for what he saw. The body of a man lying on its back, partly in the water, had obviously been there for several days. It had been half-eaten by huge blue crabs. Even as Travers approached there were several scuttling over the body. They had torn open the man's shirt and were attacking the flesh on his chest. The fingers and hands had been eaten and only the bones were left, stripped clean. The man's eyes were empty sockets and half of his face had been devoured. The crabs hadn't touched the waterlogged cigar still sticking out of the pocket of his jacket.

"The poor son of a bitch," Travers said. "They must have shot him down when he tried to land and left him for the crabs."

"Ben," Valerie whispered. "Dear, sweet Ben. Oh, Ben." Tears were rolling down her cheeks. She looked up at Travers. "Did you know? He always wanted me to call him Ben."

Chapter 31

Thurlow Anderson was standing by his desk, talking on the telephone to Secretary of Defense Walter Stevens. The late afternoon sun filtering through the windows cast long shadows on the walls of the Oval Office.

"Yes, Mr. President?" Stevens' voice was crisp, businesslike. Anderson had lured him to the Pentagon from the electronics industry in northern California, where he headed a company that was among the first to develop the silicon chip that had revolutionized the computer business.

"Walter, we have an emergency. I want the Air Force to scramble reconnaissance jets immediately to look for a convoy of missiles somewhere in the Washington area. I'm afraid I can't tell you where."

There was a stunned silence on the other end of the telephone. Then Stevens said quietly, "Whose missiles, Mr. President?"

"The agency's."

"Jesus Christ. All right, sir, I'll get the jets in the air. I'd better assemble Admiral Taylor and the Joint Chiefs in the War Room. I'll call you back from there in a few minutes."

Stevens clicked off. Grouped around the president's desk

were a worried-looking Aaron Davidow, and two of the president's military aides, Army Major General Lynn Adams, and Air Force Brigadier General Peter ("Mike") McAvoy. The third military assistant, Navy Captain Bradley Bennett, could not be found; he was said to be out playing tennis.

While the president was on the phone with Secretary Stevens, Aaron Davidow quickly filled in the military aides. When Davidow had finished, Mike McAvoy spoke up. "Have you notified SAC, Mr. President?"

"I want that done right now, Mike. Call Omaha." Just outside the door of the Oval Office, an Army warrant officer, armed but in civilian clothes, was standing by with the "football," the locked briefcase containing the codes that the president would use to order a nuclear attack. By law, only the president could push the button. But under catastrophic circumstances, if the president and his statutory successors were incapacitated in a nuclear attack, there were certain alternate, automatic procedures, authorized in advance by the president, for carrying out strategic retaliation. That was what worried Thurlow Anderson. If these highly secret procedures went into effect, Towny Black's obsolescent missiles would touch off World War III. SAC, the Strategic Air Command, had to be warned.

McAvoy was already using the phone on the little table between the two sofas, calling SAC headquarters.

The president's red telephone rang. It was Secretary Stevens, calling from the War Room, the National Military Command Center deep in the Pentagon. "The planes have scrambled, sir," he reported.

"Good. Where did they take off from?"

"Shaw Air Force Base, near Sumter, South Carolina, Mr. President. Those are the closest reconnaissance jets to Washington. We have a wing of RF-4's there. We've sent up two dozen of them. They'll fan out in different directions."

"All right, Walter. Keep me informed."

"Yes, sir. I'm with Admiral Taylor and the rest of the Joint Chiefs now. If you could brief us, sir, we'll pipe your voice over the wall speaker so we can all hear."

Quickly, Thurlow Anderson sketched in the situation for

the secretary of defense and the Joint Chiefs. Across the Potomac in the Pentagon, the military advisers were gathered around a twenty-five-foot conference table in the War Room. Mounted on the wall opposite were six screens that could, with the aid of computers, display the status and location of all U.S. forces around the globe, as well as other command information. On another wall, six digital clocks flashed the time in various world capitals. Another console showed the defense condition of all U.S. commands, with the scale ranging from DEFCON 5, "normal readiness," to DEFCON 1, "maximum force readiness," to EMERGENCY. As the president spoke, the red light was steadily flashing EMERGENCY.

Under the two-way hookup, the president could hear any of the men in the War Room. When Anderson had finished speaking, the Chairman of the Joint Chiefs responded. "This is Admiral Taylor, sir. I just want you to know that we had no knowledge of the existence of nuclear weapons outside the control of the armed forces."

"I'm sure of that, Admiral," the president replied. "Thank you."

Walter Stevens spoke. "Mr. President, I'm sitting only a few feet from the Molink terminal. I recommend we advise the Soviets."

Thurlow Anderson thought for a moment. "I've already notified SAC, Walter. But I think you're probably right about the Soviets. Go ahead and put a message on the hot line. But keep it vague. Something about a technical error that could lead to a misfiring of one or more of our missiles *inside* the United States. Emphasize that part. Give my personal regards to the chairman and tell him we'll keep him advised."

"Yes, sir."

"Admiral Taylor?"

"Yes, Mr. President."

"I want some facts on the Honest John missile. Range, nuclear payload, and so on."

"It's an old tactical missile, sir. And they could have picked a better weapon for their purpose. It's not all that reliable for pinpointing targets. General Clayton can provide the weapon characteristics. He's right here."

Charles ("Chip") Clayton, the Army Chief of Staff, had been an artillery colonel in Korea. He had fired Honest John training warheads, which were painted blue and filled with concrete, and he was generally familiar with the missile.

"The maximum range is twenty-three miles, Mr. President," General Clayton said. "The warhead payload is one hundred kilotons. That's about five times the power of the bomb we dropped at Hiroshima."

"Good Lord," Thurlow Anderson said quietly to the men in the Oval Office.

To Aaron Davidow, he said, "Get Jerry." Davidow moved to the other telephone by the sofa and dialed Jerold Wolf, the president's science adviser and one of the nation's leading physicists, who was on leave from his teaching post at MIT to work in the White House.

"If they fire one at us," Anderson said to General Clayton, "how much time until it hits?"

"I can bring that up on the computer," Clayton said. "One moment, sir." After a minute, he was back. "At maximum range, the missile would have a trajectory of 9.3 miles, sir. It would hit the White House in a hundred and ten seconds from time of launch—"

Walter Stevens broke in. "I think you should consider moving immediately to the alternate command center, Mr. President."

The president turned to Davidow. "Walter recommends we move to the Mountain. I don't think I should. It'll take too much time."

"That's up to you, sir. But if you don't, perhaps the vice-president should."

"Yes. Order a helicopter and alert the vice-president. Get him out on the south lawn."

At Fort Ritchie, Maryland, five miles from Camp David and just south of the Pennsylvania border, the president could seek the safety of his underground emergency command post, carved into a mountainside and equipped with elaborate communications equipment, medical facilities, and living quarters. But even by helicopter, the trip to the Mountain would cost him precious minutes.

To Stevens, the president said, "We can't afford the time. We'd lose twenty minutes going to the Mountain. I'm sending the vice-president."

"Very well."

Davidow tapped the president on the shoulder. "Jerry Wolf is here, sir."

Anderson sat down, turned off the intercom link with the War Room, and motioned the science adviser to a chair. Wolf was a man in his late fifties, with curly black hair turning to gray, deep furrows in his brow, and a perpetually worried expression. For once, Anderson thought, the physicist had good reason to look worried.

"I brought along some data on blast effects," Wolf said in his characteristically low voice.

"All right, Jerry. What kind of damage would they do with a direct hit?"

"It depends first of all on the height of the explosion. The missile can be set to detonate high in the air, or close to the deck, or at ground level. The effects are different in each case."

"Jerry, you're not lecturing to your students. Just lay it out for me, quickly."

Wolf flushed. He opened a black binder and consulted it. "Well, Mr. President, assuming a hundred kiloton explosion at sea level, on a clear day with the temperature in the seventies, which today is, at ground level you would get two pounds per square inch of overpressure. That could destroy wood and brick buildings, shatter glass, rupture eardrums, and create seventy-mile-per-hour winds. You'd get that blast effect out to 2.2 miles from ground zero, the center of the blast. Approximately a fifteen-square-mile area, with the White House at its center."

"What about heat and burns?" Anderson asked.

Wolf turned a page in his black book. "On unprotected skin, you would get third-degree burns causing scarring, and requiring skin grafts, out to 3.2 miles, sir. Again, assuming the blast is at ground level."

"And radiation?"

"There are two types, Mr. President. Initial or prompt

radiation, essentially neutron and gamma rays. And then the fallout which could travel for several miles and cause alpha and beta burns. But limiting the data to initial radiation, a hundred-and-sixty-five-pound man out in the open, getting a full body dose, would receive a thousand rems to 1.1 miles—"

Aaron Davidow interrupted. "What are the chances of survival with exposure to one thousand rems, Jerry?"

Wolf shook his head. "Minimal. With anything in the thousand to five thousand rem range, there is a one hundred percent chance of death in two to fourteen days from the effects of radiation on the bloodstream and the central nervous system. There's vomiting, diarrhea, and then death."

General Adams, the president's military aide, broke in. "These missiles are old, Jerry. They've been stored somewhere for fifteen years. Isn't there a good chance they will have deteriorated by now?"

Wolf ran his fingers through his hair. "I wish I could say. I can't answer that one."

"Who can?" the president snapped.

"Fritz Atwater. At the Lawrence Livermore Lab."

"Get him on the phone."

In a moment, the president was connected with Dr. Atwater, director of the weapons laboratory in California.

"This is Thurlow Anderson, Fritz. I need to know what the chances are that an Honest John missile, in storage somewhere for fifteen years, would still be operational."

"It's difficult to say, Mr. President. Normally nuclear weapons are returned to our Pantex plant every five years or so for overhauling. If they weren't cycled in, they might work, and they might not."

"In other words, there's no way to be sure?"

"That's about it, sir."

"All right, thanks, Fritz."

Jack Malloy, the president's thin, bespectacled press secretary, had slipped into the room. Malloy, a former reporter for *The Washington Post,* had not been briefed on the crisis yet. But one glance around the Oval Office and he knew that the wire service story in his hand was true.

"I'm sorry to interrupt, Mr. President, but AP has just

moved a bulletin saying that the Joint Chiefs are meeting in an unscheduled session at the Pentagon. The story speculates that we're in some sort of military emergency."

"You could put it that way, Jack," Thurlow Anderson said. "At any moment, Towny Black may lob a nuclear missile into this building."

The press secretary thought he was going to wet his pants. With great difficulty, he managed to control his bladder, but his knees felt like they were about to collapse under him. "I—I can deny the story if you want me to, sir," he stammered.

"No, damn it!" the president thundered. "We're not going to lie. There's no need to lie because we're in a crisis. Tell them you have no comment at this time. And that you'll have a statement as soon as possible. We're not going to lie."

"Yes, sir." Malloy left and headed for the little bathroom outside his office. He was thankful the bulletin had moved after his four-o'clock press briefing. He had declared a lid and most of the reporters had already left the building, which would give him a little breathing space.

The telephone rang on Thurlow Anderson's desk. He picked it up. "Yes, Beth?"

"It's Senator Owens, sir."

"Tell him I'm too busy, but Aaron will take his call."

"He insists on speaking to you, sir. He says it's urgent."

"All right, put him through." The president motioned to Davidow to pick up the other extension.

Barry Owens' voice was tense. "Mr. President, I've just received a call from Robert Travers."

"I've got Aaron Davidow on the telephone with me," Anderson said. "Go ahead. He'll take notes."

"Travers was calling from a pay phone on a place called Taylors Island. In Dorchester County, on the Eastern Shore of Maryland. He's located Site Orange, Mr. President, and he's been there. It was out in the Chesapeake Bay on James Island—"

Davidow interrupted. "What do you mean *was*?"

"That's just it. The missiles are gone. Travers says they're almost certainly moving north right now on Route Fifty, toward the Bay Bridge. They may be disguised as mail trucks."

Anderson cut in. "Thank you, Senator. We'll act on that."

The president picked up the direct line to the Pentagon.

"Walter, we've just received information indicating the missiles are moving north on Route Fifty for the Bay Bridge, possibly camouflaged as mail trucks."

"Mail trucks!"

"You heard me. Tell Admiral Taylor to get word to the reconnaissance wing and have whatever aircraft are closest to that area concentrate on Route Fifty. I want to know as soon as they're spotted."

"Yes, sir."

"Walter, we're moving down to the Situation Room. Come on, gentlemen." Aaron Davidow, Jerry Wolf, and the military aides followed the president down the corridor to the stairway. In less than a minute they were in the L-shaped Situation Room in the basement of the West Wing. It was an eerily quiet place. None of the machines in it made any noise. There were silent computer terminals and video screens. Thick gold carpeting and a low ceiling helped to mute the sound of voices.

The president turned to Mike McAvoy. "General, let's get some maps in here." The Air Force aide left on the double.

Anderson turned on an intercom, linking the Situation Room with the Pentagon. "Walter, what do you make of it?"

The defense secretary's voice was crisp and self-assured as always. "They've got to cross the Bay Bridge to get within range, Mr. President."

"Once they're over that bridge, they can hit us?"

General Dougherty, the Air Force chief of staff, responded. "Not quite, Mr. President. They've got to go another fourteen miles beyond the western terminal of the bridge to move within firing range. Somewhere around a little town called Rutland, Maryland."

McAvoy was back with a map, which he spread out on a table in front of the president.

"All right," Anderson said, "I see where Rutland is."

Admiral Taylor spoke. "One of the RF-4 pilots just radioed

in that he's spotted the convoy. They're in mail trucks, all right, a dozen of them, with support vehicles, moving pretty rapidly, about ten miles south of Easton."

"Walter, you heard that. Does the Army have any troops in that area that could stop the convoy?"

The defense secretary hesitated. "Let me check with the chiefs, Mr. President."

In a moment, Walter Stevens was back. "We don't have any ground forces that could be deployed in time to stop them, Mr. President. I'm afraid the closest combat troops we have are the Third Infantry at Fort Myer. They're too far away."

Anderson swore silently. "What about the Maryland State Police? We could have them establish road blocks north of the convoy and at the eastern end of the bridge—"

Admiral Taylor broke in: "I'm afraid the convoy could punch right through anything the state police could put up, Mr. President. We can't rely on them to stop military hardware. And there aren't enough cars on Route Fifty to create a traffic jam."

"All right. What do you recommend, Admiral?"

"An air strike, Mr. President. The First Tactical Fighter Wing, with seventy-two F-15 jets, is stationed at Langley Air Force Base, near Norfolk. They're the closest combat aircraft to Washington. They're armed with air-to-ground rockets and Vulcan twenty millimeter cannons. They can be up in the air and across the bay in a few minutes."

The president was nervously tapping a pencil on the table. "If you start shooting up that convoy, Admiral, you're going to kill some innocent people in cars on that highway, and maybe some on the ground."

"Perhaps a few," Admiral Taylor conceded. "But if you want to stop that convoy, it's the risk you have to take."

"I don't know. Damn it, Walter, what happens if one of those rockets from an F-15 scores a direct hit on one of the Honest Johns? Could it set off a nuclear explosion?"

"The chances of that are very remote," Secretary Stevens replied.

Jerry Wolf was nodding his head. "Virtually impossible,"

he said. "Unless the missile was armed, and in flight—which it won't be. Otherwise, the odds are a billion to one against the warhead being detonated by a bomb or a rocket."

Aaron Davidow was on his feet, murmuring something to the president.

Anderson nodded. "Admiral Taylor," he asked, "if one of these missiles is hit, even if there is no nuclear explosion, won't it release radioactive debris into the air?"

There was a pause while Admiral Taylor conferred with General Dougherty, the Air Force chief of staff. "Yes, sir," the chairman of the Joint Chiefs of Staff replied. "In the event of a direct hit, there probably would be a detonation of the high explosive surrounding the nuclear core. As you know, Mr. President, the warheads have a conventional explosive to trigger the nuclear explosion. If there was a conventional detonation, the nuclear core would be broken in pieces and scattered. Or it might burn. There would be radioactive material exposed on the ground and in the air."

"With what result?"

Reluctantly, the admiral admitted, "You would have a very real possibility of contaminating a wide area, Mr. President."

"Walter, you heard that. We would contaminate the whole Eastern Shore and the Chesapeake Bay, too."

"It would be a lot worse if one of those missiles is fired on Washington," Stevens replied. "Frankly, sir, I don't think you have much choice."

"Stand by. I'll be back to you in a minute." The president flipped up the "Talk" switch on the intercom, so that conversation in the Situation Room would not be broadcast to the command center in the Pentagon. Anderson paced the length of the room, and back again.

"There must be another way," he said.

"I don't think so," Davidow said softly.

"I'm afraid Admiral Taylor is right, sir," Mike McAvoy agreed.

"Aaron," the president said, "maybe this will sound crazy but—" He broke off and turned the intercom back on.

"Admiral," he asked, "those F-15's you have. Are they equipped with bombs?"

"No, sir. Rockets and cannon, like I said. They have the capability to carry bombs, but they're not equipped with racks. General Dougherty confirms that—no bomb racks."

"All right, what are the closest bombers you have to Easton, Maryland?"

General Dougherty replied, "We have a wing of F-4 Phantom jets at Seymour Johnson Air Force Base, Mr. President. Near Goldsboro, North Carolina."

"How far is it from that convoy, General?"

"I'm asking the computer. Okay, it's 258 air miles from the convoy's position."

"How long will it take the convoy to reach the eastern end of the Bay Bridge?"

"The computer can tell us that, too. Okay, the reconnaissance pilot out of Shaw reported the trucks moving north at about 45 miles per hour. That was thirteen minutes ago, which puts them in Easton now. From Easton to the bridge is—just a minute, okay—29.2 miles. That gives us thirty-nine minutes, give or take a few minutes that we've been talking."

"Can the Phantom jets get there in that time?"

Dougherty hesitated. "I believe so, sir. The Phantoms can do Mach 2, but not loaded. With bombs, once they're scrambled, they can cover that distance at four hundred knots in thirty-four minutes. It's a little tight."

"All right, General. One more question. What kind of ordnance do these planes carry?"

"Each F-4 can carry twenty 750-pound bombs, Mr. President."

"Walter?"

"Yes, sir?"

"Radio the Maryland State Police and tell them to clear the Bay Bridge of all traffic on both spans, westbound and eastbound. Tell them it's a military emergency and your orders come directly from the president of the United States."

"Yes, sir."

"Admiral Taylor?"

"Mr. President?"

"I want the Phantom jets at Goldsboro to scramble immediately, fly north, and blow up the Bay Bridge."

"My God." It was Davidow, the words soft but entirely audible in the Situation Room.

"Are you sure, Mr. President?" For once, Walter Stevens sounded less crisp and self-assured.

"You're damn right I'm sure!" Thurlow Anderson roared. "Get those planes in the air."

"Yes, *sir*," Admiral Taylor snapped.

"Walter," the president said, "it's the only way we can be sure of stopping that convoy without a nuclear accident and ghastly loss of life. Who runs that bridge anyway?"

"The Maryland Transportation Authority, Mr. President."

"Well, call them up and tell them we're sorry."

General Dougherty's voice came over the speaker. "One of the RF-4's reports the missiles are approximately five miles north of Easton at this time. They apparently know they've been seen; the pilot says the convoy is picking up speed."

"All right," Anderson said. "Keep us informed. Aaron, you'd better get Jack Malloy down here and start working on a statement for the press."

"How much do you want me to tell him?"

"Whatever he needs to know. But nothing is to be released until I've approved it."

The president was clearly in charge of the crisis, to the surprise of some of the men in the Situation Room and in the Pentagon command center. They had not realized that Thurlow Anderson could rise to the occasion, but he had.

"The Phantoms are on the way," Taylor cut in. "We've asked the FAA to clear the commercial air corridors leading into Norfolk, Richmond, Washington, and Baltimore. They're doing that now. The Coast Guard has ordered all ships from the area around the bridge."

"Very good. Mike?"

"Sir?" General McAvoy looked up from his seat across the table.

"I want you to call Barry Owens. Tell him what's going on and that his information on the convoy was vital. And tell him I'll thank him personally as soon as I can." The Air Force aide began punching the buttons on his telephone.

Walter Stevens spoke. "Mr. President, there's a reply from Moscow coming in on the hot line."

Aaron Davidow walked over to the Molink terminal in the Situation Room. "The chairman sends his personal regards and thanks the president for his timely information. He hopes the problem will be resolved without loss of life or impairment of the existing state of relations between our two peoples."

"The bastard is probably enjoying this," Anderson growled.

A worried-looking Jack Malloy came into the room carrying a yellow pad and sat down at one end of the table with Davidow, who began briefing him in a low voice as Malloy took notes.

Admiral Taylor's voice crackled over the speaker. "Mr. President, the jets are at twenty-four thousand feet north of Richmond. General Dougherty informs me that the convoy has passed Wye Mills, Maryland, and is now near Queenstown, heading west-northwest toward the Bay Bridge approaches."

The president's voice was calm. "How much time does that give us?"

General Dougherty replied. "Assuming the convoy is moving faster, about ten minutes, sir."

"Okay. Walter?"

"Yes, Mr. President?"

"Have the state police halted all traffic and cleared the bridge by now?"

"Yes, sir, they have. We have an open line to Annapolis. They've also cleared the staff people out of the toll booths and the administration building on the western end of the bridge."

"Admiral," the president asked, "where are the jets now?"

"Over the lower Potomac, sir. They're fifty miles out and beginning their descent for their final approach to the bridge."

"All right, Admiral, good luck." The president turned to Davidow. "Aaron," he asked, "did you remember to pray for me?"

To the motorists standing alongside their stopped cars on the western approach to the Bay Bridge, the Phantom jets appeared like silent silver juggernauts, all the more awesome for being totally unexpected. They streaked out of the late-afternoon sun flying directly east, and it was not until the first jet had shot overhead that the people on the ground heard the scream of the engines. One by one, the F-4's peeled off for their runs.

The first jet came in low at 500 feet. Half a mile from the bridge, it went into a steep climb and tossed a bomb. It scored a direct hit on the roadway of the new span, midway between the two steel suspension towers. Chunks of concrete and twisted steel girders went flying into the bay, 212 feet below. The jet pulled up and turned in a wide arc to the west as the next bomber commenced its run.

The bombers were clearly aiming for the suspension portions of the span, the tallest and most vulnerable part of the bridge. A second jet streaked low along the length of the 1600-foot suspension span, pulled up, and tossed two bombs. One missed and dropped harmlessly into the bay but the other struck near the east tower and snapped one of the two main cables. The damage put an unexpected strain on the vertical suspender cables, and several of them snapped as well. The torque, the enormous pressure on the steel and concrete, twisted the roadway into a grotesque angle.

One after another, the Phantom jets screamed in, letting loose their lethal missiles, each containing 386 pounds of TNT. But the proud bridge did not yield easily; for a time, its 66,000 tons of steel withstood the repeated bombardment. At 6:14 P.M., however, twelve minutes after the first jet had appeared over Sandy Point, one of the bombs sliced a gap in the north span midway between the two towers.

For a long moment, the roadway hung there. Then the second main cable snapped. The bridge began to creak and make a moaning noise. Slowly, very slowly, the concrete and steel roadway collapsed into the bay. The strain on the east tower was too much. A moment before, its great steel beams had stood 354 feet above the surface of the bay. Now, pulled down by the weight of the shattered roadway, the tower buckled and folded into the bay like a child's erector set.

The jet that had administered the coup de grace waggled its wings in triumph. It remained now only for the planes to destroy the narrower, old span to the south. Again the jets bombed the suspension portion in relays. The explosions sent more jagged chunks of steel and concrete flying in every direction. At 6:23 P.M., the second span collapsed into the bay with a roaring crash that sent enormous streams of water spouting high into the air. The jets left and an eerie silence settled over the Chesapeake, broken only by the scolding of the sea gulls wheeling and diving over the twisted wreckage of the bridge.

Senator Barry Owens rapped his gavel and the spectators jammed into the Senate Caucus Room were quickly hushed. Robert Travers sat at the witness table, which was covered with green felt cloth. In the silence, the only sound that could be heard was the whirring of the motor drives and the clicking shutters on the cameras of the still photographers, who were crouched in front of the witness. Behind the photographers, the members of the Senate Intelligence Committee sat at a long, polished mahogany table, their staff aides crowded behind them like courtiers at a king's throne. Howard Radner was whispering importantly into Senator Owens' ear.

So much history had passed through this room, Travers knew. He looked around at the marble pillars, the high ceiling, the bright chandeliers, and the even brighter television lights on the tall, unwieldy tripods along the wall. John Dean had sat in the same chair not so many years ago and destroyed a president.

Yet, Travers thought, he had come today, not to destroy but to build. Dozens of reporters from all over the world, all three television networks, and a huge, excited crowd of spectators were gathered in the hearing room. Outside the great wooden doors, in the corridors, Capitol police restrained long lines of people waiting to get in. Few of them would.

The entire nation was waiting to hear his testimony. The networks were predicting an audience of 90 million people. President Anderson's statement two days earlier was brief and cryptic, leaving many questions unanswered. The president explained that a grave crisis had arisen within the government because of the defiance of presidential authority by the director of the Central Intelligence Agency. The bombing of the William Preston Lane, Jr. Memorial Bridge had been ordered by the president to deal with the crisis. Steps had been taken to avoid any loss of life in this limited military operation. The executive branch would cooperate fully with the Senate Intelligence Committee in the congressional investigation to begin within forty-eight hours. Soon after the White House had issued the president's statement, Senator Horace Seabrook, of Alabama, chairman of the full committee, announced that he had appointed Senator Barry Owens of Colorado to conduct the televised hearings.

The photographers had dropped back and taken up positions on the floor. Travers twisted around and looked at Valerie, sitting in the front row, a few feet behind the witness chair. Their eyes met for a brief moment. He winked almost imperceptibly at his son, Jack, sitting next to Valerie, and smiled reassuringly at his daughter, Melissa, next to Jack.

Owens rapped the gavel again. "The committee will come to order," he said. "Our first witness this morning is Mr. Robert Travers. Mr. Travers, please stand up and raise your right hand. Do you swear that the evidence you shall give to the Senate Select Committee on Intelligence shall be the truth, the whole truth, and nothing but the truth, so help you God?"

"I do."

Travers sat down.

"Mr. Travers," Senator Owens intoned, "please state your full name and address for the record."

"My name is Robert Richardson Travers. I live at number 14 Bryanston Square, London, England."

"By whom are you employed, Mr. Travers?"

"The Central Intelligence Agency."

"In what capacity?"

"I am chief of the London station."

"Mr. Travers, the committee understands that you have a statement you would like to make at this time."

"Thank you, Mr. Chairman." Travers took a sip of water and a deep breath. Then, slowly and methodically, sparing no details, he began to tell the story of Operation Spectrum to the American people. He knew they were watching. He could only hope they were listening.

Home delivery from Pocket Books

Here's your opportunity to have fabulous bestsellers delivered right to you. Our free catalog is filled to the brim with the newest titles plus the finest in mysteries, science fiction, westerns, cookbooks, romances, biographies, health, psychology, humor—every subject under the sun. Order this today and a world of pleasure will arrive at your door.

POCKET BOOKS, Department ORD
1230 Avenue of the Americas, New York, N.Y. 10020

Please send me a free Pocket Books catalog for home delivery

NAME _____

ADDRESS _____

CITY _____ STATE/ZIP _____

If you have friends who would like to order books at home, we'll send them a catalog too—

NAME _____

ADDRESS _____

CITY _____ STATE/ZIP _____

NAME _____

ADDRESS _____

CITY _____ STATE/ZIP _____